Praise for Irene Hannon
and her novels

IRENE HANNON

One Special Christmas

&

Home for the Holidays

Steeple
Hill®

Published by Steeple Hill Books™

STEEPLE HILL BOOKS

Steeple
Hill®

Recycling programs
for this product may
not exist in your area.

ISBN-13: 978-0-373-65141-2

ONE SPECIAL CHRISTMAS AND HOME FOR THE HOLIDAYS

ONE SPECIAL CHRISTMAS
Copyright © 1999 by Irene Hannon

HOME FOR THE HOLIDAYS
Copyright © 1997 by Irene Hannon

www.SteepleHill.com

Printed in U.S.A.

CONTENTS

Books by Irene Hannon

Love Inspired

*Home for the Holidays
*A Groom of Her Own
*A Family to Call Her Own
It Had to Be You
One Special Christmas
The Way Home
Never Say Goodbye
Crossroads
**The Best Gift
**Gift from the Heart
**The Unexpected Gift
All Our Tomorrows
The Family Man
Rainbow's End

†From This Day Forward
†A Dream to Share
†Where Love Abides
Apprentice Father
††Tides of Hope
††The Hero Next Door
††The Doctor's Perfect Match
†† A Father for Zach

*Vows
**Sisters & Brides
†Heartland Homecomings
††Lighthouse Lane

IRENE HANNON

Irene Hannon, who writes both romance and romantic suspense, is the bestselling author of more than thirty novels. Her books have been honored with a coveted RITA® Award from Romance Writers of America (the "Oscar" of romantic fiction), a HOLT Medallion and a Reviewer's Choice Award from *RT Book Reviews*.

A former corporate communications executive with a Fortune 500 company, Irene now writes full-time. In her spare time she enjoys singing, traveling, long walks, cooking, gardening and spending time with family. She and her husband make their home in Missouri.

For more information about her and her books, Irene invites you to visit her website at www.irenehannon.com.

ONE SPECIAL CHRISTMAS

For I know well the plans I have in mind for you,
says the Lord, plans for your welfare not for woe,
plans to give you a future full of hope.

— *Jeremiah* 29:11

To my brother, Jim,
and his lovely bride, Teresa—
May all your happily-ever-after dreams come true.

Prologue

It was over in moments, yet it seemed to happen in slow motion.

The car swerved suddenly, fishtailed wildly as the driver struggled for control on the icy road. Then it skidded sideways off the steep shoulder, rolling over once before coming to rest, upright, at the bottom of the embankment.

Eric Carlson watched in horror, his hands tightening instinctively on the wheel as the accident unfolded a few hundred feet in front of him. Though he didn't doubt his eyes, the terrible scene had an odd air of unreality about it, seeming to happen in utter quiet, like an old silent movie. The sleet hitting his car roof, combined with the volume of the radio that Cindy had just cranked up, must have masked the grating sound of metal being crushed, the high-pitched crackle of shattering glass—and the inevitable screams that would accompany such a traumatic crash. But Eric could imagine them, and he swallowed convulsively as his breath lodged in his throat.

Dear God, he prayed as the full impact of what he'd

just witnessed slammed home. He slowed his car as quickly as the icy road would allow and eased it over to the shoulder.

"What are you doing?" Cindy demanded stridently.

He set the brake and reached into the back for his bag. "Exactly what you think I'm doing," he replied tersely.

"Oh, for heaven's sake, Eric, we're going to be late for the party! They're serving dinner at eight. Let's just call 911 and get out of here. Those other Good Samaritans can help," she said impatiently, gesturing toward two other cars that had also stopped.

He turned to his wife, and as he looked at her petulant expression he wondered what had drawn him to her a dozen years ago. Her blond beauty had attracted him, certainly. And he'd been flattered that someone so sophisticated had found him appealing. But surely there had been more. Hadn't her heart once been kind and caring? Hadn't the smiles she'd given him in those early days been tender and warm? Or had he seen only what he'd wanted to see, imagined what had never been there at all?

As the years had passed and the chasm between them had widened, he'd been forced to admit that perhaps it was his perception—not Cindy—that had changed. Or perhaps she had simply become more of what she had always been as she grew disillusioned with him and disenchanted with the demands of his profession—the "doctor stuff," as she demeaningly termed it. He was well aware that his dedication to his work grated on her, that she felt his devotion to his patients diminished his devotion to her. And perhaps it did. Perhaps if he had been able to give her the kind of attention she needed, their relationship wouldn't be disintegrating. Yet how could he give anything less than one hundred percent to his profession? It was a dilemma he wrestled with constantly, but always the answers eluded him. All he knew was that both of them were unhappy in their marriage.

But it was too late now to alter their status, Eric reminded himself grimly. He had meant the vows they'd made on their wedding day, including "For better, for worse." After all, as his old maiden aunt used to say, he and Cindy had made their bed. Now they had to lie in it.

Eric knew they couldn't go on like this. But his repeated suggestions that they seek counseling were always met with cold sarcasm—and a cold shoulder. As he looked at her now, in the shadowy light of the car, she seemed almost like a stranger.

Cindy shifted uncomfortably under her husband's scrutiny, and when she spoke again her tone was more conciliatory. "Look, those other people will do whatever they can until help arrives, Eric. They don't need you."

"I'm a doctor, Cindy."

"You're a pediatrician."

She didn't say "just," but the implication was there in her disparaging tone. A muscle in his jaw clenched as he handed her the cell phone. "Call 911." Then he stepped out into the darkness, turning up his collar as he strode toward the embankment, sleet stinging his face much as the familiar gibe always stung his heart.

By the time he made it down to the smashed car, slipping and sliding all the way, the other two motorists were already there. Both had flashlights and were peering into the vehicle. They glanced up when Eric approached.

"How many inside?" he asked.

"Looks like just two. A man and a woman," one replied. He eyed Eric's bag. "Are you a doctor?"

"Yes."

"Well, the woman's conscious but the man doesn't look too good," the other passerby reported dubiously.

Eric strode around to the passenger's side of the car, and with some effort the three of them were able to force open the jammed door.

"One of you give me some light," he instructed as he leaned down to look in, noting with relief that the woman's seat belt was securely in place. He touched her shoulder gently, and she turned to him, her eyes wide and dazed.

For just a moment, Eric simply stared at her. Even in the harsh beam of the flashlight, she had the face of a Madonna—a perfect oval, with dark hair and even darker eyes. She was like something out of a Raphael painting, he thought numbly, momentarily taken aback by her beauty. Her looks were classic, timeless—and marred by a nasty bump that was rising rapidly on her left temple. Abruptly he shifted his focus from her physical attributes to her physical condition.

"I'm a doctor. Can you hear me?" He spoke slowly, enunciating each word carefully.

She nodded jerkily. "I—I'm all right. Please…please take care of my husband," she pleaded.

He looked past her, noting the unnatural position of the male driver, who lay crumpled behind the steering wheel, as well as the blood seeping from the corner of his mouth. "All right. Try not to move. An ambulance is on the way."

"Can I do anything to help?" the flashlight holder asked as Eric straightened.

"The two of you can give me some light on the other side," he said over his shoulder. The other motorist had managed to get the driver's door open, and the two men focused the beams of their lights on the injured man as Eric bent down to examine him.

He wasn't wearing a seat belt, Eric noted. Right off the bat, that was a major strike against him. And the car was an older-model compact, without air bags. Strike two. Eric felt for the man's pulse. Shallow. And his respiration was uneven. He showed signs of major trauma, including head-and-neck injuries—which meant possible spinal damage, Eric noted after a quick visual scan.

Frowning, he glanced up and his gaze met that of the woman passenger. She stared at him, and he saw the fear in her eyes suddenly mushroom at his grim expression.

"He's going to be all right, isn't he?" she pleaded desperately, the stricken look on her face making his gut twist painfully. "This can't be happening! Not tonight! Not now!" She let out a strangled sob and turned her attention to her husband, reaching over to touch his face. "You'll be all right, Jack. I know you will. You have to be!" she said fiercely.

The man's breathing suddenly grew more erratic, and Eric snapped open his bag and deftly withdrew his stethoscope. As he listened to the man's fading pulse, his own heart ratcheted into double time. *God, please let the paramedics arrive soon!* he prayed.

But within seconds it became clear that they weren't going to arrive soon enough. The man's breathing grew more labored with each breath, and obviously he was fighting a losing battle to suck air into his lungs. Eric reached for his bag again. In all his years of medical training, in all his years of trauma work, he'd never had to open an airway in the field, let alone with makeshift lighting and icy sleet pricking the back of his neck. But as the seconds ticked by, it was obvious that if he didn't, this man was going to die. He couldn't let that happen—especially after seeing the anguished look in the woman's eyes.

Eric drew in a steadying breath. Then, without further hesitation, he deftly performed the procedure, aware of, but steeling himself against, the woman's startled gasp. Only when he'd finished did he glance up, noting with alarm the pallor of her face and the glazed look in her eyes. She was starting to turn shocky, Eric realized. And he couldn't handle two trauma cases at once.

Just as he began to panic, the welcome sound of approaching sirens pierced the night air. He closed his eyes and slowly he let out his breath as relief washed over him. Thank God! He needed all the help he could get—and the sooner the better.

Within moments the paramedics joined him, and he explained the situation in clipped phrases, the economy of his language honed during years of emergency-room work where every second counted. As one paramedic temporarily distracted the woman, he spoke softly to the other two.

"Probable severe neck-and-head trauma. I opened an airway, but he's still very unstable. Handle him with kid gloves."

"No problem. We've worked cases like this before," one of them assured him.

"Do you need me to stay and help?"

"We've got it covered. But thanks for stopping. Immediate medical attention can make all the difference, as you know."

Eric nodded, then straightened. He spoke briefly to the policeman on the scene, then made his way up the embankment.

As he crested the rise and stepped onto the pavement, he glanced back once more toward the accident scene, surrealistically illuminated by the police-car headlights and the rotating red-and-white beacon on the ambulance. The woman was standing now, her arms wrapped tightly around her, and though it was clear the paramedic was urging her to sit in one of the vehicles, she was adamantly shaking her head. Her gaze was locked on the two men who were carefully extricating her husband from the battered car. Eric could feel her panic, could sense her almost-palpable fear even from this distance.

Would Cindy look like that if something ever happened to him? he wondered. But even before the question formed, he knew the disheartening answer. Any love they had once shared had died long ago.

For just a moment, despite the man's severe injuries, Eric almost envied him. His wife's deep, abiding love was evident in her eyes, her expression, her very body language. Her husband was obviously the center of her world. And Eric knew intuitively that she was the center of his. Which was as it should be in a good marriage.

Finally, unable to look at the heartrending scene any longer, he turned away, his gut twisting painfully. He was reasonably certain he'd saved the man's life. But as he reached his car and slipped back inside, he wondered for just a moment if he'd done anyone a favor. Eric suspected that the road ahead would not be an easy one—for either him or his wife. That tonight was only the beginning of their trauma.

Maybe Cindy had been right, after all. Maybe he just should have driven on.

Chapter One

Five years later

"**M**rs. Nolan, the doctor will see Sarah now."

Kate glanced up from the book she was reading to her daughter and smiled. "All right. Thanks." She slung her purse over her shoulder and stood, reaching down to take Sarah's hand. "Come on, honey. It's time to go in."

"Do I have to?"

Kate gazed down into the large, dark eyes—a mirror image of her own—and with an apologetic glance at the nurse, sat back down. She pulled Sarah close and spoke gently. "You don't want to have those nasty tummyaches anymore, do you, honey? The doctor can help make them go away. And I'll stay with you the whole time. I promise."

Sarah's eyes welled with tears and she sniffed. "I don't like doctors."

"You used to like Dr. Davis, remember? And this doctor is a friend of his. So I'm sure you'll like him, too."

"He's not going to give me a shot, is he?"

"I don't think so. Not today."

Sarah's lower lip quivered. "Promise you'll stay with me?" she pleaded tremulously.

"Of course I will, honey."

She gave her daughter a quick, reassuring hug and stood again, her heart contracting as Sarah's small, trusting hand reached for hers. She couldn't even bear the thought that something serious might be wrong with her. Sarah was the only thing that gave her life any meaning or joy. Though she'd tried not to worry during the past week as she'd waited for this appointment, she'd met with little success. Nights were the worst. She kept waking up in a cold sweat as increasingly frightening scenarios played themselves out in her dreams. Sarah was all she had now, and she would do anything—anything—to keep her well and safe and happy.

She tightened her grip encouragingly and smiled down at her daughter, trying futilely to control the almost painful thumping of her heart as they followed the nurse inside. Everything would turn out fine, she told herself resolutely. It had to. Except she knew from experience that that was a lie. Everything didn't *have* to turn out fine. There were lots of times when it didn't— no matter how hard you wished for it or wanted it or prayed for it.

The nurse stopped at the door of an examining room and ushered them inside.

"The doctor will be with you in just a few minutes," she promised.

"Shall I undress Sarah?" Kate asked.

The woman glanced at Sarah's shorts and crop top, noted how tenaciously the little girl clung to her mother, and smiled as she shook her head. "I don't think so. The doctor should be able to check everything out just like that. If not, he'll let you know."

Kate watched the woman leave, then forced her lips into what she hoped was a cheery smile. "Shall we finish our story?" She held up the book she'd brought with her from the waiting room.

Sarah nodded, and as Kate sat down the youngster climbed onto her lap. Though her daughter quickly became engrossed in the story, Kate couldn't so easily forget where they were. Or why. Even when Sarah got the sniffles she worried excessively, and this mysterious ache in her daughter's stomach was making Kate's own stomach clench painfully.

When a brief knock interrupted her reading a few minutes later, she jerked involuntarily, then glanced up with a troubled gaze as the door swung open.

Eric stopped abruptly on the threshold as he stared at the woman whose face had been indelibly etched into his mind on that cold, tragic evening five years before. It was a night memorable in many ways—none of them pleasant. It had begun with the terrible accident, and had ended with his wife's announcement that she wanted a divorce. For years he'd tried to put the events of that dismal evening behind him. But the one thing he'd never been able to forget was this woman's stunning face and the desperate love he'd seen reflected in her expressive eyes.

Her face was still stunning, he noted. But her beauty was tempered now with worry and fatigue, the fine lines at the corners of her eyes and the dark smudges beneath them giving mute testimony to a life filled with unrelenting strain. Nor had her eyes lost their expressiveness—except that now they reflected disillusion and sadness instead of the love he remembered from that fateful night. Whatever burden she had carried for the past five years had clearly taken a tremendous toll on her, he concluded. She looked fragile. And achingly vulnerable. And very much alone. She seemed like a woman desperately in need of a shoulder to cry on or just a comforting hand to hold, he reflected, surprised—and disconcerted—by the unexpected surge of protectiveness that coursed through him.

Kate returned the doctor's stare, held by his compelling eyes. His gaze wasn't invasive or unfriendly—more like…unsettling. As if he knew something she didn't. Which was odd. They'd never met before, had they? she wondered, frowning slightly. Yet there *was* something familiar about him. But surely she would remember hair the color of sun-ripened wheat and eyes so intensely blue. Perhaps he just reminded her of someone from her past.

Eric realized that she didn't recognize him. Which wasn't surprising, in light of their traumatic "meeting"—if it could even be called that. And maybe it was just as well, considering his odd reaction on seeing her again. She drew him in a strangely powerful, inexplicable way;

and that scared him. His divorce from Cindy four and half years before had taught him very clearly that marriage and medicine didn't mix. Since then he'd steered clear of serious relationships. It was a rule he'd never broken. And he wasn't going to start now—with *any* woman. So, with an effort, he put his professional smile in place and held out his hand.

"Mrs. Nolan? I'm Eric Carlson."

Kate found her fingers engulfed in a firm grip that somehow felt both capable and caring. "Hello, Doctor."

"And this must be Sarah." He squatted down beside the wary little girl, who was watching him solemnly, her eyes wide, as she clung to her mother. "Hello, Sarah. I'm Dr. Eric." When she didn't respond, he tried again. "You know, I have something in my office you might like to see when we're all finished. A big tank full of beautiful fish. What's your favorite color?"

"Pink."

"Well, I have a pink fish that has a bright blue tail. Would you like to see it later?"

Sarah studied him silently for a moment. "Are you going to give me a shot?"

Eric chuckled and glanced at Kate. "Nothing like cutting to the chase, is there?" Then he transferred his attention back to Sarah and shook his head. "Nope. No shots today. I promise. So how about letting me look in your ears and peek at your tonsils? And I'll let you listen to my heart if you let me listen to yours."

Sarah tipped her head and studied him for a moment before loosening her grip on Kate. "Okay."

"That's a girl." Eric reached over and picked her up, then settled her on the end of the table. From that point on, the exam proceeded smoothly. Eric even managed to elicit a giggle or two.

Kate watched in amazement, and her respect for Eric grew exponentially from minute to minute. He had a knack for putting children at ease, for making an exam fun, and she suspected that even on those occasions when he did have to give shots, he drew little protest from his patients. He had certainly befriended Sarah, Kate conceded. Her usually shy, reserved little girl was completely relaxed.

As he worked, Eric casually asked Kate a few astute, specific questions, never shifting his focus from Sarah.

When he finished, he straightened and smiled down at his patient. "Now, that wasn't so bad, was it?"

Sarah shook her head. "It didn't hurt at all. I like you. He's nice, isn't he, Mommy?" she declared, looking over at Kate.

Kate cast an admiring glance at Eric. "Yes, honey, he sure is."

Eric felt his neck grow red at Kate's praise. Which was both odd and extremely unsettling. He never lost his cool with patients—or their mommies. To buy himself a moment to regain his composure, he lifted Sarah to the floor, then bent down to retrieve a wayward cotton ball.

Kate didn't know exactly what triggered the sudden flash of memory. Maybe it was Eric's motion of leaning so close to her, or the position of his body in conjunction with hers, or the way the overhead lighting suddenly drew out the burnished gold in his hair. But abruptly and with startling clarity she recalled another time, five years before, when this man had leaned over in exactly the same way as he'd worked on her critically injured husband in an icy wrecked car.

Her sudden gasp of recognition made Eric quickly straighten, and as their gazes met he realized that the odd link they shared was no longer a mystery to her. Her face had gone a shade paler, and he noted the sudden trembling of her fingers as her hand went to her throat.

Eric forced his gaze from hers and smiled at Sarah. "Are you ready to see that pink fish now?"

Oblivious to the sudden undertones in the room, the little girl nodded eagerly and turned to Kate. "It's all right, isn't it, Mommy?"

Somehow Kate found her voice. "Yes."

Eric took Sarah's hand and looked over at Kate discerningly. "I'll be back in a moment. Will you be okay?"

She nodded mutely, still trying to process the bizarre coincidence of today's encounter. When her own pediatrician had retired a few weeks ago, she'd simply selected the most conveniently located replacement from the list he'd provided. Eric Carlson—the man who'd saved Jack's life.

Kate had always meant to find out the name of the doctor who had stopped that night to help, intending to write him a heartfelt letter of thanks. But as the months had gone by she'd been so overwhelmed by all the other demands in her life that she had never followed through. And especially in light of the outcome, which had left her in a deep depression for almost a year. It had been all she could do after that, simply to cope. There were days even now when that was all she did—cope. But that was no excuse. This man deserved better from her, and the guilt had nagged at her for years.

Eric slipped back into the room then and shut the door before taking a seat across from Kate.

"I left Sarah in my office with one of my assistants. She'll keep her occupied until we're finished."

"You were the doctor at the accident, weren't you?" Kate said without preamble.

Eric seemed momentarily taken aback by her abrupt words, then he slowly nodded. "Yes. I recognized you the minute I came in the door."

"I never thanked you. I meant to."

He shrugged. "No thanks were necessary. I'm a doctor. That's my job."

She shook her head vehemently. "No. You didn't even have to stop, especially considering the weather. I don't remember much about that night. I had a slight concussion, and everything has always been a blur. But they told me you saved Jack's life. I always intended to find out your name and let you know I appreciated what you did."

He made a dismissive gesture. "I just opened an airway. It was enough to give him a fighting chance until he got to the hospital." He glanced briefly at her left hand, noted the ring, then proceeded carefully. "Your husband seemed to be badly hurt, Mrs. Nolan."

She swallowed and gave a brief nod of confirmation. "Yes. Two vertebrae in his neck were crushed and he had severe head injuries. At first they weren't sure if he'd even make it through the night. He was in a coma and I just lived hour by hour. But he held on somehow. And with every day that passed I grew more hopeful, despite the fact that the doctors didn't offer much encouragement. They said even if he came out of the coma, he would be paralyzed. That he'd never be the way he was before. But I was sure they were wrong. I had great faith in those days." There was an unmistakable trace of bitterness in her voice, but it was replaced by bleakness when she continued. "We never had a chance to find out, though. He died seven months later without ever regaining consciousness."

It was what Eric had feared. The desolate look in Kate's eyes, the slump of her shoulders, the catch in her voice, made his heart ache. "I'm sorry," he said helplessly, wishing he could take away her pain, offer some words of comfort. But he'd been through this before with other survivors, and he knew words did little to ease the burden of grief or the devastating sense of emptiness and loss that accompanied the death of a loved one. There

was no way to make the absolute finality of that parting
any less painful.

She blinked rapidly, and he saw the sheen of tears in
her eyes. "Thank you. You'd think after four years I'd
be able to handle it better than this, but…well, Jack and
Sarah were my whole world. Sarah was only six weeks
old when it happened, and we had so many plans, so
much to look forward to…." Her voice trailed off and
she sniffed, struggling for composure. At last she drew a
shaky breath, and when she spoke her voice was choked
and barely audible. "Everyone said I'd get over it. That
life would go on and in time I'd feel back to normal. But
you know, I don't think you ever get over it. You just get
on with it."

Eric felt his throat tighten at the abject misery in
Kate's eyes. "It takes a lot of courage just to do that,"
he told her gently, his own voice uneven.

She gave him a sad smile and shook her head. "It's
kind of you to say that, Doctor. But it doesn't take courage to simply do what you have to do. Sarah needs me.
Period. And I love her with all my heart. That's why
these mysterious stomach pains have me so worried."

Eric couldn't change the tragedy that had brought
Kate more than her share of heartache, but at least he
could set her mind at ease about Sarah.

"Well, I don't think you need to worry, Mrs. Nolan. I
can't find a thing wrong. She seems like a very healthy
little girl."

"Then what's the problem?"

He toyed with his pencil for a moment, his face
pensive. "Has there been any sort of trauma in her life
recently?"

Kate nodded slowly as fresh tears sprang to her eyes.
"Yes. My…my mother died very suddenly a month ago.

She and Sarah were very close. We all were, actually. Sort of like The Three Musketeers."

Her voice quavered, and Eric's heart went out to her. She'd had so much loss. It didn't seem fair. He longed to ease her pain, but knew there was nothing he could do. Except listen.

Kate took a deep, shaky breath. "Anyway, Mom lived with us and watched Sarah for me during the school year while I was teaching. I had to find other day care for Sarah at the last minute, and she started a couple of weeks ago, right before I went back to school. It's been a big adjustment for her. For both of us, actually. You see, I always wanted to be home until she went to school. Jack and I had agreed on that. But of course things changed when he died. Having Mom watch her was the next best thing. Now... Well, I hate leaving her with strangers. Sarah is shy, and I'm afraid she may not be mixing well with the other children." Kate bit her lip, clearly distraught.

"You know, it sounds to me like her pains may be emotionally rather than physically triggered," Eric observed. "Coping with the loss of her grandmother was probably hard enough. Coupled with being thrust into a traditional day-care situation—well, it's a big adjustment. Are there any other options?"

Kate frowned and shook her head, her eyes deeply troubled. "This was the best I could do at the last minute. Most of the really good places are booked solid and have waiting lists a mile long." She dropped her head into her hands and drew a shuddering breath. "This isn't at all what I wanted for Sarah!"

Eric's throat tightened. For a brief moment he was overcome by a powerful urge to reach over and take her hand, to give her the reassurance of a caring touch that she seemed to need so desperately. He knew that she was stressed to the limit, torn between want and necessity. At this point he was actually more worried about *her* physical and emotional state than he was about Sarah's. Children had a way of adjusting. And Sarah had the security of Kate's love. But Kate was alone, with no one to share her burdens. Though his heart told him to reach out to her, in the end professional decorum prevailed and he refrained—with great effort.

"You're doing the best you can, Mrs. Nolan, under very difficult circumstances," he reassured her gently, his voice unusually husky. "Don't be too hard on yourself."

Kate looked into his eyes, and she felt strangely comforted by the kindness and compassion she saw there. She *was* trying to do her best, and it lifted her spirits ever-so-slightly to have someone recognize that.

"Thank you. But it's obviously not good enough. I want what's best for Sarah, Doctor. There has to be a better solution than this." She sighed and wearily ran her fingers through her shoulder-length hair. "I guess I'll just have to keep looking."

Eric stared at her bowed head, his face growing thoughtful as an idea suddenly took shape his mind. If he could pull it off, several problems would be solved, he realized. Sarah would have a more personal day-care situation. Kate's guilt would be eased. And Eric's mind would be relieved of a constant worry. It was a long shot, of course. And he didn't want to raise any expectations until he had a commitment. But it just might work.

"I'm sure you'll find the answer, Mrs. Nolan. And in the meantime, remember that children are more resilient than we think. You're clearly a caring, conscientious parent, and children know intuitively when they're loved. That makes a huge difference."

Kate looked at Eric, essentially a stranger to her despite their brief, traumatic encounter five years before. Yet he seemed to know exactly the right thing to say to relieve her mind. Maybe it was a knack he had with all worried mothers. But the caring in his eyes seemed genuine—and somehow personal. Which was silly, of course. She was just another case to him. But she appreciated his kindness nonetheless.

"You have a great bedside manner, Doctor. Even if I'm not the patient," she told him with a tremulous smile. "I feel much better."

He returned the smile, and she liked the way his eyes crinkled at the corners. "I'm glad. And let me know if Sarah is still having problems in a week or so. But I think she'll adjust, given time."

"I just wish there was another option," Kate said with a sigh.

Eric didn't comment as he stood and ushered her to the door. But he had a plan. And if everything went as he hoped, Kate's wish just might come true.

Anna Carlson's hand froze, the glass of orange juice halfway to her mouth, as she stared at her son over the plate of scrambled eggs.

"You want me to do what?"

Eric had known it wasn't going to be an easy sell. Ever since his father had died six months before, his mother had shut herself off from the world, struggling not only with grief over the passing of her lifelong companion but also with a sense of uselessness. A nurturer by disposition, she had found her meaning in life by caring for the men she loved—Eric when he was younger, and in recent years her husband, as failing health made him increasingly dependent. In fact, their already strong mutual devotion had seemed to intensify as Walter's physical condition weakened.

While some women would resent the demands of living with an ill spouse, Anna had never complained. As she'd told her son on more than one occasion, "Walter took care of us for a lot of years, Eric. He worked three jobs at once when you were a baby just to make ends meet. Nothing was too much trouble if it made life easier for the people he loved. How can I do any less now, when he needs me?"

Now, with his father gone and the demands of his practice keeping him too busy to give his mother as much time as he'd like, she was adrift. The inspired idea he'd had in the office a couple of days before had seemed like the perfect solution for everyone. His mother needed someone to take care of. Sarah needed someone to do just that. Kate needed the peace of mind that a good caregiver would provide. And he wanted to help his mother find new purpose in life. It was an ideal arrangement.

But from the way she was staring at him, one would think he'd suggested she take up skydiving.

"I'd like you to consider watching one of my patients five days a week during school hours while her mother teaches," he repeated evenly.

His mother set her glass down and continued to stare at him. "Why on earth would I what to do that?"

Eric mulled over his response while the server poured him a fresh cup of coffee and decided on the direct approach.

"She needs help, Mom."

Anna frowned at him. "Who? The mother or the little girl?"

"Both."

Even if she wasn't exactly receptive, he'd at least aroused her curiosity, Eric thought. His mother hadn't looked this interested in anything since before his father had died. Their after-church Sunday-morning breakfasts had become a ritual during the last six months. It was a time he reserved exclusively for her, but usually she was subdued and barely picked at her food. Today he'd managed to snap her out of her apathy, if only for a few moments.

In fact, as she studied him now, he began to grow slightly uncomfortable. He knew that look. It was one he remembered well from his growing-up years, when she was trying to figure out what was going on in his mind, what his motivation was. Her next question confirmed it.

"Eric, in all the years you've been a doctor, I've never seen you take such a personal interest in a patient. Is there something you're not telling me about this situation?"

He had to give her credit. She was as sharp and insightful as ever. He'd never told her about the accident, but he did so now, as briefly as possible and characteristically downplaying his role. She listened with interest, and when he'd finished she looked at him shrewdly.

"And your paths just suddenly crossed again two days ago?"

"Yes."

She pondered that for a moment. "It seems odd, doesn't it?"

"Very."

"Even so, there's really no reason for you to get

involved in this woman's life, is there? You must meet a lot of parents who are facing similar dilemmas."

He couldn't argue with that. Broken families, single-parent households, stepchildren—and the many problems they entailed—he'd seen it all. And he'd never before been tempted to intervene personally. At least not to this extent. His mother was right. There wasn't any reason to get involved in Kate Nolan's life. Except maybe one: he wanted to. And at the moment he wasn't inclined to analyze his motivation.

"Let's just say that I think it would be the Christian thing to do," he replied noncommittally. "You have the time. She has the need. It's the right combination of circumstances at the right time. There's nothing more to it than that."

His mother looked skeptical, but she didn't belabor the point. Instead she glanced down at her plate and poked at her scrambled eggs, a thoughtful frown on her face. Eric waited quietly, praying that she'd at least give this a chance. It would be as good for her as it would be for Kate and Sarah.

When at last she met his gaze, her own was still uncertain. "I don't know, Eric. It's a big responsibility. And they're strangers to me. What if we don't even like each other?"

"You'll like them, Mom. I guarantee it. And they'll love you. Sarah misses her grandmother, and I can't think of a better surrogate. You were made for that role."

And this was the only chance she would have to play it. The unspoken words hung in the air between them. Eric's marriage had produced no children, much to his regret. And there wouldn't be another. He had made his peace with that. Anna never had. She thought he needed a wife, and she occasionally dropped broad hints to that effect when the opportunity presented itself. As she did now.

"I haven't given up on having a real grandchild, you know," she said pointedly.

"It's time you did."

"You're only thirty-eight, Eric. It's not too late to have a family."

"Mom." There was a warning note in his voice, which Anna ignored.

"Of course, you'd need a wife first."

"I have a wife."

"You've been divorced for almost five years, Eric."

"You know how I feel about that."

Anna sighed and glanced at the wedding band on his left hand. "Yes, I guess I do."

Eric knew that most people considered divorce a perfectly acceptable solution for a troubled union, that they found his attitude archaic. As did even his mother, who didn't take divorce lightly. But he believed in the sanctity of marriage; believed that the vows so solemnly taken were for life. He and Cindy might be divorced on paper, but in the eyes of God he believed they were still man and wife. Even Cindy's remarriage three years before hadn't convinced him otherwise. He wasn't going to judge her. He left that to the Lord. But it wasn't the right thing for him. Besides, his dedication to his career had ruined one marriage. He wasn't about to inflict that burden on another woman. In the meantime, they'd wandered far from the subject at hand.

"None of this has any bearing on our discussion, Mom," he pointed out. "If you're worried about whether you'll all get along, then how about this—I'll call Kate Nolan, and if she's interested I'll arrange for her to stop by and visit you. That way, the two of you can size each other up and you can meet Sarah. How does that sound?"

Anna nodded slowly. "I suppose I could consider it. But I'm not making any promises, Eric."

"I don't expect you to."

"I do feel sorry for her, though. So many burdens on someone so young. How old did you say Sarah was when the accident happened?"

"Six weeks."

His mother shook her head. "I can't even imagine. It's enough of a challenge for two people to raise a child. But for a single working mother… And then to lose her own mother so recently. She really does sound like she needs help, Eric."

"She does. She's been living under tremendous strain for years. I'd say she's approaching the danger level on the stress scale."

"Well, I suppose I could meet her, at least. Maybe help her out until she finds someone to take over permanently."

Eric felt the tension in his shoulders ease. "I know she'd appreciate it, Mom."

"This is all contingent on whether we get along, though," his mother cautioned.

"You'll get along fine."

"How can you be so sure?"

"Because I know you."

"But you don't know Kate Nolan. You just met her."

"Let's just call it intuition."

Eric was relieved that his mother seemed to accept that response. Even it if wasn't quite true. Because, odd as it seemed, he felt as if he *did* know Kate Nolan. But he couldn't very well tell his mother that. She would jump to all sorts of conclusions—all of them wrong, of course.

Weren't they?

Chapter Two

Kate pulled to a stop in front of the small, tidy brick bungalow and took a slow, steadying breath. She still wasn't sure how all this had come about.

Two days ago, when Eric Carlson had called to check on Sarah, Kate had been impressed by his conscientiousness. No doctor she'd seen before had ever personally followed up with a phone call after an office visit. She'd hardly recovered from that pleasant surprise when he'd gone on to say that he might have a solution to her day-care problem. To put it mildly, she'd been overwhelmed.

Even now, it was difficult to believe that he had gone to so much trouble, especially for a new patient. And by enlisting the aid of his own mother, no less! Of course, the way he'd carefully explained it to Kate, she'd be doing *him* a favor if this all worked out. Apparently his mother had been quite despondent since the death of Eric's father, and he was convinced that if she had someone to nurture—namely Sarah—she'd regain some sense of purpose in life.

He might be right, Kate mused. Feeling needed did

wonders to help one through the day. But as far as she
was concerned, *she* was the one who had the most to
gain from this arrangement. Of course, Kate had to feel
comfortable with Eric's mother. That was imperative.
But almost anything would be an improvement over her
current arrangement. Besides, she was sure the woman's
character would be impeccable. If she had raised a man
as fine as Eric seemed to be, how could she be anything
less than stellar?

The stifling heat and humidity of the St. Louis
summer slammed against Kate with a force that almost
took her breath away as she stepped out of the car. It was
a bit late in the season for such sauna-like conditions,
but then again, in St. Louis you never knew. It was too
bad the weather had decided to act up today, though. The
classrooms at the school where she taught weren't air-
conditioned, and she felt totally wilted and drained. On
top of everything else, Sarah was cranky after another
obviously unpleasant day at the day-care center—not the
best time to make a good first impression, Kate thought
ruefully. But it was too late to change the appointment
now.

"Come on, honey, it will be cool in the house," she
told Sarah encouragingly as she unbuckled her daughter's seat belt, then reached for her hand.

"I want to go home," Sarah whimpered, holding
back.

"I know, honey. So do I. But I promised Dr. Eric we'd
stop and visit his mommy. She's lonesome here all by
herself. And we wouldn't want to break our promise to
Dr. Eric, would we?"

Sarah wasn't in the mood for logic—or guilt trips.

"I don't want to," she declared stubbornly.

Kate's head began to pound. "We won't stay long. But

I promised Dr. Eric. We have to go in," she told Sarah, struggling to keep her voice calm as she gently but firmly pulled her protesting daughter from the car.

"I don't want to!" Sarah wailed, resisting Kate's efforts.

"Sarah! Stop whining!" she ordered sharply, her patience evaporating. "We're going to go in. Now. And we'll be done a lot faster if you cooperate."

Sarah was still whimpering miserably as they made their way up the brick walkway. Despite her terse tone of moments before, Kate could empathize. She was so wrung out from the heat and the stress of the last few weeks that she felt like doing exactly the same thing. Instead, she forced herself to pay attention to her surroundings. She noted the large trees and fenced backyard—a perfect place for a child, she reflected appreciatively. Lots of shade and plenty of room to run and play. And Eric's mother lived just ten minutes away from her apartment. If only things would work out! She needed a few breaks—desperately. So did Sarah.

As a result, for the first time in a very long while, Kate made a request of the Lord. For Sarah's sake. She'd stopped praying for herself long ago, when He'd ignored her entreaties and abandoned her. But maybe He'd listen on behalf of a child. *Let this work out,* she pleaded silently. *I want what's best for Sarah, and I don't know where else to turn.*

As Kate pressed the doorbell, she glanced down at her daughter. Sarah still looked hot and unhappy and ill-tempered. Kate just hoped that once inside, where it was cool, she'd settle down and give Eric's mother a glimpse of the charming little girl she usually was.

The door was pulled open almost immediately, leaving Kate to wonder if the older woman had been hovering on the inside of the door as anxiously as she was standing on the outside. For a moment they looked at each other, each rapidly taking inventory. Eric looked nothing like his mother, Kate noted immediately. This woman's hair was mostly gray, though traces of faded auburn revealed its original color—a contrast to Eric's gold blond. While Eric was tall—at least six feet—his mother was of moderate height. Five-five at the most, in heels, Kate estimated. And Eric had a trim, athletic build, while his mother was softly rounded. But she had a nice face, Kate decided. And her eyes were kind.

"You must be Kate," Anna said at last, her initial polite smile softening into true warmth.

"Yes. And this is Sarah."

Anna looked down at the little girl who eyed her warily.

"My! You're much more grown-up than I expected. I'm so glad you and your mommy decided to visit me today. It's always nice to make new friends, isn't it? Why don't you both come in before you melt and we'll have something cold to drink."

She moved aside, and Kate stepped into the welcome coolness.

"Oh, it feels wonderful in here!" she exclaimed with a sigh.

"It sure is a hot one out there today," Anna commiserated as she led the way into the living room. "Eric tells me you teach. I certainly hope the school is air-conditioned."

Kate made a wry face. "No such luck. But I'll survive. This heat can't last forever."

"Well, let me get you both something to perk you up." She looked at Sarah, who sat quietly close beside Kate on the couch. "Now, I'll just bet you're the kind of girl who likes ice cream. Am I right?" Sarah nodded. "That's what I thought. Let me see—chocolate chip, that would be my guess."

Sarah's eyes grew wide. "That's my favorite."

"Mine, too. How about a nice big bowl to help you cool off? That is, if it's okay with your mother." She glanced at Kate, who smiled and nodded. "Good. I'll just run out to the kitchen and get it ready. Would you like to come, too? I have a parakeet you might like to meet."

Sarah looked at her curiously. "What's a para— parakeet?"

"Why, it's the most beautiful bird! Sometimes he even talks. His name is George. Would you like to see him?" Sarah nodded, and when Anna held out her hand the little girl took it shyly. The older woman looked over at Kate. "I'll get Sarah settled in the kitchen with her ice cream, and then we can have a little chat. Would you like some iced tea?"

"I'd love some," Kate replied gratefully. "Thank you."

Kate watched them leave. It must run in the family, this ability to make friends so easily with children, she marveled. Eric certainly had the gift. And now she knew where he got it. She listened to the animated chatter coming from the kitchen, and took a moment to look around the living room. It was a cozy space, neat as a pin but not too fussy. The furniture was comfortable and overstuffed—made for sitting in, not just looking at. Fresh flowers stood in a vase on the coffee table, and family photos were artfully arranged on the mantel.

Kate's gaze lingered on the pictures, and she rose and moved closer to examine them. She started at one end, with a black-and-white wedding photo—probably

Anna and her husband, Kate speculated. Then came a picture of the same couple cutting a twenty-fifth-anniversary cake. Eric's father looked like a nice man, Kate reflected. And it was clear now where Eric got his looks. His father was tall, dignified, blond and blue-eyed—in other words, an older version of Eric.

But it wasn't photos of Anna and her husband that dominated the mantel. It was pictures of their son. Eric as a baby. Eric in a cub-scout uniform. Eric in a cap and gown, flanked by his proud parents. Eric with his parents again, in a shot of more recent vintage, taken on the deck of a cruise ship. And on the wall next to the mantel, a framed newspaper clipping about Eric having been named Man of the Year by a local charitable organization. Clearly, he was his parents' pride and joy.

But there was something missing from this gallery, Kate suddenly realized. Eric wore a wedding band. She remembered noticing it in the office, when he'd been playing with his pen. But there was nothing here to indicate that he had a wife, or a family. Or that he ever had. Curious.

Just then Anna returned, and Kate turned guiltily from the mantel, her face flushed. "I hope you don't mind. I was admiring your pictures."

"Not at all," Anna assured her as she deposited a tray holding iced tea and a plate of cookies on the coffee table. "That's what they're there for. Now, I think we can relax and have a chat. Sarah is trying to get George to talk, and I also left her with some crayons and paper and asked her to draw me some pictures of him. That should keep her busy for a few minutes, anyway."

"You and your son both have a way with children," Kate said as a compliment to her as she returned to her seat.

"Well, it's not hard with a lovely little girl like that."

Kate grinned. "She wasn't so lovely a few minutes ago. I practically had to drag her in here. I figured you'd take one look and say, 'No way.' I think she had a rough day at day care." Her smile quickly faded.

"I guess that's what we're here to talk about," Anna replied. "Eric tells me that your mother used to watch her, until she passed away a month ago. I'm so very sorry about that, my dear. The loss of a mother is one of life's greatest trials."

The sincere sympathy in the older woman's voice brought a lump to Kate's throat, and she struggled to contain her tears. With all the turmoil since her mother's death—the disruption in the placid routine of their days, her worry about how Sarah was handling the death, and the necessity of making last-minute arrangements for her daughter's care—she'd had little time to grieve. But the ache of loss was heavy in her heart.

"Thank you. Mom and I were always close, but during these last few years since she came to live with us we forged an even stronger bond. My dad died about eight years ago, and Mom sold the farm in Ohio where we grew up and moved to an apartment in Cincinnati. She came to help out while Jack—my husband—was in the hospital, and when he died, she just stayed on. It was the best possible arrangement for all of us under the circumstances."

"You must miss her very much."

Kate nodded. The loneliness of her life had been thrown into stark relief by the death of her mother. Even her weekly phone calls to her sister didn't ease her sense of isolation.

"It was hard enough when Jack died. But Mom was

there for me to lean on. Now... Well, it's just me. And
Sarah, of course. She's such a joy to me. A lifeline,
really. Even more precious because we never thought
she'd happen. My husband and I tried for five years
before we had her. We'd almost given up when we discovered I was pregnant. And we both agreed that I'd
stay home at least until she went to school. We were
firm believers that mothering is a full-time job."

Anna nodded approvingly. "I often think young
mothers today make a mistake when they try to have it
all. Not that you can't, of course. I just don't think you
can have it all at the same time. 'To everything there is
a season.' And children need full-time mothers, unless
there are extraordinary circumstances."

"I agree completely. But as it turned out, I was faced
with those extraordinary circumstances. I guess Eric
told you what happened."

"He filled me in on the basics. I understand you lost
your husband shortly after Sarah was born."

Kate nodded. "It was a nightmare. The accident happened on our first night out together since Sarah was
born. We'd had an early dinner to celebrate our sixth
anniversary."

"Oh, my dear! I had no idea. How awful!" Anna's
face registered shock and sympathy.

"Unfortunately, the worst was still to come," Kate
continued, her voice flat and lifeless. "Jack lived for
seven months, but he never regained consciousness. By
the time he died our finances were pretty much depleted. Long-term care is very expensive, and insurance
doesn't cover everything. So I went back to teaching,
sold our house and moved into an apartment. We've
coped till now, but when Mom died, everything just
fell apart again." Her voice caught on the last word, and

she paused to take a deep breath, struggling to keep her tears at bay. Her voice was shaky when she continued. "I just can't bear to see Sarah so unhappy. That's why I'm desperate to find a more personal, one-on-one day-care situation. Someone who can give her the love and affection and attention that I would give her if I could be there. I guess your son thought you might be willing to pinch-hit, at least until I can find something more permanent. I'm hoping the same thing," she admitted frankly.

Anna carefully set her iced-tea glass on a coaster and looked at Kate, her face concerned. "I'd like to help you, my dear. But you do understand that I'm not experienced in day care, don't you?"

Kate smiled. "You're a mother. And you raised a fine son, from what I can see. You seem kind and caring. And Sarah seems to have taken to you. Those are good enough credentials for me." Kate had decided after five minutes in her presence that Anna was the answer to her prayer.

"Well, as Eric told me, this might be my one and only chance to play grandmother," the older woman reflected. "And I would enjoy that."

Kate looked at her curiously. "What do you mean?"

"Eric's divorced. Has been for almost five years. He and Cindy never had any children. Pity, too, when he loves children so much."

"But he might remarry."

Anna shook her head sadly. "Not Eric. So perhaps I'd best take my opportunity."

Kate was curious about Anna's enigmatic comment regarding Eric, but her attention was focused on the woman's second statement. She looked at her hopefully, her own heart banging painfully in her chest. "Does that mean you'll watch Sarah?"

Anna nodded. "At least for a while. Just tell me what kind of schedule you're thinking about."

Within ten minutes the details were settled, and Kate looked across at Anna. "I can't ever thank you enough for this, Mrs. Carlson. I feel like such a great burden has been lifted from my mind."

"First of all, it's Anna. And I'm glad I can help you with this. It seems like you've had far too many trials for someone so young."

"I don't feel very young these days," Kate admitted wearily. "I may only be thirty-six, but sometimes I feel ancient."

Suddenly Sarah burst into the room to proudly show off her drawings of George. As Anna exclaimed over them, Kate settled back with her iced tea. Once upon a time, Eric had saved her husband's life. In many ways, Kate felt he had just now saved hers. And in her heart she knew that she owed him a debt of gratitude she could never even begin to repay.

"So what happened?"

"I'm fine, thanks. How are you?" Anna's amused voice came over the wire.

"Sorry," Eric apologized sheepishly. "It's just that I've had your meeting with Mrs. Nolan on my mind all afternoon, and this is the first chance I've had to call."

"It's seven-thirty. It must have been a busy day."

"It was. I had an emergency at the hospital that delayed me."

He heard her exasperated sigh. "You work too

hard, Eric. Especially since the divorce. I admire your dedication, but you need to have a life, too."

They'd been over this before—countless times. After Cindy had left and he'd decided that marriage and medicine didn't mix, he'd immersed himself in his work to the exclusion of just about everything else. He knew it wasn't healthy. He knew he needed to back off from some of his commitments, resign from a couple of the boards he was on, give some serious thought to his partner's suggestion that they bring another doctor into their practice. And he'd get around to all those things one of these days. In the meantime, he was more worried about the stress level of one beautiful-but-sad mother and her little girl.

"You're changing the subject, Mom."

"Well, I worry about you."

"Worry about Mrs. Nolan and Sarah instead. They need it more than I do."

She sighed again. "Yes, I think you're right. Oh, Eric, the minute I opened the door and looked at them, my heart just about broke. Sarah is such a precious, sensitive child. I can see where she'd feel lost in one of those big day-care centers. And Kate… Oh, dear, that poor woman. What a tragic story! And to have that accident happen on her wedding anniversary—I can't even imagine the horror. Anyway, she looked so lost and alone, standing there on the porch. And so tired and anxious. I just wanted to hug her."

Eric could relate to that. He'd felt exactly the same way. "So you agreed to watch Sarah?"

"How could I refuse? As you said, it just seemed like the Christian thing to do. Besides, I liked them both. It won't be a hardship."

"When do you start?"

"Tomorrow."

Eric's eyebrows rose in surprise. "Pretty fast action."

"Why wait? I don't have anything planned, and Kate can't get her daughter out of that place fast enough. Of course, I had to run to the store and pick up a few things. Peanut butter and jelly, ingredients for my sugar cookies, some coloring books and Play-Doh. You know, that kind of thing. I'm not used to entertaining a child."

There was a new energy in his mother's voice, an enthusiasm that Eric hadn't heard in months. Apparently his instinct that this arrangement would be good for everyone had been right on target, he thought with satisfaction.

"Do you need me to do anything?"

"No. I have it all under control, thanks."

"Well, I'll see you Sunday, then. And good luck."

"Thanks. I think things will work out just fine."

So did Eric. He was happy for his mother and Kate and Sarah—and strangely enough, for himself, as well. He wasn't quite sure why. Perhaps because now he could stop worrying so much about his mother. He could use some peace of mind on that score.

But there were other things about this arrangement that *weren't* conducive to peace of mind, he suddenly realized. Such as the link it provided with Kate Nolan. For reasons he preferred to leave unexplored, he didn't think that would necessarily lead to mental serenity.

"You know, one of these days I'm going to stop inviting you, since you never come, but Mary said I should try one more time. So…barbecue, Labor Day, five o'clock. What's your excuse this time?"

Eric slid the chart back into the folder and grinned at his partner. Frank Shapiro seemed the complete opposite of his colleague. Six inches shorter, with close-cropped, thinning brown hair and a wiry build, Frank exuded high energy in contrast to Eric's calm demeanor. While Frank was an outgoing extrovert, Eric stayed more to himself. But as they'd discovered during their residency together, in every other way— philosophical, ethical, political, religious—they were a good match. Their partnership had flourished, and Eric had only one complaint. Since his divorce, Frank had been unrelenting in his attempts to spice up Eric's practically nonexistent social life. Eric had always deflected his efforts, but he suddenly decided to throw his friend a curve.

"No excuse. I'll be there."

Frank stared at him. "What?"

"I said I'll come."

Frank tilted his head and looked at Eric suspiciously. "Are you serious?"

"Uh-huh."

"Well…gosh, that's great! Wait till I tell Mary our persistence finally paid off."

"Can I bring anything?"

"No, thanks. Except a date, that is." Frank grinned.

Eric grinned back. His friend was joking, of course. Frank knew he never dated. But suddenly Eric thought of Kate Nolan, and his expression grew thoughtful. He suspected she had even less of a social life than he did; that she rarely, if ever, allowed herself a night out, and that there was very little laughter and lightheartedness in her world. Not much of a life for a young, vital woman. Maybe he ought to ask her.

Eric frowned. Now where had that idea come from? What about his rule of keeping personal involvements at arm's length? Exceptions weren't a good idea, he told himself firmly. And yet, for some reason, ever since Kate had walked into his office he'd felt a sense of… *responsibility*—that was the word—for her. He couldn't explain it. Didn't even try. It was just there. And it nudged him to invite her. Just as a friend, of course. It would be an act of charity. Nothing more.

He laid the folder on the counter and purposely kept his tone casual. "I just might do that."

The look of surprise on Frank's face was almost comical. He stared at his partner for several seconds before he found his voice.

"Well…that's great!" He clearly wanted to ask more, but for once he seemed momentarily at a loss for words. And Eric didn't give him a chance to recover.

"On to the next patient," he declared, picking up a chart. As he walked away he could sense Frank staring after him, the dumbfounded look still on his face. And Eric couldn't help grinning. Everyone figured he was so predictable. Well, maybe it was time he started surprising a few people.

Then again, maybe it wasn't, Eric ruminated glumly as he stared at the phone in his office on Friday evening. The party was only three days away, and he still hadn't summoned up the courage to call Kate Nolan. What on earth had prompted him to make that impetuous remark to Frank? He should have been content with Frank's initial surprise when he'd accepted the invitation. There had been no need for overkill, he chastised himself.

And now he was stuck. Frank expected him to show up with a date in tow, and he'd never hear the end of it if he didn't. His partner would badger him about the "mystery" woman he'd "almost" brought. Even worse, thinking he was now willing to date, Frank would renew his efforts to set his friend up, much as he had—relent-lessly—for a year or two after the divorce. Eric closed his eyes and groaned. He loved Frank. Like a brother. But not when he played matchmaker. No, he had to show up with someone. And Kate Nolan was the only option.

Besides, there were altruistic reasons for this invita-tion, he rationalized. Kate seemed to lead far too soli-tary a life. As far as he could see, she only had Sarah. The little girl was a charmer, he acknowledged, and she seemed to adequately fulfill her mother's nurtur-ing needs. But what about Kate's other needs? Despite the tragedy that had taken the man she loved, she still needed adult companionship. And adult conversation. And someone who cared when she had a cold or a taxing day, who worried when she worked too hard or didn't eat right. He was certain those needs weren't being met. Inviting her to go with him to Frank's party wasn't a solution—but it might be a step toward a more normal, balanced life for her.

Feeling more confident, he picked up the phone and dialed her number, tapping his pen restlessly against the desk as he waited. When she answered, three rings later and out of breath, his hand stilled.

"Mrs. Nolan? It's Eric Carlson." That was odd. He sounded as breathless as she did.

There was a momentary pause, and he could sense her surprise, could imagine the look of astonishment on her face. His assessment of her reaction was confirmed by her tone of voice when she spoke.

"Hello, Doctor." He heard her draw a deep breath. "I was just opening the door when the phone rang. I had to run to answer it." *And why are you calling me?* The question, though unasked, hung in the air.

"I wanted to thank you for the note you sent me." She'd written him a warm, heartfelt letter after Anna had agreed to watch Sarah, and it suddenly seemed like a good way to open the conversation.

"Oh. You're welcome. I was very grateful for everything you did."

"I'm just glad it worked out. Mom seems much more like her old self, even though it's only been a week."

"Well, speaking for Sarah, this seems like a match made in heaven. She and your mom hit it off right from the beginning. Her morning tune has changed from 'Do I have to go?' to 'Hurry up, Mom. We'll be late for Aunt Anna's.' In fact, I'm not sure how she'll manage away from your mom for three whole days over the Labor Day holiday."

That gave him the opening he needed. "Maybe she doesn't have to."

He could hear the frown in Kate's voice. "What do you mean?"

Eric took a deep breath and willed his racing pulse to slow down. You'd think he'd never asked a woman out before, he thought with chagrin. And this wasn't even a real date, anyway.

"Well, I know this is a bit last-minute, but I was wondering if you were free Monday. My partner is having a barbecue, and I thought it might be a nice change of pace for you, after the stress of the last few weeks. And I could use a break myself."

Her stunned silence conveyed her reaction more eloquently than words. Well, what did he expect? he asked himself wryly. After all, they barely knew each other. In her position he'd probably react the same way. And he'd likely decline. So before she could do so, he spoke again, playing his trump card.

"I'm sure you're surprised by the invitation, but to be honest, you'd do me a real favor if you'd accept. Frank is a great guy, but he's always trying to fix me up and I'd like to avoid that. I'm just not interested in dating, and I can't seem to convince him of that. I usually turn down his invitations, but I figured if I came to one of his parties with a date, he might decide I could take care of my own social life after all and would lay off."

Kate stared at the phone, a frown marring her brow, her refusal dying on her lips. She wasn't in the dating mode and never would be again. What was the point, when she'd already had the best? That kind of love only came around once in a lifetime. Though Jack might be gone in body, she'd never let him go in her heart. He was her husband. He was Sarah's father. And no one could take his place. Ever. Period. She'd never even looked at another man since his death, let alone dated one. And she saw no reason to start now.

But then Eric had added that caveat:
that she'd be doing him a favor by saving him from the well-meaning-but-unwanted matchmaking efforts of his friend. Then he'd gone on to say that he wasn't interested in dating, either. His mother had implied the same thing at their first meeting, Kate recalled. And she owed him—big time, after what he'd done to help her resolve her day-care dilemma. So what would be the harm in accepting his invitation? Nothing that she could articulate. Yet somehow it didn't feel quite right. The notion of spending an evening in Eric's company made her...uneasy.

As the silence lengthened, Kate realized she had to say something. And honesty seemed the best approach. "I don't know, Doctor," she replied frankly, toying with the phone cord as she spoke. "I try to spend all my free time with Sarah. And I'd have to find someone to watch her."

"That's where Mom comes in. She'd be happy to look after Sarah."

"You mean…you already asked your mother?" She was clearly taken aback.

"Uh-huh." He'd checked with her before he'd called Kate, wanting to remove any potential stumbling blocks in advance.

"Oh. Well, wasn't she…surprised?"

"Actually, no." Which had surprised *him*. He'd expected to be plied with questions when he'd made the request. Instead, his mother had simply said, "No problem." And frankly, that had made him a little nervous. It wasn't like her. But instead of pressing his luck, he'd simply said thanks and ended the conversation as soon as possible, before she slipped back into character and launched into the third degree.

"Oh." Kate was starting to sound like George, who had a tendency to repeat the same words over and over again, she realized. "Well, I do have school the next day."

"We can make it an early night."

It was getting harder and harder to think of excuses. Eric was being absolutely cooperative and understanding. How could she say no? With a sigh, Kate capitulated. "All right, Doctor. If it will help you out."

He closed his eyes and let out a long, slow breath. When he spoke again, she heard the teasing tone in his voice.

"There's just one thing."

"What?"

"I don't think this is going to work too well if you

call me 'Doctor.' Frank might smell a rat, don't you think?"

Kate found herself smiling. "You could be right."

"So…how about if we switch to Eric and Kate?"

"I just hope I don't forget. I'm used to thinking of you as 'Doctor.'"

"I may have the same problem. Be sure to elbow me if I call you Mrs. Nolan."

But he wouldn't. Because oddly enough, since the moment she'd walked into his office she'd been "Kate" to him. In fact, he'd had to remind himself to call her "Mrs. Nolan." So this switch would be no problem at all.

"All right, Doct— Eric," she corrected herself.

They settled on a time, and as Eric replaced the receiver and leaned back in his chair, he experienced an odd combination of emotions. Relief. Satisfaction. Anticipation. Uncertainty. And last, but certainly not least, guilt.

He frowned over that last one. Why did he suddenly have this niggling sensation of guilt? He wasn't doing anything wrong. Professional ethics kept doctors from dating patients, but he knew of no such sanction against *mommies* of patients. And he hadn't exerted too much pressure on Kate. If she'd resisted too much, he would have backed off. The last thing she needed in her life was more stress. Finally, while it was true that he refrained from dating because he believed that in the eyes of the Lord he was still married, this wasn't a real date.

So why did he feel guilty? After all, he was doing this for her. Out of compassion. As a friend. He felt sorry for her. It was as simple as that.

Or was it? he asked himself. Because if his motives

were so noble and unselfish, if he was only thinking of *her,* why was *he* looking forward to the barbecue so much?

Chapter Three

Kate glanced in the mirror behind her bedroom door and absently adjusted the strap on her sundress. She'd been so taken aback by Dr. Carlson's—Eric's, she reminded herself—invitation that she hadn't thought to ask about attire. Was she too dressed up? What did people wear to a barbecue these days? It had been years since she'd been to one. To any purely social function, in fact. It actually felt odd to be dressing up for a night out. Odd—and a little uncomfortable.

Kate frowned. Even though Eric had made it clear that this wasn't a date, it had all the trappings of one. And that made her conscience twinge, as if she were somehow cheating on Jack. Which was ridiculous, of course. She loved Jack absolutely, with a devotion that was undimmed by the years. She was simply doing a favor for someone who had gone out of his way to be kind to her. There was no reason to feel guilty, she admonished herself sternly.

Resolutely she picked up her purse and stepped into the hall. Sarah glanced up from her perch on the couch and smiled as Kate approached.

"You look pretty, Mommy."

"Thanks, honey."

"I wish I could go to the party, too."

Kate's heart contracted and she sat down beside Sarah. She already felt incredibly guilty about leaving her daughter with a sitter—even if it *was* Anna—on a weekend, and Sarah's innocent comment was enough to send a pang through her heart. For just a moment she was tempted to back out on Eric. But she owed him this, she reminded herself. Just as she owed Sarah as much time as possible on her days off to make up for all the hours during the week when they had to be apart. It was a perennial dilemma, this conflict between her daughter's needs and other obligations. But she *had* promised Eric. And Sarah would be fine for one night with Anna, she assured herself.

"I wish you could, too, honey. But it's a grown-up party. And when Dr. Eric asked me to go with him I thought I should, since he was so nice to us. If it wasn't for Dr. Eric, we would never have met Aunt Anna," Kate reminded her, using the affectionate title for the older woman that she and Anna had decided upon.

"I like Aunt Anna," Sarah declared. "She said we would make cookies tonight and watch *Mary Poppins.* Have you seen that movie, Mommy?"

"Uh-huh. You'll like it. And I might even be back before it's over."

The doorbell rang, and Kate reached over to give Sarah a quick hug. "That's Dr. Eric now. Run and get your sweater and then we'll take you over to Aunt Anna's."

As Sarah scampered toward her bedroom, Kate rose and walked slowly to the door. She still felt ill at ease, but she tried to suppress her nervousness. After all, Eric seemed like a nice man. He wasn't looking for anything more than companionship. And she *had* been a pretty good conversationalist at one time, even if her skills were a bit rusty. Maybe she'd even have fun, she told herself encouragingly. But she knew that possibility was remote. Fun didn't play much of a role in her life these days. She reached for the knob and sighed. Wouldn't it be nice, though, if—

The sight of Eric's broad shoulders filling her doorway cut off her thought in mid-sentence and her polite smile of welcome froze on her face. He looked different today, she thought inanely, her lips parting slightly in surprise as she stared at him. More…human. And he exuded a virility that had been camouflaged beneath his clinical demeanor, white coat and stethoscope during their last encounter in his office. At work he looked professional and slightly remote, and his role was clear. In his present attire—khaki trousers and a cobalt-blue golf shirt that hugged his muscular chest and matched the color of his eyes—he seemed to be playing a much less precisely defined role. It was an unsettling and intimidating change. Yet his eyes—warm and genuine and straightforward, even while reflecting some other emotion she couldn't quite put her finger on—helped to calm her jitters.

Eric watched the play of emotions on Kate's face as he struggled to control his own expression. Her smile of welcome had faded to a look of surprise, and her slightly parted lips, along with the pulse that began to beat in the delicate hollow of her throat, clearly communicated her nervousness. She looked vulnerable and scared…and very, very appealing, he thought, as his heart stopped, then raced on. By anyone's definition, her simple sundress was modest, hinting at—rather than revealing—her curves. But the white piqué was a perfect foil for her dark hair and eyes. She wore a delicate gold chain at her neck, and his eyes lingered for a moment on the spot where it rested against the creamy skin at the edge of her collarbone.

Eric swallowed past the sudden lump in his throat, fighting a swift—and disconcerting—surge of panic. Until this moment he'd felt somehow insulated from Kate's beauty, gentle manner and earnest efforts to do the right thing for her daughter. He'd admired her, but he'd felt in control and able to keep a safe emotional distance. Suddenly he didn't feel at all in control. Or safe. Or distant.

But that wasn't *her* problem, he reminded himself. He'd just have to deal with his own surprising reaction later. Right now he needed to make her relax. And that would be no small chore, he realized. The pulsating shimmer of her gold chain clearly suggested accelerated respiration, indicating that she was as nervous about this setup as he suddenly was. Not a good sign.

Deliberately he tipped his lips up into a smile, and when he spoke his voice was warm and friendly—but purposely not *too* friendly. "Hello, Kate. I…"

"Hi, Dr. Eric." Sarah burst into the room, dragging her sweater by one sleeve.

He grinned at Kate as Sarah's exuberant entrance dissipated the tension in the room, then he squatted down beside his small patient and touched her nose. "Hello, Sarah. Are you still having those tummyaches?"

"No. They're all gone. You must be a very good doctor."

He chuckled. "I think maybe Dr. Anna can take the credit for your cure."

Sarah gave him a puzzled look. "Is Aunt Anna a doctor, too?"

He smiled. "In some ways. She always used to make me feel better after I fell off my bike and scraped my knees."

"I like her," Sarah declared.

"So do I."

"We're going to make cookies tonight and watch *Mary Poppins*."

"Now that sounds like fun."

"You can come, too," Sarah offered.

"I'd like to. But I promised my friend I'd come to his party. Maybe we can watch a movie together sometime, though."

"Can Mommy watch, too?"

Eric glanced up at Kate apologetically, realizing he'd put her in an awkward position. "Sure. If she wants to."

"Oh, Mommy likes movies. Don't you, Mommy?"

Kate didn't answer. Instead, she picked up her purse. "Shouldn't we be leaving? I promised Sarah I wouldn't be gone too long, and it's getting late."

He rose slowly, aware that she was laying out the ground rules for tonight. Clearly, it was going to be a short evening. Still, it was better than nothing, he consoled himself. Even a couple of hours in the company of adults, where she could laugh and relax, might help chase the haunted look from her eyes.

"Yes, we should."

As he turned toward the door the phone rang, and Kate hesitated. Then she sighed. "I'd better get it. It will only take a minute."

"No rush."

Although Sarah's chatter kept him occupied during

Kate's absence, Eric took the opportunity to glance around her modest apartment. There was a small living room, a tiny kitchenette with a counter that served as a dining table, and—judging by the three doors opening off the short hallway—apparently two bedrooms and a bath. The unit was barely large enough for two people, let alone three, he concluded with a frown. How had they managed in such a confined space when her mother was alive?

Apparently there'd been no choice. His mother had mentioned Kate's comment about her finances being depleted, and this tiny, older apartment was eloquent testimony to a tight budget. Yet she'd made it a home, he realized, noting with appreciation the warm touches that gave the rooms a comfortable, inviting feel. One of Sarah's drawings had been framed and hung on the wall. A cross-stitched pillow rested on the couch. Green plants flourished in a wicker stand by the window. And several family photos were prominently displayed.

His eyes lingered on the photo on top of the television. Kate was holding a tiny baby and a man sat next to her, on the edge of a couch, his arm protectively around her shoulders. Jack. Eric recognized him from the night of the accident. And on the opposite wall hung a wedding picture in which Kate and Jack were slightly younger—and obviously very much in love.

"That's my daddy," Sarah declared, noting the direction of Eric's gaze.

He smiled down at her. "That's what I thought. He looks very nice."

Sarah turned to study the picture gravely. "Mommy says he was. She says he loved me very much." She transferred her gaze to the photo on the TV. "That's me in that picture, when I was a baby. That's my daddy, too.

I don't remember him, though. He went to heaven right after I was born."

Eric felt his throat tighten, but before he could respond Kate spoke from the hallway.

"I'm sorry for the delay. We can go now."

He looked up, and the raw pain in her eyes tugged at his heart.

"Did you know my daddy?" Sarah asked Eric, oblivious to Kate's distress.

With an effort he withdrew his gaze from Kate's and glanced back down at Sarah. "No. I wish I had," he said gently.

"So do I. Then you could tell me what he was like. Mommy tells me stories about him, but sometimes she cries and it makes me sad."

"Sarah! That's enough about Daddy!" Kate admonished, her face flushed. When she saw Sarah's startled gaze, her eyes filled with dismay and she gentled her tone. "You don't want to keep Aunt Anna waiting, do you? She's probably all ready to make those cookies."

A slightly subdued Sarah walked to the door. "We were waiting for *you*, Mommy," she pointed out in a hurt voice that only made Kate feel worse.

Sarah talked nonstop to Eric during the short drive, and when they dropped her off, Anna wished them a pleasant evening and told them not to hurry. "We'll have lots of fun, won't we, Sarah?"

The little girl nodded vigorously, and Kate bent down beside her.

"You be a good girl, now. And Mommy will be back soon." Her voice sounded artificially bright, and the slight, almost-unnoticeable catch at the end tugged at Eric's heart.

"Okay."

It was Kate who seemed reluctant to part, he noted. Sarah seemed perfectly happy to spend the evening with his mother. Kate confirmed his impression as they drove away.

"You know, this is the first time I've ever left her with a sitter, except for day care," she admitted, her voice slightly unsteady.

"She'll be fine," he reassured her. "She and Mom get along famously."

"I know. And I'm grateful. But I feel guilty for leaving her with someone when I don't have to."

"You need a life, too, Kate," he gently pointed out. "Apart from Sarah. When was the last time you went out socially?" He caught her surprised glance out of the corner of his eye and turned to her apologetically. "Sorry. That's none of my business. But I have the impression you don't get out much, other than to your job. That's not healthy."

"Is that your professional opinion?"

"I'm not a psychiatrist. But balance is important to a healthy lifestyle."

"From what your mother has told me, it sounds like maybe you need to take your own advice."

He grimaced. "Touché. I do spend a lot of hours at work. But I also take time occasionally to socialize. Like tonight."

Kate turned to stare out the front windshield. "I *want* to be with Sarah, Eric. It's not a chore. Besides, I don't know that many people here. We lived in Cincinnati until a few months before Sarah was born. When we first moved to St. Louis we were too busy fixing up our house to socialize. And afterward… Well, I had no time to make friends. I was with Jack every minute I could spare. Since he died, I simply haven't had the interest or the energy to meet people. Besides, Sarah is all I need."

"Have you ever thought that maybe *she* needs more?" he suggested carefully.

Kate frowned. "Like what?"

"Friends her own age. Is she involved in any activities with other children?"

Kate stiffened. "There aren't many children in our apartment complex. And there's nowhere for her to play unless I take her to the park down the street. We get along, Eric. It's not ideal, but then, nothing is."

Eric could sense Kate's tension in her defensive posture. Not a good way to start their evening, he realized. It was time to back off.

"I didn't mean to be critical, Kate. You're right. Nothing is ideal. And your social life is none of my business. But I appreciate your willingness to help me out tonight. You'll like Frank and Mary. And maybe we'll both have some fun."

There was that word again. "Fun." It seemed so foreign, so distant. She could hardly remember what it was like to indulge in pure, carefree fun with other adults. And she didn't expect her memory to be jogged tonight.

But much to her surprise, it was.

Kate wasn't sure at exactly what point she began to relax and enjoy herself. Maybe it was when Frank told the hilarious story about how he and his wife met after Mary ran into his car. Or maybe it was when Mary learned that she and Kate liked the same author, then loaned her the woman's latest book, even though Kate protested that she never had time to read anymore. "Make time," Mary said, and extracted a promise that Kate would call her to talk about the book after she finished it. Or maybe it was when she got coaxed into a game of lawn darts, and much to everyone's surprise—including her own—proved that she had an incredibly accurate aim by trouncing one challenger after another.

All Kate knew was that suddenly she found herself laughing—and relaxing. It took her by surprise, but it also felt good. So good, in fact, that for a moment it made her eyes sting as she recalled the fun and laughter that had once been part of her normal, everyday existence. Nothing had been "normal" in her life for years, but tonight reminded her of what she had once had—and so often had taken for granted. This brief reprieve from the deep-seated sadness that had shrouded her existence for so long was like a life vest thrown to one adrift, and she clung to it greedily. Even if it only lasted tonight, she thought, it gave her a precious moment in the sunlight after years of darkness.

As Kate won her fourth round of lawn darts, Frank held up his hands in defeat. "That's it. I give up. I'm not a glutton for punishment. I duly declare Kate the Queen of Lawn Darts. And now I think it's time to move on to something more important. Let's eat."

Mary poked him in the ribs good-naturedly. "Is that all you ever think about? Food?"

He glanced down at her five-months-pregnant girth and grinned. "Obviously not."

She blushed and rolled her eyes. "I'm not going to touch that one with a ten-foot pole," she declared. "Let's eat."

"Isn't that what I just said?" he teased.

Kate watched their affectionate interplay with both amusement and envy. She and Jack had once shared that kind of closeness, where a look spoke volumes and a simple touch could unite two hearts. Even after all these years, whenever she saw a couple communicating in that special nonverbal way reserved for those deeply in love, her heart ached with the realization that for her those golden days were gone forever.

Eric saw the sudden melancholy sweep over Kate's face, and he frowned. He'd been keenly attuned to the nuances in her mood all evening, watching with pleasure as her initial uncertainty and subdued demeanor gave way to tentative smiles and then relaxed interaction. Eric was taken aback the first time he heard her musical laugh, then entranced by it. He was captivated when her eyes occasionally sparkled with delight. And he was charmed by her unaffected beauty and unconscious grace. It had been an incredible transformation—and he intended to do everything he could to sustain it.

"Did I hear someone say food?" he asked, coming up quickly behind her.

Mary gave him a rueful grin. "You men are all alike."

"Well, I certainly hope so," her husband countered with a wink. "Come on, we need to lead off or no one will eat." He took her arm and led her purposefully toward the buffet table.

Eric nodded toward the food line. "Shall we?"

Kate stepped forward, and he dropped his hand lightly to her waist, guiding her toward the serving table with a slight pressure in the small of her back. His touch startled her at first. She knew it was an impersonal gesture, born more of good manners than attraction, yet it sent an odd tingle racing along her spine. It had been a long time since she'd been touched like this. She'd almost forgotten the sense of protection it gave her—and how good it felt. She'd missed these simple little gestures, she realized with a pang. They went a long way toward making a person feel cared for. Yet she'd never recognized their importance until they were absent. And by then it was too late to experience again and savor those special, everyday moments that truly defined a relationship.

Eric heard her small sigh and looked at her with concern as he picked up two plates. "Is something wrong?"

She summoned a smile, but it was edged with sadness. "I was just remembering that old cliché, about how you never really appreciate something until it's gone." Her gaze strayed to Frank and Mary, who were holding hands as they carried their plates to a table. "They're a really nice couple."

Eric followed her gaze, then handed her a plate. "Yes, they are. It renews your faith in romance to see two people who are obviously in love."

They filled their plates in silence, and when they reached the end of the line he led the way toward a secluded table. Kate hesitated and glanced back toward the group.

"Shouldn't we mingle?"

"We've been doing that all night. Don't worry. Frank won't take offense." He deposited his plate on a table for two under a rose arbor and held out her chair. "This is a perfect spot for dinner, don't you think?"

Kate couldn't argue with that. It reminded her of an old-fashioned garden—the kind she'd once planned to have. Nowadays she had to content herself with a few ferns and African violets tucked into sunny corners of her apartment. She couldn't even give Sarah a proper yard to play in, she thought dispiritedly, her gaze drifting back to Frank and Mary. Their child would be blessed with two loving parents and plenty of room to stretch his or her legs—and wings, she thought wistfully.

As Eric sat down, one look at Kate's face made him realize that there was no way he could salvage her light-hearted mood. And maybe he shouldn't even try. Maybe she needed to talk about the things that had made the light in her eyes flicker and die.

"I have a feeling that watching Frank and Mary reminds you of your own marriage," he remarked quietly.

She looked at him in surprise, then gazed unseeingly at her plate as she toyed with her food. At first he wasn't sure she was going to respond. But a moment later she spoke.

"In some ways," she acknowledged softly, "Jack and I weren't as outgoing, but we had that same kind of special bond. I guess once you've experienced it, you just recognize it in others. Seeing Frank and Mary together makes me remember what I once had."

"I'm sorry about how things turned out, Kate. I guess the only consolation is that at least you had that special bond once."

She glanced at him. He was staring at his own plate now, apparently lost for a moment in his own memories. He seemed sad, and there was disillusion—and regret—in his eyes. Obviously she wasn't the only one with grief in her past, Kate realized with a sharp pang. Apparently Eric had not only gone through a painful divorce, but a painful marriage as well, devoid of the kind of love all young couples dream of. In some ways, perhaps the death of that dream was worse than living the dream and then losing it, she reflected. At least she had happy memories. His seemed depressing at best.

"Now it's my turn to say I'm sorry." She watched as, with an effort, he pulled himself back to the present.

He shrugged. "I survived—with the help of my family and my faith."

She looked down. "I had the family part, anyway."

Eric frowned. "No faith?"

"Not anymore."

"But Mom said that Sarah mentioned Sunday school."

"My mother used to take her. I feel badly that I haven't followed through, but my heart's not in it."

"What happened?"

She played with the edge of her napkin. "Jack and I went to church regularly. I used to think God really listened when we prayed," she said haltingly.

"And now?"

"Let's just say I haven't seen much evidence that He does. I prayed when Jack was injured. Pleaded, actually. And bargained. And begged. I put my trust in God's hands, always believing He'd come through for me. But He didn't. So I figured, what's the use? If God wasn't listening to me, why keep talking? That's when I stopped praying. And going to church. Mom picked up the slack with Sarah, but I've kind of dropped the ball since she…since she died. I feel guilty about it, but I just can't go back yet. Maybe I never will. I'm still too angry at God."

"You know, there's a simple fix for the guilt about Sarah, at least."

She gazed at him curiously. "There is?"

"Yes. Mom and I go to church every Sunday. We'd be more than happy to take her with us."

Kate looked at him in surprise, then frowned. "But

you've both done so much for me already. It just doesn't seem right."

"Well, then, think of it this way. We'd actually be doing this for Sarah."

She conceded his point with a slight lift of her shoulders. "I can't argue with that. Are you really sure you wouldn't mind?"

"Absolutely. We'll start tomorrow. You'd be welcome to join us anytime."

"I'll keep that in mind."

"It really might help, you know," he pressed gently. "It was a lifesaver for me. We have a wonderful minister. He's helped me through some pretty rough times."

Kate didn't want to discuss the state of her soul with anyone. She had too many conflicting emotions about her faith, too many unanswered questions. But she *would* like to know more about what had happened to turn Eric so completely off marriage. So far, he'd asked most of the questions. It seemed only fair that she return the favor.

"I take it your marriage wasn't exactly…memorable," she ventured.

An expression of pain seared across his eyes, like the white-hot flash of fireworks—brief but intense. "Oh, it was memorable, all right." Though she saw he tried to mask it, the bitterness in his tone was unmistakable.

"Is it something you can talk about? Sometimes that helps. And I used to be a good listener. I'm a little out of practice, but I can give it a try."

Even as she spoke the words, Kate was startled by their truthfulness. For the last few years she had been so focused on her own pain that she'd been oblivious to the pain of others. In one blinding moment of revelation, she realized that she had slipped, without even being aware of it, into self-pity and self-absorption. It was a disturbing insight. One of the things Jack had loved about her was her openness to others and her ability to empathize. He would hardly have recognized her now, she conceded. Since his death she'd closed herself off to everyone and everything except Sarah, her mother and her sister. And it had been an effective coping mechanism, insulating her with a numbness that made the pain in her life bearable.

But living the rest of her life in darkness and grief wasn't going to bring Jack back, she acknowledged sadly. Somehow she had to find her way back to beauty and joy and hope, because suddenly she knew she couldn't go on marking the days instead of living them. It wasn't fair to her, or to Sarah—or to the memory of Jack, who had loved life intensely and lived each day with passion and appreciation, fully embracing all the blessings the Lord had bestowed on him.

But Kate had no idea how to begin the rebuilding process. It seemed like such a daunting task. Maybe listening to Eric, as he had listened to her, would be a way to start connecting with people again.

When her gaze linked with his, she found him watching her intently and she shifted uncomfortably. Was he angry that she'd turned the tables and asked about *his* private life? she wondered anxiously. She hadn't meant to offend him. "Listen, I didn't mean to pry, Eric. I'm sorry."

"It's not that," he assured her quickly. "It's just that you— I don't know, you had a funny look on your face for a minute."

"Did I?" His perceptiveness surprised—and slightly unnerved—her. "I guess I was wondering if maybe I'd overstepped my bounds, asking about your marriage," she hedged, reluctant to reveal the personal insight that had just flashed through her mind. "It's just that talking to you about Jack and my faith helped tonight. I thought maybe it might help you to talk, too. But I understand if you'd rather not."

He looked at her for a moment before he spoke, as if assessing whether her interest was real or just polite. "Actually, I haven't talked much about it to anyone. Except my minister. Maybe because there isn't a whole lot to say. And because it still hurts after all these years. And because it's hard to admit failure," he confessed candidly. "But I'll give you the highlights—or low-lights, depending on your perspective—if you're really interested."

"I am."

He gave a slight nod. "Cindy and I met when I was in medical school," he began. "She was blond and beautiful, carefree and fun, always ready for the next adventure. I was the serious, studious type and it was exciting just to be with her. I never knew what she'd do next. All I knew was that she added a whole new dimension to my life. As different as we were, something clicked between us and I proposed a year after we met. We got married a few months later."

"Sounds like a promising beginning," Kate ventured.

"Yeah. Except things just went downhill from there. She didn't like my choice of specialty, and she grew to resent the intrusion of my career on our personal lives. We both changed through the years—or maybe we just became more of what we'd always been. In any case, the differences we once found so appealing gradually became irritating and hurtful. In the end, we were barely speaking."

He paused and looked down at his iced tea. The drops of condensation on his glass reminded him of tears, and he suddenly felt sad. "To be honest, I don't think either of us was blameless in the breakup, but I feel most responsible," he said heavily. "Cindy was right about my career—it takes an inordinate amount of my time. And it was a self-perpetuating kind of thing. As our marriage disintegrated, I spent even more time in the office and at the hospital, which only made matters worse. I don't know…. Maybe she would have been more tolerant of my schedule if I'd been doing heart transplants or something."

Kate frowned. "What do you mean?"

"Cindy wanted me to be a surgeon. That's considered one of the more 'glamorous' specialties. And when we got married, I thought I wanted to do that, too. But eventually I realized that I didn't enjoy practicing medicine in that sterile environment. I wanted to interact with people. And I love kids. Pediatrics was a natural fit for me. But Cindy hated it. It didn't have enough prestige. She was bitterly disappointed in my choice—and in me. Over time, our relationship grew strained and distant, and in the end it just fell apart." Eric didn't tell Kate about the final hurt—the reason he'd finally agreed to the divorce. Even now, five years later, it made him feel physically ill to think about it.

Impulsively Kate reached out and touched his hand. "I'm sorry, Eric."

Startled, he dropped his gaze to her slender fingers lightly resting on his sun-browned hand. It was funny. He couldn't remember a single time during his entire relationship with Cindy when she'd touched him in quite this way, with such heartfelt empathy and simple human caring. His throat tightened, and he swallowed with difficulty.

"So am I," he admitted, his voice suddenly husky. "I always believed marriage was forever, that if things got rough you worked them out. But by the time I brought up the idea of counseling, it was too late. Cindy had already given up. She finally asked for a divorce, and under the circumstances I agreed. But in my heart I still feel married. I spoke those vows in the sight of God, and I can't forget them as easily as she did."

"What do you mean?"

"She remarried a few months after the divorce became final. She and her new husband live in Denver. It's not that I'm judging her, Kate. I leave that to God. But it wasn't the right thing for me."

"So that's what your mother meant when she said she'd better take this opportunity to play grandmother," Kate mused aloud.

Eric looked surprised. "She told you that?"

"Yes. The day I met her."

"Well, maybe my message is finally sinking in. But I know she's disappointed. As the only child, I was her one hope for grandchildren," he said ruefully.

"Hey, hey, hey! This conversation looks way too heavy," Frank interrupted with a grin. "Time to liven things up a little. Okay, Kate, one more round of lawn darts. I feel renewed after that meal."

Kate smiled and glanced at her watch. "I really need to get home," she protested.

"Eric, convince her."

Eric shrugged. "He'll be a bear to work with if he doesn't get a chance to redeem himself."

Kate laughed. "Okay. One more round."

Fifteen minutes later, after she had once more soundly beaten her host, she and Eric said their goodbyes.

"He'll never live this down, you know," Eric told her with a chuckle as he escorted her to his car, his hand again placed possessively in the small of her back.

"Oh, people will forget," she replied with a smile.

"I won't," he declared smugly.

"Eric! You aren't going to use this against him, are you?"

"You'd better believe it," he asserted promptly, grinning as he opened her door. "What are friends for?"

Kate shook her head and slid in. A moment later he took his place behind the wheel. "You know, he's going to be sorry I came tonight," she predicted.

Eric smiled. "Maybe so. But do you know something, Kate?" At the odd note in his voice she turned to look at him. "I'm not. I had a really good time."

At his words, a feeling of warmth and happiness washed over her like a healing balm. "So did I," she admitted quietly. "Thanks for asking me."

"It was my pleasure." As he pulled away from the curb, he glanced over at her. "Maybe we can do it again sometime."

Again? Kate wasn't sure that was wise. It wasn't that she found Eric's company lacking. He was a great conversationalist, an empathetic listener, intelligent, well-read—not to mention incredibly handsome. She liked him. A lot. And therein lay the problem. She liked him *too* much. While she might have reached a turning point in her life tonight, she wasn't ready to deal with relationships—at least, not the male/female variety. And that included Eric—despite the fact that he wasn't even in the market for romance.

Like Eric, Kate believed in that "till death us do

part" vow. Even though she was no longer bound by it, in her heart she still felt married. Yet being with Eric tonight had awakened feelings long suppressed—and best left undisturbed, she decided firmly. Though her reactions had been subtle, they spelled danger. Intuitively she knew that Eric Carlson's very presence could disrupt her life by raising questions she wasn't yet ready to address and forcing her to examine issues she wasn't prepared to face.

She turned and gazed out into the night with a troubled frown, oblivious to the passing scenery. Even her mild reaction—or maybe *attraction* was a better word, she admitted honestly—to Eric tonight made her feel guilty; as if she were somehow betraying the love she and Jack had shared. It was *not* a good feeling. And the best way to keep it from happening again was to stay away from the disturbing man beside her.

It was as simple as that.

Chapter Four

Okay, maybe it wasn't quite *that* simple, Kate conceded the next Sunday as she waited for Eric to pick Sarah up for church. Their paths were going to cross every Sunday at this rate unless she decided to take Sarah to services herself. And that wasn't likely to happen anytime in the near future. So she'd just have to get used to seeing him once a week and maintain a polite distance.

Except that would be easier said than done, she acknowledged with a sigh. There was just something about him that drew her. Maybe it was his eyes, she mused. They were wonderful eyes. Understanding. Warm. Caring. Compelling. She'd never seen eyes quite so intensely blue before—nor so insightful. When he gazed at her she felt he could almost see into her soul.

Strangely enough, that didn't bother her, even though she'd always been a very private person. Maybe because—stranger still—she felt as if they weren't just recent acquaintances, but old friends. Which made no sense. For all practical purposes, they'd met less than two weeks ago. Nevertheless, the feeling of familiarity persisted. It was disconcerting—yet somehow oddly comforting.

The doorbell rang, and Sarah dashed to answer it. Kate followed more slowly, grateful that Eric's attention was distracted by his young greeter long enough for her to take a quick inventory—and then struggle to regain control of a breathing pattern that suddenly went haywire as she stared at him.

Kate had always known that Eric was a handsome man. He had classic Nordic good looks, and in a different age might have stood at the helm of a questing ship. Yet his gentle manner and kindheartedness were at odds with those Viking images of old. It seemed he had inherited the best of both worlds—ancient athletic virility and modern male sensibilities. It was a stunning—and extremely appealing—combination. And never had it come across more clearly than today. In a light-gray summer suit that emphasized his lean, muscular frame, and a crisp white shirt and dark blue, patterned tie, he was by far the most attractive man Kate had seen in a long time. Or maybe he was just the first one she'd *noticed* in a long time, she acknowledged with a frown.

He chose that moment to look up, and his smile of greeting faded when he saw her troubled expression. "Everything okay?"

She forced the corners of her mouth to lift and closed the distance between them. "Fine."

"Not having second thoughts?"

"No, of course not."

He studied her for a moment with those discerning eyes, as if debating whether to pursue the subject. Much to her relief, he let it rest. "We usually go to breakfast after services. Would you like us to swing by and pick you up? Make it a foursome?"

"Can we, Mommy?" Sarah asked eagerly. "I could get pancakes. I like pancakes," she told Eric.

He grinned. "So do I." He transferred his gaze back to Kate, and his expression softened. Or was it only her imagination? she wondered. "How about it, Kate?"

"I appreciate the offer, Eric, but your mom told me that's your special time together. We wouldn't want to intrude."

"Actually, it was her idea. But I had the same thought. She just brought it up first," he said with an engaging grin.

"Oh. Well, maybe another time. I really hadn't planned on going out at all today. I need to work on some lesson plans."

"Now what's that old saying? 'All work and no play makes Jack a—'" At the sudden pallor of Kate's face, Eric stopped short, his jaw tightening in self-reproach. Of all the stupid remarks! "Kate, I'm sorry. I just didn't think."

"It's…it's all right," she assured him shakily. "It's just that— Well, that saying was Jack's motto. He was a great believer in keeping things in proper perspective. He always made sure we took time for fun, and he never forgot to smell the flowers along the way."

"I have a feeling I would have liked him," Eric said quietly.

She summoned up a sad smile. "I think you might be right."

"Are we going now?" Sarah asked impatiently.

With an effort, Eric released Kate's gaze and smiled down at the little girl. "I don't think I've ever seen anyone quite so anxious to go to church," he teased. "God will be very happy."

"I just want to show Aunt Anna my new dress. Mommy bought it for me this summer and we were saving it for a special occasion."

Kate liked the deep, rich sound of the chuckle that rumbled out of Eric's chest. "Well, we won't tell God that's the reason you want to hurry. We wouldn't want to hurt His feelings."

"I want to go to church, too," Sarah assured him. "I like the singing."

"I'll walk out to the car with you," Kate said. "I'd like to say hello to Anna."

The two women exchanged a few words while Eric settled Sarah in the back seat, then he rejoined them.

"You're sure you won't come to breakfast, Kate?" Anna asked.

"Maybe another time. But thank you."

"I'll see you back to your door," Eric told her.

She looked at him in surprise. "That's really not necessary."

"Yes, it is. I have something I want to ask you."

He fell into step beside her, and she looked up at him curiously. "Is there a problem?"

He smiled ruefully. "That depends on how you look at it, I guess. I have another favor to ask, and I'd like you to consider it while we're at church." He reached up and adjusted his tie, and Kate would have sworn he was nervous. "In addition to my job, I'm on the board of several local health-related organizations. As Mom told you, I have a tendency to slightly overextend myself," he admitted wryly.

She smiled. "I think her exact words were that it's

harder for you to say no to a good cause than for a gopher to stop digging holes."

He chuckled, and a pleasing crinkle of lines appeared at the corners of his eyes. "That sounds like Mom. Anyway, next Saturday night there's a black-tie dinner dance that's the culmination of the annual fund-raising drive for one of the organizations. Usually I try to avoid these things, but I can't get out of this one. I could go alone, but to be honest, it always feels a little awkward." They reached her door, and he turned toward her. "So I wondered if you might go with me. Will you think about it while we're at church, Kate?"

She gazed up into his clear blue eyes, and for a moment she felt as if she were basking in the warmth of the summer sun under a cloudless sky. It was a good feeling—one that had been absent from her life for a long time. But it also made her nervous. She dropped her gaze, unsure how to answer. Something told her she should say no immediately. But she didn't want to hurt Eric's feelings. He had gone out of his way to be kind to her and Sarah. And besides, she had enjoyed their time together the evening before.

"Kate?"

She looked back up at him, took a deep breath and suddenly decided to follow her heart. "All right, Eric. I'll think about it," she agreed.

She was rewarded with a smile that lit up his face and made his eyes glow. A person could get lost in those eyes, she thought, mesmerized by their warmth. "Thanks, Kate. And don't work too hard while we're gone."

"N-no, I won't. See you later," she said breathlessly, then quickly slipped inside.

For a long time after he left, Kate stood with her

back braced against the front door, trying to reconcile her conflicting emotions. She felt more alive than she had in years—but she was also troubled. And she knew why. Her gaze strayed to her wedding picture, and she tenderly traced the contours of Jack's dear, familiar face. Her love for him was as strong now as it had been on that day nearly eleven years before when they'd been joined as man and wife. It had not diminished one iota.

But other things had, she thought sadly, tears welling in her eyes. Certain images and sensory memories were slowly slipping away, despite her desperate efforts to hold on to them. The funny, dismayed face Jack always made whenever she served carrots. The deep timbre of his voice during their intimate moments. The feel of his freshly-shaved skin beneath her fingertips. The distinctive, woodsy scent of his after-shave. The way he always tilted his head as he cut the grass.

All of those things were fading, like an old photograph in which all that remained were vague outlines of images that had once been sharp and clear and vibrant. Soon she would only be able to remember the *fact* that those things had once been special, not the unique qualities that made them so. She was losing Jack, bit by bit, day by day, and there was nothing she could do to stop it. The sense of distance and the ebbing of memories had accelerated in the last few months, she realized, and it left her with a sick, hollow, helpless feeling that seemed destined to plague her well into the foreseeable future.

And then, out of the blue, Eric Carlson had stepped into her life. With him, she didn't feel as hopeless and depressed. In fact, he made her feel things she'd never expected to feel again—attractive, womanly, cared for. He'd awakened in her needs that she had suppressed for five long years; needs she'd thought were forever locked within the cold recesses of her heart. Slowly, under the warmth of his gaze, those needs were beginning to thaw. And that scared her. After all, she was a lonely widow. He was a handsome divorced man. Even if the widow was still in love with her husband and the divorced man still felt married, it just didn't seem like a safe combination.

Kate wasn't sure what to do. But she knew whom to call for advice. And she intended to place that call just as soon as she poured herself a cup of coffee.

"Kate? What's wrong? I thought it was my turn to call *you* this Sunday."

"Nothing's wrong, Amy. I didn't mean to scare you," she apologized quickly, dismayed by the alarm in her sister's voice. "I just had some free time and thought I'd call you first, that's all."

"Thank God! I didn't mean to overreact, but—"

"That's okay. You have good reason. My unexpected phone calls haven't always been exactly uplifting."

"Yeah, well, hopefully those days are over. So what's the occasion? It's not my birthday or anything. How come you're springing for this Sunday's call?"

"Can't I be generous once in a while?"

"Look, neither of us can afford to be generous. Why don't I call you back tonight, as usual? It *is* my turn. Every other week, remember?"

"I remember. But I just wanted to talk. Unless... Are you getting ready for church?"

"Nope. Cal pulled a midnight shift at the park last night and is sleeping in. We're going to the second service. So I've got the time. But you haven't got the money."

"Will you quit with the money thing?"

"I'd like to. But neither of us can afford to treat money lightly—no pun intended. Just consider the facts. You're a single working mother with huge medical debts. I have three kids, my husband makes his living dressed like Smokey the Bear, we live in a log cabin and I make quilts to keep the wolf from the door. Case closed."

That wasn't quite the whole story, but Kate let it pass with a smile. "You forgot one thing."

"What?"

"You love every minute of your life."

Kate heard her sister's contented sigh. "Yeah, I do. But we'll never have money to spare. I'm always sorry we couldn't do more to help you, Kate."

"You did the most important thing, Amy. You were there. You and Mom. That was worth more than gold."

"Still, gold comes in handy sometimes. Speaking of which—how are you doing with the bills?"

"Okay. I pay off a little every month. I figure at this rate I'll be free and clear about the time I'm ready to retire." She tried for a light tone, but didn't quite pull it off.

"You know, Kate, sometimes I think that... Well, I've never said this before, but...but since things turned out the way they did, it almost would have been better if—well—if Jack hadn't..." Amy's voice trailed off.

"I've thought about that, too," Kate admitted slowly. "But at the time I was just grateful he survived the accident." She paused and took a deep breath, determined not to dwell on what might have been. She needed Amy's advice about the future, not about the past. "Actually, in a roundabout way, that's one of the reasons I called today. You'll never believe this coincidence, but the doctor who saved Eric's life at the accident scene is Sarah's new pediatrician."

"No kidding? That's weird! Did he recognize you?"

"Uh-huh. Even before I recognized him. As a matter of fact, his mother is watching Sarah for me while I teach."

"How in the world did you arrange that?"

"I didn't. He did." Kate explained, ending with Eric's offer to take Sarah to church each Sunday.

"Wow! I doubt whether my pediatrician, nice as she is, would ever take such a personal interest in *my* kids," Amy commented, clearly impressed.

"I've been really lucky," Kate acknowledged. "But I do have a sort of...dilemma."

"So tell me about it."

In halting phrases, Kate told Amy about Eric's marital situation, their evening together and his second invitation.

"So I honestly don't know what to do," she admitted at the end.

As usual, Amy honed right in on the key question. "Well, do you *want* to go?"

Kate frowned. "I—I think so. I like him, and we had a really good time. But when I'm with him I...I feel things I haven't felt in a long time. And then I feel guilty."

"You have nothing to feel guilty about," Amy declared firmly. "You're a healthy young woman who's been living in an emotional cave for way too long. Why shouldn't you go out and have a good time?"

"You know why."

"Because of Jack."

"I still love him, Amy. I still feel married. It just

doesn't seem right, somehow, to go out with another man. Even one who's not interested in romance."

There was silence for a brief moment before Amy spoke. "Can I tell you something, Kate?"

"Why do I have the feeling you will anyway, even if I say no?"

"Because you know me too well," Amy replied pertly. Then her voice grew more serious. "Look, I'll just say this straight out, okay? I know you loved Jack. And I know why. He was a great guy. We *all* loved him. And we all still miss him. We always will. As his wife, I know you feel the loss more intensely than any of us can even imagine. When I think of life without Cal… Well, it makes me understand in a very small way the pain you've had to deal with. But Jack wouldn't want you to go through the rest of your life without ever really living again, Kate. And part of living is loving. I know you have Sarah. But I'm not talking about that kind of love. You're the kind of woman who blossoms when she's loved by the right man. That's not to say you're not strong or capable or independent. You're all of those things, and you've proved it over and over again these past five years. But don't close yourself off to life—and love—because of a misplaced sense of obligation or guilt. Jack wouldn't want that, and deep in your heart you know that. Nothing can ever take away the memory of the special love you two shared. That's yours forever. But maybe it's time to start making some new memories."

For a long moment there was silence. Sometimes Kate felt that Amy, though two years younger, was really the older of the two. She was so solid, so grounded, so blessed with common sense and the ability to quickly analyze a situation and offer valuable insight. People didn't always like what Amy said. But they could rarely deny the truth of her words.

"Kate?" Amy said worriedly. "Are you still there? Look, I'm sorry if I overstepped, but—"

"It's okay," Kate interrupted. "Actually, I think you're right in a lot of ways. It's just that… Well, it's not easy to let go."

"I know, hon," Amy murmured sympathetically. "But you're going to have to let go before you can really get on with your life."

Kate played with the phone cord. "Jack's kind of slipping away anyway, you know?" Her voice broke on the last word.

"Oh, Kate, I wish I was there right now to give you a hug!"

"Yeah, so do I."

"You know, maybe this slipping away is Jack's—and the Lord's—way of telling you it's time to move on."

"Maybe. But… I don't know. I guess I'm just scared, Amy."

"That's okay. That's normal. But don't let fear stop you. It's like that old saying about ships. They may be safe in the harbor, but that's not what they're built for. I think it's time for you to set sail, Kate."

"How come you always know the right thing to say?" Kate asked, smiling mistily as she swiped at her eyes.

Amy chuckled. "My kids wouldn't agree with that."

"They will when they get older. Listen, thanks, okay? I feel a lot better."

"So are you going with Eric?"

"I guess so. But don't start getting any romantic ideas. I told you, he's not in the market."

"That's okay. At least he'll get you back into

circulation, introduce you to some new people. That's a start. And I'll want a full report next Sunday. Except *I'll* call *you*. Agreed?"

"Agreed."

* * *

"So, you've been holding out on your old pal all this time."

Eric glanced up from the chart he was reading. Frank was lounging against the door of his office, arms folded, one ankle crossed over the other, his accusatory tone tempered by the twinkle in his eyes.

"What's that supposed to mean?" As if he didn't know. He'd been waiting all afternoon for Frank to pounce and demand details about Eric's date.

"You know very well what I mean. Here I think you're a miserable, lonely, driven man desperately in need of female companionship and then you show up with a babe like Kate. Boy, you had me fooled! Where have you been hiding her all this time?"

"I haven't been 'hiding' her anywhere. And I'm not sure she'd appreciate the term 'babe,' even though I know you mean it in an entirely flattering way. How about if we just refer to her as the Queen of Lawn Darts?"

Frank grimaced. "Ouch! You would have to bring that up. I just had an off night. So…" He ambled over and perched on the edge of Eric's desk, not about to be distracted. "Tell me everything. Where did you meet this goddess? And how serious are you two?"

"We're just friends, Frank. That's it."

His partner gave a skeptical snort. "Yeah. Like Ma Barker was just a sweet old lady."

"I'm serious."

"You expect me to buy that after the way you were looking at her all night?"

Eric sent him a startled look. "What do you mean?"

"Oh, come on, man. You hung on her every word.

You made it a point to keep tabs on her whenever you were apart—which wasn't often. And you have that look in your eye."

"What look?"

"Smitten. Enamored. Head over heels. Is that descriptive enough?"

Eric frowned. "You're crazy."

"Uh-uh. I know that look. Had it once myself. Still do sometimes, in fact."

"Well, with all due respect to your powers of perception, you're way off base this time, pal."

Frank tilted his head and considered his friend thoughtfully for a moment. Then he grinned and stood. "Good try. But no sale. However, I get the message—butt out. Okay, that's fine, don't bare your soul to me, even though I'm your best friend in the world. I can read a No Trespassing sign when I see one." He ambled to the door and disappeared into the hall, but a moment later he stuck his head back inside and grinned. "But I don't pay any attention to signs. I'll wear you down eventually, you know. In the meantime, don't worry, buddy. Your secret's safe with me."

Eric stared at the doorway, then frowned and leaned back in his chair, absently playing with his pen. Frank might be a bit outspoken and on the boisterous side, but his powers of perception were keen. Usually he nailed a person's personality within five minutes of meeting him or her. He was even more intuitive about friends and associates. Sometimes it was almost scary.

Like right now.

Eric's frown deepened. Was Frank overreacting? Or had he seen something Eric had overlooked? There was no question that he liked Kate. And he *had* carried a memory of her in his mind for more than five years—but only because he'd been struck by her beauty and obvious love for her husband. Her transparent devotion had made a tremendous impact on him in light of his own disintegrating marriage. But he hardly knew her. They'd only gone out once, had spent barely four hours in each other's company socially. And it hadn't even been a real date.

And yet… Eric couldn't deny that there was at least a kernel of truth in Frank's assessment. He *was* attracted to Kate. To her beauty, certainly, but even more to her person, to who she was, to her essence. Attracted enough to want to get to know her better. And that wasn't good. Because Eric truly believed that in the sight of God he was still married. Through the years he'd never had any trouble remembering that, though countless women had made it clear they were available if he was interested. But he hadn't been. Until now.

Eric reached up with one hand and wearily massaged his temples. He wasn't going to compromise his values by allowing himself to get involved with Kate romantically, even if the lady was willing. Which she wasn't. It was obvious that her late husband had never relinquished his claim on her heart. And even if *he* was free—which he wasn't—getting involved with someone whose heart belonged to another was a recipe for disaster.

Besides, medicine and marriage didn't mix. He'd learned that the hard way. And he'd better not forget it.

Asking Kate to the dinner had probably been a mistake, Eric conceded with a sigh as he pulled the next chart toward him and flipped it open. But he couldn't retract the invitation now. All he could do was make sure it was the last one. Keeping their contact to a minimum was clearly the right thing to do—for everyone's sake.

But if that was true, why did it feel so wrong?

* * *

Kate was nervous. She'd spent the entire week second-guessing her decision to go with Eric tonight, less sure with each day that passed about the wisdom of her decision. She'd almost called Amy for another pep talk. But she already knew what her sister would say:

"You need to do this, Kate. It's time. It's a first step. Just think of it that way and you'll be fine."

And of course, Amy would be right. After all, it was just a dinner with a nice man who, for whatever reason, had found her engaging enough to want to spend a second evening with her. A man who had no interest in her beyond friendship. So why was she nervous?

"You look pretty, Mommy. Is that a new dress?"

Kate turned back to the mirror. A new dress? Hardly, she thought wryly. The limited money available for new clothes was generally spent on Sarah. Kate had foraged deep in the recesses of her closet for this dress. She'd given away most of her dressier clothes when she sold the house, having neither the room nor the need for them, but she'd kept a couple of things that were classic in style and would be serviceable for any number of functions. This sleeveless linen-like black sheath with a square neckline could be paired with a jacket for a "business" look or worn alone, accented with costume jewelry, for a dressier effect. It had made the "keeper" cut because it was practical. Tonight, a clunky hammered-gold necklace and matching earrings added some glamour to its simple lines, and she'd arranged her hair in a more sophisticated style. The outfit still might not be dressy enough for a black-tie event, Kate acknowledged, but it was the best she could do.

"No, honey. I've had this in my closet for a long time."

"From when Daddy was here?"

The innocent question made Kate's stomach clench, and she gripped the edge of the vanity. She'd bought it shortly after Sarah was born as an incentive to return to her pre-pregnancy measurements, but she'd never worn it.

"Yes, honey. It's as old as you are," she replied, struggling to maintain an even tone.

"Well, I like it. I bet Dr. Eric will, too."

The doorbell rang, and with an, "I'll get it," Sarah scampered off.

Determinedly, Kate put thoughts of the past aside and forced herself to focus on the conversation in the living room as she added a final touch of lipstick.

"Hi, Dr. Eric. Hi, Aunt Anna."

"Hello there, Sarah." Eric's deep voice had a mellow, comforting quality, Kate reflected, her lips curving up slightly.

"Hello, Sarah," Anna greeted the youngster.

On hearing the older woman's voice, Kate felt a pang of guilt. Anna had offered to keep Sarah overnight at her place so Kate and Eric wouldn't have to worry about staying out too late. But Kate had balked. Sarah wasn't even five yet, she had rationalized. It was too soon for her to be gone all night, even though it would have been more convenient for everyone.

"Mommy is almost ready. She looks really pretty. Do you think Mommy is pretty, Dr. Eric?"

There was a momentary pause, and Kate felt hot color surge to her face. But it grew even redder at Eric's husky response. "I think your mommy is beautiful, Sarah."

She had to get out there now, before Sarah asked any other embarrassing questions, Kate thought desperately.

Willing the flush on her cheeks to subside, she flipped off the light and hurried down the hall.

"Well, here's Kate now," Anna said brightly. "My dear, you look lovely."

"Thanks, Anna." Her gaze flickered to her escort. "Hello, Eric." She intended to say more, but her voice deserted her as their gazes met. He looked fabulous tonight, she thought in awe. The black tux was a perfect complement to his blond hair, and it sat well on his tall, muscular frame, emphasizing his broad shoulders and dignified bearing. Her heart stopped, then raced on. Good heavens, what was she getting herself into? she thought in panic.

Eric took in Kate's attire in one swift, comprehensive glance that missed nothing. Fashionably high heels that accentuated the pleasing line of her legs. A figure-hugging sheath that showed off her slender curves to perfection. A neckline that revealed an expanse of creamy, flawless skin. She looked different tonight, he thought, swallowing with difficulty. Gorgeous. Glamorous. And very desirable. His mouth went dry and his pulse lurched into overdrive.

As his stunned gaze locked with hers, he realized that she seemed equally dazed. Her eyes were slightly glazed and the hand she ran distractedly through her hair was trembling. But no less so than his, he realized, jamming it into his pocket. Electricity fairly sizzled in the air between them.

"Mommy, how come your face is red?" Sarah asked innocently.

Anna stepped in smoothly. "Because she put on extra blush to go with her fancy dress," the older woman replied matter-of-factly. "Now, you two better be on your way or you'll miss dinner."

With an effort Kate dragged her gaze from Eric's. "Yes, y-you're right. I'll just get my purse."

Eric watched her flee down the hall and then drew a shaky breath. He wasn't sure exactly what had happened just now. All he knew was that the smoldering look he'd just exchanged with Kate had left him reeling.

In the sanctuary of her bedroom, Kate forced herself to take several long, slow breaths. What on earth had gone on just now? She felt as if a lightning bolt had zapped her. Eric hadn't even spoken to her, yet they'd connected on some basic level that needed no words. Or had they? Maybe it was all one-sided. Could she have imagined the spark that had flashed between them? It didn't seem possible. And how could she walk back out there and pretend that nothing had happened? But she had no choice. She couldn't acknowledge a thing. The ramifications of doing so were way too scary.

She picked up her purse and walked slowly back down the hall, trying vainly to curb the uncomfortable hammering of her heart. When she stepped back into the living room, her gaze immediately sought Eric's. She searched his eyes, but it was impossible to tell if he'd been as deeply affected by the look that had passed between them as she had been. He seemed as calm and at ease as always. Good. At least one of them was in control.

"Now you two take off," Anna instructed. "And don't hurry. I'm deep into a mystery that will keep me entertained for hours after Sarah goes to bed."

"Ready, Kate?"

Did Eric's voice sound deeper than usual, Kate wondered? Was it slightly uneven? Or was it only her imagination?

"Yes." Her *own* voice was definitely unsteady, she noted with chagrin.

He stepped aside to let her pass, and when he dropped his hand lightly to the small of her back she knew that her last reply was a lie. She wasn't ready at all. Not for tonight. Nor for whatever lay ahead in her relationship with this man.

But then she remembered Amy's comment about the ship. And Amy was right, she told herself resolutely. It was time to chart a new course and set sail.

Chapter Five

As they drove to the downtown hotel where the banquet was being held, Eric could sense Kate's tension. It mirrored his own. To pretend that nothing had happened just now in her apartment would be foolish. To acknowledge it would be dangerous. There was clearly only one way to deal with it: stay away from situations where it might happen again. Frankly, he didn't need the temptation. And she didn't need the stress. His earlier decision to make this their last social excursion was clearly the right one, he told himself resolutely.

However, they still had to get through tonight. He risked a sideways glance at her. She was staring straight ahead, her brow marred by a slight frown, the lines of her body taut with strain. Not good, he concluded. He had been hoping for a repeat of their first outing, when she had relaxed and laughed and had seemed, at least for a little while, less weary and burdened. But tonight they were definitely not off to a good start. This might be their last pseudo "date," but he wanted her to enjoy it. She deserved a pleasant evening. He needed to distract her, introduce a subject that would take her mind off the unexpected chemistry that had erupted between them a few minutes before.

"You know, Mom already seems more like her old self in just the two weeks she's been watching Sarah," he said conversationally.

Kate turned to him. "Does she? I'm glad. It's worked out well for us, too. Sarah looks forward to the time she spends with Anna. What a difference from our brief day-care-center experience!" She sounded a bit breathless, and her tone was a little too bright, but Eric persisted.

"I know there are cases like yours where mothers have to work, but I often think it's a shame that so many of today's kids are being raised by strangers just so the parents can bring in two incomes to support a more extravagant lifestyle. I really think kids would rather have time and attention from their parents than material things."

Kate nodded eagerly, warming to the subject. "You know, that's exactly how Jack and I felt! We waited a long time for Sarah, and we decided that if the Lord ever blessed us with a child, he or she would have at least one full-time parent. That's why I quit my job when she was born. Jack had a good job—he was an engineer—so he was able to provide for us comfortably. Nothing lavish. But then, we didn't need 'lavish.' We just needed each other."

She sighed and turned to stare out the front window, but her eyes were clearly not focused on the road ahead of her. "It was the way I was raised, I guess. We never had a lot when I was growing up," she said softly. "But we never felt poor, either. Because our home was rich in love. That's what Jack and I wanted for our child. A home filled with love. You know, it's too bad more parents don't realize that kids would rather have your time on a daily basis than a week at some fancy tennis camp in the summer. Sometimes I think parents today spend so much on material things for their children out of guilt—as a way to appease their conscience for the *time* they should have spent instead."

"I couldn't agree more."

Kate looked at him curiously. "I hope you don't think I'm prying, Eric, but… Well, you obviously like kids. And they just as obviously like you. Yet you never had your own."

A flicker of pain crossed his face, but he hid it by turning briefly to glance in the rearview mirror as he debated how to answer Kate's implied question. Hedge or be frank? It was a painful subject, one he'd discussed with only a few trusted, longtime friends. Kate was new in his life. Yet he trusted her. And so he chose to be frank.

"You're right about my feelings with regard to children," he said quietly. "I always assumed that if I ever got married, I'd have my own family. And I guess I also assumed that most people felt that way. Cindy and I somehow never discussed the issue directly. I tried a few times, but as I recall, her answers were always a little vague and noncommittal. I should have pursued it, but I suppose I was afraid of what I'd hear if I pressed the issue. And I didn't want to risk hurting our relationship by upsetting her. I'd figured that once we were married it would just be a natural next step, and any reservations she might have had would evaporate.

"As it turned out, I was wrong. About a lot of things, actually. Cindy didn't want kids, period. They would have 'cramped her style,' as she so succinctly put it. And as much as I wanted children, I didn't want them to have a mother whose heart wasn't in the job. Besides, as she often reminded me, if I was too busy with my career to spend time with her, how would I ever find time to spend with children? And I suppose she had a point," he conceded wearily. "But I still wanted children. Giving up that dream was very difficult."

Kate thought about all the joy Sarah added to her life; how even in her darkest hours, when her heart grieved most deeply for Jack, her daughter had always been the one bright ray of sunlight able to penetrate to the dark, cold corners of her soul and remind her that joy and beauty still lived. But on Eric's darkest days he had struggled alone, not only with disintegration of a marriage but also with the loss of a dream for a family. And now he would always be alone. It was such a waste, she thought, her heart aching for him.

"You would have made a good father, you know," she said gently.

He gave her a crooked grin. "You think so?" His tone was light, but there was a poignant, wistful quality to it that tugged at her heart and made her throat tighten with emotion.

"Yes. As my sister Amy would wisely say, you can tell a lot about a man by the way he treats children. And you can tell a lot about a man by the way children treat *him*. According to her, children have almost a sixth sense about people. Using Sarah—who's generally very shy around strangers—as a yardstick, you stand pretty tall. So, yes, I think you would have made a great dad."

Eric felt his neck redden at the compliment. Very few things made him uncomfortable, but praise was at the top of the list. So he quickly refocused the attention on Kate. "I can hear the affection in your voice when you mention your sister. I take it you and she are close?"

"Yes. It's too bad she lives in Tennessee. We have to

be content with weekly phone calls," she told him with a sigh.

"Tennessee isn't too far. Don't you visit occasionally?"

"Not as often as we'd like. Her husband, Cal, is an attorney *and* a part-time ranger in Great Smoky Mountains National Park, so his busy season is summer. They can never get away then, and I'm teaching the rest of the year. Besides, it's tough traveling with three small children—four-year-old twins and a six-month-old."

He gave a low whistle. "She *does* have her hands full."

Kate smiled. "That's putting it mildly. She also hosts a bi-weekly program on a Christian cable station in Knoxville. Anyway, Sarah, Mom and I always went down in the spring, and then again at Thanksgiving. But that's about it."

"Thanksgiving in the Smokies sounds nice," he remarked with a smile.

"It is. Especially at Amy's. She's become quite the earth mother. They live in a log cabin, and she makes quilts and bakes homemade bread and cans vegetables. It's an amazing transition, considering that in her twenties she was an absolutely gung-ho career woman who liked bright lights and traveling in the fast lane and thought life simply ceased to exist outside the city limits."

"What happened?"

"Cal."

"Ah. True love."

"Uh-huh. It wasn't that she changed for him. She just discovered that all that time she'd been living a lie. Somewhere along the way she'd bought into the notion that success is only measured in dollars and prestige and power. But she was never happy, even though she had all those things. It took Cal to make her realize that."

"That's quite a story, Kate. Sort of reaffirms your belief in happy endings."

She smiled softly. "Yeah, it does. They're a great couple." As Eric turned into the curving drive of the hotel, Kate sent him a startled look. "You mean we're here already?"

"See how times flies when you're having fun?" She smiled, and he was gratified to note that she now seemed much more relaxed. "Shall we go in and be wined and dined?"

"I think that's what we're here for," she replied.

Eric didn't have Kate to himself again until after dessert. As a board member, he knew many of the guests and it seemed that all of them wanted to spend a few minutes talking with him during the cocktail hour. Throughout the meal Kate was kept occupied by an elderly man seated to her right. Only when their dinner companions rose to mingle with other guests did Eric have a few minutes alone with her.

"You seem to have made a friend in Henri," he remarked, nodding toward the older man who was now greeting some guests at a nearby table.

Kate followed Eric's glance and smiled. "He's a fascinating person. You'd never guess by looking at him that he was an underground fighter with the French Resistance in World War II, would you?"

Eric stared at Kate. He'd known Henri Montand, a major contributor to this event, for ten years. But it seemed that Kate had learned more about his background over one dinner than he had in a decade.

"You're kidding!"

"No. You didn't know?"

He shook his head ruefully. "Speaking of having a way with people... I may be pretty good with kids, but you obviously have a knack with adults." Kate flushed at his compliment, and he found that quality in her endearing—and utterly appealing. "So, are you having fun?" he asked, trying unsuccessfully to minimize the sudden huskiness in his voice. Fortunately, Kate didn't seem to notice.

"Oh, yes! This is a lovely event." She glanced around appreciatively at the fresh flower arrangements on the tables, the crystal chandeliers and the orchestra just beginning to tune up.

"The fund-raising committee generally does a nice job. But most importantly, the organization does good work. Abused kids need all the help they can get."

"You really take your commitment to children seriously, don't you? On and off the job."

"It's pretty hard to leave it at the office," he admitted. "But I do too much sometimes, I guess. That's what Cindy always said, anyway. And since the divorce, I've gotten even more involved. Frank's always saying that I'm a driven man. Even Mom's been telling me to get a life. And they're right. My terms on two boards are up at the end of the year and I've already decided not to renew them. But I'll stay involved with this one. I've been on the board for almost ten years and—"

"Eric! Kate!"

They glanced up, and Kate recognized the man bustling toward them as an energetic, fortyish board member Eric had introduced her to earlier. "Listen, help us out, will you? We need some people to kick off the dancing. I think if I get five or six of the board members out on the floor, everyone will loosen up. Thanks, guys." Without giving them a chance to respond, he hurried off.

Kate stared after him, then glanced at Eric uncertainly. "I haven't danced in years."

"Neither have I."

She gave a nervous laugh. "Honestly, Eric, I don't even think I remember how. That was about the only thing Jack couldn't do. I haven't danced since my wedding."

"I haven't danced in six or seven years."

"So should we just pass? I mean, I'd like to help out, but…" She lifted her shoulders helplessly.

Eric looked at her thoughtfully. It would be easy to agree. And probably wise. But as he gazed at Kate, bathed in golden light from the centerpiece candle, the creamy skin of her neck and collarbone glowing warmly, the delicate curve of her neck illuminated by the flickering flame, he was suddenly overcome by a compelling need to hold her in his arms and sway to romantic music. It would be a memory of their brief time together that he could dust off when the nights got long and he was in a melancholy mood, or on those rare occasions when he let himself indulge in fantasy and wonder how differently his life might have turned out if he'd met someone like Kate a dozen years ago.

"I'm willing to give it a try if you are."

Her eyes grew wide. "Are you serious?"

"Absolutely."

"But I'm really not very good, Eric. I'll probably step all over your feet."

"I'm more worried about stepping on yours. Come on, we'll muddle through." He stood and held out his hand.

Kate hesitated. It was true that her dancing skills

were extremely rusty. And it was also true that she was worried about looking awkward and embarrassing Eric. But she was even more worried about the close proximity that dancing entailed. It was one thing to sit next to this virile man in the car or at the table, and quite another to be held in his arms. She wasn't exactly sure how she would handle the closeness. But there seemed to be no way to gracefully decline. So she took a deep breath and placed her hand in his.

"You may be sorry," she warned, her voice not quite steady.

"I don't think so."

As he led her out to the dance floor, the orchestra began playing "Unforgettable." He glanced down at her and grinned. "You know, if we're both as bad as we claim, that's exactly what this dance might be."

Her insides were quaking, but she managed to smile. "You could be right."

As it turned out, the dance really was unforgettable. In every way.

From the moment he drew her into his arms, she felt as if she'd come home. They danced together perfectly, moving effortlessly to the beat of the music. And once she realized she didn't have to worry about her feet, she was able to focus on other things—the spicy scent of his after-shave, the way he tenderly folded her right hand in his left, tucking it protectively against his solid chest, and the strong, sure feel of his other hand splayed across her back, guiding her firmly but gently.

Kate closed her eyes and let his touch and the romantic music work their magic. It had been a long time, such a very long time, since she'd been held this way; since she'd felt so safe and protected and—the word *cherished* came to mind. Which was strange. After all, she barely knew Eric. But something about the way he held her made her feel all of those things. Of course, it might just be her imagination. But, real or not, she intended to enjoy the moment, because it might never come again. With a contented sigh, she relaxed against him.

Eric felt Kate's sudden relaxation, and instinctively he drew her closer, tilting his head slightly so that her lustrous hair brushed his cheek. Then he closed his eyes and inhaled, savoring the faint, pleasing floral fragrance that emanated from her skin. She felt good in his arms, he reflected; soft and feminine and very, very appealing. He swallowed with difficulty. *Dear Lord, why did you send someone like this my way?* he cried silently, overcome by a sudden sense of anguish and regret. *I made a vow in Your sight on my wedding day that I don't want to break. But I'm lonely, Lord. And Kate is getting harder and harder to resist. Her sweetness and values and kind heart are like a ray of sun in my life. I'm drawn to her, Lord. Powerfully. Please help me find the strength to do what is right.*

By the time the music ended, Kate was fairly quivering. And Eric didn't look much steadier, she reflected, as—with obvious reluctance—he released her. The hand that rested at the small of her back as he guided her toward their table felt about as unsteady as her legs.

"Eric! I knew you were here somewhere but I just couldn't seem to find you in this crowd."

They turned in unison as a man in his mid-fifties with salt-and-pepper hair approached them.

"Hello, Reverend Jacobs." Eric's voice sounded husky, she noted. But at least it was working. She wasn't sure about her own. "It's quite a turnout, isn't it?"

"It gets bigger every year, which is very gratifying."

"Reverend, I'd like you to meet Kate Nolan. Kate, Reverend Carl Jacobs, my minister."

"Nice to meet you, Mrs. Nolan." The man extended his hand, and Kate found her fingers engulfed in a firm, somehow reassuring clasp. She stared at the minister, struck by the kindness and serenity in his eyes. He radiated calm, like someone who was at peace with life, who understood the vagaries of this world and had not only accepted them, but had found a way to move beyond them. He seemed, somehow, like a man with answers. The kind of answers Kate had been searching for.

Their gazes held for a long moment, until at last Kate found her voice. "It's nice to meet you, too. Eric has spoken very highly of you."

"And also of you. I've met your daughter. She's charming."

"Thank you."

Suddenly Eric reached inside his jacket and retrieved his pager. He scanned the message, then frowned. "Would you two excuse me while I make a quick phone call?"

"Of course," Kate replied.

"I'll keep Mrs. Nolan company," the reverend promised.

They watched as Eric threaded his way through the crowd, then disappeared.

"He works too hard," Reverend Jacobs remarked. "But it's difficult to fault such dedication. And he's a fine doctor."

"I agree."

"Eric has mentioned you, Mrs. Nolan. Have you known each other long?"

"Please call me Kate. Actually, Eric and I have a somewhat unusual history. We met—if you could call it that—five years ago, when my husband was seriously injured in a car accident. Eric saved his life."

The minister's eyebrows rose. "Is that right? Eric never mentioned it. But then, I'm not surprised. To use an old cliché, he isn't one to blow his own horn. But I understood from Eric that you were a widow."

"Yes. My husband lived for several months after the accident, but he never regained consciousness."

"I'm so sorry, Kate. It must have been a very difficult time for you. Sarah would have been just a baby, I'm sure."

She swallowed and nodded. "She was six weeks old. She needed me, and so I managed to get through the days. But it was almost like my own life ended in some ways when Jack died," she said quietly.

"I know what you mean. I lost my wife of thirty years to cancer just five months ago. She left a void that can never be filled."

Kate's face softened in sympathy. "I'm so sorry, Reverend."

"Thank you. It's been a difficult time. But the Lord has sustained me."

A flash of pain and bitterness swept through her. "I wish I could say the same. I always felt He'd deserted me."

"Many people feel that way in the face of tragedy," Reverend Jacobs returned in an understanding tone that held no censure. "But often the opposite actually happens. We think the Lord hasn't answered our prayers, so we turn away. But you know, He always does answer us. It's just that sometimes it's not the answer we want to hear."

Kate frowned. "I've never thought of it quite that way before. But why would He take someone like Jack, who was so young and had so much to offer? Why would He not only take my husband, but deprive Sarah of a father? What sense does that make?"

"The Lord's ways are often difficult to understand, Kate. And I certainly don't have all the answers," the minister said gently. "But maybe together we could find a few. I'd certainly be happy to talk things through with you. Why don't you stop by some day?"

Kate thought about Eric's comment at the barbecue— that Reverend Jacobs had helped him through some difficult times. Might he be able to do the same for her? Help her find the sense of peace that he so obviously had, even in the face of a recent, tragic loss? It seemed like an option that might bear exploring.

"I just might do that, Reverend."

"Please do." He extracted a card from his pocket and handed it to her, then glanced over her shoulder. "Well, here comes your host." He waved at Eric, who was weaving through the crowd, then turned to Kate and extended his hand. "I have several more people to see before I leave tonight. It was a pleasure to meet you. And do think about stopping by."

"I will."

Eric rejoined her a moment later, and the concern on his face made her breath catch in her throat. "What's wrong? Is Sarah…"

"Sarah's fine," he reassured her quickly, noting her sudden pallor. "That was my exchange. I'm on call tonight. One of my patients has been in an accident, and her parents are on their way to the hospital with her now. I promised to meet them. Normally I'd just let the emergency room handle it, but she's got asthma as well and I thought a familiar face might help calm her down. She's only eight."

"Of course." She reached for her purse and tucked the minister's card inside.

"Kate, I'm sorry about this," Eric said regretfully. "I wanted us to have a nice evening."

"But we have! The dinner was lovely, and we even got to dance. That's more than I've done in a long time. Please don't worry about it."

He gazed down into Kate's sincere eyes and felt a lump form in his throat. He remembered Cindy's attitude on occasions when they'd had to cut a social evening short—resentful, put-upon, angry. It had put a strain on their relationship for days. Of course, Cindy had been through it many times. This was a first for Kate. Maybe, in time, she'd grow to feel the same way. But somehow he didn't think so. Not that the theory would ever be put to the test, he reminded himself firmly.

"Thanks for understanding," he said quietly.

She shrugged off his gratitude. "Don't be silly. If I was a parent with an injured child, I'd want *my* doctor there. It's the right thing to do."

"Nevertheless, I appreciate it. I'd take you home first, but the hospital is so close. How about if I call you a cab?"

"Why don't I just go with you?"

That was an offer he'd never heard before. "To the hospital?" he asked in surprise.

"Would that be okay?"

"Sure. I'd appreciate the company," he said honestly. "But it could be a while," he warned.

"If you're delayed I can just get a cab from there. I don't mind waiting, Eric." Which was true. She really didn't want their evening to end just yet.

"Okay, if you're sure."

As they turned to go, she expected him to place his

hand at the small of her back and guide her toward the door, as had become his custom. But instead, he surprised her by taking her hand in his, linking their fingers and squeezing gently. The smile he gave her was warm and somehow intimate.

"Thanks for being a good sport."

As he led her out of the ballroom, Kate savored the feel of his strong fingers entwined with hers. And she wondered about Cindy's customary reaction to an interruption such as this. Not good, apparently, considering how grateful—and taken aback—Eric had been by her acceptance of it. She was beginning to form a picture of his married life. And it wasn't pretty.

A movement on the other side of the waiting room caught her eye, and Kate looked up from her magazine. The young couple whose daughter had been injured had risen anxiously, privy to something in the corridor hidden from Kate's view. A moment later Eric entered and walked toward them. Though they spoke in low tones, their voices carried clearly.

"How is she, Doctor?" The man's face was lined with anxiety, and Kate could tell even from across the room that his wife had a death grip on his hand. Her heart contracted in sympathy, and she blinked back sudden tears. She knew what it was like to wait in a cold, sterile anteroom for news about someone you loved.

"She'll be fine, Mr. Thomas. Let's sit down for a minute. Mrs. Thomas?" Eric nodded toward a cluster of chairs and gently guided the mother toward one, clearly attuned to the woman's emotional distress. Kate was impressed by his astuteness—and his thoughtfulness. In a medical world that was often clinical and impersonal,

Eric appeared to be an admirable exception. Which somehow didn't surprise her.

When they were seated, he spoke again, his tone calm and reassuring. "Emily has lots of scrapes and bruises, but nothing requiring stitches. Her arm is broken—in two places, actually—but they're clean breaks and should heal just fine. Dr. West is a fine orthopedic surgeon and he took care of everything. She was having a little trouble with her breathing when I first arrived, but we got that under control very quickly. Once I started talking to her about your vacation to Walt Disney World, she calmed down and the asthma wasn't a problem. We'd like to keep her overnight just to make sure she's not in too much pain and monitor her breathing. There should be no problem with her going home in the morning."

The relief on the young couple's faces was visible from across the room, Kate noted discreetly.

"I can't thank you enough for coming in tonight, Doctor," the woman said gratefully, her voice thick with tears. "We told her all the way here in the car that you were coming, and that helped to keep her calm. We were so afraid she'd have an attack!"

"No thanks are necessary, Mrs. Thomas. I'm just doing my job."

"You do a lot more than that," the girl's father corrected him. "Most doctors just send you to the emergency room. They don't show up themselves. This means a lot to us. Especially when it's obvious we interrupted a special event." He nodded toward Eric's tux.

"I was glad to do it. I'll stop by in the morning and check on Emily, and by lunchtime she'll be ready to go home. Just tell her not to play soccer quite so aggressively in the future," he said with a grin.

"Do you think maybe we should take her off the team?" the man asked anxiously.

"Not at all. We've got her asthma under control. And kids need to run and play and stretch their wings. Reasonable caution is prudent. Excessive caution is stifling. Sometimes accidents happen, but that's part of living." Eric rose. "They're getting ready to move her to a room, so let me take you down to her and you can walk with her."

Eric glanced at Kate and smiled as he ushered the couple out, mouthing, "I'll be right back." She nodded.

When he reappeared a few minutes later, she was waiting at the doorway. He smiled at her ruefully. "You look ready to leave."

"Let's just say hospitals aren't my favorite places," she replied lightly, but he heard the pain in her voice. His gut clenched at the echo of sadness in her eyes and he frowned.

"I'm sorry, Kate. I didn't even think about that. I shouldn't have let you come. Instead of leaving you with pleasant memories of tonight, I've dredged up unhappy ones."

"I wanted to come," she insisted. "And I'm glad I did. It wasn't as hard as I thought it might be."

He took her arm and guided her purposefully toward the door. "But there's no reason to hang around now. It's my second trip today, anyway." He glanced at his watch and his frown deepened. "It's probably too late to go back to the dance. Would you like to stop and get a cup of coffee on the way home?"

She looked up at him. He'd mentioned he was on call this weekend. And that he'd already made one trip to the hospital today. There were fine lines at the corners of his eyes, and slight shadows beneath them. Much as she'd like to extend the evening, she shook her head. "It's been a long week, Eric. And there's no reason to keep your mother up any later than necessary. Let's head back."

He studied her for a moment. "Are you sure?"

"Of course. But I had a good time tonight, despite the interruption."

He chuckled. "I guess we should look on the bright side," he said as they reached his car and he opened the door for her.

She glanced at him curiously. "What do you mean?"

"Well, we may have ended up at a hospital, but at least it wasn't because of any broken toes."

She smiled. He had a good sense of humor. And he wasn't afraid to laugh at himself. She liked that. "Good point. Actually, I think we did quite well for two very out-of-practice dancers."

Eric almost suggested that they polish up their skills another night, but he caught himself in time. There wouldn't be another time, he reminded himself soberly. It was too dangerous, because Kate was easy to be with, and he knew with absolute certainty that she could very easily become a part of his life—an important part. But given his situation, all he could offer her was friendship.

And his feelings were already running way too deep for that.

Chapter Six

Kate drew a deep breath, then reached up and rang the bell on the parsonage. She wasn't sure exactly why she had followed through and made an appointment with Reverend Jacobs, except that she had been struck by the calm and peace he radiated even in the face of personal tragedy. She sensed that he had found the answers to some of life's harder questions, and that he might also have some of the answers *she* needed. It couldn't hurt to find out, especially since Anna had agreed to keep Sarah for an extra hour after school so Kate could take care of some "personal" business.

The door swung open, and Reverend Jacobs smiled at her kindly. "Kate. It's good to see you again. Come in."

She stepped into the foyer, and as the minister led her toward his office he paused beside an older woman seated at a word processor.

"Kate, this is Margaret Stephens. She's been with me for…how long, Margaret?"

The woman smiled indulgently. "Twenty-two years, Reverend."

"That's right, twenty-two years. She keeps my professional life in order. I'd be lost without her. Margaret, Kate Nolan."

They exchanged greetings, then the minister ushered his visitor into the office and closed the door. "I know you're on a tight schedule, Kate. Please make yourself comfortable." He indicated a small sitting area off to one side. "Can I offer you some coffee?"

"No, thanks. I've had my one cup for the day. My husband was the real coffee drinker in the family," she said, her lips curving up in affectionate remembrance.

Reverend Jacobs filled a mug and sat in a chair at right angles to hers. "Would you mind telling me a little bit about him, Kate? I can see that he's still a very important part of your life. I have a feeling that to know you, I also need to know him."

"I—I hardly know where to begin, Reverend," she faltered, her smile fading.

"How about telling me how you met?"

Under his gentle questioning, Kate found herself recounting their first meeting, courtship and eventual engagement. Halting phrases eventually gave way to a flood of words as she spoke about their wedding, their early years as a married couple, and their joy at Sarah's birth. Only when she came to the accident, the subsequent seven-month nightmare and her feelings of confusion and abandonment, did she once more struggle to find words.

"At first I refused to accept the prognosis," she said, her voice subdued and laced with pain. "I just couldn't believe the Lord would allow Jack to be paralyzed or to…to die. I prayed constantly, not only for my sake, but for Sarah's. I didn't want her to grow up without a father. I had faith, and every time I went to the hospital I believed there would be a breakthrough. But the months went by with no change, and eventually Jack was moved to a long-term-care facility. That's when I began to lose hope. Seven months after the accident, he died."

"Tell me about how you felt then, Kate," Reverend Jacobs said gently.

She lifted her shoulders wearily. "Numb. Devastated. Angry. Guilty. Confused. A whole tangle of emotions. I still feel a lot of them."

"Can you talk to me about the anger and guilt?"

She drew a deep breath. "I was angry at God," she said slowly. "I still am. And I was angry at Jack—which was totally illogical and only made me feel guilty. The accident wasn't his fault. But I still felt as if he'd deserted me. And then I kept thinking, if only he'd worn his seat belt. I should have reminded him to buckle up. I usually did. But it just didn't occur to me that night. So that added to the guilt."

"None of those feelings are abnormal, Kate. I experienced many of them myself when my wife died. I felt guilty, too, thinking that if only I'd insisted she go to the doctor sooner, she might have lived. And when she died, I was angry. She was taken from me just when we were reaching the stage in our lives when we'd planned to travel and spend more time together. All of the thoughts and emotions you mentioned are part of the natural grieving process. Knowing that others have gone through the same things often helps. Have you shared your feelings with anyone?"

"No. I just…couldn't find the words. And then I kept trying to figure out why God would take Jack from us. It just didn't make sense. I began to think that maybe… maybe I was being punished for something I did wrong," she said in a small voice.

The minister nodded sympathetically. "People often feel as you did when they lose someone they love—that it's their own fault in some way. But that's not the case, Kate. Jack's death had nothing to do with you. It was simply his time to go to the Lord. We can spend our lives asking why about such things, but that's an exercise in futility. The better path is to simply let go and admit that even though we can't understand the Lord's ways, we accept them. That's the only way to find peace in this world. But it's not always easy."

She nodded, and hot tears welled in her eyes. "I know. I've been trying to find that peace for a long time."

"You took a good first step today."

Kate shook her head sadly. "I'm not sure about that, Reverend. To be frank, I only came because I'm desperate. You found peace because your faith is strong. Mine isn't, or it would have sustained me through this trial. Instead, it died with Jack. So I guess on top of everything else, I've failed God." Her voice broke on the last word.

Reverend Jacobs leaned forward intently. "Let me tell you something, Kate. Doubts and despair don't make you a bad person. They just mean you're human. That's how the Lord created us, with all the weaknesses and frailties that entails. He doesn't expect perfection. He knows we stumble and lose our way. In fact, the history of Christianity is filled with holy men and women who experienced a dark night of the soul at some point in their lives. The Lord didn't disown them because of that, even when they disowned Him. He just patiently waited for them to come home. That's the beauty of our faith, Kate. The Lord is always ready to welcome us back, no matter how far we wander, once we open our hearts to Him."

Kate saw nothing but sincerity and compassion in the minister's eyes, and a little flicker of hope leaped to life in her soul. "I'd like to believe that, Reverend. I'd like to try to find my way back. But I—I don't know how."

"As I said, you've already taken the first step by coming here today. And I'll do all I can to help you. May I also suggest that you join your lovely little girl at Sunday services? Just hearing the words of Scripture may offer you some comfort and guidance. You probably won't find what you're seeking in one or two visits, but if you persist, in God's time you will."

Kate wasn't convinced. But clearly Reverend Jacobs was. And her faith *had* been important to her at one time. Perhaps, with the minister's help, it could be again.

Kate nervously adjusted the belt on her navy blue knit dress, then ran a brush through her hair. She knew Eric would be surprised when he discovered he had two guests for services today. She probably should have called and warned him. But she hadn't decided for sure about going until this morning. And besides, he *had* told her she was welcome anytime. She hoped that was still true, considering she hadn't heard from him since the night of the dinner dance, a week before. But then, why should she? Their outings had been defined as "favors," not dates. He probably didn't need any more of those. Neither of them was in the market for romance, but she had hoped that maybe they could be friends.

The doorbell interrupted her thoughts, and she headed toward the living room. "I'll get it," she told Sarah as she passed the bathroom. "You finish up those teeth."

When she reached the door, she took a deep breath

to steady her suddenly rapid pulse, then smiled before she pulled it open. "Good morning, Eric."

His own smile of welcome turned into a look of inquiry as his gaze swept over her. "You're awfully dressed up for grading papers."

She flushed. "Actually, I thought I might— That is, if the invitation is still open I'd like to join you for church today."

For a brief moment before he shuttered his emotions she thought she saw a flash of apprehension—and dismay—in his eyes, and her stomach clenched painfully. She stepped aside to let him enter, then turned to face him nervously.

"I stopped by to see Reverend Jacobs Friday after school, and we had a long talk. You were right. He's a good listener. I felt better about…about a lot of things after we spoke. He suggested I try coming back to church, so I decided to join you today, if that's okay."

"Mom will be delighted."

A telling response, she reflected, suddenly acutely embarrassed. His *mother* would be delighted. Not him. She hadn't imagined his reluctance. For some reason he was pulling back, retreating from the relationship he'd initiated with her, she realized as a flush rose to her cheeks.

"Listen, Eric, maybe this isn't such a good idea. After all, I have my own car. It isn't as if we have to go together. I don't want to impose and take you out of your way when there's no need. I should have called you earlier and just said we'd see you there. I'm sorry to—"

The words died in her throat as he reached over and touched her arm.

"Kate."

She stared at him with wide, uncertain eyes. He

looked down at her, frowning. She'd obviously picked up on his sudden discomfort, he realized. His resolve to stay away from her was shaky at best, but he'd figured it would hold if he just stopped by once a week to pick up Sarah and only saw Kate long enough to say hello. Her unexpected decision to go to church complicated things tremendously. But that was *his* problem. He *had* invited her to join them. She didn't strike him as the kind of woman who reached out easily, and his response had been far from enthusiastic. He needed to reassure her without telling her the real reason for his hesitation.

"You surprised me, that's all. I think it's great you've decided to go back to church."

She looked into his eyes, searching for the consternation she'd seen earlier, but it was gone. Had she imagined it? she wondered in confusion.

"We can go on our own in the future," she offered, her voice still uncertain. "I just thought it might be easier this first time to be with people we know."

His hand still rested on her arm, and its warmth seeped through the thin fabric of her dress as he gave her a gentle squeeze. "We'll talk about the future later, okay? Let's just worry about today for now."

It was a vague answer, but his voice was kind and his smile genuine. Besides, the future might not even be an issue. She might never go back to church again. She wasn't convinced that it would make that much difference, despite Reverend Jacobs's confidence.

But half an hour later, sitting in a pew beside Eric, she had the oddest sense of homecoming. As she listened to the words of Scripture, joined in the old familiar hymns and reflected on the sermon appropriately titled "All You Must Do Is Knock," she was surprised at just how much the experience touched her heart. And Reverend

Jacobs's warm greeting afterward made her feel good—and welcome.

"I'm so glad you came, Kate," he said, taking her hand in a firm grip.

"So am I."

"Eric, Anna, good to see you both. Hello, Sarah."

"Hello," the little girl said shyly, staying close beside Kate.

"You know, I bet you'd enjoy our Sunday school," he told the youngster before turning back to Kate. "The fall session is just starting. Sarah would be most welcome."

"Thank you. I'll think about it."

"Just give us a call if you'd like to enroll her."

They moved on then, so others could speak with the minister, and she reached for Sarah's hand as Eric cupped her elbow.

"You'll join us for breakfast, won't you?"

"Can we, Mommy?" Sarah asked eagerly.

Kate glanced quickly at Eric, but his face was unreadable.

"Of course you can," Anna chimed in. "We won't take no for an answer, will we, Eric?"

"Absolutely not," he replied firmly.

"I really don't want to intrude on your time together," Kate protested.

"It's three-to-one, Kate," Eric said with a smile that made her feel warm all over. "Give it up."

She swallowed. "Okay, you win. For today, anyway."

"Oh, goody!" Sarah exclaimed, hopping from one foot to the other. "Can I have pancakes?" she asked Eric.

"Of course."

"This is the best Sunday I can ever remember," she declared happily.

Kate didn't respond. It was one of her best Sundays in a long time, too. But she had an uncomfortable feeling that it wasn't one of Eric's. And for some reason that made her spirits, which had been buoyed by the church service, take a sudden nosedive.

"Did you and Kate have some sort of misunderstanding?"

Eric frowned and positioned the phone more comfortably against his ear as he closed the chart in front of him. "Hello, Mom," he replied wryly.

"Oh. Hello. Well, did you?"

"Did I what?"

"Have a misunderstanding with Kate," she repeated impatiently.

"No."

"Then why won't she go to church with us this Sunday?"

Eric's frown deepened. "You mean she isn't?"

"No. She stayed for a cup of tea today when she picked up Sarah and told me that they would be going by themselves from now on, and to please let you know and thank you for all your help."

Kate had obviously picked up on his momentary panic last Sunday when she'd announced that she was going to accompany them. But maybe that was for the best, he reasoned. He didn't want to hurt her, but he couldn't afford to get too close, because if he did, they could *both* be hurt. Badly. Given his marital status and the demands of his profession—which had ruined one marriage already—she was a temptation he didn't need.

"Eric? Are you still there?" his mother prompted.

"Yes."

"So did something happen between you two to upset her?"

"I haven't even talked to her all week, Mom."

"Why not?"

"I hardly know her."

"Well, I'd hoped you'd be trying to remedy that. Women like Kate don't come along very often, you know. She's a wonderful person."

"She's also still in love with her husband."

"Of course she is. I'm sure she always will be. Love like that doesn't die, Eric." His mother's voice suddenly grew subdued and sad, and his heart contracted in sympathy—and in shared loss. His father's death had been extremely hard on both of them, leaving a gap that could never be filled. "But that doesn't mean you can't ever love anyone else. And I just thought…" Her voice trailed off.

Eric sighed. He knew what she thought—that he needed to find someone new. But aside from the fact that he still considered himself married, there were other pitfalls to a relationship: namely, the demands of his profession.

"That's not an option, Mom," he said gently but firmly.

"But Eric, you've been divorced for almost five years," she argued. "Cindy is remarried. It doesn't seem right for you to be alone. You should have a wife and family."

"I tried that once. It didn't work."

There was a brief hesitation before she quietly declared, "Maybe it was just the wrong woman."

Eric's eyebrows rose in surprise. Though his mother

was usually outspoken in her opinion, she'd never before come this close to saying what he'd always suspected she felt about his marriage: that he and Cindy had not been a good match.

"Maybe," he admitted. "But it's too late now for second-guessing."

Her sigh came clearly over the wire. "Sometimes I think you're too hard on yourself, Eric. I'm sure the Lord doesn't expect you to spend the rest of your life alone when the divorce wasn't even your fault. As I recall, Cindy was the one who wanted out. You were willing to work at it."

"I'm not blameless, Mom. I have a demanding career, and it got in the way of our relationship. Marriage and medicine just don't seem to mix."

"That's nonsense," she declared briskly. "Most doctors are married and they manage just fine. Look at Frank."

"Well, maybe he knows some secret I don't."

"There's no secret, Eric. It just takes love and understanding on both sides."

"I can't debate that with you, Mom. All I know is that it didn't work for me. And even if I was free, I'm not willing to take that risk again. Besides, Kate obviously isn't interested. So let it rest. It's probably for the best."

Eric knew his mother wasn't happy with his response. She wanted him to have another chance at love. And as he hung up the receiver, he had to admit that he wanted that, too. Especially now. The hours he'd spent in Kate's company had given him a glimpse of the life he might have had with the right woman. But his error in judgment had cost him dearly, he thought with a disheartened sigh. And he was still paying the price.

* * *

Kate read the thermometer gauge worriedly. One hundred and two.

"I don't feel good, Mommy," Sarah whimpered.

Kate smoothed the hair from her daughter's damp forehead with a slightly unsteady hand. "I know, honey. I'm going to call Dr. Eric right now. You just lie here and be very quiet, okay?"

Kate tucked the blankets around Sarah, then headed for the phone to call Eric's exchange. She also spoke with Anna to let her know she was keeping Sarah home tomorrow.

"It's probably just a flu bug, Kate," the older woman reassured her. "Don't worry too much. Children get these things, you know. They bounce back quickly. When did she get sick?"

"A couple of hours ago, right before dinner. It just came on suddenly. She was fine this morning and had a great time at Sunday school."

"Oh, you must have gone to the later service, then. Eric was concerned when we didn't see you at church."

Was he? Kate wondered with a wistfulness that surprised—and disconcerted—her as she rang off. Deep inside she'd like to think his concern was prompted by more than polite consideration. After all, they'd spent two very enjoyable social evenings together. And she liked him. A lot. Too much, maybe, because the feelings he awakened in her made her feel disloyal to Jack. And she wasn't sure how to deal with that. But since he seemed to be putting a distance between them, it apparently wasn't something she needed to worry about, she reminded herself firmly.

But he wasn't putting distance between them today,

Kate realized when she opened the door forty-five minutes later and found Eric. Her eyes widened as she noted
the well-worn jeans that clung to his long, lean legs
and the blue cotton shirt with rolled-up sleeves, open
at the neck. Kate had never seen him dressed so infor-
mally before, and the effect was…well, stunning. In this
rugged clothing, he literally took her breath away. She
clung to the edge of the door and stared at him.

"Kate? Are you okay?"

Okay? No, she wasn't okay. In fact, her hand on the
edge of the door was trembling. Which was ridiculous!
She tried to get a grip. She barely knew this man, she
reminded herself. They were practically strangers. Yes,
he was handsome. Yes, he was nice. Yes, she found herself attracted to him at some basic level that she didn't
understand. But he wasn't in the market for romance,
and neither was she. She needed to remember that. She
drew a shaky breath and somehow found her voice.

"Yes. I'm fine. But Sarah's not."

"That's why I'm here."

He held up his black bag, which had somehow
escaped Kate's notice. Her gaze had gotten stuck on
his broad shoulders and muscular chest. "A house call?"
she said in surprise, her voice slightly breathless.

He smiled and shrugged. "Mom said you sounded
really worried."

Kate stepped aside and motioned him in. "I am. But
I didn't expect you to come over. It's your day off, isn't
it? The answering service said Frank was taking the
calls this weekend."

"He is. But I told him I'd handle this one."

"Why? I mean, you don't do this for all your patients,
do you?"

He gazed down at her, and the blue of his eyes seemed to intensify. "No, Kate, I don't."

She stared at him, and her mouth suddenly went dry. He'd answered her second question, but not her first. Which was probably just as well, because she wasn't ready to deal with the answer she might get. At least, not yet. Nervously she tucked her hair behind her ear and looked away. "Well, I—I appreciate it, Eric. Sarah's back here."

Eric followed as she led the way down the short hallway. He was glad she hadn't pressed for an answer to her first question, because he wasn't sure himself why he had come. There had been no need to make a house call. Frank could easily have dealt with the situation by phone. But he'd experienced such a letdown when he didn't see Kate in church this morning that he'd grasped at the first excuse to see her. It wasn't wise, of course. But when it came to her, his heart seemed more in control of his actions than his mind was. Which was a problem he needed to address—and soon.

"Dr. Eric came to see you, honey."

Eric smiled at Sarah as he followed Kate into the charmingly decorated little girl's room and sat down on the bed beside his patient. "Hello, Sarah. I heard you were sick."

"Uh-huh. I threw up."

He glanced at Kate.

She nodded. "Twice in the last hour. And her temperature is still a hundred and two."

"Well, that doesn't sound like much fun." He snapped his bag open as he spoke. "I'd better take a look. Is that all right with you, Sarah?"

"I guess so. You aren't going to give me a shot, are you?"

He chuckled. "Not today. I'm just going to listen to your heart and look in your ears and check out those tonsils."

He conversed easily with Sarah while he did a quick exam. When he finished he removed the stethoscope from around his neck and placed it back in his bag.

"Well, little lady, I think you have the flu. But you know what? You should feel a whole lot better by tomorrow. In the meantime, I want you to drink a lot of soda and water and juice and take aspirin whenever your mom gives them to you. Okay?"

"Okay."

He turned to Kate. "Do you have any white soda?"

She nodded. "I'll get some—and the aspirin."

As Kate disappeared down the hall, he turned back to find Sarah studying him quite seriously. "Dr. Eric, do you have a little girl of your own?" she asked suddenly.

A pang of regret ricocheted through him, almost painful in its intensity, but he managed to smile. "No."

"Do you wish you had a little girl?"

"Sometimes."

"Sometimes I wish I had a daddy, too." She pointed to a picture of Jack on her bedside table. "He was my daddy. Mommy says he watches out for me from heaven now, but I wish I had a daddy who could hold me in his lap and tell me stories."

"I wish you did, too, Sarah." Eric reached over and smoothed the hair back from her flushed face as his throat constricted. If everything had gone the way he'd planned, he would have his own children right now, and a wife who loved him. But he'd never have the former. Nor had he ever had the latter, he thought sadly. Through the years he had gradually come to realize that Cindy had never really loved him—not in the fullest sense of that word. It had been a hard thing to accept. It still was.

"Maybe you could be my daddy," Sarah said brightly. "Then you could read me stories at night and—"

"Sarah!"

Eric turned to find Kate in the doorway, her face flushed.

"What's wrong, Mommy?" Sarah asked innocently, her eyes wide.

Eric watched silently as Kate drew a deep breath. "Nothing's wrong, honey. But you need to drink your soda so you can go to sleep. Then you'll be all better tomorrow, just like Dr. Eric said."

Eric stood as Kate moved into the room. She avoided his eyes, and bright spots of pink still burned on each cheek.

"I'll let myself out," he said quietly.

"No." She looked up at him, obviously still embarrassed by Sarah's remark, though good manners took precedence. "I put the kettle on. Please stay and have a cup of tea or coffee. And some cake. It's the least I can do after you came over here on your day off."

He hesitated, then nodded. "All right. I'll wait for you in the living room."

Kate watched him leave, then turned back to Sarah and helped her sit up enough to drink the soda.

"Are you mad, Mommy?" Sarah asked in a small voice.

"No, honey. Of course not."

"You seemed mad when you came back in the room."

Kate shook her head. "I wasn't mad, Sarah. I heard what you and Dr. Eric were talking about, and I just got sad for a minute because your daddy isn't here with us. He loved you very much, honey. Before you were born we used to plan all the things the three of us would do together. I'm just very sorry he can't be here to do them with us." Kate picked up the photo from the bedside table and gently traced Jack's face with her finger. "Don't ever forget how much he loved you, Sarah. He's part of you. See? You have his eyes. And you have that little dimple in your cheek, just like he had. So part of Daddy will always be with us in you."

Sarah studied the photo for a moment. "He was pretty, wasn't he, Mommy?"

Kate blinked to clear the sudden film of moisture in her eyes. "Yes, Sarah. He was very pretty."

"Do you think he misses us up in heaven?"

"I'm sure he does."

"But he can't come back, can he, Mommy?"

"No, honey."

"Do you think he would be mad if I got a new daddy sometime? Just for while I'm down here?"

Would he? Kate wondered, as she replaced the photo. She'd never thought of it quite that way. And in that context, she knew the answer. Jack wouldn't want Sarah to grow up without the influence of a kind, caring father in her life. They had always talked about how they wanted her to experience all the joys of a real family—two loving parents and at least a sibling or two. Jack would still want that, even if he couldn't be the one to provide it.

"No, Sarah," Kate replied slowly. "I don't think he'd mind. Your daddy would want you to have a father."

"But how would I get one?" Sarah asked, clearly puzzled.

"Well, I would have to get married again."

"Would you do that, Mommy?"

"I don't know, honey. Your daddy was a very special man. It would be hard to find someone like him again."

"Is Dr. Eric like him?"

Kate glanced toward the bedroom door and dropped her voice. "I just met Dr. Eric, honey. I don't know him well enough to answer that question."

Sarah scooted down in the bed and pulled the covers up to her chin. Already her eyes were drifting closed. "Well, then I think you should get to know him better," she declared sleepily.

Kate adjusted the covers, then reached over and touched the photo of Jack, her gaze troubled. For several long moments she just sat there. She didn't want to do anything that would diminish the love they had shared. It was a beautiful thing, and she would always treasure it in her heart. But it was only a memory now. And memories could only sustain one for so long.

Kate sighed as she reached over and turned off the light. Even if she was ready to move on—and she wasn't convinced that she was—Eric wasn't available. He'd made that eminently clear. In his mind, he still had a wife. And after his first disastrous marriage, he truly believed that medicine and marriage didn't mix. So, if and when she decided to consider romance again, she'd have to look elsewhere.

Except, for some strange reason that plan held no appeal.

Chapter Seven

Eric listened to the murmur of voices as he restlessly roamed around Kate's living room. He couldn't distinguish the words, but he could guess what they were talking about. Sarah's last remark had clearly embarrassed Kate. And probably upset her, as well. He suspected that she'd done everything she could to make Jack as real as possible for Sarah. But it was a hard thing to do when the little girl had no memory of him. To her he was only an image, like the characters in her storybooks, with no basis in reality. What she wanted was a real daddy— someone who could hold her hand and share her life. Kate was fighting a losing battle, Eric thought with a sigh. Sarah was too young to be comforted by stories of a father she had never known.

Eric wandered into the kitchen, shoving his hands into the pockets of his jeans as he glanced around. The room was small but homey, with several of Sarah's drawings displayed on the refrigerator. The remains of a hardly touched dinner lay strewn next to the sink— macaroni and cheese, green beans, salad. Sarah must have started to feel badly before they ate more than a few bites.

His gaze swept over the eat-in counter that separated the living room and kitchen, taking in the pile of half-graded school papers, a copy of the church bulletin—and a loan statement at his elbow reflecting a balance of nearly six figures. Eric frowned and quickly glanced away. The latter was obviously private business. But he knew what the debt most likely represented: Jack's medical bills—probably for the extended-care facility where he'd spent his last months. Eric had seen too many instances where insurance covered only certain expenses in situations like that, leaving the survivors deep in debt. He could make a reasonable guess at Kate's salary, and he knew it would take her years to repay the loan. It just didn't seem fair, he reflected, his frown deepening as his eyes strayed back to the statement. He could write a check for the entire amount and not even miss it. To Kate, it was obviously a fortune.

"She's sleeping now."

Eric's gaze flew guiltily to hers and hot color stole up his neck. Kate glanced down at the counter, and a flush reddened her cheeks as she moved to gather up the papers, putting the statement at the bottom of the stack.

"Sorry. The place isn't usually so cluttered."

"I wasn't looking, Kate. It was just lying there," Eric said quietly. To pretend he hadn't seen the piece of paper would be foolish.

She sighed and her hands stilled, but she kept her eyes averted. "I know."

"For Jack's care, I assume?"

She hesitated briefly, then nodded. "The health insurance covered a lot, and the life insurance helped—later.

But the expenses piled up so quickly. The debt was absolutely staggering. It still is. And with nothing to show for it," she added wearily, her voice catching in a way that tugged at his heart.

There was silence for a moment, and then she straightened her shoulders and looked up at him. "But you didn't come here tonight to hear about my problems. Let me get you that cup of coffee and cake I promised."

Actually, he wished she *would* share her problems with him. But he understood her reluctance. Their acquaintance was still too new. So he let it drop, nodding instead toward the sink. "It looks like you haven't even had dinner yet."

She glanced disinterestedly at the remains of the meal. "I had enough. I haven't been that hungry lately, anyway."

Eric frowned as she moved to the stove to fill the kettle, his gaze sweeping over her too-thin figure. "You can't afford to skip too many meals, Kate."

She shrugged as she set out two plates. "I eat when I'm hungry."

"Do you rest when you're tired?"

She paused in surprise, holding the knife motionless above the cinnamon coffee cake, and sent him a startled look. Then she turned back to her task. "I rest when there's time."

"Why do I think that's never?"

She turned to face him again, the smile on her face tinged with sadness. "You sound like my mother."

Eric didn't *feel* like her mother. Far from it. As his gaze took in her ebony hair tumbling around her face, her dark eyes shadowed with fatigue, her slender, deceptively fragile-looking form, he felt a fierce surge of protectiveness sweep over him—as well as something else he tried to ignore. He cleared his throat.

"You're the only mother in this room, Kate. And father, too, for that matter. It can't be easy, raising a child alone, trying to play both roles."

Her eyes grew troubled, and she turned away to reach for the kettle as it began to whistle. "Listen, Eric, I'm sorry about what Sarah said. She has a way of coming out with things that aren't always...well, discreet."

He waved her apology aside. "Don't worry about it, Kate. I hear all kinds of things from kids. Most of it I don't take seriously."

She placed their cake on the counter, then reached for her tea and his coffee, pushing aside the school papers as she sat on a stool next to him.

"Looks like you have some work ahead of you," he commented, nodding toward the pile.

"That's the lot of a teacher, I suppose. A never-ending stream of papers to grade. I usually work on them after Sarah goes to bed so I don't have to give up any of my time with her."

He looked at her. She was seated only inches away from him—so close he could clearly discern the faint lines of strain around her mouth. "Does sleep enter into the equation anywhere?" he asked gently. "You look tired, Kate."

The concern in his voice touched her, and her throat tightened as an unaccustomed warmth swept over her. "I catch up on my sleep in the summer," she replied, striving for a light tone. The truth was, she needed to take a summer job as well, at least something part-time.

"I have a feeling you're the kind of woman who never gives herself a break."

She propped her chin in her hand and played with her

tea bag, swirling it in the amber liquid. "Jack always said I was too intense," she admitted quietly. "That I took everything too seriously. But that's just the way I am. If I commit to something, I can't do it halfway. Like teaching. I didn't want to go back to it. I wanted to stay home with Sarah. But that wasn't to be. So as long as I have to work, I intend to give one hundred percent. The same with raising Sarah. I want to be the very best mother possible under the circumstances. That's why I spend every spare minute with her. It's why I grade papers and do lesson plans at night." She paused and looked over at him speculatively. "You strike me as being equally committed to your profession, Eric. I can't imagine you ever doing anything halfway."

He conceded the point with a nod. "You're right. But maybe that's not the best way to be. Sometimes I wonder if…" His voice trailed off and he stared down pensively into his coffee.

Kate knew he was thinking about his failed marriage, and impulsively she reached over and lightly touched his hand. The simple contact jolted him. "I have a feeling you're being too hard on yourself about…the past," she said quietly.

He stared down at her delicate hand as its warmth seeped into his very pores. It took only this simple innocent touch, filled with tender compassion, to remind him how lonely and empty his life had become. That reminder left a feeling of bleakness in its wake. Carefully he removed his hand on the pretext of reaching for his fork.

"How did we get into such a heavy discussion?" he asked, forcing his lips up into the semblance of a smile as he speared a bite of cake.

"I don't know. I think we started off talking about food."

"Well, then, let's get back to that topic," he declared, "because this cake is wonderful. Did you make it?"

"Uh-huh."

He devoured another large bite, clearly savoring the dessert. "You know, the only time I ever have home baking anymore is at Mom's. I could live on this cake. What it is?"

"Sour-cream cinnamon streusel coffee cake," she recited with a smile. "It was one of my mom's favorite recipes. Kind of a family standard."

"Well, you can bake this for me anytime. I'd make more house calls if I always got treats like this in return."

"Do you actually make house calls?"

"Once in a great while."

"Well, I'm glad you did tonight. Although my checkbook might not be," she teased with a smile.

Eric stopped eating for a moment and looked at her. "There's no charge for this, Kate."

Her smile faded. "Wait a minute. This was a professional call, Eric. I expect to be billed. You don't owe me any favors. And I always pay my debts."

He finished off the last of the cake, then stood. "Okay, then bake me one of these sometime and we'll be even."

"That's not…"

"Kate." He picked up his bag and turned to her. "I know you pay your debts. I saw evidence of that tonight. If you want to repay me, then do me a favor. Bake me one of these—" he tapped on the cake plate, then turned to look at her "—and get more rest. You're doing a great job taking care of Sarah. Now you need to take care of yourself."

She followed him to the door, prepared to continue the argument, but when he turned there was something in his cobalt-blue eyes that made her protest die in her throat. Their expression was unreadable, but the warmth in their depths was unmistakable. And when he spoke, his voice was slightly husky.

"Good night, Kate. Call me if Sarah isn't a lot better by tomorrow."

She swallowed, with difficulty. "I will. And thank you, Eric."

"It was my pleasure."

He looked at her for a moment, his gaze intense, and her breath got stuck somewhere in her chest. Slowly he reached up and touched her face, and she felt every muscle in her body begin to quiver. His fingers were gentle, the contact brief and unplanned, but as their gazes locked for an instant, Kate saw a flame leap to life in his eyes. Her stomach fluttered strangely, and she remembered Sarah's words to her earlier—*"I think you should get to know him better."*

Her mouth went dry and she seemed unable to move. Eric's gaze seared into her soul—assessing, discerning, seeking. She stopped breathing, not at all sure what was happening. Or if she could stop it. Or—most disturbing of all—if she even *wanted* to.

And then, abruptly, he turned away, striding quickly down the stairs. Kate stared after him, her heart hammering painfully in her chest as she thought about what had just happened. Had Eric been thinking about kissing her? Or had she only imagined it? But she hadn't imagined his touch. Her cheek was still tingling where his hand had rested.

And what did that touch mean? she wondered with a troubled frown as she slowly closed the door. And why had he done it?

Why did you do that? Eric berated himself as he strode angrily toward his car. He tossed his bag onto the passenger side and slid behind the wheel, his fingers gripping its curved edge as he stared into the darkness, struggling to understand what had just happened.

The self-control he'd carefully honed through the years had slipped badly tonight, he admitted. He wasn't normally an impulsive man. But as he'd looked at Kate's willowy form silhouetted in the doorway, he had been overwhelmed by a powerful urge to touch her, to reassure her in a tactile way that she wasn't as alone as she seemed to feel. He had wanted to tell her that she could always call on him, for anything. Had wanted to pull her into his arms and hold her. Had wanted to kiss her, to taste her sweet lips beneath his.

Eric let out a ragged breath and closed his eyes. Thank heaven he hadn't given in to that impulse; that he'd resisted his instincts and confined himself to a simple touch. But it hadn't been easy. And he had a sinking feeling in the pit of his stomach that the next time, it would be even more difficult.

Eric knew that he should strengthen his resolve to keep their contact to a minimum. He knew that just being around Kate was a dangerous temptation he didn't need. But he also knew it was a risk he was going to take—as soon as he regained his equilibrium and self-control. He figured that would take a week, maybe two. It wouldn't be easy to wait that long to see her again, he acknowledged. But he would manage it.

* * *

Three days later, Eric was already trying to think of an excuse to call Kate. So much for resolve, he thought grimly as he pulled into the attached garage of his modest bungalow, then headed down the driveway to retrieve the mail. She hadn't contacted him, so he'd assumed Sarah was feeling much better. Which had meant no more house calls. That was good, of course. For Sarah, anyway.

Eric reached into the mailbox and withdrew the usual assortment of bills and ads, flipping through the stack disinterestedly until a letter with his former sister-in-law's return address caught his eye. He frowned. Odd. He hadn't heard from Elaine since the divorce, more than four years ago. He closed the garage door and entered the kitchen, tossing the bulk of the mail on the counter and loosening his tie before slitting open the envelope and scanning the letter.

I know you will be surprised to hear from me, Eric, but I was reasonably certain that unless I wrote, you might never hear about Cindy. I know there was no love lost between the two of you by the time your marriage ended, but I think it's only right to let you know that she died a month ago. She was diagnosed with lung cancer a year ago—so far along that it was hopeless from the start. I guess her chain-smoking finally caught up with her.

Cindy never talked much about the divorce, although she did say that it was her idea. She was my sister and I loved her, but I want you to know that I always felt she had thrown away something pretty wonderful when she left you. I'm sure there was fault on both sides—there always is—but I suspect, much as I loved Cindy, that the bulk of it lay with her. I can only imagine what a devastating experience the breakup was for you, knowing what I do of you from our contact during your marriage.

I hope life has treated you more kindly since the breakup, Eric, and wish you only the best in the future.

Elaine

Eric stared numbly at the paper, then slowly sat down at the table. Cancer was a devastating disease that ravaged its victims physically. He couldn't even imagine how Cindy, who had always taken such care with her appearance, had coped with that—not to mention all the pain and suffering that cancer inflicted.

For a moment he allowed himself to recall how she had looked at their wedding, her blond beauty absolutely radiant and perfect; and how his heart had been so filled with love on that dream-come-true day. But over the next few years he'd watched that dream slowly disintegrate, until the night of the accident, when it had become a nightmare.

Eric raised a shaky hand and raked his fingers through his hair. He hadn't thought about that night in a long time, had purposely kept the memory of their confrontation at bay. But now the scene came back with startling clarity, the sequence of events unfolding in his mind as if on a movie screen.

At Eric's insistence, they'd cut their evening short. He hadn't been able to get the accident out of his mind, and the smoke at the party had actually begun to make him feel nauseous. Usually he'd deferred to Cindy at such events, enduring them until she was ready to call it a night. But that evening he'd simply told her they were leaving. She'd fumed all the way home in the car, then had confronted him the moment they walked in the door, turning on him in cold fury.

"Okay, do you want to tell me what that caveman act was all about?"

Eric wasn't up to a fight. But her tight-lipped, pinched features and belligerent tone told him there was no avoiding a confrontation.

"I just couldn't handle it tonight, Cindy. Not after the accident. It all seemed so...shallow. And the smoke was making me sick."

She uttered an expletive that made him cringe. "Why do you have to take everything so personally, anyway?" she demanded harshly. "You did your best. More than you needed to, probably. Why can't you just walk away? It's only a job."

He thought of the accident scene, of the woman's devastated face, the man's mangled body. And of his wife's inability to understand, even after all this time, that walking away simply wasn't in his nature. "It's not that easy, Cindy," he replied wearily.

She reached for her purse and extracted a cigarette, staring down his look of disapproval defiantly as she lit it and inhaled deeply.

"You and I need to talk, Eric."

She was right. But he was too tired tonight for the kind of discussion she had in mind. "Tomorrow, Cindy."

"No. Now."

There was an odd note in her voice, and he looked at her with a frown. Her gaze flickered away from his, as if she was suddenly nervous, and his frown deepened. He suddenly felt sick again—not from the smoke, but from a premonition that whatever Cindy had on her mind was going to change their relationship forever. And he didn't want to hear it. Not tonight.

"Look, can't this wait?"

"No. It's waited too long already." She moved restlessly to the other side of the room, paused as if gathering her courage, then turned to face him.

"Eric, this isn't working anymore, if it ever did. You know that. Let's face it. This marriage was a mistake from the start. We're not a good match. You can't have enjoyed these last six years any more than I have."

Eric wanted to pretend that this wasn't happening. But the tenseness in his shoulders, the sudden feeling of panic, the hollowness in the pit of his stomach, made it all too real.

"We took vows before God, Cindy. We can't just toss them aside. Remember the 'For better, for worse'?"

She gave a brief, bitter laugh. "Oh, I know all about the 'for worse' part. When do we come to the 'for better'?"

That hurt. There had been some moments of happiness, at least at the beginning. "We had some good times."

"A few," she conceded with an indifferent shrug. "But not enough to sustain this relationship. And I want more, Eric. In this marriage I'll always be competing for your attention with a bunch of sick kids. And I'm tired of losing."

"You knew I was a doctor when you married me."

She dismissed the comment with an impatient gesture. "I thought you were going to be a *surgeon,* Eric. With decent hours most of the time. Doing really important work. I didn't know you were going to turn into the pediatric version of Marcus Welby, always on call, always ready to jump every time some kid has a runny nose."

Eric's mouth tightened. Cindy had always made her opinion clear on the subject, but she'd never before used such hateful language.

Something in his expression must have registered, because when she spoke again she softened her tone. "Look, Eric, let's not make this any harder than necessary, okay? Let's just agree to call it quits and go our separate ways."

"You're asking for a divorce."

"Yes."

"Why now?"

She shot him an assessing look. "You want the truth?"

Suddenly he wasn't sure he did, but he nodded nonetheless.

She took a deep breath and reached down to tap the ash off her cigarette. "Okay. I've met someone I... like...a lot. There's potential there. And I want to be free to explore it." She paused, and as she watched the color ebb from his face, she spoke again. "I'm not having an affair, if that's what you're thinking. I wouldn't go that far, not while we're married. You know that."

He didn't know much of anything at the moment. He just felt shocked—and numb. He sat down heavily and dropped his head into his hands.

"Look, Eric, it's not that bad. Lots of marriages fail. This way we can both be free to try to find someone who is more compatible."

Slowly he raised his head, his face stricken, and looked at her. "I married for life, Cindy." His voice was flat, devoid of all emotion.

"I thought I did, too. But it didn't work out. I don't think God expects people to stay in miserable marriages."

"I think He expects people to try as hard as they can to make it work."

"I did try," she replied defiantly. "And it still didn't work. I'm sorry, Eric."

But she didn't sound sorry, he thought dully. She sounded almost...relieved. As if she'd made up her mind about this a long time ago and had been waiting for the right moment to tell him.

When he didn't reply, she glared at him impatiently. "So are you going to make this easy, or am I going to have to fight you on it?"

He raked the fingers of his hand through his hair and his shoulders drooped. "I'm tired of fighting, Cindy. I can't hold you if you don't want to stay."

"Good." The relief in her voice was obvious. "I'm glad you're being sensible. It's for the best, Eric. Maybe you'll find someone in the future who'll make you a better wife."

He looked at her sadly. "I already have a wife, Cindy. We may be able to break the bonds of our marriage in the eyes of the law, but in the sight of God we'll always be married. 'Till death us do part.'"

Eric returned to the present with a start and stared at the letter from Elaine. "Till death us do part." The words echoed hollowly in his heart. He'd remained faithful to that vow, but the cost had been deep-seated loneliness and episodes of dark despair. Now he was free. He wasn't sure what that meant exactly. But there would be time to think about it later. Right now he needed to talk with the Lord. He closed his eyes and bowed his head. *Dear Lord, be with Cindy,* he prayed. *Show her*

Your infinite mercy and understanding. And forgive me for all the times I failed her. May she find with You the peace and happiness I couldn't provide her with in this life. Amen.

Kate peered at the mailbox, verified the address, then pulled up to the curb and parked. She surveyed the small bungalow, surprised at its modest proportions and its location in this quiet, family-oriented neighborhood. She'd assumed that a successful doctor like Eric would live in more ostentatious surroundings.

She reached for the coffee cake, then paused as her nerves kicked in. She knew Eric hadn't really expected her to follow through on his "payment" suggestion for the house call. But it had given her an excuse to see him again. Just being in his presence made her feel good. In fact, since he'd come into her life she felt better than she had in a long time. Thanks to him, she was taking steps to renew her relationship with the Lord. Thanks to him, she'd found a wonderful caregiver for Sarah. And thanks to him, the spot in her heart that had lain cold and empty and dead for five long years was beginning to reawaken.

Actually, she wasn't sure whether to thank him for the latter. In fact she wasn't sure how to handle it—especially considering that Eric was off-limits. He'd made that very clear. Plus, she didn't know if she was ready to say goodbye to her past yet, despite Amy's advice. But something had compelled her to come here today. It might not be wise, but she had listened to her heart. She only hoped that it would guide her through the encounter to come. After their parting on Sunday night, Kate wasn't at all sure what to expect when Eric opened the door.

What she hadn't expected was his shell-shocked appearance. There were deep furrows between his brows, his hands were trembling and his face was colorless. She looked at him in alarm, her own trepidation forgotten as panic set in.

"Eric? What is it? What's wrong?"

He stared at her for a moment, as if trying to refocus. "Kate? What are you doing here? Is Sarah all right?"

"She's fine. I dropped her off at church for Christmas-pageant practice, and I wanted to stop by and repay you for the house call." She held up the coffee cake. "But... well, you look awful! Are you sick? What happened?"

He sighed and wearily passed a shaky hand over his eyes. "I had some...unexpected news. Come in, Kate." He stepped aside to let her enter, but she hesitated.

"Look, I don't want to intrude, Eric. Maybe I should come back another time."

"You're not intruding. And I'd like you to stay, actually. I could use the company."

Kate searched his eyes, but his invitation seemed sincere rather than just polite, so she stepped past him into the hallway.

"I was just going to make some coffee. Can I offer you some tea?"

"Thanks. But why don't you let me make it? You look like you should sit down."

He smiled wryly at her concerned expression as he led the way to the kitchen. "Don't worry, Kate. I'm not sick. Just shocked. But you look tired. Go ahead and sit down and I'll put the kettle on." He indicated a sturdy antique wooden table and chairs in a large bay off to one side of the kitchen.

She complied silently, watching as he stepped between the stove and the oak cabinets. He moved with an easy grace, a quiet competence that was restful and reassuring. She glanced around her. The kitchen was a lovely spot, cheerful and bright, with big windows that offered views of what appeared to be a large tree-shaded backyard. But the room itself was somewhat sterile, with few personal items other than a letter addressed to Eric on the table. Though Cindy had been gone a long time, Kate was surprised that there was so little evidence of the decorating touches usually initiated by the woman of the house. But the room was comfortable and clearly had great potential.

"I like your house, Eric," Kate remarked as he set plates and forks on the table.

"Do the honors on the cake, would you, Kate? And thanks. The house *is* nice. It's the kind of place I always wanted."

"Me, too. Jack and I had a house something like this when we first moved to St. Louis."

Eric heard the wistful tone in her voice, and it tugged at his heart. He knew from his mother that Kate had sold the house after Jack died. She'd needed the money for other things—like paying medical bills. But he didn't want her dwelling on the past.

"The only problem with this place is the decorating—or lack thereof. It needs to be warmed up, but I'm not even sure where to begin."

"I'm surprised Cindy didn't do more," Kate admitted.

"Cindy never lived here, Kate. I bought this place after the divorce."

"Oh. I'm sorry."

"No need to be. Believe me, this wasn't her style. We lived in a condo in West County when we were married. It was what she wanted, and it suited her."

But what about you? Kate wanted to ask. *Didn't your wants count? What about whether it suited you?* But she remained silent, for he suddenly grew pensive as his gaze came to rest on the letter. Kate suddenly realized that whatever it contained accounted for his recent shock. And that it had something to do with Cindy.

She looked over at him, and their gazes met. She didn't want to pry, but she wanted him to know that she cared. "I'm a good listener, Eric," she said quietly.

He studied her for a moment, then sighed and turned away to retrieve their mugs. Kate tried not to be hurt by his silence. After all, they were recent acquaintances. She couldn't blame him for wanting to keep his problem private. But when he sat down he surprised her.

"That letter is from Cindy's sister."

Kate looked at him curiously but remained quiet.

"Cindy died a couple of weeks ago."

Kate stared at him in shock. Now she understood why he had looked so shaken when he answered the door. "What happened?"

"Lung cancer. I was always afraid her smoking would kill her."

"I'm so sorry."

He sighed. "I am, too. For her. For what might have been. For all the mistakes we both made. My strongest feeling at the moment is regret. It's odd, Kate. I have no sense of personal loss. No grief in that way. Cindy and I parted long ago, even before the divorce. By the end of our marriage we were really no more than strangers."

Kate couldn't imagine the living hell of that kind of relationship. She and Jack had had arguments on occasion, but deep down they'd always known that their marriage was rock solid, that it would endure, no matter what obstacles life put in their path. Eric had clearly never enjoyed that kind of relationship.

Impulsively she reached over and laid her hand on his, just as she had three nights before. "I'm so sorry, Eric," she repeated. "Not only for Cindy's death, but for the death of your marriage. In some ways, I think that would be even harder to bear than the physical death of a loved one. I was devastated when Jack died, but I had wonderful memories to cling to and sustain me. I'm sorry you never had that."

Eric looked into Kate's tear-filled eyes and something deep within him stirred. It was such a foreign emotion that it took him a moment to identify it as hope. Here, with this special woman, he suddenly felt that his future no longer needed to be solitary and devoid of love. Which was strange. Because though he might now be free to marry in the eyes of the Lord, there were still major obstacles to overcome before he could even begin to consider a future with Kate. First of all, she was still in love with Jack. That was no small hurdle. And second, he was still a doctor, committed to a profession that didn't seem to mix with marriage—or at least, not for him. There seemed no way around that barrier.

And yet…Eric couldn't suppress the optimism that surged through him. It was as if a heavy burden had been lifted from his shoulders, as if the floodgates had opened on a parched field. Yes, the problems were significant. But all things were possible with the Lord. And maybe, with His help, out of the darkness of these past years a new day was about to dawn.

Chapter Eight

"So...I hear I have some competition in the baking department."

Kate took a sip of her tea and smiled at Anna. "Hardly."

"I don't know." The older woman's tone was skeptical, but there was a twinkle in her eye. "The way Eric raved about that coffee cake—it must be something special. It was nice of you to make one just for him."

"It was the least I could do after he stopped by to see Sarah—and on a Sunday night." Kate poured herself another cup of tea and sighed contentedly. "Mmm. This is the perfect antidote to a long, drawn-out teachers' meeting. Thanks for watching Sarah later than usual, Anna."

"My pleasure. She's a delightful little girl and no trouble at all." They simultaneously glanced out the window toward the patio, where the youngster was engrossed in some make-believe game, wringing every moment out of the rapidly diminishing daylight. "She's so excited about the Christmas pageant at church. It's all she's talked about for the last two days. If you need any help with the angel costume, I'd be more than happy to lend a hand."

Kate smiled and shook her head. "Speaking of angels—how did I get lucky enough to find you?"

"Well, you can thank my son for that. And it wasn't luck at all. It was just part of God's plan."

"What plan is that?" Kate inquired with a smile.

The doorbell rang before the older woman could reply. "Goodness! I don't usually have visitors at this hour," she remarked, a flush rising to her cheeks. "Will you excuse me for a moment, my dear?"

"Of course. We need to be leaving anyway." Kate started to get up, but Anna put a hand on her shoulder.

"Not yet!" There was an anxious note in her voice, and Kate looked at her curiously. Anna's flush deepened and she quickly backtracked. "At least finish your tea first," she said, before quickly leaving the room.

Kate stared after her, a sudden niggling suspicion sending an uneasy tingle down her spine. The older woman was up to something, she concluded. But what?

She had her answer a few moments later when Anna reentered the kitchen followed by Eric, who was toting two large white sacks.

"Well, look who stopped by," Anna declared, feigning surprise.

Kate sent her a chiding look, which the older woman ignored. Kate was beginning to realize that Anna was a matchmaker at heart and now seemed to be directing her efforts at her son and the mother of her young charge. Of course, she wouldn't get very far without the cooperation of said son, Kate reflected, directing her glance his way. And he wasn't in the market for romance. But as their gazes connected she somehow got lost in his blue eyes and warm smile and forgot all about conspiracy theories.

"Hi."

How did he manage to impart such a warm, personal tone to a single word? Kate wondered as she distractedly returned the greeting.

He held up the sacks. "I heard you were working late tonight and thought maybe we could all share some Chinese. I brought chicken fingers and fries for Sarah."

Kate smiled, touched by his thoughtfulness. "She'll love that. It's not a treat she gets too often."

"How about you, Kate? Is Chinese all right?"

"Perfect. A treat for me, too."

Anna looked from one to the other with a satisfied expression. "I'll just call Sarah," she offered, heading toward the back door.

Kate rose to get some plates and eating utensils while Eric unpacked the bags. "You're going to spoil us, you know," she told him over her shoulder.

"You could use some spoiling."

She turned to him in surprise, and as their gazes met, a faint flush rose in her cheeks. There was something... different about Eric tonight, she decided. She couldn't quite put her finger on it. He seemed less tense. Less worried. And definitely less distant. Which shouldn't surprise her, considering how much he'd shared with her Wednesday night about the deep-seated hurts and disappointments of his marriage. In fact, she'd been surprised by his openness. Most men she'd met kept their feelings to themselves—especially the darker ones—as well as their doubts. Even Jack. Despite his outgoing nature, he'd had a hard time talking about feelings, preferring instead to express them.

But Eric had told her things that many men's egos

would never have let them admit—his sense of failure when the marriage had faltered, his doubts about the compatibility of a family and his career, his sense of betrayal and deep hurt when Cindy had asked him for a divorce and told him she'd met someone new. It touched her deeply that he'd chosen to share his feelings with her. And as she'd left he'd looked at her as he had the prior Sunday, and had touched her cheek in just the same way.

Kate had thought about that evening a great deal over the last two days. She'd wondered what it meant, where it would lead. Now she was beginning to get a clue. Eric's visit tonight had clearly been planned. He was making an effort to see her, to get to know her better, to spend time with her. In other words, he was letting her know he was interested in her. At the same time, she sensed that he would wait for her to give him a sign that she wanted their relationship to move to a deeper level.

But Kate wasn't prepared to do that yet. She needed more time to sort through her conflicting emotions—and loyalties. With a self-conscious smile, she turned back to the cabinet and busied herself with the plates and glasses.

Eric got the message. Kate wasn't ready to cross the line from friendship to anything else yet. And frankly, he wasn't sure he was, either. So he would wait. And in time the Lord would show them both the way.

Somehow the Friday-night dinners became a regular event. So did Sunday church, with breakfast afterward. And Eric began calling her during the week to share amusing stories about his young patients and to ask about her day. Sometimes he would drop in unexpectedly for coffee, or sweep everyone off to an impromptu dinner out, much to Sarah's delight—not to mention her mother's.

Occasionally their evenings would be interrupted by Eric's pager, and though he always apologized, Kate assured him that she didn't mind. His deep compassion and fervent commitment to his work were part of who he was. To change that would be to change his very essence. And she liked him just the way he was.

By late October, he had become so much a part of their lives that the loneliness of the last five years began to recede in her mind until it was only a dim, unpleasant memory. In fact, not only did she begin to forget what life had been like before Eric, it was becoming harder and harder to imagine a future without him.

"Okay, partner, we need to have a talk."

Eric glanced up from his paperwork as Frank strode in with a determined look on his face, then dropped into the chair across from Eric's desk.

"What's up?" Eric asked mildly.

"We need to add a third physician to this practice," he declared without preamble.

Eric's eyebrows rose. "We've talked about this before."

"I know. And you were always reluctant. But that was when we were just getting established and *needed* to work twelve hours a day. We're past that now. We have a thriving practice. There's plenty of work for a third doctor. Plus, we'll only have to cover calls every third weekend instead of every two. With the baby coming, Mary thinks I need to lighten up my work schedule so I have more time to spend with the family. And I agree."

"So do I."

Frank opened his mouth to argue, stared at Eric, and shut it. "What did you say?"

"I said I agree."

"Just like that? No protest? No litany of reasons why this isn't a good time?"

"Nope."

Frank stared at him, his expression slowly changing from astonishment to smugness as the light dawned. "Oh, I get it. It's Kate."

"Kate?"

"Don't give me that innocent act. Of course it's Kate. Things are heating up, huh?"

Eric thought about their basically platonic relationship and smiled ruefully. "I wouldn't say that exactly."

"Oh, come on, buddy. You can tell me. Just because I haven't pestered you with questions about her lately doesn't mean I forgot the way you looked at her at the barbecue. I knew then something was in the wind. You're seeing her a lot, aren't you?"

"As a matter of fact, yes."

Frank grinned. "I thought so. Listen, I think that's great. It's about time you had something more in your life than a job and charity work. I'm glad for you, pal. This third partner will help us *both* out."

"Do you have someone in mind?"

"Absolutely. Carolyn Clark."

Eric knew her. She was one of the hardest-working pediatric residents he'd ever met, and her educational credentials were impressive. She'd be a good fit. "Is she interested?"

"Yep."

"Let's talk to her, then."

Frank shook his head incredulously. "You know, I

thought I was going to have to do a real sell job on you about this."

Eric chuckled. "Not this time."

"So...I take it things are going well with Kate." Frank leaned back and crossed an ankle over a knee, clearly settling in for a long interrogation.

Eric looked at his friend speculatively as he recalled something his mother had said to him weeks ago about his partner's ability to balance marriage and medicine. He hesitated for a moment, then spoke carefully. "Can I ask you something, Frank?"

At the serious tone in Eric's voice, Frank straightened. "Sure. Shoot."

Eric steepled his fingers and sighed. "I guess it's no secret that Cindy and I made a mess of our marriage. And one of the biggest problems was my career. She hated how it intruded on our relationship and interrupted our private life. It was a major problem, and I just couldn't seem to solve it. If I had been able to, our marriage might not have fallen apart."

Frank's eyes narrowed. "It wasn't just *your* problem, Eric."

"What do you mean?"

Frank spoke slowly, obviously choosing his words carefully. "Doctors' lives—whatever their specialty—don't belong completely to them. That's just the nature of the job. And good doctors—the ones who really care, who take the Hippocratic oath seriously—always serve two masters. Yes, we care for our families and the people we love. But we also have an obligation to do our best for the people we serve. Our patients' lives are literally in our hands. You don't have to marry a doctor to realize that. Cindy knew what she was getting into, Eric. Don't beat yourself up about that. She just wasn't willing to play second fiddle—ever. I think that reflects more on her than on you."

Eric wanted to believe Frank. But the doubts went too deep and were of too long a duration to be dispelled so quickly by his partner's reassurance. "What about you and Mary, Frank? How do the two of you deal with the demands? Doesn't Mary ever resent them?"

"Honestly? No. Which doesn't mean she isn't disappointed on occasion when my professional obligations interfere with our plans. But she accepts it as part of what makes me tick. And she knows I do everything I can to put her first the rest of the time and make time for us as a couple—like pushing for a third partner," he said, flashing a grin. "So we've never had any problems."

Eric looked at Frank silently for a moment, then sighed. "I wish I could be sure it worked like that for everyone."

Frank stood, his expression serious. "Don't let one bad experience stop you from having a good one, Eric. I don't know Kate very well. But I liked what I saw. Cindy's gone now. There's nothing except fear to keep you from moving forward. And let me say one more thing. You're just about the most conscientious, caring person I know. If you couldn't make a marriage work, nobody could. And if you ever tell anybody I got this mushy, I'll deny it," he finished with a smile as he exited.

Eric stared after him thoughtfully. He and Frank had been friends for a long time. Usually his colleague hid his deeper feelings under an umbrella of humor. But just now he'd spoken from the heart. Eric appreciated his flattering words, as well as his honesty. And Frank was right. He *was* afraid. Now the question was, could he get over those fears enough to take another chance on love?

* * *

Anna handed Kate another pin, then backed up and critically surveyed the hem of Sarah's angel costume. "I think that will do it. I'll run it up for you on the machine tomorrow, Kate."

Kate stood and lifted Sarah down from the sturdy kitchen chair, giving her a hug as she lowered her to the floor. "You're a beautiful angel, honey."

"Are we going to make the wings next week?" the little girl asked excitedly.

"Absolutely. Dr. Eric said he'd get some wire for us at the hardware store for the frame."

"Mommy's been working on the wreath for my hair at night after I go to bed," Sarah told Anna. "It's really pretty!"

"I think you'll be the loveliest angel there ever was," Anna declared with a smile. "Now let's get that gown off so it stays clean. Angels always look nice and neat, you know."

"I can't thank you enough for all your help, Anna," Kate said warmly when Sarah scampered off to play. "In a way, I feel that Sarah has a brand-new grandmother."

"Well, it's a role I always wanted to play," Anna reminded her as she laid the gown over the sewing machine. "I love taking care of her. It's given me a new sense of purpose. I still miss Walter every day, of course, but it's easier to bear, somehow, knowing that you and Sarah are counting on me." She paused and turned to the younger woman. "And speaking of watching Sarah—I know this is rather short notice, Kate, but my cousin called last night. She and a friend were planning to go on a cruise the week of Thanksgiving, and her friend had to back out at the last minute. She asked me to go instead. I've always wanted to take a cruise, and this seemed like a providential opportunity. So I told her yes. But I'm afraid that means I can't watch Sarah on Monday and Tuesday of Thanksgiving week."

"Oh, Anna, don't give it another thought!" Kate assured her. "I'm thrilled for you! And Thanksgiving is still three weeks away. I have plenty of time to make other arrangements."

"Actually, I spoke with my neighbor—a lovely young woman, very responsible, with two small children of her own. Sarah's played with them on occasion. She said she'd be happy to watch her. I know you're leaving for your sister's Wednesday, and I'll be back Sunday night. So it's only for two days."

Kate was touched by the older woman's consideration. "Thank you, Anna. That sounds perfect," she said warmly. "And I hope you have a wonderful time on your cruise."

"Oh, I expect we will. Except…"

"Except what?" Kate prompted when Anna's voice trailed off.

"Well, I'm a little concerned about Eric. He'll be by himself on Thanksgiving, and I'm afraid it will be hard for him. It's always been the three of us on holidays. But when I spoke to him last night about the trip, he encouraged me to go and assured me he'd be fine. So I suppose I shouldn't worry. He'll probably go to Frank's."

Kate frowned. Eric wouldn't be spending the holiday with Frank because they were going to Mary's parents' house. He'd probably end up working the whole four-day weekend. Unless…

"Is something wrong, dear?" Anna asked, eyeing the younger woman with concern.

Kate forced herself to smile. "Not a thing." There was

no sense mentioning the idea that had just popped into her head. Especially when she wasn't sure she would follow through on it, anyway.

"Hi, Amy."

"Kate? It's my Sunday, isn't it?"

"Yes. But Eric is stopping by in a little while, so I thought I'd just go ahead and call. Are you in the middle of something?"

"You mean other than the usual mayhem around this place?"

Kate chuckled. "What's going on now?"

"A friend of Cal's had to go out of the country on business for a few weeks and somehow conned my good-natured husband into baby-sitting his iguana. The twins are fascinated. Personally, when it comes to pets I prefer the warm, cuddly variety. However, as long as I don't have to touch it, I suppose I can put up with a reptile in my house for a limited time. But speaking of 'warm and cuddly'—how are things with Eric?"

Kate flushed. She'd tried to downplay their relationship, but Amy wasn't inclined to buy the "just friends" routine. Which, in a way, might make it easier to broach the subject that was on her mind. "Things are fine."

"'Fine,' hmm. Would you define that?"

"I see him a lot. We go to church together and all of us eat dinner at his mother's every Friday night. Sometimes he drops over. Like tonight."

There was silence for a moment. "Look, Kate, I don't want to pry—or push. So if you want to tell me to mind my own business, it won't hurt my feelings in the least. But is it really just a friendship thing with you two?"

Kate played with the phone cord. "Yes. Although sometimes I... Well, I think maybe he'd like for it to be more. I mean, I know he still has concerns about mixing medicine and marriage. He got burned pretty badly the first time he tried that. So he's gun-shy. But I have a feeling if I gave him some encouragement he might be willing to at least...consider it."

"And I take it you haven't?"

"No. I'm still trying to put my own past behind me," Kate admitted, her gaze coming to rest on the wedding picture that hung over the couch. "It's really hard to let go, you know? Even after all this time."

"Yeah, I know." Amy sighed. "I guess you just need to listen to your heart and do things at your own pace, Kate. You'll know when it's the right time to move forward."

Kate took a deep breath. "Actually, that's one of the reasons I called. I think maybe it *is* the right time. At least to take a few small steps." Kate explained Anna's Thanksgiving plans and her concern about Eric being alone. "So I wondered if maybe... Well, I thought that—"

"Invite him," Amy interrupted promptly.

"Honestly?"

"Of course. One more mouth to feed in this household won't even be noticed. And there's plenty of room. We'll kick out the iguana if we have to."

Kate laughed. Amy had always had a knack for making her feel better. "You're a pretty terrific sister, you know that?"

"Just paying back an old debt. Seems to me you were a pretty good sounding board once when I really needed guidance. If it wasn't for you I might never have married Cal and ended up living in the heart of Tennessee. You know, come to think of it..."

Kate smiled at her teasing tone. "You wouldn't trade your life for anything and you know it."

"You're right about that. Listen, you bring that over-worked doctor down here and we'll show him a Thanksgiving he won't forget."

"Thanks, Amy."

"My pleasure. Just do me a favor, okay? Warn him about the iguana."

Kate didn't mention the holiday that night when Eric stopped by for cake and coffee. In fact, it took her a whole week to work up the courage to broach the subject. And when she did, it was at the last minute, as he walked Sarah and her to the door after Sunday services.

Kate fitted her key in the lock and ushered Sarah inside, then turned to Eric, struggling to get her suddenly-too-rapid pulse under control. "Thanks again for the ride. And for breakfast," she said a bit breathlessly.

"You're welcome."

Though there was a chill in the early-November air, his smile warmed her all the way to her toes. "Uh, Eric…"

He looked at her curiously, alerted by something in her tone. "Yes?"

"I'm glad your mother is going on that cruise."

"So am I. It will be a nice change of pace for her. She sounds like a kid when she talks about it—which is most of the time. I didn't think we'd get a word in edgewise at breakfast today."

"I know. She's so excited! But… Well, what about you? It won't be much fun to spend the holiday alone."

He shrugged dismissively. "I'll be fine."

"Your mom is kind of concerned about you being by yourself."

He tilted his head and eyed her quizzically. "Did she tell you that?"

"Uh-huh."

He frowned. "I told her not to worry."

"That's how mothers are. It's in the job description." She paused and took a deep breath. "To be honest, I'm not too happy about the situation, either. So I thought you might like to... Well, I talked to Amy and...you know we always go there for Thanksgiving, and there's plenty of room—Amy said so. Except she did tell me to warn you about the iguana. Cal's watching it for a friend of his. Amy's not too happy about that, but the kids love it and—" Her nervous babbling ceased abruptly when Eric laid his hand on her arm and gazed down at her.

"Kate, are you asking me to spend Thanksgiving with you and your family?" he asked quietly.

She swallowed with difficulty and nodded. "Listen, I know it's kind of a long trip and they're all strangers to you, so it's okay if..."

"I accept."

She looked at him in surprise. "Really?"

"Really. Because between you and me, I *wasn't* looking forward to spending this holiday alone. And I can't think of anywhere I'd rather be on this Thanksgiving than with you. And Sarah. And Amy and her family... and the iguana," he teased, a twinkle springing to life in his eyes.

Kate's gaze was locked on his, and she watched, mesmerized, as the twinkle suddenly changed to an ember that quickly ignited, deepening the color of his eyes. Her breath caught in her throat as he slowly reached over and touched her face, letting his hand linger before gently raking his fingers through her hair.

Though the touch was simple, its effect on Kate's metabolism was anything but. She longed to lean against his solid chest, to feel his arms protectively and tenderly enfold her. She closed her eyes and sighed softly, instinctively swaying toward him.

Eric read her body language, recognized the invitation she was unconsciously issuing, and fought down the sudden urge to pull her close. *Dear Lord, give me strength,* he prayed, his heart hammering in his chest. He wanted to hold her tightly, to touch her, to caress the soft waves of her ebony hair and the silky smoothness of her cheek. He wanted to press his lips to hers and taste their sweetness. Bottom line, he wanted a whole lot more than he *should* want at this point, he reminded himself as he struggled to control his desires. Get a grip, admonished himself sharply. This is not the time. Or the place.

With a triumph of willpower that surprised him, he dropped his hand and stepped back, drawing a long, shaky breath as he did so.

Kate opened her eyes and blinked, as if trying to clear her vision, then reached out to grip the doorframe as she stared at him.

"I'll call you," he promised, his gaze locked on hers.

She nodded jerkily. "Okay." It was barely a whisper.

He held her gaze for a moment longer, then with obvious effort turned and strode quickly away. Not until he was out of her sight did he pause for a moment to take a deep, steadying breath. He knew that Kate was close to reaching out to him. The real question now was whether they were both ready. During the last couple of weeks he'd thought a lot about his conversation with Frank, and he was gradually beginning to believe that maybe…just maybe… marriage and medicine could mix—with the right woman. Namely, Kate. But even if he resolved his own issues, there was still Jack. Could she let him go? And could she ever find it in her heart to love someone else as intensely as she'd loved her husband?

Eric wasn't sure. And that uncertainty left him discouraged. For if he truly set out to win the heart of this special woman, he realized he could face a daunting task. The simple fact was, his experience in dealing with *living* rivals was extremely limited. And he was at a total loss about how to deal with a dead one.

Chapter Nine

Kate glanced over her shoulder at Sarah, whose excited chatter had finally been silenced by sleep, and smiled. Her gaze connected with Eric's as she turned back, and he glanced briefly in the rearview mirror, his own mouth lifting at the corners.

"Looks like the sandman finally won."

"Thanks for being so patient, Eric. I'm sure you would have preferred a quieter drive."

"Honestly? No. Most of my drives are far *too* quiet. This was a nice change."

"Well, Sarah isn't usually this wound up. It's just that she's been so excited about the trip. She was up at dawn, ready and waiting."

"Which means her mother was up at dawn, as well."

She shrugged. "I had things to do anyway."

"You must be tired, Kate. Why don't you grab a nap, too?"

The sudden tenderness in his voice made her stomach flutter, but she tried to ignore the sensation. "I'm okay. The fact is, I'm excited, too. I've been looking forward to seeing Amy and her family as much as Sarah has.

The kids are cute, Cal is great and Amy... Well, Amy's special. I hope you like her, Eric."

"I'm sure I will. Especially if she's anything like you."

She felt a warm flush rise to her face. "Actually, we're pretty different," she replied, striving to maintain a conversational tone. "Amy has always been more outgoing and self-confident, sort of a take-charge kind of person—in the best sense of the term. She's a doer and an organizer and always has things under control. Unlike me."

Eric frowned and glanced over at her. "I think you're selling yourself short."

Kate gazed unseeingly into the deepening dusk. "'Control' isn't a word I would apply to my life in recent years," she said quietly.

"The things that happened were *beyond* your control, Kate," Eric reminded her gently but firmly. "You coped admirably under extremely difficult circumstances and through it all you've been an exceptional mother. That ranks you pretty highly in my book."

Kate turned to study his strong profile, trying unsuccessfully to read his expression in the dim light. "I have a feeling you're just being kind, Eric, but in any case, thank you."

His gaze flickered momentarily to hers. "I'm not just being kind, Kate. Trust me."

That tender, intimate quality was back in his voice, and her heart stopped, then raced on. "You know, Dr. Carlson, you're going to turn my head with all these compliments. Pretty soon I'll have to add conceitedness to my list of faults," she quipped, unwilling yet to deal with the implications of his flattery—and his tone. She was relieved when he picked up on her cue and responded with a chuckle.

"Why do I doubt that?" he countered.

They lapsed into companionable silence then, and by the time they pulled into the drive that led to Amy's log house it was after ten. The crunch of the tires on the gravel announced their arrival, and as they pulled to a stop, the front door was flung open to reveal a silhouetted, jeans-clad figure.

Kate smiled softly. "Amy's been watching for us."

Before Eric could respond, the woman in the doorway called something over her shoulder, then raced down the steps, bypassing the last one with a leap. Kate pushed open her door, and the two women met in front of the car, clinging to each other in a fierce hug.

"Oh, Kate, it's so good to see you!" Amy said fervently.

When Kate replied there was a trace of tears in her voice. "I've missed you so much!"

Eric leaned against the car and folded his arms across his chest as he silently watched the reunion. Though it was difficult to see much in the dim light, there were definitely some physical differences between the two women. Amy was taller than Kate, and her hair wasn't nearly as dark. While Kate was softly rounded in all the right places, Amy's build seemed more angular and athletic. And her movements suggested a more boisterous, impulsive nature than Kate's. But whatever their physical or personality differences, it was clear that the sisters shared a strong emotional bond. He felt touched—and honored—that Kate had included him in this family gathering.

When Amy at last extricated herself from the hug,

she strode toward him and extended her hand. "You're obviously Eric. Welcome."

He straightened quickly and took her fingers in a firm grip. "And you're obviously Amy. Thank you for inviting me. I'm looking forward to being part of your holiday."

Amy tilted her head and planted her hands on her hips. "I hope you still feel that way when you leave on Sunday. Kate did tell you about the iguana, right?"

He smiled. "I've been duly warned about your temporary guest."

"Well, I'm glad you used the term 'temporary,'" she confessed with relief. "We're eccentric enough without having strangers think we regularly keep weird animals in our house. You'll be happy to know that Wally isn't sleeping in your room."

"'Wally'?"

"The iguana." She rolled her eyes. "An iguana named Wally, can you believe it? The next time Cal agrees to—"

"Did I hear my name mentioned?"

A tall, dark-haired man slipped his arm around Amy's shoulders and she turned to look up at him. Her expression softened, though her tone was teasing. "You did. We were discussing Wally."

Cal grimaced good-naturedly. "Why do I think I'll never hear the end of this?"

"Because you won't," she replied pertly. "But enough about Wally for the moment. Eric, this is my husband, Cal. Cal, Eric Carlson."

While the two men shook hands and exchanged greetings, Amy slipped from under Cal's arm, peered inside the car and grinned. "Looks like someone nodded off."

"About a hundred and fifty miles ago," Kate informed her.

"Well, I'm sure you're all exhausted after that long drive. Are you hungry?" She glanced from Kate to Eric, and they shook their heads.

"We stopped for dinner along the way," Kate told her.

"Okay. Then let's get you all to bed. We can visit tomorrow."

By the time everyone was settled, it was nearly eleven. Sarah and the twins were happily rolled into sleeping bags in the living room, while Kate took the twins' room. Eric was assigned the sleeper sofa in the den.

"Now, is there anything else you need tonight?" Amy asked.

"We're fine," Kate assured her. "Get some rest yourself."

Amy chuckled and glanced at her watch ruefully. "Fat chance. Believe it or not, Caitlin still likes a midnight bottle. My six-month-old," she explained to Eric.

He smiled. "A healthy appetite is a good sign."

"I'll remind myself of that while I'm feeding her in the wee hours," she replied with a wry grin. "Good night, you two."

They watched her disappear up the rough-hewn split-log stairway, and then Eric turned to Kate. The warmth in his eyes banished the evening chill. "Sleep well," he said huskily.

She opened her mouth to reply, discovered she'd somehow misplaced her voice, and forced herself to take a deep breath before trying again. "I usually do when I'm here. I like being in the country."

"I do, too. This seems like a perfect spot to celebrate

an all-American holiday. Thanks again for inviting me, Kate."

She smiled. "Like Amy said, save your thanks until we leave. It can get pretty crazy around here with all the kids."

"It's a good kind of crazy, though."

Her smile softened. "Yeah, it is."

Kate expected him to turn away then, but instead he propped a shoulder against the doorframe and shoved his hands into the pockets of his jeans. He drew a deep breath, and in the dim light of the hall Kate could see twin furrows etched between his eyes.

"Is something wrong?" she asked in concern.

He glanced down at her, and his frown eased. "No. I'm just thinking how nice it is to be in a home so obviously filled with love. Amy and Cal seem to have created something really special in this house. I can feel it, even in the short time I've been here. It's heartwarming to see such a successful marriage."

"They do happen, Eric. I know."

He looked down into her eyes and nodded slowly. "I know you do. I guess the question is…"

His voice trailed off, and Kate felt her breath catch in her throat. She could guess what he was thinking, and she knew she ought to leave his comment alone. But she spoke anyway. "The question is what?" she ventured hesitantly.

Eric gazed at her for a long moment. Then, instead of replying, he withdrew one of his hands from his pocket and reached over to cup her chin, his thumb stroking her cheek. It was a casual, uncomplicated gesture. But the warmth of his gentle touch, the compelling look in his eyes, turned it into so much more. A deep yearning surged through Kate, and she felt her heart pause, then race on. She wanted more, she realized. She wanted him to hold her in his strong arms, to tenderly claim her long-neglected lips. Instinctively Kate knew Eric's briefest kiss would transport her to a land of emotion from which she had long been estranged.

Eric saw the longing in Kate's eyes and could no longer ignore—or suppress—the attraction that sparked between them. It was time to test the waters. Slowly he leaned toward her, his gaze locked on hers. His own pulse was none too steady, and he closed his eyes as their lips came whisper close, eager to taste the sweetness of—

"Oh, I'm glad you're both still up. I forgot—"

Kate heard Eric's sharply indrawn breath and pulled back, startled. She felt hot color suffuse her face as she turned to her sister.

Amy paused on the bottom step and quickly assessed the situation. "Uh, listen, leave it to me to barge right in at the wrong time. I just wanted to let you know that we planned to go to services tomorrow morning at ten, if that's okay with you two."

"Th-that's fine. Thanks." Kate tried unsuccessfully to control the tremor in her voice.

"So…good night again. This time for good," Amy promised as she made her way up the stairs. A few seconds later a door very deliberately clicked shut.

There was a long moment of awkward silence. Then Kate wrapped her arms around her body and tried to smile. "Amy always did have impeccable timing," she said shakily.

Eric let out a long breath and raked the fingers of one hand through his hair. "That's for sure."

"Listen, it's getting late anyway. We're both tired. Maybe… maybe we should just call it a night."

He looked down at her for a moment, the haze of desire still evident in his eyes. Finally he sighed and nodded. "I guess you're right. But remember one thing." His voice was husky as he reached over and touched her cheek.

"Wh-what?" she stammered, her gaze locked on his.

"To borrow a line from *Gone With the Wind*, 'Tomorrow is another day.'"

And with that enigmatic comment, he turned and disappeared down the hall.

Tomorrow was, indeed, another day. But it was a family affair—from the pancake breakfast to the church service to the dinner preparations, when everyone was recruited to help. Eric found himself peeling potatoes after Amy slapped a paring knife into his hand and said she figured if he could handle a scalpel, he could handle that.

The meal itself was a joyous, boisterous affair, and afterward everyone pitched in on the cleanup. They paid their respects to Wally, admired the gazebo Cal was building in a grove of rhododendrons at the back of the property, and stayed up late, reminiscing and playing board games. The next day was equally busy, and the evening not conducive to privacy—Amy was up till all hours with a fussy Caitlin. On Saturday Cal took them into Great Smoky Mountains National Park for a "VIP tour," as he laughingly called it.

"This isn't the best time of year for the park, but it has its beauty in all seasons," he told them as they wandered down a particularly lovely path by a crystal-clear stream. As the children ran ahead, and Cal and Amy strolled arm in arm, Caitlin sleeping—finally!—in the carrier on Cal's back, Eric slowed his pace and turned to Kate.

"Alone at last," he declared with a grin.

She gave him a wry glance. "Hardly."

"Why do I think this is as good as it's going to get while we're here?"

Kate looked up at him apologetically. "It's been a bit overwhelming, hasn't it? I'm sorry, Eric. I guess I didn't realize that—well, that you were hoping for some time alone."

He reached over and deliberately laced his fingers with hers. A tingle ran down her spine at his touch, and she felt warm color rise in her cheeks when he spoke. "I guess I didn't, either—until the night we arrived. As you've probably realized by now, I tend to be the slow-moving, cautious type when it comes to relationships. Maybe too much so. At least that's what Frank says."

Kate smiled understandingly. "I'm the same way. Just ask Amy. I like to be sure about things, and sometimes… sometimes that holds me back."

"I know. Unfortunately, life doesn't seem to offer many certainties."

"Maybe…maybe there are times when you just have to trust your heart."

He looked down at her, his eyes serious. "I haven't been willing to do that for a long time," he admitted honestly.

She gazed up at him, searching his eyes, wanting to ask the question that hovered on her lips but feeling afraid to do so. Yet he seemed to read her mind, and answered it.

"I've felt…differently about a lot of things since I met you, Kate," he told her quietly.

"So…so have I," she confessed haltingly. "But I'm

still not sure about what to do. Reverend Jacobs has been really great, though, in helping me sort out my feelings. And I've been following his advice to pray for guidance."

He smiled and squeezed her hand. "Since I've been doing the same thing, why don't we leave it in the Lord's hands for the moment? He'll show us the way in His own time."

She nodded. "I think that's a good plan. But can I tell you something?" she added impulsively. "I hope He doesn't wait too long."

Eric chuckled. "You and me both."

"Okay, I put Cal in charge of Caitlin's midnight feeding and very firmly told him that it was now or never for our sister-to-sister tête-à-tête. Here's your hot chocolate. Let me throw another log on the fire and then we're all set," Amy said briskly.

Kate tucked her feet under her and smiled as Amy joined her on the couch a moment later. "This is nice."

Amy sighed contentedly and nodded. "Yeah, it is, isn't it?" She settled herself comfortably into the cushions and took a leisurely sip of her hot chocolate, then turned to find Kate grinning at her. "What's wrong?"

Kate chuckled and reached over to wipe the sticky marshmallow mustache from her sister's upper lip. "It's nice to see that some things never change," she teased.

Amy grinned impudently, but a moment later her face grew melancholy. "Too bad other things do, though," she reflected wistfully.

Kate's expression sobered. "You're thinking about Mom, aren't you?"

"Yeah. It seemed so strange not to have her here for Thanksgiving. It's like a puzzle with a missing piece. She was always such a rock. No matter what scrapes I got into, I could always count on her to get me back on the straight and narrow, or to point me in the right direction when I was lost. Now I feel kind of like a ship adrift without an anchor. And on top of everything else, I missed her gravy at dinner. No one made it like Mom."

Kate nodded. "I thought about that, too."

"It must be doubly hard for you, Kate," Amy reflected with a frown. "She was part of your everyday existence. I can't even imagine the gap her death left in your life."

Kate blinked back her tears and turned to gaze into the fire. "It was pretty awful. Sometimes, in those first few weeks, I'd get so lonely… You'll think I'm crazy when I tell you this, Amy, but there were times I actually talked out loud to Mom. Like she was still there. Meeting Anna has helped a lot, though. It's not the same as having Mom, of course, but in many ways she reminds me of her. And she's taken Sarah and me under her wing. It was a godsend that she came into our lives when she did. I was grieving so much for Mom and at my wit's end about the day-care situation. Then she just appeared, out of the blue. I'll never get over it."

"The timing was pretty incredible," Amy concurred. "I'm glad you met her. And Eric, too." She took a sip of her hot chocolate and then spoke carefully. "I know you insist that your relationship is pretty platonic, but I have to say things didn't look like 'just friends' the other night when I interrupted you two."

Kate blushed and gazed down into her mug. "I think maybe it won't be platonic for much longer," she admitted quietly.

"Can I say I'm glad?"

Kate looked at her curiously. "Why?"

"Because I like what I've seen of Eric these few days. Because Sarah obviously adores him. And most of all because I think it would be good for you to let love back into your life. The question is, are you willing to open that door?"

Kate nodded slowly. "I think so, Amy. In fact, I think I'm... Well, I think I'm falling in love with Eric. But I still love Jack. Sometimes I feel so confused. I mean, how can I love them both?" she asked helplessly.

"How does a mother love more than one child? The heart has an infinite capacity for love, Kate. We can love many people in our lives, all in different ways. The love you have for Jack will always be there. Part of your heart will be his and his alone until the day you die. But that doesn't mean there isn't room for someone else. Love Eric for himself—for all the special qualities that are uniquely his. That won't diminish in any way the love you have for Jack. It's just different. A new dimension of love, if you will."

Kate reached over and took Amy's hand. In the firelight her eyes shimmered with tears. "Thank you, Amy."

"For what?"

"For understanding. For trying to help me find a way to let go."

Amy squeezed her hand, and when she spoke her voice was slightly unsteady. "It's time, Kate. In your heart I think you know that. And I have a feeling that one very special doctor is waiting for you to close the door on the past and open the one that says Future. Because until you do, things will go nowhere. There's no place for him in your past. But unless I'm way off the mark, I think he'd very much like to be part of your future."

Kate glanced toward the passenger seat and her lips curved up into a tender smile as she gazed for just a moment at that very special doctor, who was now sleeping quite soundly. In repose his face looked younger, more relaxed, more endearingly vulnerable. Reluctantly she turned her attention back to the road. Though she'd insisted they take her car for the trip, he'd been equally insistent about driving them down. But for the trip back she'd convinced him that they'd both arrive more rested if they took turns. She'd even encouraged him to sleep on this final lap, and he'd taken her up on it. In fact, both of her passengers had drifted off.

Absently Kate switched on her wipers as a soft drizzle began to fall. She was actually glad to have some quiet time to think. Since her conversation with Amy the night before, she'd felt a new sense of peace and resolution. Everything suddenly seemed more clear. Months before, when her pediatrician had retired, she could have chosen any number of doctors as a replacement. But she'd selected Eric, a man who had once saved her husband's life. Though some would dismiss it as an odd twist of fate, Kate believed there was more to it than that. Things happened for a reason. The Lord had guided her toward Eric, and through him, to Anna. Both had enriched her life tremendously. And now it seemed that she was being given the chance to find love once again. The choice about whether to pursue it was hers; but the opportunity had come from the Lord. And, with His help, she resolved to start building the future Amy had referred to.

The rain intensified, and Kate's full attention snapped

back to the road. Ever since the accident five years before, she'd hated driving in bad weather, especially at night, and avoided it whenever possible. But she could handle a little rain, she told herself encouragingly.

Twenty minutes later, however, when the rain turned to sleet, her confidence faltered. As the small ice particles zinged against the windshield, she frowned worriedly and tightened her grip on the wheel. She detested sleet. It brought back the nightmare of the accident with harrowing intensity. Her heart began to thump painfully, and she risked a quick glance at Eric, who was still sleeping soundly. She knew he'd take over in a minute if she asked him to, but she hated to wake him. He worked too hard and slept too little as it was. And she wasn't at all sure he'd gotten much rest on this trip, between the sleeper sofa and Caitlin's nighttime fussiness. She glanced at her watch. They were less than an hour away from home. She could do this if she took it a mile at a time, she told herself firmly. Her fears were irrational, after all. She had to get over them sooner or later. She might as well take the first step tonight.

Eric wasn't sure exactly what awakened him. But as he slowly came back to reality an odd noise registered in his consciousness. He frowned, struggling to identify the sound. Once he opened his eyes, the icy buildup on the windshield quickly gave him his answer. Sleet. His gaze flickered to the road. Judging by the glaze, the freezing rain had been coming down for some time.

Eric quickly straightened and turned to Kate. Though the car interior was dim, the tension in her body was evident in her rigid posture and white-knuckled grip on the wheel. She was driving slowly and cautiously, with absolute concentration, and seemed completely oblivious to everything but the task at hand. These conditions must be a stark reminder of a similar night five years before, he realized, suddenly filled with compassion.

"Kate." He spoke softly, trying not to startle her, but she jumped nonetheless as her gaze jerked toward his.

"Oh! You're awake." Her voice sounded tight and was edged with panic.

"How long has the weather been this bad?" he asked with more calm than he felt. It was obvious that he needed to get her out from behind the wheel as quickly as possible. She was terrified. The hazardous conditions had clearly brought back the traumatic memories of the accident.

With a hand that shook badly, she reached up and tucked a strand of hair behind her ear. "About…about half an hour."

"Why don't you pull onto the shoulder and let me take over?" he suggested quietly.

"It's too icy to stop here. And there's…there's a drop-off at the edge." There was a note of hysteria in her voice now.

"There's plenty of room, Kate," he reassured her soothingly. "Just take it slow and easy. There's no one behind us. I'll help you." He placed his hand protectively over hers on the wheel, alarmed by her frigid fingers. "Come on, sweetheart, just guide it over real gently. That's right."

With his help she edged the car halfway onto the shoulder. Eric glanced into the rearview mirror as they rolled to a stop, and was relieved that there were no other vehicles in sight. "Can you just slide over here, Kate? I'll go around to the driver's side."

Jerkily she nodded. By the time he'd slipped and slid around the front of the car and settled himself behind the wheel, she was huddled into the passenger seat. Her face was totally devoid of color, a thin film of perspiration beaded her upper lip and her breathing was shallow. He frowned as he reached over to take her cold hands in his.

"Kate?" She turned to him, her eyes slightly dazed. "Everything's going to be fine. We're almost home. You'll be back in your apartment in less than an hour. Okay?"

She nodded mutely.

He released her hands reluctantly. What he wanted to do was take her in his arms until her trembling ceased. But he suspected the best way to calm her was to get her out of the car and into her apartment.

The remaining drive was made in silence, though he glanced her way frequently. She stared straight ahead, her hands clenched in her lap, her posture still rigid. And, in truth, her concern—if not its intensity—was valid, Eric admitted. The roads were slick and hazardous, and continued to worsen as the minutes passed. He didn't realize how tense *he* had become until they pulled into a vacant spot in front of her apartment and he shut off the engine. Only then did the knotted muscles in his shoulders and the tension in his neck register. He took a deep breath and turned to Kate.

"Home at last," he said quietly.

Shakily Kate reached up and brushed her hair back from her face. "Th-thank you for driving, Eric. I'm sorry you had to take over."

"I didn't mind, Kate. I just wish you'd woken me up sooner."

"Are we home?" A sleepy voice from the back seat interrupted them.

Eric turned, lightening his tone. "Indeed we are, Miss Sarah."

She rubbed her eyes and stared out the window. "Oh! It's snowing!"

"Not yet. But it wouldn't surprise me if we didn't wake up to a winter wonderland tomorrow. Right now it's just ice. And very slippery. So I'm going to carry you up to the apartment, okay?"

"Okay. Can I build a snowman tomorrow if it snows, Mommy?"

Eric glanced at Kate. "Your mommy's awfully tired right now, honey. She drove for a long time. We'll decide about the snowman tomorrow." He turned to Kate and reached over to rest his hand on her knee. "Sit tight, okay? I'll take Sarah in and come back for you."

"I can manage, Eric."

"Humor me, okay? I don't think we want any trips to the emergency room for broken bones on a night like this."

He had a point. "Okay." She reached for her purse and fumbled around for her keys.

He squeezed her shoulder as she handed them over, then opened his door and carefully stepped out. The pavement was like a newly cleaned skating rink, he concluded, moving with extreme caution as he reached in for Sarah. "Hold on tight, sweetie."

He was back more quickly than Kate expected, his collar turned up against the pelting sleet. "Take it slow and easy, Kate," he cautioned as he opened her door and held out his hand. "Walking is pretty treacherous."

She took his hand and stepped out, steadying herself on the car door. "What about the luggage?"

"I'll come back for it. First I want to get you inside where it's safe and warm."

She didn't argue. At the moment, anywhere safe and warm sounded like heaven.

Eric kept a firm grip on her arm as they made their way slowly up the steps from the parking lot and along the walk. He was right—the night was too dangerous for either walking *or* driving, she reflected. Not until she'd stepped inside did she finally relax, her shoulders drooping as she drew a weary sigh.

"I've never been all that thrilled with this apartment, but right now I could get down and kiss the floor," she admitted, summoning up a shaky smile.

"I have a better idea." He took her hand and led her to the couch, then gently urged her down. "Sit for a minute and take a few deep breaths. You'll feel a lot better. I'll get the luggage and then head back to my place before it gets any worse."

"But Eric, it's too dangerous to drive!" she protested in alarm.

"Why can't Dr. Eric stay here tonight, Mommy?" Sarah piped up. "He can sleep on the sofa bed, just like you used to do before Grandma went to heaven."

Kate looked up at Eric. His eyes were unreadable. "Would you consider it?" she asked uncertainly. "I'll be so worried if you try to drive home. It's not safe out there."

Eric studied her. She seemed so vulnerable, her eyes huge in her white face, her body still trembling, her dark hair loose and mussed around her face. She was right about the danger outside. But suddenly he was a whole lot more worried about the danger inside.

Chapter Ten

The sudden whistling of the kettle bought him a moment's reprieve. "I put the water on to boil when I brought Sarah in," he said over his shoulder as he headed for the kitchen. "I figured you could use a cup of tea. Let me make it and then we can discuss the situation."

Except what was there to discuss, really? he thought as he mechanically pulled a mug from the cabinet and added water and a tea bag. The weather was terrible. It didn't make sense to take risks. But what about the risks right here? he countered silently. Kate was an extremely desirable woman. He'd been attracted to her for weeks. So far, past experience and a conviction that marriage and medicine didn't mix had allowed him to exercise some discipline in their relationship. But this weekend he'd almost kissed her. And though Amy's untimely interruption had effectively derailed his passion, the desire was still there. It might not be wise to stay. But common sense told him that venturing out again tonight would foolish.

With sudden decision he picked up the mug and stepped out of the kitchen, frowning as he glanced around the deserted living room. A moment later, Sarah's girlish giggle, followed by the low murmur of voices, echoed down the hall and he headed in that direction.

Kate looked up guiltily when he entered Sarah's bedroom. "I know you asked me to wait, but I wanted to get Sarah into bed as quickly as possible. It was a long trip for her."

He handed her the mug, noting the lingering quaver in her hand. "It was also a long trip for her mother," he replied quietly. "Go on back into the living room and relax. I'll put Sarah to bed."

"Oh, goody!" the little girl exclaimed, clapping her hands. "Will you read me a story, too?"

"A short one, if you get your pajamas on really quick."

As she scampered down the hall to the bathroom, Kate looked up at Eric. "Are you sure you don't mind doing this?"

"Not in the least. Go back out there and put your feet up. Doctor's orders," he added, flashing her a grin.

She rose slowly. "Listen, Eric, I'm sorry Sarah put you on the spot about staying tonight. And I understand if you don't want to. But the weather is so bad and..."

He reached over and gently grasped her upper arms, effectively stilling her voice. "I'm staying, Kate," he said deliberately. "I was just taking a minute to...think about it."

His gaze was locked on hers, and Kate stared up at him silently, certain he wasn't referring to the weather. A swarm of butterflies suddenly took flight in her stomach.

"Oh. Well, okay. I'll...I'll be in the living room."

And then she fled.

At first, as Kate waited for him to join her, she sat

perched on the edge of the couch, her shoulders hunched nervously, her hands tensely gripping the mug. But as she slowly sipped the soothing liquid and listened to the voices in the back bedroom—Sarah's high and excited, Eric's deep and mellow—she gradually began to relax. It was an odd feeling, to let someone take care of *her* for a change and help her with her daily chores, she mused. And it suddenly occurred to her that she could get used to this.

But she had better not, she warned herself. After all, the man had never even kissed her. Not that he hadn't tried, she conceded, her lips curving up into a smile. It was ironic that Amy, who had been the one urging her to put some romance back in her life, had also been the one to derail Kate's first romantic encounter in years.

Eric had thrown her the classic line from *Gone With the Wind* as they'd parted that night. Was tonight the "tomorrow" he'd referred to then? she wondered, as a warm surge of adrenaline shot through her. It had been such a long time... She wasn't even sure she remembered *how* to be amorous. Her only consolation was that Eric was equally rusty. She shook her head ruefully. They were quite a pair.

"Want to share the joke?"

Startled, Kate looked up to find Eric smiling at her from the doorway. She tried vainly to stifle the flush that rose to her cheeks, desperately searching for a truthful but evasive response.

"I was just thinking about...about Amy."

"Hmm." She wasn't sure he believed her, but fortunately he let it pass. "Let me get a cup of tea and I'll join you."

She scooted over to make room for him, noting as she placed her mug on the end table that her hands were once again trembling. She clasped them together tightly in her lap and took several long, deep breaths. This was ridiculous, she scolded herself. After all, she was a grown woman. She could handle this situation. Okay, so maybe she was a little out of practice. But if she just remained calm, she'd be fine. Eric was probably just as nervous as she was, she told herself consolingly.

Except he didn't look in the least nervous as he settled down comfortably beside her, she noted enviously. In fact, the man looked totally relaxed.

"Feeling better?" he asked.

She nodded stiffly. "Uh-huh. The tea helped a lot. Thank you."

"My pleasure." His gaze swept over her face appraisingly. She did look better now, he decided. There was more color in her cheeks and the dazed look had left her eyes. "I'm just sorry you had to go through that."

She sighed, and her eyes grew troubled. "You'd think after all these years I'd have gotten over my fear of being in a car in bad weather. But I can't seem to shake it. Even here in town I try to avoid driving when the roads are slick. Especially at night. Sometimes I have to, of course, but it always shakes me up."

"I noticed."

She flushed. "It's so embarrassing. I feel like I should be able to put that night behind me and move on. But I can't seem to get past it."

Eric draped an arm loosely over her shoulders and gently massaged her stiff muscles. "Don't apologize, Kate. You weren't just involved in a fender bender. It was a nightmare situation. That kind of trauma can linger for years. In fact, you may never get over it completely. You'll probably always be extra careful in winter-weather driving—which isn't necessarily a bad thing, by the way. But eventually the fear should subside to a more manageable level. There's no need to rush it. Things usually happen in their own time."

His reassuring comments and the soothing touch of his hand went a long way toward easing Kate's tension. She sighed and relaxed against his arm.

"That feels good," she murmured. "I guess I was more tense than I realized."

He set his cup on the coffee table. "Turn around and I'll do both shoulders."

She did as he instructed, angling herself on the couch so that her back was to him. With a gentle but firm touch he massaged her shoulders, her upper arms, her neck, until the tension at last evaporated.

"Has anyone ever told you that you have great hands, Doctor?" she asked languidly, dropping her head forward.

Eric stared at her slender shoulders, at the dark hair spilling over his fingers, and drew a deep breath. "Not lately," he replied, his voice suddenly husky.

Kate heard the different nuance in his tone and felt her pulse quicken as his touch changed subtly from therapeutic to sensual.

"You have beautiful hair, Kate. Has anyone ever told *you* that?"

"Not lately," she echoed breathlessly.

Slowly she drew in her breath and held it as he combed his fingers through her hair. A moment later a jolt of electricity shot through her when she felt his lips on the back of her neck.

"You taste good, too," he murmured.

Kate closed her eyes and uttered a small, contented sound deep in her throat as he moved her hair aside and let his lips travel across the full width of her neck. "Oh,

Eric," she breathed. "I'd forgotten how good this could feel!"

"Me, too." He turned her then, urging her to face him with gentle hands on her shoulders. Their gazes connected, and she could see the fire smoldering in the depths of his eyes. "But I'd like to remember," he continued. "And I'd like to make some new memories. With you."

She stared at him, mesmerized by the profound emotion and honesty she saw reflected in his eyes. Her throat contracted with tenderness. "I'd like that, too," she whispered, and was rewarded with a smile that warmed her through and through. Slowly he reached over to touch her face, but stopped when she backed off slightly.

"What's wrong?" he queried in concern.

She blushed self-consciously. "It's just that I'm…I'm really out of practice. And I guess I'm a little bit afraid that I won't be…that you won't like… I haven't kissed a man in years, and I feel so awkward and schoolgirlish and— Boy, I'm really blowing this, aren't I?" she finished artlessly.

Eric's expression eased and he chuckled. "Can I tell you something? I have exactly the same fears. So what do you say we both just relax? I have a feeling everything will turn out fine."

Kate forced her trembling lips into a smile. "If you say so."

He reached out to her again, and this time she remained still, letting her eyelids drift closed as his fingers made contact with her skin.

Eric moved slowly, taking time to savor the feel of her skin beneath fingertips that were suddenly hypersensitive as he traced the sweet contours of her face, memorizing every nuance. She felt so soft—so good. He knew that they were breaking new ground in their relationship tonight; knew that there was no turning back once they started down this path. And part of him was still afraid. The wounds from his first marriage had left scars that ran deep. But somehow he sensed that with Kate, things would be different. He'd prayed for guidance, had asked the Lord to give him the courage to trust his heart, and so now he stood poised at a crossroads: he could either stay on the safe, predictable, lonely path he'd been following, or move in a new, uncharted direction that could bring love. The choice was his.

He gazed tenderly down at Kate's upturned face, at the soft fanning of her dark lashes against her cheeks. There was a fineness to her; a goodness that radiated from deep within. It wasn't in her nature ever to be hurtful or selfish or inconsiderate. He knew that as surely as he knew the sun rose in the east. She was a kind, caring woman who had shown great courage and endurance in the face of tragedy. She was also a loving and conscientious mother. And though she had strayed from her faith for a time, she had eventually found her way home again.

And then there was her beauty. With her flawless complexion, lovely features and slender, toned body, she looked closer to twenty-five than thirty-five. And her hair—it was soft and full and made for a man's hands to tangle in, he thought, combing his fingers through the wavy tresses.

In short, she was an incredibly desirable woman.

And yet…she'd remained alone for five long years, true to the memory of her dead husband. That, too, he admired in her. Loyalty and enduring love were qualities to be respected and honored. He knew she was still struggling to reconcile the possibility of a new relationship with her devotion to Jack, and was reluctant to do anything that diminished the memory of their love and commitment. So he felt deeply honored that she was willing to open her heart to him. Not to mention deeply attracted. Until Kate, he hadn't so much as *considered* the option of falling in love again. Now it wasn't just an option; it was a very real possibility.

Eric let his other hand drop to her waist and closed the distance between them. He felt her begin to tremble again, and he knew she was afraid, just as he was. Where would this lead? Were they making a mistake? Would they both end up hurt? Eric didn't know. But there was only one way to find the answer to those questions. Taking a slow, deep breath, he leaned toward her and tenderly claimed her lips.

Though his touch was gentle, Kate was momentarily stunned by the electric sizzle that shot through her. At the same time, she felt as if she'd been waiting for this moment for years. And maybe, in a way, she had. There had always been physical affection in her life—as a daughter, a mother, a sister. But this kind of affection had long been absent. And she'd missed it. A sweet shiver of delight swept over her and her heart soared with an almost-forgotten thrill as Eric's lips moved tenderly over hers, igniting long-dormant desires deep within her. Without consciously realizing what she was doing, she put her arms around his neck and pulled him even closer.

Eric was momentarily taken aback by her complete surrender to his embrace and by her ardent, uninhibited response. He'd expected her to be tentative and uncertain. Instead, she was giving herself fully and willingly to the kiss. And he was delighted. Because it meant that she not only cared for him, but also trusted him. And he had no intention of betraying that trust.

Kate felt his firm, sure hand on her back, through the thin fabric of her turtleneck. She could feel the hard, uneven thudding of his heart. She could feel his ragged breath. But most of all she could feel his lips, hungry yet tender. And she responded willingly, reveling in the embrace of this wonderful, caring man.

At last, with obvious reluctance, he drew back enough to gaze down at her.

She stared up at him, able to utter only one, breathy word. "Wow!"

His lips tilted up into an unsteady, crooked grin. "Yeah. Wow!"

She touched his face wonderingly, hesitantly reaching out to trace his lips with her fingertip. His sudden, sharp intake of breath made her pause, and she started to withdraw her hand. But he grasped it and held it firmly in place.

"Don't stop," he said hoarsely, closing his eyes.

Slowly she continued her exploration, her fingertips memorizing the planes of his face. Only when she'd finished did he open his eyes. He held her gaze compellingly as he lifted her hand to his lips and kissed the palm.

This time it was her turn to gasp. He paused and raised his eyebrows questioningly.

"Don't stop," she murmured, echoing his words.

He kissed each fingertip before enfolding her hand protectively in his, his fingers warm and strong around hers. Then he drew a long, ragged breath. "You know what you said earlier, about being out of practice?" he reminded her with a crooked grin. "If this is what you're like when you're rusty, I have serious concerns for my blood pressure when you're up to speed."

She blushed and smiled shyly. "I guess I got a little carried away."

"Hey, I'm not complaining! I just didn't expect things to get so…intense…so quickly."

"Me, neither."

"Are you sorry?" His tone was serious now, his face concerned.

She considered the question for a moment, finding it hard to concentrate when one of his hands was stroking her nape and the other was entwined with hers. "No. I think in my heart I realized at some point that this was inevitable. And we're not exactly strangers on a first date. We've known each other for over three months, Eric. This evolution of friendship into romance—well, it feels right to me. And natural. And comfortable. Not to mention…exciting." Her face grew warm, and he gave a relieved chuckle.

"I'm glad you added that last adjective. For a minute, there, I was beginning to feel like a pair of old slippers," he teased.

She smiled. "'Old slippers' is hardly the way I would describe you. More like a pair of fancy shoes I once bought—classy and sophisticated and guaranteed to make a woman feel drop-dead gorgeous and desirable."

"Well, you're definitely all of the above. And I plan to do everything I can to make you feel that way every day from now on."

Kate looked up at him, and the tenderness in his eyes made her throat constrict with happiness as her heart soared with hope. For the first time in years she began to think that maybe, just maybe, she wouldn't spend the rest of her life alone.

The smell of freshly brewing coffee wafted into the bedroom, slowly coaxing Kate awake the next morning. But even though the aroma was appealing, she fought the return to full consciousness. She wanted to hold on to this lingering, inexplicable feeling of contentment—most likely a remnant of some already forgotten dream—for just a little longer.

But she couldn't ignore the knock on her door a few minutes later. And she especially couldn't ignore the husky male voice that accompanied it.

"Are you decent?"

Her eyelids flew open and she stared at the ceiling in shock. The feeling of contentment *wasn't* an illusion, after all. It was as real as the man standing on the other side of her door. She struggled to a half-sitting position and frantically pulled the blanket up to her neck, clutching it against her chest with both hands as her pulse skyrocketed.

"Y-yes. Come in."

Eric opened the door, a coffee mug in one hand, and paused for a moment to smile at her. His gaze, intimate and tender, lingered on her face, then did a leisurely inventory of the dark mass of hair tumbling around her shoulders, the demure neckline of her gown, the cheeks still flushed from sleep. With her wide eyes, slightly parted lips and endearingly modest posture, she looked vulnerable...and beautiful...and very, very appealing.

With a jolt that rocked him to his core, Eric suddenly realized that he wanted to wake up beside this special woman every morning for the rest of his life. But how could things have progressed so quickly? he wondered in confusion. When he'd claimed Kate's lips last night, he'd considered it a first step down a new path in their relationship. Yet he now realized that it hadn't been a first step at all. It had simply verified what his heart had known for weeks. He was in love with her. But was he ready for that kind of commitment?

And then she smiled—a tentative, endearing smile that tugged at his heart and chased away his doubts. Yes, he *was* ready, he realized. Maybe past ready. But he wasn't so sure about her. Though she'd responded fully to his overtures last night, she might be having second thoughts in the light of day. He knew she still had issues to deal with, and he couldn't push her. But he also knew with absolute certainty that one day in the not-too-distant future he would ask her to be his wife. It was just a matter of waiting for the right time.

"Hi, Mommy." Impatient about the delay in seeing her mother, Sarah squeezed past Eric and plopped on the bed beside Kate.

Lost in the intensity of Eric's gaze, Kate needed a moment to refocus and respond. "Hi, sweetie. Do I get a good-morning hug?" She leaned over to kiss her daughter, holding her close for a long moment as she willed her breathing to calm. She glanced at the clock as she released Sarah, and her eyes grew anxious. "Oh, no! I forgot to set the alarm last night. I'll be late! I've got to get up!"

Eric moved beside her and placed a hand on her shoulder. "Your school declared a snow day. You're a lady of leisure today."

Her posture relaxed and she drew a deep breath. "It must be pretty bad out there. They never call snow days."

"It is."

He handed her the coffee, and she gave him a warm smile. "Thank you. I'm not used to such service. Do you do windows?" she teased.

He chuckled and gave her a wink. "Depends what the job pays."

She flushed but was saved from having to reply when Sarah spoke up.

"Are you staying here all day, Dr. Eric?"

"I wish I could," he declared regretfully. "But kids still get sick when it snows. So I need to go and take care of them."

Kate looked at him worriedly. "What are the roads like?"

He shrugged. "Manageable in daylight. The radio said the main routes are clear and I'll be careful, Kate," he promised gently, reaching out to touch her cheek.

She swallowed. "Okay."

"I'll call you when I get to the hospital."

She gave him a grateful look. "Thank you."

"Take it easy today, okay? Get some rest."

She nodded mutely.

He hesitated, then turned to Sarah. "Do you think you could find a piece of paper and a pencil for me in the kitchen, honey?"

"Uh-huh." She scooted off the bed and skipped down the hall.

As soon as she was out the door, Eric looked back at Kate. "I enjoyed last night," he said huskily.

"So did I."

"And I couldn't leave without doing this." He leaned over, and her lips stirred sweetly beneath his promise-filled kiss. "I wish we had more time," he admitted. His breath was warm on her cheek as he reluctantly broke contact.

"There's always tonight."

He gazed down at her with a warm, amused smile. "Is that an invitation?"

"Yes."

"I accept."

At the sound of running feet, he quickly turned to the doorway.

"Is this okay, Dr. Eric?" Sarah asked, holding out a tablet and pencil as she reentered the room.

"That's perfect, honey." Eric took it and scribbled something, then handed it to Kate. "That's my pager number, just in case you need me."

Her spoken reply was a simple, "Thank you," but in the silence of her heart another voice responded differently. "I'll always need you," it said.

For a moment, Kate was taken aback by those words. Though they were simple, too, their implication was not. And suddenly she knew that the time had come to put her past to rest. Only then could she give herself a chance at a future that included this very special man.

Kate climbed onto the kitchen chair she'd dragged into her bedroom and carefully withdrew a box from the top shelf of her closet. As she deposited it in the living room, she glanced at the clock. Sarah had gone to the park down the street with the little boy next door and his mother, which meant Kate had about an hour to herself. That should be plenty of time, she decided, as she made herself a cup of hot chocolate and put on the CD of classical music that Amy had given her last Christmas.

Kate settled herself comfortably on the couch, took a deep breath and lifted the lid of the box. The familiar cream-colored envelope on top produced the usual melancholy pang, though it wasn't quite as intense this year. She fingered the envelope gently, then withdrew the formal invitation. As her eyes scanned the conventional wording, she found it hard to believe that eleven years ago today she had walked down the aisle as a radiant bride. So much had happened since then. So much had changed. In many ways, she felt like a different person. The youthful girl in white, so optimistic, so filled with dreams for the future, so deeply in love with her husband-to-be, seemed almost like a stranger, or a character in a story she had read—not actually lived.

She set the invitation aside and reached for the album, pausing to take a sip of her hot chocolate as she flipped open the first page. It was an annual ritual that she and Jack had begun on their first anniversary. They would usually open a bottle of champagne and slowly work their way through the photos, sometimes laughing, sometimes stopping to kiss, sometimes pausing to offer toasts. She'd continued the tradition after his death, substituting hot chocolate for the champagne.

When Kate reached the last page—a close-up portrait of the two of them—her eyes misted as her gaze lovingly traced Jack's handsome, dear face. He had been a wonderful husband. There had been no one else like him—no one who touched her heart in quite the way he had, no one who had his knack for making her find that special place inside herself where the child still lived. And there never would be again. She knew that with absolute certainty. And she accepted it.

With Reverend Jacobs' help, she had also accepted Jack's death, had made her peace with the Lord's decision to call him home sooner than either of them had expected. She felt ready, at last, to move forward with her life—and her relationship with Eric. Much of the credit for that went to Amy, who had put into words what Kate had begun to feel in her heart: that her love for Eric in no way diminished what she and Jack had shared. That time in her life—those memories—stood apart and belonged always to them. She and Eric would create something new that was theirs alone, touch places within each other that no one else had ever touched. They would move forward together, leaving doubts and guilt behind, and face tomorrow with hope.

Suddenly Kate remembered the counted-cross-stitch sampler she'd worked on at Jack's bedside during the months he'd been in the long-term nursing facility. With a frown, she tried to recall where she'd put it. Somewhere in her closet, she was sure. A few minutes later, after rummaging around on the floor, she emerged triumphantly with a dusty bag. She waited until she was seated again on the couch before she carefully withdrew her handiwork and gazed at the partially stitched words from Jeremiah. She read them once, twice, a third time. They had given her hope as she'd sat by Jack's side, she recalled, but she'd bitterly put the sampler away unfinished—just like her life—after he died.

Kate looked again at their wedding portrait on the last page of the album, and her throat tightened with emotion. For she knew that this ritual, which had helped sustain her during the last few years, was now coming to an end.

"I love you," she whispered, her voice catching. "I always will. You were my sunshine, Jack. You filled my life with joy and beauty and laughter. I'll never forget that. And I'll never let Sarah forget what a wonderful father she had in you. But it's time now for me to let you go. I know you're with the Lord, and that you've found the contentment and wholeness that only comes when we are one with Him in heaven. But I still have a road to travel here. And I don't want to make the journey alone. I think Eric is going to ask me to marry him soon, and I'm going to accept. He's a wonderful man. You would have liked him, I think. And it's my most fervent prayer that you'll always know I love you no less because I also love him." She paused as her eyes misted with tears. "Goodbye, my love. Until we meet again."

And then, very gently, she closed the album.

Chapter Eleven

"I'll get it!" Sarah called as she raced from the living room to the front door.

Kate smiled and wiped her hands on a dish towel. It might have taken *her* a long time to figure out where Eric fit in the scheme of things, but for Sarah, who had no memories holding her back, he had immediately meshed seamlessly and naturally into their lives.

"Hi, sweetie. Did you build a snowman today?" she heard Eric ask.

"Yes. Mark and me and his mommy went to the park and made a gigan—gigan—really big snowman with a carrot for a nose and charcoal for eyes."

Kate liked the sound of his chuckle—deep, rich and heartwarming. "Now that sounds like a first-class snowman. Did your mommy go, too?"

"No. She said she had stuff to do."

Kate stepped into the living room then and smiled at Eric. The snow had started up again, and delicate white flakes clung to the shoulders of his dark wool coat. He looked rugged and masculine, she thought, as her heart skipped a beat.

"Hi."

He glanced up to return her greeting, but the words died in his throat. She looked absolutely radiant tonight, he thought in awe. On a peripheral level he noticed her deep blue angora sweater and black stirrup pants, and her hair, brushed loose and full, lying softly on her shoulders. But it was the glow on her face that stunned him. For the first time in their acquaintance she seemed truly relaxed and at ease, he realized. There was a profound calmness, a serenity about her that reached out and touched his very soul. Something about her had changed—and changed dramatically—in the hours since he'd reluctantly left her to enjoy her snow day. It was as if an event of great significance had occurred. But what?

Kate saw the sudden look of speculation on his face and flushed. Was her newfound inner peace so obvious? But Eric was a perceptive man. She should have realized he'd immediately sense the change in her, just as she should have realized that he'd quickly notice the changes in the room, as well. In one quick, discerning sweep his gaze passed over, then returned to the spots where photos of her and Jack had once been displayed.

Sarah's powers of perception were none too shabby, either, Kate acknowledged wryly. The little girl was watching the proceedings with interest, and quickly noted the direction of Eric's glances.

"Do you like our new picture?" she piped up.

His brain was so busy trying to process the significance of Kate's redecorating efforts that it took a moment for the question to register. When it did, he transferred his attention from the Monet print behind the couch to Sarah. "It's very pretty."

"I like it, too," she declared. "It was in the hall closet.

Mommy said it was too pretty to keep hidden away. So she took the wedding picture down. She said sometimes you have to put things away to make room for new things."

Eric turned to Kate, whose cheeks were tinged with warm color.

"Mommy let me put the picture from the TV in my room, too," Sarah continued, oblivious to the intense atmosphere. "She said we're going to get some tulip bulbs in pots to put there instead, and that we can watch them grow all winter. She said they'll help us keep spring in our hearts even when it's cold and snowing outside. Isn't that right, Mommy?"

Eric's gaze remained locked on hers. "That's right, honey," Kate replied unsteadily, reaching up distractedly to push her hair back from her face. And that was when Eric noticed the most significant thing of all.

The ring finger of her left hand was bare.

"Aren't you going to say hi to Mommy?" Sarah demanded when the silence between the two adults lengthened.

Once again, it took him a moment to collect his chaotic thoughts. "Of course I am. In fact, I'm going to do better than that." His gaze never leaving Kate's, he closed the distance between them, hesitated long enough to give her time to protest, then leaned over and kissed her.

"Hi," he greeted her huskily, one hand resting lightly at her waist. "I missed you."

"We missed you, too," Sarah added. "But Mommy said you'd be back."

"Mommy was right."

"We're having chicken and dressing and biscuits tonight," she announced. "And chocolate cake!"

"And broccoli," Kate reminded her daughter.

"Sounds like a celebration. Broccoli and all," Eric remarked.

Kate's flush deepened and she turned toward the kitchen, trying to steady her staccato pulse. "Sarah, you have just enough time to finish watching your video before dinner."

"Okay." The little girl happily returned to the TV set and sat down, cross-legged.

As Kate walked toward the counter, she was aware of Eric close behind her. And she wasn't at all surprised when he placed his hands on her shoulders and leaned close, his breath warm on her neck.

"I like the redecorating."

She took a deep breath as she turned to face him, and he looped his arms loosely around her waist. They were only inches apart, and she felt lost for a moment in the depths of his deep blue eyes. "It was time," she replied quietly.

"You're sure about this?"

She nodded. "I don't want to live in the past anymore, Eric. I'll never forget my life with Jack. And I'll always love him," she added honestly. "But memories can only sustain you for so long. I've tried to hold on to them, but as a result I've ended up putting my *life* on hold. I've felt like a hollow, empty shell for too long. There was a time when my life was rich and full and filled with promise. I want to feel that way again. I want to move forward and make new memories."

She didn't say, "With you," but somehow she had a feeling he knew what was in her heart. And his next words not only confirmed that, but sent her hopes soaring.

He reached over and tenderly cupped her face with

his strong, capable hands. "I feel the same way, Kate," he told her huskily. "What do you say we start making those memories together?"

Kate couldn't remember a Christmas season so filled with joy and breathless anticipation. For once she didn't mind the cold weather, and moved with renewed energy and a lightness of step. Her daily chores, formerly dreary, no longer seemed burdensome and endless. Because always, at the end of her day, there was Eric. Whether it was a simple dinner at her apartment or an impromptu meal out, whether it was a "family outing" with Sarah and Anna, or quietly sipping hot chocolate with Eric by the tree after Sarah went to bed, each moment was golden. And Kate treasured every single one, storing them in a special place in her heart reserved just for Eric. Their relationship, so long purely friendship, blossomed rapidly into a genuine romance.

Once, Kate paused in surprise as she passed a mirror, hardly recognizing for a moment the woman with the sparkling eyes, flushed cheeks and animated face who stared back her. She shook her head and smiled ruefully. There was no hiding it, she admitted. It was there for all the world to see. She was in love.

Even Sarah noticed. As Kate tucked her daughter into bed one night after Eric had been summoned to the hospital for an emergency, the little girl suddenly looked up at her, her expression quite serious.

"Are you going to marry Dr. Eric?" she asked solemnly, without preamble.

Kate's heart stopped, then tripped on. She'd been expecting this question, but she still wasn't sure how to answer it—or the others that would inevitably follow.

Slowly she sat down on the bed and took Sarah's hand, silently asking the Lord for guidance.

"He hasn't asked me yet, honey."

"But what if he does?" she persisted.

"Well, what do you think I should do?"

She considered for a moment. "Would he live with us if you got married?"

"We'd all live together. Probably at Dr. Eric's house."

"Would he be my daddy?"

This was the tough one. Kate struggled to find the right words—words that would keep Jack's memory alive but leave room for Eric, as well. "Actually, Sarah, you'd have *two* daddies." She reached over and picked up the photo of Jack. "When you were born, this was your daddy. He's in heaven now, so you can't see him, but he still loves you very much. And so does Dr. Eric. He'd be your daddy here. So you see how lucky you would be? You'd have a daddy in heaven and one here on earth."

"Do you still love my first daddy?"

Tears pricked her eyes, and Kate swallowed. "Of course, honey. I always will. He was very special to me. But he wouldn't want us to be lonesome. And I know he'd like Dr. Eric. I think he would probably be very happy if Dr. Eric took care of us, since he can't be with us himself."

Sarah thought about that for a minute. "You know something, Mommy?" she said at last.

"What, sweetheart?"

"I would really like to have a daddy I could see. If Dr. Eric asks you to marry him, I think you should. Then we could be a real family. And that would be my best Christmas present ever!"

As Kate bent over to kiss Sarah, her heart gave a silent, fervent reply.

And mine as well.

"Kate? Eric. Listen, I've got a problem at the hospital."

Kate frowned and glanced at her watch. Sarah had to be at church in forty-five minutes for the Christmas pageant, and Eric had planned to take them.

"Kate?" Eric prompted when she didn't reply.

"I'm here. Will you be tied up long?"

She heard his weary sigh over the line. "Possibly. I've got a little boy who was just diagnosed with meningitis."

Kate's throat tightened and she closed her eyes. She'd read stories about the dangerous, fast-moving illness. "Oh, Eric! I'm sorry. How old is he?"

"Seven. Even worse, he's an only child. The parents are panic-stricken."

"How bad is he?"

"Bad."

She swallowed. The tone of his voice said everything. "Listen, don't worry about tonight, okay? I'll take Sarah. Maybe you can meet us later if things improve."

"Kate, I'm sorry. Sarah will be so disappointed."

He was right. Her daughter had been looking forward to having all three of them—Kate, Eric and Anna—in the audience. "Like a family," she'd told Kate happily. But it couldn't be helped.

"I'll explain it to her, Eric. Don't worry."

"I wish Mom hadn't agreed to go early to help set up refreshments." She heard the frustration in his voice. "At least you could have ridden together, then."

"Please, Eric. It's okay. We're fine. Just do what you can for that poor child and his parents."

"Thanks, Kate."

"For what?"

"For understanding. For not making me feel guilty. For not hating my work and resenting the demands and the disruption."

Once again Kate had a glimpse of the hell he must have lived through with Cindy.

"Eric, your profession is part of who you are," she said quietly. "Your conscientiousness and caring are two of the things I lo—" She paused and cleared her throat. "Things I respect in you and find appealing. So stop worrying and go do your job, okay?"

"Okay. And I'll get there as soon as I can. You'll explain to Sarah? Tell her I'm sorry?"

"Yes. Everything will be fine. We'll see you later."

"Count on it."

As Kate slowly replaced the receiver, Sarah trailed excitedly into the kitchen, holding her halo. "When do we have to leave, Mommy?"

Kate took her hand and drew her into the living room, tucking her under her arm as they sat down. "In about fifteen minutes. Honey, you know how Dr. Eric was supposed to take us?"

Sarah looked up at her with wide eyes that were suddenly troubled. "Yes."

"Well, he's at the hospital. There's a very sick little boy there who needs him very much. And his mommy and daddy are very worried and they need Dr. Eric, too. So he has to stay with them for a while and try to help that little boy get well so he can go home for Christmas."

Sarah's lower lip began to quiver. "Isn't Dr. Eric coming to see me in the Christmas pageant?"

"He's going to try his very best, honey. But he isn't sure he'll be able to get there in time. This little boy needs him. Just think if you were sick and had to go to the hospital. Wouldn't you want Dr. Eric to stay with you?"

"Yes. But he said he'd come to my show. And I need him, too."

"I know, honey. And Dr. Eric knows, too. It's just that sometimes, when you're a doctor, other people need you more. This little boy is so sick that he might die if Dr. Eric doesn't stay with him."

"You mean like Daddy?"

"Yes. Just like Daddy. And then his mommy and daddy would be all alone, just like we were after Daddy went to heaven."

"And they would be very sad, wouldn't they? Like you used to be?"

"Yes, they would."

Sarah bit her lip and struggled with that idea. "I guess maybe they do need Dr. Eric more," she said at last in a small voice.

Kate's heart swelled, and she pulled Sarah close. "Oh, sweetie, I'm so proud of you. You're such a big girl! Why don't we say a prayer for the little boy so that God will watch over him?"

"Okay."

As they held hands on the couch and sent a heartfelt plea to the Lord, Kate also took a moment to silently give thanks—for the wonderful, caring man who had come into her life, and for a precious daughter who had shown a compassion and unselfishness beyond her years.

* * *

"Oh, my, will you look at that!"

Anna stood at the window of the church hall and gazed outside. A mixture of sleet and snow had begun to fall during the program, and the roads were already covered. Kate, who stood at her elbow, felt the color drain from her face. Eric hadn't made it to the pageant, and there was still no sign of him. The road would only get worse the longer she waited, and even though the social was just beginning, she decided to call it a night.

"I think I'm going to head home, Anna," she said, trying to control the tremor in her voice. "I'm not much for driving in bad weather."

Anna turned back to her. "Well, I can't say I blame you. But you'll have to pry Sarah away from the dessert table."

Kate glanced at her daughter, whose obvious delight in the wonderland of sweets brought a fleeting smile to Kate's face. "We'll just have to get a plate to go. How about you? Will you be okay getting home?" she asked worriedly.

"Oh, absolutely. Fred and Jenny have a four-wheel drive. In fact, if you want to wait, you could ride with us and just leave your car here."

Kate considered the offer for a moment, then regretfully shook her head. "Thanks, Anna. I'd love to take you up on that, but I need the car for school tomorrow."

"Well, you be careful then, okay?"

"I will."

By the time Kate and Sarah were strapped into their older-model compact car, the icy mixture had intensified. Kate glanced nervously at Sarah, but fortunately she was so busy sampling her smorgasbord of desserts that she seemed oblivious to her mother's tension. Which was just as well, Kate concluded. With any luck, they'd be home before Sarah even made a dent in her plate of goodies.

Eric swung into the church parking lot, skidding slightly as he made the turn. For the first time he realized that it was sleeting. He'd been so distraught since he'd left the hospital that he hadn't even noticed the weather. He'd simply turned on the windshield defroster and made the drive to the church on automatic pilot, his mind in a turmoil.

Was there anything else he could have done? he asked himself for the dozenth time in the last hour. Had he reacted quickly enough? Had he pushed the tests through as rapidly as possible? Would it have made any difference if they'd made the diagnosis even half an hour sooner? And dear God, how did you explain to two grief-stricken parents that you'd let their only child die? They'd stared at him numbly, in shock and disbelief, and all he'd been able to say was, "I'm sorry." "Inadequate" didn't even come close to describing those words.

Eric parked the car and took a long, shaky breath. Even after years of dealing with scenarios like this, he'd never gotten used to it. Some doctors learned to insulate themselves from the pain. He never had. On nights like this it ripped through him like a knife, leaving his heart in shreds, his spirits crushed.

Wearily he climbed out of the car and made his way toward the church hall. He wasn't in the mood to see anyone, not even Kate, but he'd promised to come if he could. And he wasn't a man who gave his word lightly. So when he'd left the hospital he'd just automatically headed in this direction.

"Heavens, Eric, are you all right?"

Anna met him inside the door, her face a mask of concern.

He jammed his hands into the deep pockets of his jacket. "Not especially."

"Kate told me about your patient. Did he…"

"He didn't make it." His voice was flat and lifeless.

Anna's eyes filled with tears and she reached out to touch his arm. "Oh, Eric, I'm sorry. I know how losses like this tear you up."

"I'm in great shape compared to the parents."

"I know you did all you could," Anna said quietly.

He sighed and wearily raked the fingers of one hand through his hair. "I hope so." He glanced around the room and frowned. "Is the pageant over?"

"It's been over for twenty minutes. Would you like some coffee?"

Distractedly he shook his head, his gaze once more scanning the room. "Where's Kate? And Sarah?"

"They left about five minutes ago. Kate said she didn't want to wait in case the weather got any worse."

For the first time since leaving the hospital his mind switched gears. Kate hated to drive in this kind of weather. And now she was out there on roads that were rapidly becoming treacherous, probably as terrified as she'd been on the drive home from Tennessee. His frown deepened and he turned toward the door.

"I'll call you tomorrow, Mom," he called over his shoulder, not waiting for a reply.

As Eric set off on the familiar route from the church to Kate's apartment, his heart began to hammer against his rib cage. He drove as quickly as the deteriorating conditions would allow, peering ahead, his hands gripping the wheel. *Please, Lord, watch over her,* he prayed. *Let her feel Your presence and Your guiding hand.*

By the time he caught sight of her, she was only about a mile from her apartment. She was driving slowly and cautiously, but she was safe, he reassured himself, his shoulders sagging in relief. In a couple of minutes he'd be right behind her, and a few minutes after that, she'd be home.

Eric watched as Kate stopped at an intersection. She took plenty of time to look in both directions, then continued across. But for some reason she stopped right in the middle. Or perhaps her car stalled or got stuck on the ice. He wasn't sure. All he knew was that he suddenly saw headlights approaching too quickly, heard the squeal of brakes, and then watched in horror as the other car slammed into the passenger side of Kate's vehicle.

For the second time in a handful of hours, Eric felt as if someone had kicked him in the gut. He stepped on the accelerator, oblivious to the road conditions, and skidded to a stop with only inches to spare. The other driver was already out of his car and clearly unhurt.

"Do you have a cell phone?" Eric shouted as he slipped and slid across the icy surface. The man nodded. "Call 911," Eric barked harshly.

He didn't want to look inside Kate's car. But he had no choice. Hiding from what was inside the car was as impossible as hiding from what was in his heart.

He tried Sarah's door first, but it was too smashed to budge and he couldn't tell how seriously hurt she was by peering in the window. All he knew was that she was crying.

Eric moved around to the driver's side as quickly as the icy conditions would allow, and when he pulled open the door the wrenching sound of Sarah's sobbing spilled out. Kate was leaning across the seat, frantically trying to unbuckle her daughter's seat belt, but she was too constrained by her own. Eric reached in and unsnapped it, freeing her.

"Kate, are you all right?"

If she heard him, she didn't respond. Her attention was focused solely on her daughter.

He tried again, this time more forcefully, his hands firmly on her shoulders, a touch of desperation in his voice. "Kate, look at me. I need to know if you're all right."

She turned then, her eyes frantic. For a moment she didn't even seem to recognize him, and when she did, her face crumpled. "Eric? Oh, God, where were you? We needed you! Please…help us! Help Sarah!"

Eric felt as if a knife had just been thrust into his heart and ruthlessly twisted. Those few words, and the look of hurt and betrayal on her face, sent his world crashing so rapidly that it left him reeling. But he couldn't think about that now. There were other, more pressing things that demanded his attention.

"Kate, are you hurt?" he repeated, his voice broken and raspy.

Jerkily she shook her head, then clutched at his arm. "No. I'm okay. Please…just help Sarah!"

"I'm going to. Can you get out? I can't get in from her side."

Kate nodded and scrambled out, swaying unsteadily as she stood. He reached for her, but she shook him off impatiently, clinging to the frigid metal of the car as the sleet stung her face. "Go to Sarah."

Eric climbed into the front seat and reached over to touch Sarah, speaking softly. "Sarah, it's Dr. Eric. I'm going to help you, okay? Sarah? Can you look at me?"

Her sobbing abated slightly and she turned to him,

her eyes wide with fear. At first he thought the dark splotches on her face were blood and his stomach lurched. But then he noticed the plate of cake and cookies on the floor and realized it was chocolate. He drew a steadying breath.

"Sarah, can you tell me what hurts?"

"M-my ar-arm," she said tearfully.

"I'll tell you what. I'm going to unbuckle your seat belt and take a look, okay?" He tried to keep his voice calm and matter-of-fact, but it took every ounce of discipline he had.

"I want my mommy," Sarah declared, her lower lip beginning to tremble.

"I'm here, Sarah." Kate leaned into the car. "Do what Dr. Eric says, okay?"

She sniffled. "Okay."

"Sarah, honey, can you turn toward me? I just want to take a look at your arm. I promise I'll try not to hurt you." Eric reached over and unsnapped her seat belt as he spoke, holding it away from her body as it slid into its holder.

She angled toward him slightly, her sobs subsiding. Fortunately she was wearing a down-filled parka, he noted. It had probably padded her somewhat from the impact. But it also hampered his exam. He reached over and took her small hand in his, forcing himself to smile.

"It looks like you had chocolate cake tonight. Was it good?" he asked, gently manipulating her arm.

"Yes. But I didn't get to finish it."

"Well, we'll just have to get you some more. Maybe your very own cake."

Her eyes grew wide. "Really?"

"Really." He unzipped her parka and eased it off her shoulders. "Do you want chocolate or yellow?"

"Chocolate."

"Ah. A woman after my own heart." He carefully pressed her arm in critical places through the thin knit of her sweater, slowly working his way up. "I think that's a good choice. Chocolate or white icing?"

"Chocolate. And maybe it could have— Ouch!" She gave a startled yelp when he reached her elbow.

"I'm sorry, honey. Does it hurt up here, too?" Carefully he pressed along her upper arm to her shoulder. Silently she shook her head.

"How is everything in here, Doctor?"

Eric turned, suddenly aware of the flashing red lights reflecting off the icy pavement. A police officer was looking into the car.

"Nothing too serious, as far as I can tell."

"Should I call an ambulance?"

That would only upset Kate and Sarah even more, he decided. "I'll take them to the hospital."

"Okay. I'll send one of my men over to take a statement."

Eric nodded, then turned back to Sarah and draped the parka over her shoulders. "I don't want to hurt your arm, honey. Can you scoot over and put your other arm around my neck?"

Sarah nodded, and a moment later he eased himself out of the car, with Sarah in his arms. Kate reached out to her daughter and touched her face, then turned anxious eyes to Eric.

"I don't think there's any real damage," he said reassuringly. "But I'd like to get you both checked out at the hospital, just to be sure."

Kate shook her head. "I'm fine. I'm just worried about Sarah."

Kate didn't look fine. She looked terrible. Her face was colorless and she was visibly shaking. But he wasn't about to stand around in the sleet and argue.

"Hold on to my arm. We'll take my car."

She frowned. "What about my car? Is it drivable?"

"Yes, ma'm," the police officer replied, coming up next to them. "The keys are still in the ignition, so if you'll give us your address, we'll drop it off when we're finished here."

Kate complied, and a few moments later they were on their way to the hospital. Though Eric tried to convince Kate to be examined, she refused.

"I told you, Eric. I'm not hurt. Just shaken up. I'll feel much better when I know for sure that Sarah is all right."

Which she was, except for a badly bruised elbow, Eric concluded after a complete exam at the hospital. Kate's shoulders sagged with relief when he told her, and she lifted a weary, trembling hand to her forehead as tears spilled out of her eyes.

"Thank God!" she whispered fervently.

Eric wanted to reach out to Kate, wanted to take her in his arms and comfort her. Wanted to feel the comfort of *her* arms. But he held himself back. Her words at the accident scene, though spoken in a moment of panic and fear, had seared themselves into his soul, "Where were you? We needed you!" In circumstances like that, people often said what was truly in their heart. Cindy had just been more direct about it. "You're never there when I need you," had been her frequent refrain. And she had been right. Just as Kate had been right a couple of hours before. If he'd attended the pageant,

as he'd promised, the accident would never have happened. They would have stayed for the social, and their
paths would never have crossed with the other driver.
Once again, his profession had gotten in the way of his
private life—and with consequences that could have
been so much worse. And it could very likely happen
again. Which led Eric to the disheartening conclusion
he'd reached long ago.

Marriage and medicine didn't mix.

Chapter Twelve

Something was very wrong.

Kate frowned and slowly replaced the receiver, then turned to stare out the window at the leaden skies and the barren trees cloaked in a dull, gray fog. *Everything* suddenly looked gray to her, she realized, her eyes misting with tears—including the future that so recently had seemed golden.

Ever since the accident four days ago, Eric had been like a different person. He'd brought Sarah her own miniature chocolate cake, just as he'd promised in the car on the night of the accident. He'd offered to drive Kate anywhere she needed to go, even though she had a rental car while her own was being repaired. He checked daily to see how she and Sarah were doing. In fact, she'd just hung up from his call. But in many ways she felt as if she'd been talking to a polite stranger. There was a distance between them, an almost palpable separation that made her feel cold and afraid.

At first Kate thought it was because of the little boy he'd lost. And that probably *was* part of it, she reflected. He wasn't the kind of man who would ever be able to insulate his heart from such a tragedy. But the distance she felt was due to more than that, she was sure. For some reason the accident that had damaged her car had also damaged something far more valuable—their rela-tion- ship. And she wasn't sure why. She'd tried to bring it up a couple of times, but Eric had simply said that he was busy at work, and they could talk about it after the holidays. Which did nothing to ease her mind.

Restlessly Kate rose and began to pace, her worry deepening. Eric was slipping away. She could feel it as surely as she'd felt the sting of sleet against her cheeks on the night of the accident. And she couldn't let that happen. Not without a fight, anyway. Not when she'd begun to build her whole future around this special man. But how did you fight an unknown enemy? How did you tackle a phantom, a shadow?

Kate didn't know. But suddenly she thought of some-one who might.

"Kate! This is a surprise!" Amy exclaimed. "Did you change your mind and decide to come down for Christmas? You know you and Eric and Sarah are more than welcome. And you won't even have to put up with Wally this time. I'm pleased to report that our guest has thankfully been returned to his owner in good health and with good riddance, just in time for the holidays. Hallelujah!"

Kate found herself smiling despite her anxiety. "Since you did such a good job, maybe Cal's friend will ask you to iguana-sit again next year."

"Bite your tongue!" Amy declared in horror.

"Just a thought."

"And not a good one. But speaking of good thoughts, I'm serious about the invitation. Do you think you can drag that hardworking doctor down here for a quick visit?"

Kate played with the phone cord. "Frankly, I doubt I could convince him to visit anyone. Even me."

There was a moment of silence while Amy processed this information. When she spoke, her voice was laced with concern. "Do you want to tell me what happened?"

"I honestly don't know," Kate admitted, struggling to control the tears that suddenly welled in her eyes. "It's just that ever since the accident, he…"

"Whoa! Back up! What accident?" Amy demanded in alarm.

A pang of guilt ricocheted through Kate. She should have told Amy sooner, but she'd had other things on her mind—namely her relationship with Eric. "It wasn't bad, Amy. Don't worry. Some guy ran into our car the other night on the way back from the Christmas pageant. It was sleeting, and he lost control."

"Are you and Sarah all right?"

"Sarah's elbow is bruised, but it's nothing serious. I'm fine."

"How about Eric?"

Kate frowned. "What do you mean?"

"Was he hurt?"

"Oh. He wasn't in the car. He was delayed at the hospital. By the time he got to church we'd left, so he followed us. He was right behind us when the accident happened."

"You mean he saw the whole thing?"

"Yes."

"Wow! That must have played havoc with his nerves. It gives me chills just to think about it. And that's when things changed between the two of you?"

"Yes."

"Maybe he's just upset, Kate," Amy speculated. "Watching something like that unfold in front of your eyes, seeing people you care about in danger and not being able to do anything about it… It probably shook him up pretty badly."

"I know. And to make matters worse, he'd just lost a patient." Kate briefly explained about the little boy with meningitis.

"Oh, Kate!" Amy exclaimed in horror. "Having met Eric, I imagine he was devastated."

"Yes, he was."

"Okay, so let's try to piece this together," she reasoned. "He'd already had a terrible day at the hospital. Then, not only did he disappoint Sarah, who was looking forward to having him at the pageant, but he wasn't able to drive you. You told me once that his first marriage was more or less a disaster, largely because of conflicts between his career and personal life. And that for a long time he was afraid marriage and medicine didn't mix. Maybe those old fears have resurfaced. He probably figures that if he had taken you, the accident might never have happened. But his job got in the way." She paused, and when she spoke again her voice was thoughtful. "You know, I'd lay odds that right now he's waging a pretty intense battle with guilt. And fear."

As usual, Amy's analytical mind had distilled the essence of the situation. "You might be right," Kate conceded.

"Maybe he thinks you're upset because he didn't make the pageant. Maybe he thinks you blame him for what happened."

"But that's ridiculous! It wasn't his fault!"

"Did you tell him that?"

Kate frowned. No, she hadn't. In fact, what *had* she said to him the night of the accident? The whole incident was still so fuzzy. She remembered him pulling open her door, and she recalled the immense relief she'd felt, and her silent "Thank God!" But she hadn't said that. Nor had she said, "I'm so glad you're here," though she'd thought that, as well. She struggled to remember her first words to him, and was almost sorry when she did, for her heart sank.

"Oh, no! I couldn't have..." she whispered bleakly, closing her eyes, wishing with every ounce of her being that she could take back those accusatory words, spoken without thinking, in a moment of panic.

"Kate? What is it?"

"I just remembered what I said when Eric arrived on the accident scene," she said in dismay.

"What?"

Kate drew a deep breath. "Basically, I implied that he wasn't there for us when we needed him. Which of course only played right into the guilt he was already feeling. Big time. Oh, Amy, what am I going to do? I didn't mean it the way it came out! I was just so frightened and worried about Sarah. I don't even know where those words came from. He must have felt like he was reliving a nightmare. Just when he was starting to believe that marriage and medicine *could* mix, I say something stupid like that and blow the whole thing. He had enough guilt laid on him in his first marriage to last a lifetime. He's sure not going to put himself in that position again. No wonder he backed off!"

"You do have a problem," Amy conceded soberly. "Up until that point, do you think things were getting pretty...serious?"

"Very. In fact, I think he was..." She swallowed past

the lump in her throat. "I think he was going to ask me to marry him, Amy."

"Were you going to accept?"

"Yes."

"Then you can't let this setback stand in the way," she declared resolutely.

"But I can't take back those words. And he isn't likely to forget them."

"I agree. What you need now are some more words."

"Do you want to explain that?"

"Let me ask you something first, Kate. How much do you love Eric?"

"So much that I can't even imagine a future without him anymore," she replied softly, without hesitation.

"Then you love him enough to do something totally out of character?"

"What exactly do you have in mind?" Kate asked, suddenly cautious.

"Just answer the question."

Kate drew a deep breath. She wasn't sure she was going to be comfortable with whatever Amy was going to suggest. But she also knew that her sister's advice would be sound. It always was. "Yes."

"Good," Amy declared with satisfaction. "Because I have a plan."

Eric frowned as he pulled up in front of his mother's house. Why was Kate's car here? He and Anna were supposed to pick up Kate and Sarah later, in time for Christmas Eve services, and they were all going to spend the day together tomorrow. Kate had canceled her usual holiday trip to Amy's when they'd made those arrangements. If she hadn't, he would have begged off from the whole thing. It was bound to be awkward.

Eric knew that Kate was confused and troubled by the change in their relationship. The intimacy they'd begun to create had been replaced by polite formality, the closeness by distance. In fact, if Christmas hadn't been only days away, he'd have cut the ties entirely by now, as painful as that would be. God knew, it wasn't what he wanted to do. But he felt he had no choice. During the last few weeks he'd gradually begun to believe that with Kate, things could be different; that she wouldn't come to resent the demands of his profession—and ultimately him—as Cindy had. And yet, in a moment of crisis, at a time when the heart often spoke truths even *it* hadn't recognized, she'd voiced a resentment, a blame, that had pierced him to his very core. He doubted whether she even recalled what she'd said. But though *she* might not remember her words, they were ones *he* could never forget.

Eric closed his eyes and gripped the steering wheel as his gut twisted painfully. With all his heart he wished there was a way out of this dilemma, an answer to the same question that had plagued him during his marriage to Cindy: where did his first loyalty lie? It was a conflict he'd never been able to reconcile. Cindy had made her opinion clear. And—intentionally or not—so had Kate. He desperately wished he could promise her it would never happen again, but that would be a lie. It *would* happen again. And again. And again. Until finally she, too, grew disillusioned and bitter. He couldn't do that to her. Or to himself.

Wearily Eric climbed out of the car. For everyone's sake he needed to be upbeat for the holiday. There would be time for sadness, for dealing with the loss of a dream, later. But getting through the next thirty-six hours with even a semblance of holiday cheer wasn't going to be easy.

The fragrant smell of pine mingling with the aroma of freshly baked cookies greeted him as he stepped inside the door, and he paused for a moment to let the warm, comforting holiday smells work their soothing magic. They took him back many years, to the happy days of his boyhood, and his lips curved up at the pleasant memories. If only life could be as simple as it had been in those idyllic days of youth, when the most pressing question he faced was whether there would be a shiny red bike under the tree, come Christmas morning.

"Eric! I thought I heard you," Anna greeted him with a smile as she stepped into the small foyer.

"Hello, Mom." He bent and kissed her cheek. "Merry Christmas."

"Merry Christmas to you. I'm glad you came early."

"You asked me to."

"So I did. It's nice to see you still listen to your mother once in a while," she teased.

"You know I'm always at your beck and call. But I'm surprised to see that Kate and Sarah are here," he remarked, striving for a casual tone. "I thought we were picking them up for services later."

"Well, when Kate called earlier, she sounded awfully lonesome. She and Sarah were all by themselves, so I invited them to come over early. I figured, why not spend the time together? I baked a ham, and there's plenty for two more. I didn't think you'd mind," she teased.

Eric hadn't said anything to his mother about his plans to stop seeing Kate, and tonight wasn't the time to break the news—not when he knew she had hopes for a wedding in the not-too-distant future. It would ruin her Christmas. And one ruined Christmas was enough. "Of course not."

"Hi, Dr. Eric!" Sarah dashed into the hallway and launched herself at him.

He reached down and swept her up. "Hi, yourself, sweetie. How's that elbow?"

She cocked it for him to see. "It's still kind of blue." Then she put her small arms around his neck and smiled. "You know what?"

His throat tightened. This was something else he was going to miss—the trusting touch of a child who loved him. "What?"

"This is the best Christmas ever!"

Eric's gut clenched again. How he hated to hurt this child! He was sure Kate would find a way to explain their breakup without making him sound like a villain. That was her way. But he sure *felt* like one. And as he looked into Sarah's happy, guileless face, so filled with the optimism of youth, he suddenly felt old.

"Sarah, honey, are you ready to decorate that next batch of cookies?" Anna asked.

"Yes. Do you want a cookie, Dr. Eric? Aunt Anna made them, and I decorated them," she told him proudly.

"I'll have one a little later," he promised as he set her down. He glanced at his mother as Sarah scampered back to the kitchen. "Where's Kate?"

"Right here," she replied breathlessly, coming up behind Anna.

As always, Eric was moved by the translucent beauty of her face. These last few weeks it had seemed almost luminous, filled with a soft light and a peace that

reflected a soul at rest. But today she seemed a bit...
different. He couldn't quite put his finger on it. Her eyes
were a little too bright, for one thing. And her face was
flushed. There was also an unusual energy radiating
from her, making her movements seem agitated. He
frowned, both curious and concerned.

"Are you all right?" he asked.

Her flush deepened. "Yes, of course. A little warm
from all that cookie baking, though. Anna, I think I'll
take a walk. I love this crisp weather, and I feel a touch
of snow in the air. I won't be gone long," she promised,
opening the hall closet to retrieve her coat.

"Kate, dear, do you think you should?" Anna asked
worriedly. "It's getting dark."

"I'll be fine. A little fresh air will do me good."

Anna turned to Eric with a frown. "I'm not crazy
about her walking alone, even if it is Christmas Eve."

"Please don't worry, Anna. I won't be gone long. Just
down to the park and back," Kate reassured her as she
pulled on her gloves.

Eric wasn't crazy about the idea, either. But Kate
seemed determined to go. He frowned, waging an internal debate. Spending time alone with her was the last
thing he wanted to do. The temptation to touch her, to
feel her melt into his arms, was hard enough to resist
when there were other people present. He wasn't sure his
self-control would hold when it was just the two of them.
Despite recent events and his subsequent resolve to end
their relationship, he still loved her. He still wanted her
to be his wife. And deep in his heart, he still wanted to
believe they could work out the conflict between their
personal life as a couple and his career. But his confidence had been badly shaken. He just couldn't find the
courage to trust his heart—or his judgment. They had

betrayed him once. How could he be sure they wouldn't again?

"Eric, I really don't like this," Anna prompted more forcefully.

His gaze swung from Kate to Anna's concerned face, then back to Kate. He didn't, either. It wasn't safe for Kate to be wandering around in the dark by herself. There was really no choice.

"Why don't I go with you?" he suggested. "If you don't mind the company."

Did her smile seem relieved? Or was it just his imagination?

"I don't mind in the least. Thank you." She picked up a tote bag, slung it over her shoulder and gazed expectantly at Eric.

He hesitated for a moment, then pulled open the door and stepped aside. "We won't be long, Mom," he said as Kate moved past him, leaving a faint, pleasing fragrance in her wake.

"Don't hurry. We won't eat for at least an hour," she assured them.

Kate waited while he shut the door, then fell into step beside him as they headed down the sidewalk. Dusk was just beginning to fall, and the lights from Christmas trees twinkled merrily in the windows. Few cars passed, leaving the peace and stillness of the evening largely undisturbed.

"I've always liked Christmas Eve," Kate said softly. "I remember as a child it was filled with such a sense of wonder and hope and anticipation. As if great, exciting things were about to happen. Was it like that for you?"

Eric shoved his hands into the pockets of his overcoat. His breath made frosty clouds in the cold air, but his heart was warm as he thought of Christmases past. "Yes, it was. Thanks to Mom and Dad. They made me feel that somehow anything was possible during this magical season. It's a shame we have to grow up and lose that belief in endless possibilities."

They strolled for a few minutes in silence, and just as they reached the park a few large, feathery flakes began to drift down. The distant strains of "Silent Night" floated through the quiet air as carolers raised their voices in the familiar, beloved melody.

"My favorite Christmas song," Kate murmured, her lips curving up sweetly. "Could we sit for a minute?" She nodded toward a park bench tucked between two fir trees bedecked with twinkling white lights.

Eric hesitated. He was already pushing his luck, going on this walk. He'd had to fight the impulse to reach over and take her hand every step of the way. Sitting on a park bench, where the shimmering lights were sure to add a luster to her ebony hair and bring out the sparkle in her eyes, was downright dangerous. "It's getting awfully dark, Kate," he objected.

"Please, Eric? We don't have to stay long. But the song is so beautiful."

There was no way he could refuse her when she looked at him like that, her eyes soft and hopeful, her face glowing. He drew a deep breath and slowly let it out. "Okay."

Kate led the way to the bench and sat down, carefully setting the tote bag beside her. He joined her more slowly, keeping a modest distance between them. As they sat there quietly, listening to the distant, melodic voices, Eric stole a glance at Kate. She seemed oblivious to the snowflakes that clung to her hair like gossamer stars, giving her an ethereal beauty. Her gaze was fixed on something in the distance, and he wondered what she was thinking.

Please, Lord, give me the courage to go through with this, Kate prayed silently. *I've never been the bold type, but I think Amy's right. This may be the only way to convince Eric how much I care. Please, let me feel Your presence and help me to find the right words.*

As the last strains of "Silent Night" faded away, her heart began to hammer painfully against her rib cage. So before her courage could waver, she clasped her hands tightly in her lap, took a deep breath and turned to him.

"Eric, I've been thinking a lot about what happened the night of the accident. And I think we need to talk about it," she said as firmly as she could manage, considering her insides were quivering like the proverbial bowlful of jelly.

Startled, he jerked his gaze to hers. Confrontation wasn't her style, yet there was a touch of that in both her voice and the determined tilt of her chin. And she was right, of course. They did need to talk. But he didn't want to do it on Christmas Eve. "Kate, can't we put this on hold until after…"

"No." Her tone was quiet but resolved. "My life has been on hold too long, Eric." She reached into the tote bag at her feet, withdrew a flat, rectangular package and held it out to him. "Let's start with this."

He stared at the gift wrapped in silver paper. "Kate, I…"

"Please, Eric. Unlike Amy, I'm not really good at this assertiveness thing, so just humor me, okay?"

The pleading tone in her voice, the strain around its edges, tugged at his heart, and without another word he took the package and tore off the wrapping. He angled the counted-cross-stitch sampler toward the light from the bushes as he slowly read the words from Jeremiah that had been so carefully and elaborately stitched around a motif of the rising sun. "For I know well the plans I have in mind for you, says the Lord, plans for your welfare not for woe! Plans to give you a future full of hope."

"I started working on this when Jack was in the hospital," Kate told him quietly, her gaze resting on the sampler. "I came across the passage one night when I was idly leafing through the Bible, and it seemed to speak directly to my soul. Because after the accident I felt that there must have been something I did—something wrong—to deserve such a tragedy and loss. Taking Jack away was the Lord's way of punishing me, I thought. So whenever I started to feel overwhelmed, I'd pull this out and work on it to remind me that the Lord was *for* me, not *against* me. And it also encouraged me to look to the future with faith and hope. It made me believe that things would get better, that tomorrow my life would again be filled with joy."

Kate paused and transferred her gaze from the gift to his deep blue eyes. "When Jack died, I put the sampler away. I felt empty and hollow inside, and the words seemed to mock me rather than offer comfort. For a long time I lived in an emotional and spiritual vacuum. The guilt became all-consuming again, and I lost hope that the kind of love I shared with Jack, which had made my world so bright, would ever touch my life again. All I could see in my future was an endless string of dark days. And then you came along."

She drew a steadying breath, willing her courage to hold fast. "Eric, the simple fact is that until I met you, my life was like this sampler—on hold and unfinished.

But you made me realize that it was time to tie up the loose threads and move on. So I did exactly that—literally and figuratively. Because when I took this out of storage, I took out my heart, as well. For the first time in five years, I let myself not only believe again in the endless possibilities of life, but I opened myself to them. I want you to have this because I think you've been held captive by the same demons that plagued me for years—guilt and hopelessness. And I think it's time for you to do what I did—put your past to rest so you can create a new future."

She paused and reached into her bag again, this time withdrawing a smaller, square box, which she handed to him. She noticed that her hands were trembling, and clasped them tightly in her lap as Eric silently unwrapped the second package, then lifted the lid. Nestled on a bed of tissue lay a delicate, heart-shaped blown-glass Christmas-tree ornament with a loop of green satin ribbon at the top, anchored with sprigs of holly.

"Just as today we celebrate the birth of a baby who brought new life to the world two thousand years ago, I'd like us to celebrate our own rebirth of hope and faith that this day symbolizes," Kate said softly. "When Jack died, I never thought I'd love again. But the Lord seemed to have other ideas when he sent you my way. Because how could I help but fall in love with your tenderness and caring and sense of humor and those deep blue eyes and all of the thousands of things that make you so very special and unique? I love you, Eric Carlson, and I can't imagine my future without you in it. So I give you this ornament as a sign of what you've already claimed—my heart. And I would be very honored if…if you would marry me."

Eric stared at her, speechless, then looked down at

the shiny red ornament cradled in his hands. It was so fragile and so easily broken—just like her heart. Dear God, had she really offered to entrust it to his care? Or was he caught up in some sort of Christmas Eve fantasy? His confused gaze moved to her hands, clasped tightly in her lap, and he could sense the tension vibrating in every nerve of her body as she waited for his reaction. So it was real, after all.

A rush of tenderness and love and elation swept over him, so swift and powerful that it took his breath away—and scared him out of his wits. There was no question that he returned her love, with every ounce of his being. Yet doubts about making a success of marriage, given the pressures of his career, remained. He struggled against the urge to throw caution to the wind and pull her into his arms and shout "Yes!" for all the world to hear. It was what his heart told him to do. But he had to make sure she understood the dangers.

"Kate, I—" His voice broke and he cleared his throat.

Kate felt the bottom drop out of her stomach. She'd obviously shocked him into speechlessness, and her courage suddenly deserted her. How could she possibly have asked this man to marry her? Amy's bold plan had seemed reasonable when they'd discussed it, but given his reaction, it was way off base. Now she needed to find a way to smooth over the awkwardness she'd created.

"Listen, Eric, I'm sorry," she said jerkily. "Y-you don't have to answer that question. I understand if…"

He reached out and took her hand, his look so tender and warm that her voice deserted her. "I *want* to answer the question. I was just…overwhelmed for a minute. No one's ever proposed to me before." His lips quirked into a crooked grin.

Although the ardent light in his eyes set her heart hammering, she sensed a hesitation in his manner. She had hoped her bold question would assuage any doubts he might have about her willingness to accept the demands his job would make on their life, but apparently it hadn't, she realized with dismay.

"I—I understand if you need to think about it," she stammered, stalling for time, suddenly afraid to hear his answer. If he was going to refuse, she didn't want to know tonight. Not on Christmas Eve. She averted her gaze and reached for the tote bag. "Like you said, we can talk about this after Christmas."

She started to stand, but he restrained her and pulled her trembling body close beside him, into the shelter of his arm. "You can't just drop something like that on a man and then walk away, you know. Let's talk."

She lowered her head and stared at the snowflakes falling gently to the ground, willing the peace of that sight to calm the turbulence in her heart. "I don't know what else to say," she responded softly, her voice choked with emotion.

Eric reached over and with gentle pressure urged her chin back up until their gazes met. "Then I'll start. First of all, I love you, too," he said huskily.

Kate's throat constricted, and joy flooded her heart. Those were the words she'd been praying to hear for weeks! And yet…he hadn't accepted her proposal. She searched his eyes, afraid to ask but knowing she had to. "I sense a 'but' there," she ventured, her voice quavering.

He laced his fingers with hers and absently stroked his thumb across the back of her hand.

"There is," he conceded. "I'm just not sure marriage would be good for either of us."

"How can you say that, when we love each other?"

"Because love implies certain obligations. Like being there for a child's Christmas play. And making sure the woman you love doesn't have to deal with her private terrors alone. And protecting the people you love from danger. And honoring promises. And a million other things that my profession won't always allow me to do. What happened four days ago could happen again, Kate. I can't promise you it won't."

"I'm not asking you to. I admire your dedication to your work, Eric. It's part of what makes you who you are. Don't you think I know that you're torn between what you see as conflicting loyalties, that you anguish over balancing the two responsibilities? I wish you wouldn't let it tear you up inside. Yet one of the reasons I love you is that you care enough to *feel* anguish. And my feelings about *that* will never change."

He wanted to believe her. Desperately. But experience had been a harsh teacher. "I'd like to think that's true, Kate," he said wearily. "And I know you believe it is—right now. But I'm afraid that in time you'll come to resent my work. Whether you realize it or not, you were upset the night of the accident because I wasn't there for you."

"You're thinking about that stupid comment I made when you opened my door, aren't you?" she said quietly.

He looked surprised. "You remember what you said?"

"Yes. And obviously you do, too. Eric, I don't know where those words came from. I was distraught. And shaken up. And afraid Sarah was hurt. I wasn't even thinking straight. Do you know what my *thoughts* were when you appeared? 'Thank God.' I can't even find the words to describe the relief I felt when I saw you. I know my words didn't reflect that. But that was what was in my heart." She paused and took a deep breath. "Believe it or not, Eric, I can handle the fact that you have a demanding career that sometimes requires you to make difficult choices. I may be disappointed sometimes if your duties take you away from us, but I'll never stop loving you. Because I know you'll always do your best to *give* your best. To us *and* your job. I would never ask for any more than that. And I truly believe that if we trust in the Lord, He'll show us the way to make this work."

Eric gazed into the face that had become so precious and dear to him during these last few months. The sincerity in her eyes, and the love, were unquestionable. What had he ever done to deserve a woman with such an understanding heart, and an inner beauty that surpassed even her physical loveliness? he wondered, his throat tightening with emotion. She seemed so sure, so confident about their future. Why couldn't he put his own doubts and fears to rest, as well?

"You seem to have such faith," he said quietly.

She looked at him steadily. "Enough to move mountains. I'm not Cindy, Eric. I love you for who you are— not in *spite* of who you are. And on this Christmas Eve, for the first time in years, I believe great, exciting things are about to happen. I believe that anything is possible. And I believe in you. And us."

Eric looked at her, his heart so full of love that for a moment he couldn't speak. She was everything he'd always wanted, and he suddenly knew with absolute certainty that he'd be a fool to pass up this chance for happiness. As if to confirm his sudden lightness of heart, the distant voices of the carolers came once more through the air, jubilantly proclaiming, "Joy to the World." As he reached over and touched her face with infinite tenderness, his doubt was replaced by a gladness and peace that truly reflected this most joyous, holy season.

"When I got to Mom's tonight, Sarah said that this was the best Christmas ever," Eric told Kate huskily. "And you know something? She's absolutely right."

Kate studied him cautiously, trying not to infer too much from his tender tone of voice and the promise in his eyes. Yet she was unable to stop her hopes from soaring. "Is that a yes?" she ventured.

He chuckled as his own spirits suddenly took wing. "That is most definitely a yes. And even though this proposal wasn't exactly traditional, I think we should seal it in the traditional way. Don't you agree?"

The sudden flame of passion in his eyes made her tingle. "Most definitely, " she concurred.

He reached for her, and she went willingly, savoring the haven of his strong arms and the wondrous feeling of homecoming. And in the moment before his lips claimed hers, the words of the distant carol echoed in her ears, making her heart rejoice.

"Let heaven and nature sing. Let heaven and nature sing. Let heaven, and heaven, and nature sing."

Amen, she said silently. *And thank you.*

Epilogue

Five months later

It was a perfect day for a wedding.

Kate gazed out the window of Amy's log cabin at the blue-hazed mountains, fresh with spring. New green shoots decorated the tips of the spruce trees, and the masses of rhododendrons and mountain laurel on the hillsides were heavy with pink-hued blossoms. A cloud of yellow swallowtail butterflies drifted by, undulating playfully in the warm morning sun, while classical flute music played a duet with the splashing water from a nearby stream.

Kate smiled and slowly drew in a deep breath. The peaceful setting, reflecting the beauty of God's creation and the rebirth of nature after a long, cold winter, seemed symbolic; within a few moments, she and Eric would start a new life together after their own long, cold winter of the heart.

"You look happy."

Kate turned at the sound of Amy's voice. Her sister stood in the doorway with Sarah, holding two bouquets of mountain laurel still beaded with silver drops of dew.

"I am."

"And beautiful."

Kate flushed and turned to look in the full-length mirror beside her. The simple but elegant style of her A-line, tea-length gown enhanced her slender figure, and the overlay of delicate chiffon that flared out near the hem softly swirled as she moved. Long sleeves—sheer and full, cuffed at the wrist—emphasized her delicate bone structure, and the deep blue color was a perfect foil for her dark hair and flawless complexion.

"I *feel* beautiful," she admitted. And young. And breathless. And hopeful. And all the things every bride should feel on her special day, she thought with wonder.

"Do I look pretty, too, Mommy?" Sarah asked.

Kate turned to her daughter and smiled. In her white eyelet dress, with a basket of flowers in her hands, she would fit right in at a Victorian garden party.

"You look lovely," Kate replied, kneeling down to hold her close. Without Sarah, she knew she would never have survived the months following Jack's death. Only her daughter's sunny disposition and innocent laughter had kept her sane and grounded in the present, prevented her from slipping into the abyss of total despair. She hugged Sarah fiercely, thanking God for His gift of the precious child who had filled her life with a special love during the difficult years when she'd felt so deserted and spiritually alone.

When Kate finally released her, Sarah lifted her basket and pointed to a bluebell. "I picked that flower for Dr. Eric. Aunt Amy says I can give it to him later."

Kate smiled, deeply grateful that Sarah adored Eric. And equally grateful that the feeling was returned.

"I'm sure he'll like that. It's just the color of his eyes."

"Well, if you two ladies are ready, I don't think we should keep the groom waiting any longer," Amy announced.

Kate gave Sarah one more quick hug. "I love you, honey," she whispered.

"I love you, too, Mommy."

Kate rose and Amy handed her one of the bouquets. For a long moment their gazes met and held.

"You know how happy I am for you, don't you?" Amy said softly.

Kate nodded, and when she spoke her voice was choked with tears. "I know. And thank you, Amy. For everything. For your love and support and for always being there. You and Mom were my lifeline for so many years."

Amy's own voice was none too steady when she replied, "I always will be, Kate. But I'm more than happy to share the job with someone else. Especially Eric."

The flute music suddenly changed, and Kate recognized the melody of the hymn they'd chosen for the opening of the ceremony.

"It's time," Amy said.

Kate nodded. Amy took Sarah's hand and they preceded Kate down the steps and out the door. She waited for a few moments, then stepped out into the sunshine and walked slowly toward the gazebo banked by blossoming rhododendrons and surrounded by the people she loved most in the world.

Anna was there, of course, beaming with joy. Cal smiled at her and winked, juggling Caitlin in one arm while the twins clung to his leg and stared wide-eyed at the proceedings. Frank grinned and gave a subtle thumbs-up signal.

And Eric—her breath caught in her throat as she gazed at him. He looked incredibly handsome in a dove-gray suit that hugged his broad shoulders. The morning sun had turned his blond hair to gold, and as she gazed into his face—so fine and strong and compassionate and caring—tears of happiness pricked her eyes. His own eyes, so blue and tender, caught and held hers compellingly as she drew closer. They spoke more eloquently than words of the passion and love and commitment in his heart, and she trembled with wonder that God had blessed her with a second chance at love.

As the pure notes of "Amazing Grace" drifted through the mountain air, she was glad once again that they'd chosen this hymn to begin their wedding ceremony. For she had, indeed, once been lost. But now she was found. And today, as she prepared to start a new life with the man she loved, she felt filled with God's amazing grace.

Eric watched Kate approach, and his own heart overflowed with joy. The significance of the song wasn't lost on him, either. He knew that without the Lord's help, he wouldn't be standing here today. On his own, he would never have had the courage to take another chance on love. But God had sent him Kate, whose sweetness and understanding had broken through the barriers he'd erected around his heart and made him believe once again in endless possibilities. And as Kate stepped up into the gazebo and took his hand, her eyes shining with love and faith and trust, he knew beyond the shadow of a doubt that they would have a rich, full marriage. For the Lord would always help them, just as His grace had led their hearts home.

* * * * *

Dear Reader,

As I write this, the rustle of autumn is underfoot. Winter—that season of rest and renewal for a slumbering world—will soon be upon us. But like the beautiful scarlet cardinals twittering in the tree beside my bench, and the gloriously blooming impatiens oblivious to the inevitable frost that will soon make them only a memory, I am reluctant to let the warm weather go.

Yet sometimes letting go is the only way to move forward. For without winter, we would never appreciate the joys and promise of spring. And without saying goodbye to the past, we can never say hello to the future. Eric and Kate discovered that in this book. And they also discovered that life is filled with endless possibilities if we open our eyes—and hearts—to them.

This upcoming Christmas season, may each of you experience the joy that comes from believing in the endless possibilities that keep life always new.

Irene Hannon

HOME FOR THE HOLIDAYS

Come to me, all you who labor and
are overburdened, and I will give you rest.
Shoulder my yoke and learn from me,
for I am gentle and humble in heart,
and you will find rest for your souls.

—*Matthew* 11:28–29

To Tom

My Friend, My Hero, My Love

Chapter One

$Nick$ Sinclair felt his blood pressure begin to rise and his spirits crash. A few moments ago he'd been on a high, elated by the news that he'd won the commission to design a new headquarters building for the Midwest Regional Arts Center. It was a coup destined to move his architectural career into the limelight.

Then George Thompson dropped his bombshell. On behalf of the building committee, he had strongly suggested—more like mandated, Nick thought grimly—that the firm of Sinclair and Stevens use some unknown landscaping company to design the grounds.

"Taylor Landscaping?" Nick cleared his throat. "I don't believe I've heard of them," he said in a pleasant, conversational tone that betrayed none of his turmoil.

"You will," George replied with a decisive nod. "Great company. Small. Relatively new. But dynamic. Creative, yet practical. I like that." George always spoke in clipped sentences, a habit that Nick suddenly found irritating.

"How do you know about them?"

"Several of the board members have used them. Did

the landscaping at my new house, in fact. Wonderful job! My wife said they were great to work with. Very professional. And stayed right on budget, too."

Nick struggled to keep his face impassive as a wave of panic washed over him. On his own, he knew he could assemble a team of contractors that would do the firm of Sinclair and Stevens proud. But one weak link was all it took to ruin an otherwise great job. Or, at the very least, to make his life miserable.

Nick carefully smoothed down his tie. Not that there was anything out of order in his appearance. His navy blue pin-striped suit, starched white cotton shirt and maroon-and-gray paisley tie sat well on his just-over-six-foot frame. Broad shouldered, with dark hair and even darker eyes, he didn't particularly care about clothes one way or the other, but he'd invested a good number of his thirty-six years to reach this point in his career, and he was smart enough to know that appearances *did* count. Today he looked every bit the part of a rising young architect, and nothing was amiss— including his tie. But that little maneuver bought him a few seconds of time—all he needed to recover from his surprise at George's suggestion and to rapidly formulate his response.

"Well, I'm sure they're very competent, but commercial landscaping is on an entirely different scale than residential," Nick said smoothly. "Now, I've worked with an established firm for several years that I think you'll find very—"

"Nick." George held up his hand, cutting the younger man off. "Providing opportunities for young talent is in keeping with the philosophy of the Arts Center. And it's one of the reasons we chose *your* firm to design it.

I think it's only fair that we at least give this company a chance, don't you?"

Nick looked at the man across from him in silence. Checkmate, he thought grudgingly. George Thompson's years as a respected trial attorney served him well in the business world. You couldn't raise an objection that he hadn't already considered.

And, Nick had to admit, he was right. The Arts Center board could have chosen a well-established architectural firm for this project. Instead, the board members—all of whom were influential business people in St. Louis—were giving him a shot at it. He couldn't argue the point that this Taylor Landscaping deserved a chance, too. It was just that he didn't relish the idea of some wet-behind-the-ears firm getting its chance at his expense. However, it looked as if he didn't have a choice.

"I see what you mean," he said, his even tone revealing nothing of his frustration.

"Good, good. Give them a look, get a bid…I think you'll be impressed."

"I'll get in touch with them immediately," Nick promised. "Now, about the schedule…"

By the time Nick left George's office, all of the details had been finalized. He should have been on top of the world. Instead, the sudden gust of cold March wind and the overcast, threatening sky that greeted him when he stepped through the glass doors better matched his mood, and he scowled at the dark clouds overhead.

There had to be a way around this, he reasoned as he climbed into a sleek red sports car parked in the visitors' lot. Obviously, the board wanted a first-class job. The Arts Center would be a St. Louis showpiece, and anything less than the best would reflect poorly on the city. Just as obviously, the board members were convinced this landscaping firm could handle the job. And maybe they were right. But *Nick* wasn't convinced. Not yet, anyway. And before he agreed to work with this company, he had to feel confident in its abilities. George *had* given him an out. A slim one, true, but it was there. And he intended to use it unless Taylor Landscaping did one terrific sell job on him.

Suddenly Nick found himself walking through the door of his office, with no recollection of the drive from downtown. For a man who prided himself on his alertness and attention to detail, it was an unsettling experience. Frowning, he nodded distractedly to the receptionist, glanced at the two part-time draftsmen at work in a large, airy room and stuck his head into his partner's office.

Jack Stevens glanced up from his drafting table and grinned hopefully, his short-cropped sandy hair giving him a fresh-faced, all-American-boy look. "Well?"

"Well what?"

"How'd it go?"

"Fine."

"You mean you got the job?"

"Yeah."

Jack tilted his head quizzically. "Well, try to contain your enthusiasm," he said dryly.

Nick shook his head impatiently and raked his fingers through his hair, jamming his other hand into the pocket of his slacks. "There's a complication."

"What?"

"Have you ever heard of Taylor Landscaping?"

Jack frowned thoughtfully. "Taylor Landscaping… No, I don't think so. Why?"

"Because the board of the Arts Center *strongly* recommended them to do the landscape design."

Jack leaned against the drafting table, propping his head on a fist. "Is that bad? What do *you* know about Taylor Landscaping?"

"Nothing. That's the point. It's some new outfit that's probably fairly inexperienced."

"Sort of like Sinclair and Stevens?" Jack said with a mild grin.

Nick glared at him. "Don't you start, too. That's exactly what George implied."

Jack shrugged. "Well, it's the truth. Why don't you keep cool until you check them out? Might be the proverbial diamond in the rough."

"It also might be a lump of coal."

"Maybe. Then again, maybe not."

Nick gave him a disgusted look. He was in no mood for humoring, not with the commission of his career facing potential disaster at the hands of an inept landscape designer. "Aren't you just a little worried about how this might affect the future of Sinclair and Stevens?" he said tersely. "Most people will only see the outside of the Arts Center, and a bad landscaping job could ruin the lines."

"You're really worried about this, aren't you?"

"You better believe it." Nick walked restlessly over to the large window on one wall and stared out unseeingly for a long moment before he turned back to his colleague. "You of all people know how hard we've worked to get this far. Fourteen-hour days for three long years, working in a cramped office with barely room for two drafting tables. It's beyond me where you ever found the time or energy to have two kids along the way! We've done okay, but you know as well as I do that we've been waiting for our real break, the one job that will move us into the big leagues. This is it, Jack. It may sound dramatic, but our future could depend on this commission. This is what will make or break our reputation with the people who count in this town. We blow it—we might as well close up shop because we'll never get another chance."

Jack stared at his partner thoughtfully for a few minutes, his demeanor now just as serious as his friend's. "I'm sorry, Nick. I didn't mean to make light of it. I realize how important this is. But if this landscaper doesn't cut it, we don't have to use them, do we? You said the board *recommended* them. So at least the door's open to other possibilities if they don't work out, isn't it?"

"Yeah. About half an inch."

"Look, before we jump to any conclusions or panic unnecessarily, why don't you check out this Taylor Landscaping? I trust your judgment. If you're not satisfied with them, we just have to tell George. I'll back you up, but this project is really your baby, Nick. You went after it and you did the preliminary design that the committee selected. I know it's coming out of the Sinclair and Stevens shop and I'll help peripherally, but you're the one who needs to feel comfortable with this company because you're the one who'll have to work with them."

"Yeah, I know. And you're right. I need to check them out. I'm condemning without a trial, and that's really not fair." He glanced at his watch and gave an exasperated sigh. "Six o'clock! Where did the day go?" He shook his head. "It's too late to do anything today, but I'll follow up on this first thing in the morning."

At nine o'clock the next morning Nick punched in the number for Taylor Landscaping. He waited with an impatient frown as the phone rang once, twice, three times. By the sixth ring he was drumming his fingers on the desk. What kind of an outfit was this, anyway? Every business office he knew of was open by this hour. Hadn't anyone ever told this company that an unanswered phone meant lost business? Nick was just about to hang up when a slightly breathless voice answered.

"Taylor Landscaping."

"This is Nick Sinclair from Sinclair and Stevens. I'd like to speak with Mr. Taylor."

There was a long pause at the other end of the line. "Do you mean the owner?" There was a hint of amusement in the voice.

Nick bit back the sarcastic retort that sprang to his lips, confining his response to a single, curt syllable. "Yes."

"Well, everyone's out at the job site right now."

Nick debated. He could just leave a message. But it might not be a bad idea to see this outfit at work. "All right. Just give me the address," he said in a clipped, authoritative tone.

"Well, I guess that would be okay." The voice sounded uncertain. "Hang on a minute." A sound of papers being shuffled came over the line, and after several interminable minutes the information was relayed. Nick jotted it down. A residential job, in a nice area of large homes and expansive grounds. But not a commercial commission.

"Thanks," he said.

"My pleasure." The amused tone was back.

Nick frowned at the receiver, perplexed by the woman's attitude. But he wasn't about to waste time trying to figure it out. Instead, he glanced at his watch. If he hurried, there was time to pay a quick visit to Taylor Landscaping before his eleven o'clock meeting.

A half hour later Nick pulled up at the address provided by the woman on the phone. Four people, dressed in jeans and work shirts, were visible. Two wrestled with a large boulder. Next to them, a guy with a mustache fiddled with a jackhammer. Another slightly built worker, who appeared to be only a teenager, stood apart with a hose, watering some freshly planted azalea bushes.

Nick had no idea who the owner was, but the kid with the hose was closest to the street. Besides, he had no desire to approach the group with the jackhammer. It was now in use, and the bone-jarring noise was already giving him a headache.

Nick stepped onto the lawn and took a moment to look over the grounds. It was a new house, built on a vacant lot in an already established neighborhood. The ground had been cleared during construction, and it was obvious that a complete landscaping job was under way. The work appeared to be just beginning, and it was difficult to tell whether a cohesive plan had been developed. But a well-maintained pickup truck bearing the name Taylor Landscaping stood parked in the circular driveway, and the crew seemed energetic.

The jackhammer stopped momentarily, and Nick

opened his mouth to speak. But before he could make a sound the annoying noise started again. Shaking his head in irritation, he moved forward and tapped on the shoulder of the teenage boy who held the hose.

It happened so quickly Nick had no chance to step aside. The boy swung around in instinctive alarm, maintaining a death grip on the hose and drenching him in the most embarrassing possible place. Nick was stunned, but not too stunned to lunge for the hose and yank it in a different direction. He glanced down at his soggy gray wool slacks, and for the second time in less than twenty-four hours he felt his blood pressure edge up.

"Just what exactly were you trying to do?" he demanded hotly. "Of all the stupid antics…"

"I'm…I'm really sorry," the teenager stammered.

Nick removed his pocket handkerchief and tried to sop up the moisture, a task he quickly realized was futile. "Yeah, well, that really solves everything, doesn't it?" he said sarcastically. "I have an important meeting in less than forty-five minutes. How do you suggest I explain this?"

The teenager stared at him blankly.

"You could say you had an accident," replied a mildly amused voice.

Nick glanced up. The worker who had offered the suggestion wore a baseball cap and dark sunglasses.

"Very funny," he said icily. "Which one of you is Mr. Taylor?"

His question was met with silence, and he frowned in irritation. "I'm looking for the owner," he said through gritted teeth.

"Well, why didn't you say so," the worker in sunglasses spoke again, the husky voice now even more amused. The baseball cap was flipped off, releasing a cascade of strawberry blond hair caught back in a pony-tail. She removed the glasses to reveal two startlingly green eyes. "You're looking at her."

Nick stared at the woman across from him. Several moments passed while he tried to absorb this informa-tion. And in those few moments Laura Taylor quickly summed up the man across from her. Rude. Arrogant. Overbearing. No sense of humor. Probably a male chau-vinist, judging by his reaction to her gender.

"Laura, I—I'm really sorry."

Laura turned her attention to the young man holding the hose. He looked stricken, and she reached out and gripped his shoulder comfortingly. "It's okay, Jimmy. No permanent damage was done. But those azaleas could use some more water. Why don't you finish up over there." She turned to the other two men. "I'll be with you guys in a few minutes. Just do what you can in the meantime."

They nodded and headed back to work, leaving Laura alone with the stranger. She tilted her head and looked up at him, realizing just how tall he was. At five-eight, she wasn't exactly petite, but this man made her feel...vulnerable. It was odd...and unsettling. And it was also ridiculous, she told herself sharply.

"What can I do for you?" she asked, more curtly than she intended.

Nick stared down into the emerald green eyes that now held a hint of defiance. How had he failed to notice, even from a distance, that one of the workers was a woman? Sure, the glasses and the cap had effectively

hidden two of her best features, but the lithe, willowy figure definitely did not belong to a man!

Laura saw the quick, discreet pass his eyes made over her body, and she resented it. She put her hands on her hips and glared at him. "Look, mister, I don't have all day. I've got a lot of work to do."

It suddenly occurred to Nick just what kind of work she was doing, and he frowned. "You shouldn't be trying to move that boulder," he said. "Why isn't he doing the heavy work?" He gestured toward Jimmy, the young man with the hose.

The question took Laura by surprise, and she answered without even considering the appropriateness of the query. "He's only sixteen. It's too much for him."

"And it's not for you?"

"I'm used to this kind of work. He isn't."

"How can you run this company if you're out in the field actually doing the manual labor?"

Her eyes narrowed. "Not that it's any of your business, but we happen to be one person short today."

"As a matter of fact, it does happen to be my business."

Laura frowned. "I'm not following you."

"I'm Nick Sinclair, of Sinclair and Stevens. We're designing the new Regional Arts Center, and you happen to own the firm of choice for the landscape portion, or so George Thompson tells me."

Now it was Laura's turn to be shocked into stunned silence. She stared at the man across from her, her initial elation at the news suddenly evaporating as her stomach dropped to her toes. What had she done? The Lord at last had answered her prayers, sending a dream commission her way, and she'd blown it by insulting the man who held the key to that dream. Why couldn't she have overlooked his bad manners long enough to find out his business?

Nick saw the conflicting emotions cross her face, debated the merits of trying to put her at ease and decided against it. Let her sweat it out. He certainly was. From what he'd seen so far, he wasn't impressed with Taylor Landscaping. Not by a long shot. He'd started the day off with the disorganized receptionist and then arrived on the scene to find that half of the crew consisted of a high school kid and a woman. Not a promising first impression.

Nick remained silent, his arms crossed. He noted the flush of color on her face, the look of despair in her eyes, the nervous way she bit her lower lip. His resolve began to waver. After all, he was the one who had appeared on the scene uninvited and disrupted what otherwise seemed to be a relatively smooth operation. And then he'd behaved arrogantly over a simple mistake. Not to mention his reaction to the discovery that a woman owned Taylor Landscaping. What had come over him? He wasn't a chauvinist. At least, he didn't think he was. But this woman sure must think so, and he couldn't blame her.

Nick had just decided that maybe an apology was in order when the woman across from him took a sudden deep breath, distractedly brushed a few stray wisps of hair back from her face and fixed those green eyes unflinchingly on his darker ones.

"Do you think it might be a good idea if we start over?"

"It couldn't hurt."

A quick look of relief crossed her face. She wiped her hand on her jeans and held it out. "Mr. Sinclair, I'm Laura Taylor. And as you've already discovered, I own Taylor Landscaping."

Nick took the hand that was offered, surprised by the firmness of the grip.

"Look, I'm sorry about that," she said, gesturing vaguely in the direction of the embarrassing water spot. "I guess Jimmy didn't hear you coming up behind him because of the jackhammer."

"Maybe not, but isn't sixteen a little young to be working in a crew like this?" he asked pointedly.

As if to say, can't you afford more experienced help, Laura thought.

She bit back her first reaction, then shrugged. "I hired Jimmy through Christian Youth Outreach. Have you heard of it?"

"No, I don't think so."

She sighed. "Unfortunately, not enough people have. It's an organization that provides support for young people from troubled homes," she explained. "A lot of the kids have been abused. Anyway, Jimmy is part of a work-study program sponsored by Outreach. He just works for me part-time, to earn money for college." She looked over at him, a frown marring her brow. "He'll need all the help he can get. I'm just doing my bit."

Nick felt embarrassed now by his question. He took a closer look at the woman across from him. She was older than he'd first thought. Early thirties, probably. A fan of barely perceptible lines radiated out from her eyes, and there were faint shadows under her lower lashes. Although she'd stopped frowning, slight creases remained. She seemed tense and serious, and he had a strong suspicion that she'd worked very hard to get where she was. Yet she still found time to help others. All of which was admirable. But it didn't alleviate his concerns about Taylor Landscaping's role in the Regional Arts Center. Hard work was important, but talent and creativity were the critical components. He still had no idea how her company would fare on that score, and he had to find out before he made any commitments.

"Ms. Taylor, I suggest that we defer our discussion about the Regional Arts Center to another time. You're obviously busy, and—" he glanced at his watch with a frown "—I'm late for a meeting. How about tomorrow at one?"

"That would be fine."

He withdrew a business card from his pocket and handed it to her. "Sorry for the interruption today."

"And I'm sorry about that." Again she gestured vaguely toward his slacks.

"Well, as someone suggested, I'll just say I had an accident."

Laura caught the faint teasing tone in his voice and looked at him in confusion. Was this the same arrogant man who had been ranting at them less than ten minutes ago? It didn't seem possible.

Unsure how to respond, she chose not to. Instead, she reached back and twisted her hair up, securing it firmly under the baseball cap before once more settling the dark glasses on the bridge of her nose.

"I'll see you tomorrow, then."

Nick was taken aback by her abrupt goodbye, and watched for a moment as she strode back toward her crew. Despite the fact that she'd been unfailingly polite once the purpose of his visit had been revealed, she obviously didn't like him. His attempt to lighten the mood at their parting had been clearly rebuffed. As he turned toward his car, the jarring reverberations of the jackhammer started up again, and the headache he'd had earlier returned with a vengeance.

The partnership of Taylor Landscaping and Sinclair and Stevens was definitely off to a rocky start.

Chapter Two

Nick turned sharply, swinging neatly into his reserved parking space. As he set the brake, he glanced at his watch with a frown. He was twenty minutes late for his meeting with Laura Taylor, and judging by the unfamiliar, older-model hatchback in the small parking lot, she was waiting for him.

For some odd reason, he still felt off balance from their meeting the previous day. From the moment he'd arrived at the job site, things had gone wrong. And being twenty minutes late for their meeting today wasn't going to help.

Nick strode into the reception area and stopped at the desk to pick up his messages.

"Laura Taylor is here," the woman behind the desk told him, confirming his assumption about the Toyota's owner. "I was going to have her wait here, but when you weren't back at one Jack came out and got her. I think they're in his office."

"Thanks, Connie. Did any of these sound urgent?" he asked, waving the stack of pink message slips in his hand.

"No. I told everyone it would probably be late afternoon before you got back to them."

"Thanks. Would you handle my calls until Ms. Taylor leaves?"

"Sure."

Nick heard the sound of voices from Jack's office as he paused at his desk to deposit his briefcase. He couldn't make out the conversation, but Jack's sudden shout of laughter told him that his partner and Laura Taylor had hit it off. Good. Maybe if Jack had kept her entertained, she'd be less judgmental about his tardiness. He shrugged out of his jacket, rolled up the sleeves of his crisp white cotton shirt and loosened his tie, flexing the muscles in his shoulders. He wasn't in the mood for another encounter with Laura Taylor, not after the marathon lunch meeting he'd just attended with a difficult client, but he didn't have a choice.

As Nick approached Jack's office, the sounds of an animated conversation grew louder. Through the open door he could see half of Jack, who was leaning against his desk, ankles crossed and arms folded over his chest. But he gave his partner only a passing glance, directing his attention to Laura Taylor instead. She was sitting in one of the chairs by the desk, angled slightly away from him, legs crossed, her attention focused on Jack. Nick stopped walking, taking a moment to watch her unobserved. She was dressed the same as yesterday, in worn jeans and a blue cotton work shirt, her feet encased in heavy tan work boots. The baseball cap was missing, and her hair was once again caught back in a ponytail, the severe hairstyle emphasizing the fine bone structure of her face. Her full cotton shirt was neatly tucked in, a hemp belt encircling a waist that seemed no more than a hand span in circumference. The worn jeans molded themselves to her long, shapely legs like a second skin, he thought as his eyes leisurely traced their contours. It suddenly occurred to him that even in this workmanlike attire, Laura Taylor radiated more femininity than most of the women he knew, freshly manicured and dressed in designer clothes.

Manicures were obviously not part of Laura Taylor's life, he thought as his gaze moved to the hands that rested quietly on the arms of her chair. He remembered the strength of her handshake, and noted with surprise the long, slender fingers. Her nails were cut short and left unpolished, and her hands looked somewhat work worn. He thought again about her struggle with the boulder yesterday, and frowned. She was too fragile looking for that kind of work. He eyed her more critically, noting that despite her fabulous shape, she bordered on being too thin. The dark shadows under her eyes that he'd noticed yesterday were still there, speaking eloquently of tension and hard work and lack of rest. A powerful, unexpected twinge deep inside brought a frown to his face. Now what was that all about? he wondered, jamming a hand into the pocket of his slacks.

The sudden movement caught Laura's attention, and her gaze swung to the doorway. The image she saw was not comforting. Nick Sinclair stood frowning at her, and her stomach began to churn. She was painfully aware of the poor impression she'd made on him yesterday, but at least he'd agreed to meet with her today. She couldn't blow it. She couldn't! *Please, God, let him give me a chance with this project,* she prayed silently.

Nick's eyes locked on hers, and she returned the gaze unflinchingly, although it took all of her willpower.

Based on his expression, it appeared that he might already have had second thoughts about using her company, she thought dispiritedly. He was an intimidating figure, even in shirtsleeves. The angular planes of his face and prominent cheekbones held a no-nonsense look, and his dark eyes seemed fathomless—and unreadable. At the same time, there was an almost tangible magnetism about him that seemed somehow... unsettling.

Jack, sensing the change in mood, leaned forward to look out the door.

"Nick! Come on in. Laura and I were just getting acquainted."

Nick tore his eyes away from the deep green ones locked on his. "Sorry about the delay. My lunch meeting took a lot longer than I expected. I hope the wait doesn't inconvenience you," he said, turning his attention back to Laura.

Laura struggled to present an outward facade of calm as questions and doubts raced through her mind. Had he changed his mind about giving her a chance? Was her behavior yesterday going to cause her to lose this job? Were his chauvinistic attitudes going to work against her? She struggled to control her inner turmoil, and when at last she spoke her voice sounded cool and composed.

"No. I've enjoyed chatting with Jack. I'm just going back to the job site when I finish here."

"Still one person short?"

"Yes."

He nodded curtly. "Then let's try to make this as brief as possible." He turned back to his partner. "Do you want to sit in, Jack?"

"I'd like to, but I have a two o'clock that I need to prepare for."

"Okay. Ms. Taylor, why don't we go into the conference room? There's more space to spread out the plans," Nick smoothly suggested.

"It's Mrs.," she corrected him, noting that his eyes automatically dropped to her left hand, which displayed no ring. "I'm ready whenever you are," she said, ignoring the question implicit in his look. She reached for the portfolio beside her chair and stood. "Jack, it was nice meeting you," she said, holding out her hand. Her voice was tinged with a husky warmth Nick had never heard before, and he noted that they were on a first-name basis.

"My pleasure."

Nick stepped aside for her to pass, catching Jack's eye as he did so. Jack grinned and gave a thumbs-up signal, but Nick just gave a slight shrug. Jack might have been impressed with Laura Taylor personally, but Nick was more interested in her abilities as a landscaper.

He followed her down the hall, conscious of a faint, pleasing fragrance that emanated from her hair. Again he felt a disturbing stirring deep within, which irritated him. "Right here," he said, more sharply than he intended. She shot him a startled look. "Go on in and I'll grab the plans from my office," he added, purposely gentling his tone.

She nodded and disappeared inside. He returned to his office, pausing to lean on his desk, palms down, and take a deep, steadying breath. For some reason, Laura Taylor had the oddest effect on him. She seemed so cool and composed, so strong and independent, yet she'd shown moments of touching vulnerability—yesterday when she'd found out who he was, and just now when he'd spoken to her in an unexpectedly harsh tone.

He couldn't quite get a handle on her. She was a small-business owner, apparently with enough smarts to weather the many pitfalls inherent in that situation. You had to be tough to survive, and he had seen the results of that struggle in many of the women he dated. He was inherently drawn to women who displayed independence, toughness, intelligence and drive. Women who were savvy and sophisticated in the business world, but who knew exactly what buttons to push to turn him on after hours. The only problem now was that these very qualities seemed to make his relationships mechanical, gratifying on a physical level but lacking some essential ingredient.

Lately his thoughts had been turning to a more serious involvement, to marriage and the kind of family Jack had. The only problem was that the women he'd been involved with put their careers first and relationships second. Like Clair. He was beginning to feel as if he was just one more appointment on her calendar. Their dates were always penciled in, and it was understood that if a business conflict arose, the personal commitment would be sacrificed. Nick understood that—he'd lived that way himself for the past ten years—but now he wanted—needed—something more. Once or twice he'd thought about suggesting marriage to Clair, but he'd never been able to bring himself to do it. Because, while he admired her and was physically attracted to her, he knew deep in his heart that she would never put her first priority on their relationship—as he intended to do with the woman he married. As a result, he saw her less and less. She was so busy with her own independent life that he sometimes wondered if she even noticed that he rarely called anymore.

Nick walked over to the window and ran his fingers through his hair, uncertain why his emotional dilemma had surfaced just now, in the midst of a business meeting. He supposed Laura Taylor had triggered it in some way, but he wasn't sure why. Maybe it was those intriguing glimpses of vulnerability, a surprising contrast to her usual businesslike demeanor. That vulnerability wasn't something he usually saw in the professional women of his acquaintance. Yet she obviously didn't let it get in the way of her business.

Impatiently Nick walked over to his desk and picked up the rolls of plans. An analysis of Laura Taylor's psyche was not on his agenda today, he told himself firmly.

Laura was grateful to have a few moments alone. It gave her a chance to compose herself and prepare for her next encounter with the unpredictable Nick Sinclair. She had no idea why he'd spoken to her so sharply just now. But she did know that this job was a once-in-a-lifetime opportunity, and she *had* to get it. *She* knew she could handle it—the question was, how could she convince the man in the next room?

As she often did when faced with a question or situation or decision that baffled her, Laura closed her eyes and opened her mind and heart to the One who had guided her so well in the past. Her faith had always been important to her, but only in the difficult years, when it had been put to the test, had she realized how powerful an anchor it could be. It had provided calm in the midst of turbulence, hope in the face of despair. She had learned to accept God's will without always understanding it, and she knew that whatever happened today was part of His plan for her. All she could do was her best and leave the rest in His hands.

Laura took a deep breath and opened her eyes. The panic was gone, and she felt ready to once more face the intimidating Nick Sinclair.

By the time Nick returned, Laura was bent over studying the model of the Regional Arts Center. She straightened up when she heard him enter, impressed despite herself by the clever integration of contemporary and classical features. "Very nice," she remarked.

"Thanks."

With an unconscious grace, she moved around the conference table and unzipped the portfolio that lay there, taking another deep, steadying breath before she spoke.

"I think it makes sense for us to be honest with each other about the possibility of working together. I realize that you probably have no idea of the capabilities of Taylor Landscaping, and based on our encounter yesterday I have the distinct impression that our services are being—to put it bluntly—shoved down your throat. So I thought it might be helpful for you to see some examples of our work. I've brought some drawings and photographs of some of our jobs over the past two years. While there's nothing in here on the scale of the Regional Arts Center, I have every confidence that we can do an exceptional job for you. I've also brought a list of all of our jobs since the business began six years ago, as well as a review of my academic and professional credentials."

As she talked, Laura arranged the contents of her portfolio on the table, keeping her eyes averted from the man across from her. Last night, as she'd prepared for bed, she'd had a chance to think about their encounter yesterday. It had become clear to her that Nick Sinclair was probably extremely uncomfortable with the whole arrangement. If he was like most architects, he had established relationships with a group of proven, reliable contractors. Naturally, for a prestigious job like the Regional Arts Center he would have preferred to use one of those firms. Laura understood that. She also understood that he might still do so, providing he could justify it to George Thompson and the Arts Center board. So she had come prepared. This commission was vitally important to her business, and she wasn't about to let it slip away without a fight. She carefully finished arranging the contents of her portfolio on the table before she spoke again.

"Now, what would you like to see first?" she asked, looking up at last.

Nick Sinclair's attention was entirely focused upon her now. His grim expression made her feel uncomfortable, as if he was sure she'd never measure up. She dropped her eyes, a faint flush staining her cheeks.

Nick saw the look on her face and slowly settled himself on the edge of the conference table across from her. He opened his mouth to speak, then closed it. This project obviously meant as much to her as it did to him—maybe more, he thought, his jaw tightening as he once again pictured her struggling with the boulder.

"Let's look at some of the photos first," he suggested quietly.

Laura glanced up, their eyes locked and she saw nothing but sincerity. Maybe he'd give her a fair chance after all, she thought, pulling the photos toward her.

They worked their way through the photos and the designs, and then Nick quickly scanned the list of projects, spending more time on the sheet with her credentials. He was impressed by her background and by the quality of the jobs Taylor Landscaping had done, but he still wasn't honestly convinced that her firm could handle a job the magnitude of the Arts Center.

"What I've seen here looks very good," he said carefully, his eyes meeting hers as he handed back her list of credentials. "But most of what you've done is residential work, with the exception of a few small commercial jobs. Do you really think you're equipped to handle the Arts Center?"

"Yes," she said steadily. "I realize we'll have to expand. I've been wanting to do that anyway, but I was waiting for the right commission to come along. And as for our ability to do the design itself, all I'm really asking for is a chance to give you some ideas. I won't even charge for spec time."

"No one is asking you to work for free."

"I'll do anything it takes to convince you that we can handle this job," she said steadily, her gaze locked on his.

She wants this assignment so much, Nick realized with a sharp pang of sympathy. He knew what it felt like to be in that position. But earnestness didn't guarantee talent or results, he reminded himself.

"Suppose we take a look at the plans," he suggested. "You've already seen the model, and I'll fill you in on the terrain."

"I've already been to the site," she informed him.

He looked at her in surprise. "You have?"

She nodded. "This morning. I knew where it was

from all the articles in the paper, so I went over there early and walked around a bit. But I had no idea what you have in mind architecturally, or even what direction you want the building to face, so I need to see the plans before I can talk intelligently about the landscaping."

Nick nodded, impressed by her initiative. "Of course." He unrolled one of the elevations, and for the next two hours they worked their way through the plans. Laura's questions were astute, and the preliminary ideas she voiced were intelligent, appropriate and interesting. She took extensive notes as they talked, and Nick couldn't help notice the enthusiastic sparkle in her lovely green eyes.

When the last of the elevations had been rerolled, Laura leaned back in her chair. "I'm impressed," she said honestly. "It's a spectacular building, and I like the use of natural materials. This will lend itself beautifully to landscaping that features native plants and trees. I can just imagine the entrance in the spring if we do a design with dogwoods and azaleas and redbuds. And the reflecting pool in front could be flanked with gardens that feature seasonal flowers." She paused thoughtfully, and then looked over at Nick. "Those are just preliminary thoughts, of course. I'd like to get some rough designs on paper and then meet with you again before you make a decision on your landscaper."

Despite her calm, professional tone, Nick saw the strain around her mouth and eyes, and could sense the tenseness in her body as she waited for his answer. He had a totally illogical urge to reach over and smooth away the smudges under her lower lashes with his thumb, which he firmly stifled.

She's married, for heaven's sake, he chastised himself. Get a grip, pal. That's really not your style.

He cleared his throat and forced himself to glance away from those mesmerizing eyes. "That would be fine," he said, gathering up the plans. "I'll have a set of prints run for you. When would you like to get together again?"

"How about a week from today?"

He looked up in surprise. "Will that give you enough time?"

She shrugged. "Enough to do some preliminary work. It won't be detailed, but it should be sufficient for you to decide whether you want my firm for this job."

"All right. Should we try one o'clock again?"

"That will be fine."

"And next time I promise to be punctual," he said, his eyes twinkling.

She gave him a fleeting smile and then shrugged. "I enjoyed chatting with Jack. He's a nice guy."

"Give me a minute and I'll have those copies made for you."

By the time he returned, Laura had gathered up all of her material. He handed her the copies and she slipped them inside the portfolio, zipping it before extending her hand.

"Thank you, Mr. Sinclair. I appreciate the chance you're giving me."

"It's my pleasure. I do have one favor to ask, though."

"Yes?" she asked quizzically.

"Could we use first names? This Mr. and Mrs. business is too formal for me."

She shrugged. "Sure."

He smiled. "Good. Then I'll see you next week, Laura."

Three nights later, the phone's persistent ringing finally penetrated Laura's awareness. She sat bent over the drawing board in a corner of her living room, working on the Regional Arts Center designs, and had no time for social calls. And it had to be a social call, she thought when a quick glance at her watch showed that it was after seven. So she ignored it and went back to work.

An hour and a half later, the doorbell rang. Laura looked up and sighed. She'd promised designs in a week with full knowledge that the commitment would appreciably lengthen her already long work days. But they were going to be even longer if she had too many interruptions.

The bell rang again, and this time the caller kept the button depressed. With a frown Laura slid off the stool where she'd been perched and, massaging her neck muscles with one hand, made her way to the door. Her eyes widened when she glanced through the peephole.

"Sam!" she said, swinging the door open. "This is a surprise! Come in."

The slim, fashionably dressed woman on the other side sauntered over the doorway and glanced around. "Have you had your phone fixed yet?"

"My phone?" Laura asked blankly, shutting and bolting the door.

"Well, it must be out of order. I keep calling, and it just keeps ringing. And you're obviously here."

"Oh." Laura's face flooded with color. "Sorry," she said apologetically. "I just didn't pick up. I'm on a deadline for what could be the commission that will finally put Taylor Landscaping on the map, and I just don't have time for anything else until next week."

"Including food?" Sam asked.

"I've been eating," she hedged.

"What did you have for dinner?"

"Well, I haven't had dinner yet," Laura admitted. As Sam pointedly glanced at her watch, her shoulder-length red hair swung across her face. "May I ask at just what hour you plan to dine?"

"When I get hungry."

"You're not hungry yet? You must have had a big lunch," Sam persisted.

"Not exactly." Suddenly Laura realized she felt ravenous. She'd eaten only an apple for lunch, and that had been hours ago. As enticing smells emanated from the brown sack that Sam held Laura felt her empty stomach growl.

"You wouldn't want to share some Chinese with me, would you?" Sam asked, waving the bag under Laura's nose.

Laura grinned. "I could probably be persuaded. Why are you eating so late?"

"I was showing a house and my clients had to poke into every nook and cranny."

"Well, I'm glad you decided to share your dinner with me," Laura admitted as Sam opened cartons and doled out Mongolian beef and cashew chicken, with healthy servings of rice. "Although I never have understood this mothering complex you have," Laura teased. Sam certainly didn't look like the nurturing type, but she watched over Laura like a mother hen. "Not that I'm complaining, you understand. But I really can take care of myself," Laura mumbled around a mouthful of food.

"Right," Sam said with mild sarcasm. "That's why you don't eat right and work such long hours."

"Getting a business off the ground isn't easy, Sam," Laura said, spearing a piece of green onion. "Mmm, this is delicious," she said with a smile, closing her eyes. "Anyway, right now I don't care if I have to stay up every night until two in the morning for the next week. It will be worth it."

"Is that when you've been going to bed?" Sam asked. "How long can you keep up this pace?"

"As long as it takes. Sam, this could be it! You know the new Regional Arts Center that's going to be built?"

"Yeah, I've read about it in the paper."

"Well, I may get a shot at doing the landscaping!"

"No kidding!" Sam said, duly impressed. "How did this come about?"

Laura explained briefly, concluding with the day she'd met Nick Sinclair at the job site. "Although I haven't yet figured out how he knew where I was," she said with a frown.

"I think maybe I can enlighten you on that," Sam said slowly.

Laura looked at her in surprise. "You can?"

She nodded. "Uh-huh. When I stopped by your office the other morning to drop off the book you loaned me, the phone rang and I just answered it automatically. That was the guy's name—Nick Sinclair. He asked for *Mr.* Taylor and didn't seem to take my amusement too kindly. Anyway, your job schedule was right there, and I didn't think it would hurt to give him the address. You know," she said thoughtfully, "he was pretty heavy-handed, but he did have a really intriguing voice. What does he look like?"

Laura frowned. "I don't know," she said with a shrug. "He's attractive enough, I guess. Mid to late thirties, pretty tall, dark hair, high cheekbones, brown eyes. But to be honest, Sam, I've been so intimidated the two times we've met it's everything I can do to speak coherently let alone take inventory. After all, we didn't exactly get off to a good start," she said, a touch of irony in her voice.

"Hmm" was all Sam said.

"What does that mean?" Laura asked suspiciously.

Sam shrugged. "Nothing. But do me a favor, kiddo. Next time, take inventory."

"Why?"

"Why do you think?" she asked with an exasperated sigh.

"Sam, for all I know the man is married! Besides, we've been over this before," Laura warned.

"Yes, and I still haven't changed my mind. After all, it's been nearly ten years, for Pete's sake! You could do with some male companionship."

"I can do *without* it," she said emphatically.

Sam sighed dramatically. "I wish you would at least make an effort. Is this guy nice?"

Laura frowned. "He wasn't the first time we met. He was arrogant and rude, and when he found out I was the owner his shock was almost comical."

"Well, after all, the man had just been doused with a hose," Sam reminded her.

"That's no excuse," Laura said.

"What about the second time you met?" Sam persisted.

Laura shrugged. "He seems to be a good architect. The plans for the Arts Center are very impressive."

Sam rolled her eyes. "Why don't I just give up? Laura, was he nice?"

Laura remembered the way he'd patiently looked at all the material she'd brought, and then spent two hours explaining the plans, finally agreeing to let her have a shot at the job. But she also remembered the way she felt around him—intimidated and uncertain. "He makes me nervous," she said.

"Well, it's a start," Sam said optimistically.

Laura smiled and shook her head, reaching for a fortune cookie. "Don't get your hopes up," she said, breaking it open.

Sam watched her friend's face turn slightly pink as she read the slip of paper. "What does it say?" she asked curiously.

In reply, Laura crumpled the paper between her fingers. "These things are stupid," she said.

"What does it say?" Sam repeated.

Laura sighed. "If I tell you, will you promise not to make any comments?"

"Sure."

Laura looked at her friend skeptically, and then read, "His heart was yours from the moment you met."

Sam didn't say a word. She just smiled.

Chapter Three

The harmonies of the string quartet could barely be heard above the voices of the crowd, driven under the large tent by a sudden June shower. Nick, alone for a moment, grimaced as he adjusted his bow tie. The late-afternoon air felt unusually muggy and warm, even for St. Louis, and his glass was almost empty. Not that he could stomach much more of the bubbly champagne being served, anyway. Maybe he could find something more thirst quenching if he made a search, he thought halfheartedly. But it didn't seem worth the effort of fighting his way through the dense crowd. Besides, he preferred to remain on the sidelines for the moment. The ground-breaking party for the Arts Center had brought out all of the "beautiful" people, the wealthy St. Louisans who could be counted on as patrons for anything arts related. He'd said hello to all the right people and smiled for the photographers, and now all he wanted to do was go home, shed his tux and relax. It had been a long week. Despite the festive surroundings, his spirits felt as flat as the residue of champagne in his glass.

It was odd, really, that he wasn't in a more upbeat mood. His plans had been given enthusiastic praise in the press, and the ground-breaking party today for the project he'd worked so hard to win should have left him filled with excitement and energy. Instead, he was suddenly bone weary.

Nick's gaze swept over the crowd once more and, with a sudden jolt, he realized that, unconsciously, he was doing what he'd been doing ever since he'd arrived—searching for Laura. That realization also revealed the surprising reason for his glum mood—he had needed her presence to make this party a success.

Nick frowned, honest enough to admit the truth but still taken aback by it. He readily acknowledged that he enjoyed Laura's company. Ever since he'd awarded Taylor Landscaping the job two months ago, he'd seen her regularly as she more fully developed her plans and brought them to the office for his approval. He had grown to look forward to their meetings, to respect her intensity and creativity, and to experience a sense of satisfaction every time he elicited one of her rare smiles.

And *rare* was an appropriate word, he thought grimly, shoving his free hand into the pocket of his slacks. She worked too hard. He'd suspected as much at their first encounter, and the suspicion had been confirmed at subsequent meetings. Not that she ever complained. It was more subtle than that. Like the time he'd asked if he could keep the designs and review them after his full day of meetings, and she'd assured him she could just stop by on her way home from the office that evening about eight to pick them up.

But why wasn't she here today? He knew she'd been

invited, and she deserved a party after the work she'd
put into this project. A chance to get out of her customary jeans and— Suddenly his thoughts were arrested by
a startling possibility. Maybe she didn't have anything
to wear to a black-tie occasion! He knew she oper-
ated on a shoestring, and it was conceivable that her
budget was too tight to allow for frivolities like cocktail
dresses. He still had no idea what her husband did for
a living, although he obviously wasn't involved in the
landscaping business. Maybe he was ill, or out of work,
leaving Laura to carry the burden of support.

"Nick! Here you are! Just wanted to say congratula-
tions again on an outstanding job. I've heard nothing
but compliments from everyone who's looked at the
model."

The familiar voice brought Nick back to reality, and
he turned to smile at George Thompson. "Thank you.
It's been a great party."

"All except for the weather. But it's brightening up
now. Well, enjoy yourself. I'll see you soon, Nick."

The fickle weather had, indeed, changed once again.
Rays of sun peeped through the clouds, and the guests
began to make their way out of the tent. Nick breathed
a sigh of relief as the crowd thinned and his eyes began
to scan the gathering again, this time hoping to spot
a waiter with a fresh tray of something other than
champagne.

His eyes had completed only part of their circuit
when they were arrested by a tantalizing view. A woman
was seated in the far corner of the tent, angled sideways.
Her body was blocked from his view by a tuxedoed
figure, but her crossed legs were clearly revealed under
a fashionably short black skirt. His appreciative gaze

wandered leisurely up their shapely length, his thirst forgotten for the moment. This was the most enjoyable part of the event so far, he thought with a wry smile.

Suddenly the legs uncrossed and the woman rose. She now stood totally hidden from his view by the man in the tuxedo, and Nick shook his head ruefully. So much for that pleasant interlude, he thought.

He was just about to go in search of a drink when he saw the woman attempt to move out from behind the man, only to have him take her arm and forcibly restrain her, backing her even farther into the corner.

Nick frowned. He didn't fancy himself a Sir Galahad, and besides, most women today were quite capable of taking care of themselves in situations like this. His intrusion could only cause unpleasantness. The man was probably her husband or, even worse, someone very important who it would not be wise to offend. Yet he was unwilling to leave the woman unassisted if she actually needed help.

Nick hesitated uncertainly. He watched the woman make another attempt to walk away, moving to one side. The glimpse he caught of her face made the swallow of champagne catch in his throat, and he almost choked as he stared in disbelief. It was Laura!

No wonder he hadn't noticed her earlier, he thought. She wore a black crepe cocktail dress, with double spaghetti straps held in place by rhinestone clips on the straight-cut bodice. The dress gently hugged her figure, ending well above her knees. She was gorgeous, Nick thought, stunned. Loose and full, her hair fell in soft, shimmering waves against the creamy expanse of her exposed shoulders. Her subtle makeup enhanced her picture-perfect features and wide eyes. She looked chic and sophisticated and polished, and she seemed as comfortable here as she did on a construction site.

Nick's perusal was abruptly interrupted as Laura made yet another futile attempt to extricate herself from the man's grasp. His indecision evaporated and he surged forward, adeptly maneuvering his way through the crowd, his eyes never leaving her face. She looked pale, and though poised and obviously trying her best to be polite, he also saw that a trace of fear lurked in her eyes. His stomach tightened into a hard knot, and as a waiter passed, he removed two glasses of champagne from the tray, never stopping his advance.

"Laura! I've been looking everywhere for you. I finally found the champagne," he greeted her, forcing a pleasant, conversational tone into his voice.

Laura's eyes flew to his, and he could see the relief flood through them. "Thanks, Nick. I wondered where you went." Her voice sounded a bit unsteady, but she took his lead gamely. His hand brushed hers as he offered her the champagne, and he noted that her fingers felt icy as she took the glass, holding it with both hands.

The fortyish, balding man looked from Nick to Laura, his flushed face indicating that he'd had his share of the freely flowing champagne. "You two are together? Sorry. Why didn't you say so?" he mumbled, his hands dropping to his sides. Nick saw the red mark his grip had left on Laura's arm and his jaw tightened. "I think I'll go find some more champagne," the man said, glancing around fuzzily.

"Maybe you've had enough," Nick suggested curtly, but the man had already turned and disappeared into the crowd.

Laura carefully set her champagne glass down on the table next to her and took a deep breath. "Thank you," she said quietly.

"I didn't do much." He watched her closely, aware that she was deeply upset.

"Well, your timing was perfect," she replied, a forced lightness in her tone. She reached for her purse, unsnapped the clasp and retrieved a mirror. "I think I'm about to lose an earring," she said, buying herself some time while she regained her composure. She reached up and tightened the already secure rhinestone clip.

She was putting on a good show, Nick thought. But he wasn't fooled. He could hear the strain in her voice and he could see the unsteadiness of her hands. "Maybe you should drink this," he suggested quietly, picking up her glass of champagne.

She looked at it distastefully and shook her head. "No, thanks."

He glanced in the direction of her "admirer." "I guess I don't blame you."

She shrugged. "I don't have anything against moderate drinking," she said. "But I have no tolerance for abuse." Her eyes dropped to the silver filigreed mirror in her hands, and she played with it nervously before setting it on the table. She took a deep breath, and when she spoke again there was a husky uncertainty in her voice. "I do appreciate your help, Nick. I—I'm not very good at handling those kinds of situations."

"You shouldn't have to be," he said, with an edge to his voice that made her look up in surprise. "No woman should."

She was taken aback by the vehemence of his tone, given that she'd labeled him a male chauvinist. "Yes, well, it sounds good in theory." She paused and took a deep breath. "Look, Nick, I think I'm going to head home. It's been a long day."

"Did you work all day?"

She nodded. "Up until about three hours ago."

"That hardly looks like your usual work attire," he said, hoping that the warmth of his smile would ease some of the tension he sensed in her body. "If I may say so, you look stunning."

"Well, you didn't expect me to come in my jeans, did you?" she asked, unexpectedly pleased by his compliment. When he didn't reply, her eyes widened in disbelief. "Or did you?"

"No, of course not," he said quickly. He didn't tell her that he thought she might have stayed away due to lack of appropriate attire rather than lack of taste. "It's just that I've never seen you wear anything but work clothes."

She tilted her chin up slightly, and there was a touch of defensiveness in her voice when she spoke. "Jeans and overalls suit my job. This outfit would hardly be appropriate at a construction site. I don't have an office job, Nick. And I'm not afraid to get my hands dirty."

Nick frowned at her misinterpretation of his remark. "I realize that," he said quietly. "I didn't mean to offend you, Laura. My comment was meant as a compliment, not a criticism."

Laura looked at him, lost for a moment in the depth of his eyes. What else did he realize? she wondered. Did he realize that for some unaccountable reason her heart was hammering in her chest? Did he realize that her breathing had become slightly erratic? And did he realize that neither of those reactions was a result of her unpleasant encounter? Distractedly she pushed the hair back from her face. "I've really got to be going," she said, retrieving her purse from the chair at her side.

"Are you here alone?" Nick asked in surprise.

"Yes."

"Well, can I at least walk you to your car?"

"I'm fine, really. But thanks for the offer. Good night, Nick."

He hesitated, reluctant to let her leave alone, knowing he couldn't stop her. When Laura looked at him curiously, he found his voice. "Good night, Laura."

He watched her thread her way through the thinning crowd, frustrated by his inability to…to what? he wondered. He'd done all that was necessary by helping her out of an offensive situation. Yet he felt she'd needed something more, something he couldn't give. She'd seemed unaccountably shaken by the encounter, and he doubted whether she'd fully recovered. Certainly it had been unpleasant, but there'd been no real danger. Yet he'd caught the glimmer of fear in her eyes, of vulnerability. He wished she had at least let him walk her to her car. And where was her husband? he wondered, suddenly angry. She did have one. Or at least he assumed she did. Yet she always seemed so alone.

He continued to stare pensively into the crowd long after she'd disappeared from sight. Only when he realized that the majority of guests had departed did he rouse himself to do the same. It was time to call it a day.

Nick turned to set his glass on the table, and his eyes fell on Laura's silver mirror, obviously forgotten in her haste to depart. He picked it up and weighed it thoughtfully in his hand, turning it over to examine it more closely. It looked quite old, perhaps a family heirloom, he mused. He'd have to call Laura immediately and let her know it was safe. Hopefully he could reach her even before she realized it was missing. She'd had enough stress for one day, he thought, a muscle in his jaw tightening.

And then an idea slowly took form in his mind. Why not drop it off on his way home? That way he could assure himself that she had gotten home all right and, perhaps in the process, meet the elusive Mr. Taylor.

Nick slipped the mirror into the pocket of his jacket and turned to go, only to find a board member at his elbow. His patience was stretched to the breaking point by the time he could tactfully disengage himself from a discussion of the importance of art to the St. Louis community. Then it took another ten minutes to find a phone directory so he could look up Laura's address. With a frustrated sigh, he glanced at his watch. Seven o'clock. Laura was probably home by now. He *could* just call and let her know he had the mirror, he told himself. There was no urgency about returning it. But somehow that wasn't good enough. He *wanted* to go. And he wasn't going to waste time analyzing the reasons why.

Laura stirred the spaghetti sauce, raising the spoon to her lips for a taste. Perfect, she thought with a satisfied smile. But then, Grandmother's recipe never failed. It was one of those things you could always count on. And there weren't a lot of them in this world, she mused, her smile fading. There was her faith, of course. It had been her anchor in the difficult years of her marriage and the struggle for survival that followed. Her trust in the Lord was stable, sure and strong, and even in her darkest hours, it had offered her hope and comfort. The Lord had always stretched out his hand to steady her when she felt most shaky and lost. Yes, she could count on her faith.

She could also count on her family. And Sam. But certainly not men. Or at least not her judgment of them. How could she have been so wrong? she asked herself again, as she had countless times before. But the answer always eluded her.

As her mood started to darken, Laura fiercely took herself in hand. She refused to become melancholy over a stupid little incident that she'd blown out of all proportion, she told herself angrily. Okay, so the man's steel grip on her arm and the smell of liquor on his breath had brought back painful memories. So what? She wasn't the only one in the world with painful memories, and it was about time that she laid hers to rest.

At the same time, she had made progress, she consoled herself. She turned the spaghetti sauce down to simmer, removed her large white apron and headed for the bedroom to change clothes. Three or four years ago she probably would have been a basket case after that scene. She'd held up all right. Of course, if Nick hadn't come along…

Nick. Her arm froze as she reached around to unzip the black cocktail dress. Thoughts of him were almost as disturbing as thoughts of the unpleasant encounter. Both caused her breathing to quicken and her pulse rate to accelerate. Both made her stomach churn and her legs grow weak. Both made her nervous and uncertain.

But for very different reasons, she acknowledged honestly. Ever since Sam had planted the seed of romance in her head about Nick, Laura had reacted like a skittish colt whenever she was around him. And the explanation was simple. She felt attracted to him. Heaven help her, but she did. There was simply no way to honestly deny it, and Laura had learned through the years that being honest with herself was essential to her survival.

Slowly she unzipped the dress, stepped out of it and made her way toward the closet. When she passed the full-length mirror behind her door she hesitated, and then glanced at her reflection. It wasn't something she did often; for too many years she had disliked herself and her body so intensely that she avoided mirrors whenever possible. She was still much too thin, but at least her self-image had improved enough in the past few years that she could now look at herself without cringing.

One thing for sure, she thought with a wry smile, her job might be physically demanding, but it helped keep her in shape. Her body was that of a twenty-year-old—muscles toned, stomach flat, thighs firm. Joe had enjoyed her body once, she thought, allowing a moment of wistful recollection. At least he had until the problems started and she'd begun to lose weight. Then he'd started making fun of her thinness. And her looks. And her ambition. And her faith.

His loss of faith and belittlement of hers had been one of the most painful things to endure during those last difficult months. As their relationship had deteriorated, she'd turned more and more to her faith to sustain her, finding great comfort in the Bible. Joe, on the other hand, had found no solace there, had laughed when she suggested they spend some time each evening

reading a few verses out loud. It was almost as if he
was jealous of her faith, resenting the consolation she
found there. She had tried to help, tried to share her
faith with him, but he had resisted every attempt she'd
made. In the end, his ridicule of all she had been raised
to believe in had killed whatever love still survived in
their relationship.

A lump formed in her throat, and she forced herself
to swallow past it. The power of love—both construc-
tive and destructive—never ceased to amaze her. Her
faith had survived, but little else had, including her
self-esteem. Even now, more than ten years later, she
was still self-conscious about her body. "Bony," Joe
had called her. She'd gained a little weight since then,
but she was still probably too thin to be desirable. Not
that she'd cared about that over the years. But for some
reason Nick had activated hormones that she'd thought
had died long ago. After Joe, Laura had been convinced
that she would never be attracted to another man. With
a shudder she recalled how the sweetness of their young
love had gradually soured, how in the end lovemaking
had become an ordeal, an act devoid of all tenderness,
to be endured, not enjoyed. Even now the memories
filled her with shame and disgust. It had taken her
years to accept emotionally what she'd always known
intellectually—that Joe's actions had been the result of
his own sickness rather than anything she had done. She
had dealt with the guilt—as much as she would ever
be able to, knowing that some would always remain.
And she had stopped asking the "what if?" questions
ten times a day. But she had never recovered enough
to risk another relationship.

Until she met Nick, Laura had been content to live

the solitary life she'd created for herself, a life where no one made demands of her, no one belittled her, no one hurt her. It was a safe, if insulated, existence. Sam had been after her for years to reconsider her self-imposed physical and emotional celibacy, but, until Nick, Laura had never even been tempted. The idea of opening up again to any man had turned her off completely, and her passionate side was kept firmly under wraps.

So why were her hormones kicking in now? she wondered. Sure, Nick was a handsome man. And he seemed nice enough. After their initial confrontation, he'd proven to be a fair and considerate business associate. But until this afternoon she'd never related to him on anything but a professional level. Not that she should consider today's encounter very significant, she reminded herself. He had simply helped her out of an awkward situation, his action prompted more by good manners than personal interest. Yet the way he'd looked at her, as if he sensed the trauma of the situation for her and cared how she felt, had sent shock waves along her nerve endings and filled her with an almost forgotten warmth.

Laura took a deep breath and closed her eyes. What was wrong with her? Had she suppressed her needs for so long that even the slightest kindness and warmth from a man sent them clamoring for release?

Impatiently Laura pulled on a pair of shorts and a T-shirt. She had to get a grip on her emotions. Nick was a business associate. Period. Her reaction to him was just the result of long-suppressed physical needs. She would never again give herself to a man, now or in the future. It was simply too dangerous. No matter what Sam thought!

* * *

By the time Nick turned down Laura's street, it was nearly seven-thirty. He'd grown more uncertain with every mile he'd driven. Maybe her husband wouldn't appreciate his visit. And the last thing he wanted to do was cause Laura any further distress.

He still felt undecided when he pulled up in front of her apartment. He parked the car but remained behind the wheel, glancing around the neighborhood. Not the best part of town, he thought grimly. She lived in a four-family unit in the south part of the city, on a side street lined with similar brick flats. The buildings in this part of the city were probably at least seventy years old, and judging by the cars lining the street, it was not an affluent area. In fact, the longer he sat there, the more he began to realize that the surroundings were actually a little seedy. He frowned. He'd known money was tight, but she had a nice storefront office, albeit small, in one of the nicer suburbs, so he hadn't expected that she would live in such a run-down area.

He thought of his own West County condo, with its tennis courts and swimming pool and health club, and a surge of guilt washed over him. Nick was certain that Laura worked just as hard—if not harder—than he did, and she obviously had much less to show for it. Even in his leaner years, Nick's life-style had never been this impoverished.

He glanced at Laura's apartment building, still undecided. Why was he agonizing over a simple decision? he asked himself impatiently. After all, the worst that could happen would be that he would be treated as an unwelcome intruder. If so, he could make a hasty departure. It was no big deal.

Determinedly, Nick stepped out of his car, which was attracting interested glances from a few teenagers gathered on a neighboring porch. He felt them staring at the back of his tux as he bent to carefully lock the door, and he paused uncertainly, fiddling unnecessarily with the key. Was it wise to leave the car unattended? But he wouldn't be staying long, he assured himself. He strode inside, found that Laura lived on the top floor and took the steps two at a time.

Laura heard the doorbell and frowned, glancing at the clock. Sam was out of town until tomorrow, so it couldn't be her. Curiously she walked over to the door and peered through the peephole.

Her eyes widened, and with a muffled exclamation she stepped back from the door in alarm, her hand going to her throat. She began to take deep breaths, trying to steady the staccato beat of her heart. This wasn't good. This wasn't good at all. Not after the thoughts she'd just been having. Maybe she could just ignore him, she thought hopefully. Surely he'd go away if she didn't answer the door. But then logic took over. Why was he here? It must be something important for him to track her down at home. Was there a problem with the Arts Center, something he'd discovered after she'd left the party? That must be it, because he hadn't even bothered to change out of his tux. He'd come directly from the party. It had to be urgent.

Laura took another deep breath and stepped forward, sliding back the bolt and swinging the door open. "Nick! Is something wrong?" she asked without preamble.

Nick stared at the woman across from him. Her hair still swung loose and full, but she'd changed into shorts that snugly hugged her hips and revealed even more of her incredible legs than the cocktail dress had. A T-shirt clung softly to her upper body, the sea blue color complementing her hair and eyes. Suddenly aware that the silence was lengthening noticeably, he cleared his throat. "That's not the most enthusiastic welcome I've ever received," he said, flashing a quick, uncertain grin.

"Sorry," she said, flushing as she stepped aside. "Come in."

He hesitated. "I don't want to intrude…"

"I'm just making dinner."

"Well, only for a minute." He crossed the threshold into a tiny foyer and Laura shut the door behind him, sliding the bolt into place.

"Make yourself comfortable," she said, gesturing toward the living room, and Nick stepped into the softly lit room, which Laura had decorated in an English country style. Floral-patterned chintz covered the couches and chairs, and an old trunk served as a coffee table. Baskets of dried flowers and the soft yellow walls gave the room a warm, homey feel. A drafting table stood in one corner, with a wooden desk nearby, and lace curtains hung at the windows. There was a dining nook to one side, separated from the galley kitchen by a counter, and a glance down the hall revealed a bathroom door slightly ajar and a closed door that must be a bedroom.

"You've done a good job with this place," he said approvingly. "These older buildings are hard to decorate."

He regretted the words the moment he said them, thinking she might interpret his comment as criticism, but he was wrong.

"Thanks. It's amazing what a little paint, a needle and thread and some elbow grease can do."

She seemed skittish, not offended, and Nick wondered if her husband was in the bedroom or expected soon. He'd better do what he came to do and get out, he decided, withdrawing the mirror from his pocket and holding it out to her.

"I think you forgot this."

"Oh!" She gasped softly and reached for it.

"I thought you might be worried. It looks like it might be valuable."

She shrugged. "I have no idea about its monetary worth. But it has a lot of sentimental value." Her voice grew soft. "My grandfather gave this to my grandmother on their wedding day." She shook her head. "I can't believe I forgot it."

"Given the situation, I can. You were pretty upset."

She looked at him and took a deep breath. It seemed foolish to deny what had clearly been quite apparent. "Was it that obvious?" she asked quietly.

"Mmm-hmm."

"Like I said, I'm not very good at handling that sort of thing. Would you like to sit down for a minute?"

"The offer is tempting," he hedged, his eyes traveling around the room. "You've made this a very welcoming place." His eyes fell on the dining table and he noted with surprise that only one place was set. So Laura was here alone. But why? He decided to probe, knowing it was a gamble. "It's too bad your husband couldn't join you today," he said casually, strolling over to one of the overstuffed chairs. "That scene probably would have been avoided."

His back was to her when he spoke, and as he turned

he caught the sudden look of pain in her eyes. Then they went flat, and she turned away. "My husband is dead," she said in a curiously unemotional voice. "Will you excuse me for a minute? I need to check something in the kitchen."

Nick felt as if he'd been kicked in the stomach. He had wondered if she was divorced, although divorced women rarely asked to be called Mrs. anymore. Yet the idea that she might be a widow had never entered his mind. He'd satisfied his curiosity all right—at her expense, he thought, gritting his teeth. He jammed his hands into his pockets, his fists tightening in frustration at his lack of tact.

When Laura reappeared a few moments later, he turned to her, feeling that some comment was called for. "Laura, I'm sorry. I didn't know."

She looked at him, startled, as if surprised he'd reopened the subject. Then she shrugged. "No reason you should have. Please, sit down."

Nick hesitated for a moment, and then settled his large frame into a chair, noting that she perched nervously on the edge of the couch. Why was she so tense? Was it his presence that made her uncomfortable? And if so, why? He'd given her no reason to be nervous. In fact, since their first explosive encounter he'd gone out of his way to treat her with consideration.

"Laura, is there something wrong?" he asked quietly, knowing he was taking a chance but willing to accept the consequences.

The deep, mellow tone of his voice had a curiously soothing effect on Laura, and she looked down at the hands clasped tightly in her lap. At last she glanced up, aware that Nick's relaxed posture was at odds with the intensity of his eyes, which seemed to say "I care." And for just the briefest moment she felt tempted to pour her heart out to this man who was practically a stranger. But before the urge grew too strong to resist, she abruptly stood.

Nick seemed taken aback by her sudden movement, but he remained seated, waiting for her to speak.

Now that she was on her feet, Laura was at a loss. It was important that he leave, she knew that much. Never mind that she'd just invited him to sit down. Something intuitively told her that he represented danger. "No, everything's fine," she lied. "Except dinner. I'm afraid it will burn if I don't get into the kitchen." Her voice was pitched above normal, and even to her ears it sounded strained.

Nick remained seated. "It smells good," he said with a smile.

Dear Lord, why couldn't the man take the hint and just leave? Laura thought desperately. But she forced a bright smile to her lips. "Thanks. It's an old family recipe. I really hadn't planned to fix dinner tonight, but I didn't get a chance to eat much at the party," she said, trying to talk away her nervousness.

"Me neither."

Laura stared at him. Good grief, he was angling for a dinner invitation! This was great. Just great. She was trying to get rid of him and he wanted to stay. They were obviously not on the same wavelength. But how could she ignore the blatant hint without sounding ungracious? After all, he had come to her assistance today, and he'd gone out of his way to return the mirror.

Logic told her to ignore the prickling of her

conscience. But good manners—and something else she refused to acknowledge—told her to listen. She sighed, capitulating.

"Would you like to stay for dinner?"

Nick smiled, the tense muscles in his abdomen relaxing. "As a matter of fact, yes." Then, suddenly, a shadow of doubt crept into his eyes, which narrowed as they swept over her too-thin form. "On second thought, maybe I won't. I don't want to take part of your dinner."

This was her out! All she had to say was "Maybe another time," and she'd be safe. But other words came out instead. "Oh, there's plenty. I made a whole batch of sauce and I was going to freeze what I didn't use. It's just a matter of cooking a bit more spaghetti."

Relief washed over his features, and he smiled. "In that case, I'll stay."

Laura smiled back. At least, she forced her lips to turn up into the semblance of a smile. But something told her she'd just made a big mistake.

Chapter Four

"What can I do to help?" Nick asked, his engaging smile making her heart misbehave.

"There's really nothing," Laura said vaguely, still off balance by the unexpected turn of events. A visitor for dinner was the last thing she'd expected—especially this particular visitor.

Nick placed his fists on his hips, tilted his head and grinned at her. "Were you going to make a salad? I'm not too great on cooked stuff, but I can handle a head of lettuce."

Laura found herself responding to his lighthearted warmth, and a smile played at the corners of her mouth. "Well, I wasn't planning to. But since you offered…"

Nick gestured toward the kitchen. "Lead the way."

Laura was conscious of him close behind her as she walked toward the tiny kitchen, and she was even more conscious of him as they worked side by side in the cramped space, only a few inches apart. She suddenly felt all thumbs as she stirred the sauce and put the spaghetti into the boiling water. Nick, on the other hand, seemed totally relaxed. He was humming some nondescript tune under his breath as he worked, detouring occasionally to peer in her refrigerator and withdraw some other ingredient. So far she'd watched him chop lettuce, cut up tomatoes, slice red onion, sprinkle cheese and add croutons, all with a dexterity that surprised her. She had never expected him to be so at home in a kitchen.

"Voilà! A masterpiece!" he exclaimed finally, turning to her with a smile. "I just hope your spaghetti lives up to the standards of this creation," he said with an exaggerated French accent and an aristocratic sniff.

Laura found herself unexpectedly giggling at his comic antics, but her face quickly sobered when she saw an odd expression in his eyes. "What's wrong?" she asked uncertainly.

"Nothing. It's just that you should do that more often," he said quietly, suddenly serious.

She frowned in confusion. "What?"

"Laugh. It makes your face come alive."

Laura turned away, embarrassed, and stuck her head in the freezer on the pretense of looking for something. In reality, she hoped the cool air would take the flush from her cheeks. "Thanks, I think," she said over her shoulder, her voice muffled.

"You're welcome."

Her eyes fell on a package of garlic bread, and she reached for it gratefully. "I thought I had some of this left," she said glibly. "Should be perfect with our menu."

"Looks good," he agreed.

Suddenly the kitchen seemed even smaller than before. Nick leaned against the counter, his arms folded across his chest, one ankle crossed over the other. His cool confidence unnerved her, especially at this proximity. He was so close that if he wanted to he could simply reach over and pull her into his arms, she realized, quickly trying to stifle the unbidden thought. But it remained stubbornly in place, and her heart rate took a jump.

"Um, Nick, maybe you could set another place," she suggested. Anything to get him just a few feet farther away! she thought.

"Sure," he said easily, straightening up and walking around to the other side of the counter. "If you hand the stuff through, I'll take care of it."

Laura breathed a sigh of relief, feeling somehow safer now that they were separated by a counter. "Okay." She stood on tiptoe to open the overhead cabinet, unaware that when she reached up for the extra plate and glass, her T-shirt crept up to reveal a bare section of creamy white midriff and a perfectly formed navel.

Nick took a sharp, sudden deep breath and reached up to loosen his tie.

"Oh, you must be warm in that outfit," Laura said innocently as she handed the plate through. "I'm sorry I don't have the air on. I usually only run it during heat waves. Why don't you take off your tie and jacket?"

Nick swallowed with difficulty. "I think I will," he said, turning away, needing a minute to compose himself. Did Laura have any idea just how attractive she was? Even in shorts, her face now almost wiped free of makeup from the steamy kitchen, there was an appeal about her that he found strangely compelling.

He pulled off his tie and undid the top button of his shirt, slipping his arms out of the jacket and automatically rolling his sleeves to the elbows in his customary fashion. His hand hesitated for a fraction of a second on the cummerbund, and then he unsnapped it. He'd be a whole lot more comfortable without it.

Laura watched the cotton fabric of the shirt stretch across his broad shoulders as he went through these maneuvers, and a profound yearning surged through her. It had been so long, so very long...

With harsh determination she turned away and opened a cupboard to search for some cloth napkins. Her eye fell on an unopened bottle of red wine, a Christmas gift from a client. She'd been saving it for a special occasion. Thoughtfully, she reached for it, then hesitated. Was she asking for trouble? This wasn't a romantic tryst, after all. It was just a thank-you, and Laura didn't want Nick to read any more than that into this invitation. Still, wine would be a nice complement to the meal. With sudden decision, she grasped the bottle firmly and pulled it out. She was already flirting with danger merely by having him here. Why be cautious now?

Laura turned to find Nick in the doorway, and she paused, her eyes drawn to the V of springy, dark hair revealed at the open neck of his shirt. She clutched the bottle to her chest, suddenly at a loss for words, sorry now that she'd taken the wine out.

Nick glanced at the bottle curiously. "I'm surprised," he commented. "After your encounter today, I wouldn't think you'd be inclined to drink."

"I told you, Nick. I have nothing against alcohol. Wine goes great with some food. But I can't tolerate abuse. It freaks me out."

"So I noticed," he said, watching her closely, searching for a clue to the reason why.

Laura's eyes flew to his, then skittered away at their intensity. "Well, shall we eat?" she asked a bit breathlessly.

He took the hint gracefully and dropped the subject, and Laura's heart stopped hammering quite so painfully. Nevertheless, she was sure she wouldn't be able to swallow a bite of food. Her stomach was churning, and even as he held her chair—an unexpected courtesy—she was fighting waves of panic. She was having a pleasant, intimate dinner with a man for the first time in more than a decade—never mind the circumstances. It would have been nerve-racking enough with any man. But it wasn't just any man. It was Nick Sinclair, the man who only this afternoon had awakened her dormant hormones.

Nick sat down across from her and smiled. "Shall I pour?" he asked, picking up the bottle of wine.

"Yes, please."

"Everything smells delicious," he commented, aware of her tension, struggling to put her at ease. "Your grandmother must have been some cook."

"Yes, she was."

"Was she Italian?"

Laura found herself smiling. "Hardly. She just loved to experiment with dishes from foreign lands. And in Jersey, Missouri, Italy is about as foreign as you can get."

"Jersey," he mused. "I don't think I've ever heard of it."

"Not many people have. It's a tiny town in the southern part of the state."

"Is that where you grew up?" he asked.

"Mmm-hmm."

"It must have been nice growing up in a small town. I've spent all of my life in big cities. I grew up in Denver."

"Small-town life has some advantages," Laura said. "But not many opportunities."

"I suppose that's true. So how's the salad?"

Laura looked down in surprise at her half-empty plate. Nick's gentle, nonthreatening conversation had made her relax and she'd begun to eat without even realizing it. "It's very good," she said.

"Well, you don't have to look so surprised," he said in mock chagrin.

She laughed. "Sorry. You just don't look like the type of man who would spend much time in the kitchen," she admitted.

"As a bachelor, it's a matter of survival to learn some of the basics," he said.

As the meal progressed, Laura found that the tension was slowly ebbing from her body. She realized how much Nick's quiet, attentive, undemanding manner had calmed her. With a little prompting, she even found herself telling him about her work with Christian Youth Outreach and sharing her views about the importance of a Christian influence on young people and the difference it could make in troubled lives.

By the time the last crust of garlic bread had been eaten, Laura felt mellow and relaxed, and she smiled at Nick, no longer intimidated or frightened. He was easy to be with, she realized.

"I'm afraid I can't offer you dessert," she apologized. "I don't keep sweets in the house. It's just too much of a temptation."

"Well, I have a suggestion."

She looked at him curiously. "What?"

"How about Ted Drewes?"

Laura hadn't been to the South Side landmark in years, but the famous frozen custard was considered the ultimate summertime treat for many St. Louisans.

Nick watched her surprise turn to delight, and he grinned. "Why do I think this won't be a hard sell?"

She smiled back. "I must admit that I've always had a weakness for Ted Drewes," she confessed. "But it is getting late."

Nick glanced at his watch and let out a low whistle. "Is it actually ten o'clock?"

"I'm afraid so."

Nick looked up and saw the disappointment in her eyes. "Well, this is the peak time for Ted Drewes on a Friday night," he reminded her. "I'm game if you are."

"Nick…are you sure?" she asked uncertainly. "You've already gone to so much trouble for me today…"

He reached over and covered her hand with his, his touch sending sparks along her nerve endings. "Laura, I'm doing this for *me*," he said softly.

She looked into his eyes, trying to read his thoughts, but all she saw was a warmth and tenderness that made her breath catch in her throat. His hand still rested on hers, and she loved the protective feel of it. She'd almost forgotten that a touch could be so gentle.

"Well…in that case…okay," she said, her voice uneven.

"Good." He squeezed her hand and then released it. "I'm parked out in front."

"Let me just get my purse," she said, feeling as nervous as a teenager on her first date.

When Laura reached the sanctuary of her bedroom she groped in her purse for her lipstick and applied it with shaking hands. Then she ran a comb through her hair. All the while Nick's words kept replaying in her mind. *I'm doing this for me.* They made her feel good…and scared, all at the same time. But maybe that was okay, she thought. Maybe it was the Lord's way of reminding her to be cautious and move slowly.

When Laura returned to the living room Nick stood waiting, his jacket slung casually over his shoulder. He smiled as she walked toward him, and Laura felt nearly breathless. He really was a very handsome man. Maybe too handsome, she reflected.

"Ready?"

"Yes."

He opened the door for her and stepped aside as she carefully locked it, then followed her down the steps. When they reached the ground floor she found his hand at the small of her back as he guided her toward the red sports car, which was thankfully still in one piece, he noted.

Laura let him lead her to the car, enjoying his touch, impersonal though she knew it was. She sank into the cushions of the two-seater, the unaccustomed luxury making her smile.

"Nice car," she said, reverently running her hand over the leather cushions.

Nick flashed her a grin. "Thanks. It was a splurge, but we all deserve those now and then, don't you think?" He suddenly remembered her older-model hatchback and clenched his jaw, realizing that she probably had little discretionary income. He was afraid he might have offended her, but when she spoke her voice was friendly and conversational.

"Of course! What good is success if you can't enjoy the fruits of your labors?" she replied promptly. Her tone held no resentment, no envy, no self-pity that her own financial situation was not yet secure enough to allow for such luxuries. She was quite a woman, Nick thought—not for the first time that day.

As always, the lines at Ted Drewes stretched nearly into the street, and a good-natured crowd milled about. Families, couples young and old, teenagers in groups, all mingled. A stretch limo was even pulled up to the curb, but that was not an uncommon sight.

"This place never ceases to amaze me," she said with a smile, shaking her head as Nick jockeyed for a parking place.

"It's pretty incredible," he agreed, stopping by a spot that was being vacated. "We're in luck," he said triumphantly, skillfully pulling into the tight slot. By the time he turned off the ignition and started to come around to open Laura's door, he discovered that she'd already alighted, and he stopped in midstride.

Laura looked at him guiltily. It had been so long since she'd dated that she'd forgotten the niceties. Over the years she had grown accustomed to doing everything herself.

"Sorry," they said in unison.

Laura smiled. "Why are you sorry?" she asked.

He shrugged sheepishly. "I thought maybe you were one of those women who felt offended by men opening doors and holding chairs. I've run into a few who let me know in no uncertain terms that they considered such behavior the height of chauvinism. But my mother did a good job training me, and now it's a habit. If I offended you, I'm sorry."

"No, it's not that," Laura assured him quickly. "As a matter of fact, I enjoy it. I just..." Her voice trailed off. How could she tell him that it had been so long since she'd been with a man that she had simply forgotten the rules? "I'm sorry," she finished lamely, seeing no way she could possibly explain her behavior without telling him things that were better left unsaid.

"No problem," Nick assured her with a smile. "I just want to make sure we're on the same wavelength."

After braving the long line at the order window they returned to Nick's car, leaning against the hood as they ate their chocolate chip concretes, so called because of their thick texture. As they enjoyed the frozen concoction Nick kept her amused with comments and outrageous speculations about various people in the crowd.

"See that guy over there? The one in the Bermuda shorts who looks like he's made too many visits here? He's a spy," he said solemnly.

"How do you figure that?" Laura asked, smiling up at him.

"It's elementary, my dear. Spies are picked to blend in with the crowd. Would *you* think he was a spy?"

"No," she admitted.

"Well, there you have it."

Laura giggled. "Nick Sinclair, you're crazy. Has anyone ever told you that?"

"I've been called a few things in my life," he admitted. "But 'crazy'...no, that's a new one. Should I be insulted?"

"No. You're crazy in the best sense of the word," she said, laughing.

"Well, it must not be so bad if it makes you laugh," he said softly, his voice suddenly serious.

Laura was thrown off balance by the change in mood, preferring the safe, easy banter of moments before. She shifted uncomfortably and focused on scraping the last bite of custard out of the bottom of her cup.

Nick sensed her withdrawal. For some reason, relationships with men made her uncomfortable, he realized. She seemed fine when the give and take was light and friendly, but introduce an element of seriousness or intimacy and she backed off, retreating behind a wall of caution. Why? He felt certain there was an explanation. And probably not a pleasant one. But he was equally sure that at this stage in their relationship she was not about to share it with him. He'd have to earn her trust first. And pushing or coming on too strong were not the right tactics, he warned himself. In fact, he instinctively knew that doing so would be the surest way to lose her.

"Well, I see you've managed to polish off that entire concrete," he said lightly, peering into her now empty container. His head was so close that Laura could smell the distinctive scent of his aftershave, could see the few flecks of silver in his full, incredibly soft-looking hair.

"Uh, yes, I did, didn't I? And on top of all that pasta, too." She groaned. "This was not a heart-healthy meal. And it wasn't so great for the waistline, either."

"You don't have to worry about that," he assured her.

Laura looked at him sharply. "What do you mean?"

Nick was taken aback by her prickly reaction. "It was

a compliment, Laura. You don't have an extra ounce of fat on your entire body."

She looked down dejectedly, playing with her spoon. So Nick thought she looked scrawny, too. And scrawny was not attractive.

"Laura?" Nick's voice was uncertain. When she didn't look up, he reached over and gently cupped her chin in his hand, turning her head, forcing her to look at him. He gazed into her eyes, which suddenly looked miserable and lost, and felt an almost overwhelming desire to pull her into his arms. He resisted the urge with difficulty. "Laura?" he repeated questioningly, his voice now husky. "What is it?"

She couldn't lie, not when his eyes were locked on hers with such intensity. "I'm just sort of paranoid about being skinny," she said softly. "It's not very…very—" she searched for the right word "—appealing," she finished.

Nick frowned. Good grief, did Laura think she was unattractive? It wasn't possible. No one could look like her and be unaware of her effect on the opposite sex. Or could they? he wondered incredulously. She didn't seem to hold a very high opinion of her physical attributes. Yes, she was on the thin side. But most models would kill to have her figure. And he personally preferred slender women. Voluptuous beauty had never appealed to him.

"Laura, you can't be serious," he said quietly, deciding that honesty was the only tactic. "You are a gorgeous woman! You knocked me off my feet today at the party in that slinky little black dress you had on." Usually he didn't lay his cards out on the table so early in the game, but her need for reassurance outweighed his need to protect his ego.

Laura's eyes reflected disbelief. "You're being very kind, Nick, but—"

"Laura, stop it," he said fiercely, cutting her off abruptly. Her look of shock made him soften his tone. "Look, I am not giving you empty compliments. I respect you too much for that. I'm telling you the truth. You are an extremely attractive woman, and if I wasn't looking into your eyes right now and reading the uncertainty, I'd think you were just fishing for compliments. It's almost beyond my comprehension that someone who looks like you should have any doubts about her attractiveness."

Laura swallowed past the lump in her throat and felt hot tears forming behind her eyes. She wanted to believe Nick. Wanted to desperately. But life had made her wary. And you didn't lose that wariness overnight, no matter how kind a person was.

"It's a long story, Nick," she said softly.

"I figured it might be." He casually draped an arm around her shoulders. "Sometimes it helps to talk," he offered.

"Sometimes," she agreed, conscious of the warmth of his fingers gently massaging her shoulder. His simple touch made her yearn for too much too soon.

"But not now?" he suggested.

"Not yet," she amended, knowing she was leaving the door open for the future.

"I'll settle for that," he said. "Ready to call it a night?" At her nod he stood and, extending a hand, drew her to her feet. He kept his hand familiarly in the small of her back as they walked around the car, releasing her only after he'd opened the door and she made a move to slip inside.

"Thank you," she said, suddenly shy.

"You're welcome."

The ride home was brief and quiet, but it was a companionable silence. Only when he pulled up in front of her apartment and came around to open her car door did he speak, glancing around as he did so.

"It's not very well lit here, is it?" he said.

"I've never thought about it," she replied truthfully.

"You don't wander around here at night, do you?" he asked worriedly.

"No. Nick, it's a safe neighborhood, if that's what you're asking," she assured him.

"If you say so," he replied, but he sounded unconvinced.

They walked up the dimly lit stairway to her second-floor apartment, and Nick silently took the key from her hand and fitted it into the lock.

Laura looked up at him, her eyes suddenly sad. She'd had a wonderful evening, an evening she'd never expected to have again. Now she felt a little like Cinderella at midnight as the chiming clock broke the magic spell, knowing that today had been a chance encounter that was unlikely to be repeated.

Nick saw the melancholy look steal over her eyes and reached up to brush a few stray strands of hair back from her face. Laura's breath caught in her throat at his intimate touch, and her heart began to pound.

"You look suddenly unhappy, Laura," he said, his voice edged with concern. "Didn't you have a good time tonight?"

"Oh, yes! I did! I'm just sorry it's over," she admitted. "It's the nicest evening I've had in a long time," she told him honestly. "I just hope I didn't disrupt any of your plans. This was so unexpected."

"Yes, it was. And yes, you did. But I'm not complaining," he said with a gentle smile that warmed her right down to her toes.

"Well…" Should she ask him to come in? she wondered. What was the protocol? Did an invitation to come in automatically include an invitation for more? She'd been out of the dating world too long to know. What she *did* know was that casual intimacy wasn't her style. It went against everything she believed as a Christian.

Nick, sensing her dilemma, solved the problem. He would have liked nothing better than to follow her through that door, to hold her in his arms until she melted against him, to leisurely taste her sweet kisses. But now was not the time, and he knew it.

"I'll see you soon, Laura," he said, his voice strangely husky. "Get a good night's sleep."

Nick hesitated. He knew she was scared. He didn't know why, but her fear was real. And he knew he couldn't push her. At the same time, he had to let her know that tonight's chance encounter had turned into a great deal more than that for him.

Carefully, so as not to frighten her, he lifted her hair back from her face, letting its silky strands slip through his fingers. He caressed her cheek with his thumb, his eyes locked on hers. He thought he detected desire, but if so, it was so tangled up with fear that the two were indistinguishable. Suddenly fearful himself, he slowly leaned down and gently pressed his lips to hers in a brief but tender kiss. He had followed his instinct, which told him to do that. But the same instinct told him to do no more. So with one last stroke of his thumb, exercising a degree of self-control that surprised him, he reluctantly stepped back.

"Good night, Laura," he said with a smile. "Pleasant dreams."

And then he disappeared down the dim stairway, leaving her filled with a deep, aching emptiness tempered only by the tender new buds of a frightening, uninvited hope.

Chapter Five

"I haven't heard you mention our friend, Nick Sinclair, lately," Sam said, helping herself to another potato skin.

Laura glanced around the popular eatery, crowded on Saturday night with singles, and shook her head. "Why in the world did you pick this place?" she asked, the incessant din of high-pitched voices and laughter giving her a headache.

"It's a hot spot," Sam informed her.

"It's a meat market," Laura replied flatly.

Sam shrugged. "Same difference. So how's Nick?"

Laura sighed. "Sam, do you ever give up?"

"Nope," she replied without apology, taking a bite out of a potato skin and chewing it thoughtfully. "That's the problem with you, you know. You've given up."

"Given up?"

"Yeah. On men."

"How is it we always end up talking about men?"

"Because good friends should discuss important things. And men certainly fall into that category."

"Sam, you've been married—right?"

"Right."

"And it was a disaster, right?"

"Right."

"So how come you want to find another man and repeat the mistake?"

"Laura," Sam said patiently. "Just because we married two losers doesn't mean all men are bad. So, we got unlucky. There are plenty of good men out there who would love to meet a wholesome, hardworking woman like you and a straightforward, slightly kooky woman like me. And I bet if we found the right ones, they'd treat us like queens."

"Yeah?" Laura said skeptically. "Well, I'm not willing to take the chance. By the way, how did your date turn out last night? Who was it this week? The accountant?"

"Jay. The engineer. It was okay," Sam said with a shrug. "We went to a movie, stopped for a drink, had a few laughs. You know, the usual."

"No. I don't know," Laura replied.

"You could if you wanted to."

"Maybe," she said skeptically. "Anyway, that's not the point. I *don't* want to."

"That's precisely the point. This may not be your scene," Sam said, gesturing to the bar, "but there are other ways to meet men. I'm not saying you need to go out twice a week. But twice a month would be nice. Just for diversion. How about twice a year?" she teased her.

"I don't have time for diversions," Laura replied matter-of-factly. "But I must admit I'm in awe of your technique. How do you do it?"

"Do what?"

"Find all these men you go out with."

"I *look,* Laura. That's your problem, you know. You don't look. Even when there's a perfectly good specimen right under your nose, do you notice? No. Which reminds me…what about Nick?" she prodded.

"What about him?"

"Do you see him much?"

"When necessary." And sometimes when not, she added silently, recalling the previous night's impromptu dinner and trip to Ted Drewes.

Sam gave a snort of disgust. "When necessary," she mimicked. "Laura, for Pete's sake, you've got to let a man know you're interested or you'll never get anywhere!"

"I don't want to get anywhere," she insisted firmly.

"Of course you do. You just don't know you do. So when did you see him last?"

"Sam." There was a warning note in her voice.

"What? Is it a state secret? I only asked a simple question."

"Okay, okay. Last night."

"Last *night?* As in after work?"

"Yes," Laura admitted. "The ground breaking for the Arts Center was yesterday, and I forgot my mirror there. You know, the one my grandmother gave me?" At Sam's impatient nod, Laura continued. "Well, anyway, he dropped it by the apartment after the party."

"And?"

"And what?"

"What happened?"

"Nothing."

"You mean he just handed you the mirror at the door and left?" Sam asked, disappointed.

"Well, not exactly. Neither of us ate at the party...and he...well, he smelled the spaghetti sauce and...I mean, he did go out of his way. I—I couldn't very well not ask him to stay," Laura stammered.

"Are you telling me you invited him to dinner?" Sam asked incredulously.

"Yes," Laura admitted reluctantly. "But don't jump to any conclusions," she warned quickly. "I felt like I owed him a favor. And besides, he practically invited himself."

"You don't have to justify it to me," Sam assured her. "I think it's great! So what happened then?"

"What do you mean?"

"Laura, it is like pulling teeth to get any information out of you," Sam said in frustration. "I mean, you ate, you talked...then what?"

"We went to Ted Drewes for dessert," Laura offered.

"Good. He extended the evening. Did you have a good time?"

"Yes. Well, sort of. Sam..." She took a deep breath. "I was really nervous," she admitted, playing with her glass.

"That's okay," Sam assured her. "It's perfectly natural. You haven't dated for a while."

"Try fourteen years," Laura said wryly.

"Well, there you go. You're just out of practice. Do you think he'll ask you out again?"

"What do you mean, 'again'? He didn't ask me out this time."

"Laura, you know what I mean."

Laura shrugged. "I don't know. I think he had a good time," she said cautiously.

"Is he attached?"

"I—I don't think so. Sam, he...he kissed me goodnight," she said, her cheeks turning pink.

"And you let him?" Sam asked incredulously. "Well, hallelujah!"

"But, Sam, I'm not ready for this yet!" Laura protested.

"Laura, you're past ready. You're ripe," Sam said with her usual blunt, earthy honesty.

Laura smiled. Leave it to Sam to home right in on the problem. The woman across from her might be too outspoken for some, but she'd been a true friend and a real lifesaver to Laura during the rough times. Sam could always be counted on to remain steadfastly loyal and supportive.

"I'm not sure I'd go that far," Laura replied with a smile.

"Well, I would. So tell me, what does he look like? I assume you've taken inventory by now."

Laura flushed. "Sam, I'm not good at describing people."

"Well, does he look like anyone here?" Sam persisted.

Laura let her gaze roam over the room, first through the restaurant and then through the adjoining bar. "No. I'm not good at seeing resemblances. I told you that... Oh, no!"

"Laura, what is it?" Sam asked, alarmed by her friend's sudden pallor.

"I don't believe this," Laura muttered incredulously, sinking lower into the booth.

"What's wrong?" Sam asked again.

"It's him!"

"Him?"

"Yes. Him!"

"*Him* him?" Sam's head swiveled. "Where?"

"Sam! Will you please turn around," she hissed. "Maybe he won't see us," she said hopefully.

Nick leaned against the bar, swirling the ice in his drink, trying to figure a way to make his escape without looking rude. He fervently hoped that this was the last bachelor party he ever had to attend. They were so predictable and boring. He was tired of the singles scene, tired of going home alone every night, tired of wondering if he would ever find someone to spend his life with, as Jack had. He envied Jack and Peggy their satisfying existence. Sure, Jack complained good-naturedly about being nothing more than a Mr. Mom and a general handyman, but Nick knew he was deeply content. And that was the kind of life Nick wanted.

He let his eyes idly roam around the room, sipping his gin and tonic. His contacts were already drying out from the cigarette smoke that hung in the air, and he sighed wearily. At least there was a no-smoking area in the restaurant, he thought enviously, his gaze sweeping over the crowd. The faces were just a blur until his eye was caught by a redhead openly staring at him. She was attractive enough in a flamboyant sort of way, and he smiled lazily back. For a moment he thought she was alone, and then he realized there was another woman slumped in the booth beside her. Nick could only see the back of her head, but the unique strawberry blond hue caught his eye. Laura had hair that color, he thought. And then he frowned. Could it be her? he wondered. He tried to dismiss the possibility as too much of a coincidence, but he had a gut feeling that it really was her. Should he check it out? And what if he was wrong? Well, what if he was? he asked himself impatiently. He had nothing to lose. He could just make some innocuous remark to the redhead and beat a hasty retreat. It was worth a try.

"Sam," Laura hissed again, this time more urgently. "Will you please turn around? He's going to notice you if you keep staring."

"Too late," Sam replied. "He just smiled at me."

Laura moaned. "Well, will you at least stop encouraging him?" she pleaded.

"You didn't tell me he was such a hunk," her friend said accusingly, still looking over her shoulder. Suddenly she straightened up. "Hey! He's coming over!"

Laura gave her a panic-stricken look, and then searched wildly for an escape. But they were wedged in a corner booth, and the only way out would take her directly in Nick's path.

"Laura, chill out," Sam advised, aware that her friend was panicking. "You spent hours with him alone last night. This is no big deal."

"Maybe not to you," Laura replied tersely, her heart banging painfully against her rib cage. What was she going to say to him? she wondered. Would he mention last night? Oh, why hadn't Sam picked some other place!

"Hello, Laura. I thought it was you." Nick's deep, mellow voice intruded on her thoughts and she slowly raised her eyes. He smiled at her, looking utterly relaxed, dressed in a pair of khaki trousers and a striped cotton shirt. He held a drink in one hand and nonchalantly leaned on the corner of their booth. He looked fantastic, as always, and Laura suddenly wished she'd dressed in something more flattering than twill slacks and an oversize cotton sweater.

"Hello, Nick."

There was a moment's awkward pause while Nick waited for her to ask him to join them and Laura prayed he would go away.

Sam looked from one to the other, decided it was time to step in and salvage the situation and smiled brightly.

"I don't believe we've met. I'm Sam Reynolds," she said, extending her hand.

Nick took it, looking at her quizzically. "Are you sure we haven't met? Your voice sounds familiar."

"Not exactly," Sam said with an impudent grin. "But we have spoken before."

"We have?"

"Mmm-hmm. I've had a spare key to Laura's office ever since she locked herself out a couple of years ago, and I answered the phone the day you called looking for her."

Nick had the grace to flush. "Then I think I owe you an apology. As I recall, my manners were somewhat lacking that day."

"Well, I would hardly have described you as Mr. Congeniality," Sam agreed. "But that's okay. I survived."

"Well, maybe we can start over. After all, Laura gave me a second chance, and I was even more rotten to her," he said with an engaging grin.

"I don't know…" Sam said, pretending to think it over. "What do you think, Laura?"

Laura couldn't think, period. "Sure. I guess so," she mumbled.

"All right. If Laura says it's okay, then I guess it is. Would you like to join us?"

Laura gave her a venomous look, which Sam ignored.

"As a matter of fact, yes. Thanks." Nick slid into the booth next to Laura, and she quickly tried to move over, only to find her progress blocked by Sam who had relinquished just a few measly inches of the seat. Nick didn't seem to mind the close proximity, but Laura was all too aware of his body whisper-close to hers.

"Help yourself to some potato skins," Sam offered.

"No, thanks. I've been eating bar food all night."

"I hope we're not taking you away from your friends," Sam said.

"No. It's a bachelor party, and like they say, if you've seen one, you've seen them all. I was about to make my excuses, anyway."

"Good. Then you can stay awhile. Isn't that great, Laura?"

Laura felt Sam's elbow in her ribs and realized that she hadn't taken any part in the conversation. "Oh. Yes, that's nice."

Nick casually draped his arm across the back of the booth, and the tips of his fingers rested on Laura's shoulder. She tried to move slightly away, but Sam had her wedged in.

"Can I buy you ladies a drink?" Nick asked.

"Thanks. I'll have a tonic water," Sam said.

"Laura?"

"Iced tea, please."

Nick signaled to the waitress and relayed the orders before resuming the conversation.

"So what brings you two to this mecca for swinging singles?" he asked.

"What do you think?" Sam said pertly. "We're looking for men. Are you available?"

Laura looked horrified, but after a moment of stunned silence, Nick chuckled. "Your friend here doesn't pull any punches, does she?" he said to Laura with a smile.

"Sam's pretty direct," Laura agreed. "But that's *not* why we're here. At least, *I'm* not. Sam picked this place."

"And I'm glad she did," Nick replied smoothly. "Otherwise there wouldn't have been anyone to rescue me from that bachelor party. And, Sam, to answer your question, yes, I am." He turned to look at the bar for a moment. "Would you excuse me for a minute? I think the group is leaving and I need to give the groom my best wishes."

"Sure," Sam said. "We'll still be here."

"Will you?" Nick asked quietly, directing his question to Laura. He was aware of her tension and he wouldn't put it past her to bolt the moment he was out of sight.

The thought had crossed her mind, and she flushed guiltily. It was almost as if he'd sensed her impulse to flee, and now he was asking for a promise to stay. But as long as Sam was here, what could be the harm? "Yes."

He smiled at her. "Good. I'll be right back."

The moment he was out of earshot Laura turned on Sam. "Sam, how could you? First you invite him to join us, then you ask personal questions. I'm not only a nervous wreck, I'm embarrassed."

"Why?" Sam asked innocently. "He didn't seem to mind. And you should thank me. Now you know for sure that he's available," she said smugly.

"So what? Available and interested are two different things."

"Oh, he's interested," Sam said confidently.

"How do you know?"

"Because."

"That tells me a lot," Laura retorted.

"Look, he came over here because he thought it was you. The man wasn't exactly trying to avoid an encounter—he arranged it. And when he talks to you there's a soft, gentle look in his eyes that makes me feel mushy inside," she said dreamily. "Yeah, the man's interested."

"Well, maybe the woman isn't."

"Oh, she's interested, too."

"What are you, a mind reader?"

"No. It doesn't take a sixth sense to pick up the vibrations between you two. Laura, you're scared, right?"

"Yes."

"And why do you think you're scared?"

"Because I haven't been around a man for a very long time."

"Nope. Wrong answer, kiddo. Not just any man could make you feel like this. It's Nick. Because you're attracted to him, too, and for the first time in years you sense a threat to that insulated existence you've created for yourself. You're not scared because he's a man. You're scared because he's Nick—a very special man.

And by the way, I approve. He's not only a hunk, he's got a great personality and a good sense of humor."

Nick chose that moment to slip back into the booth, giving Laura no time to respond. She had been about to protest Sam's quick assessment, but in retrospect she had to admit that maybe Sam was right.

"Did you miss me?" Nick asked with a grin.

"Oh, were you gone?" Sam asked, feigning surprise.

"Well, that's a surefire way to deflate a man's ego," Nick replied good-naturedly.

Laura listened with envy to the exchange. Sam was so at ease with Nick, while she was a mass of vibrating nerves. She couldn't even think of any witty remarks to add to the repartee. Miserably she stirred her iced tea. The ice was slowly melting and diluting the color, washing it out to a pale image of its former self. Sort of like her, she thought. Sometimes, emotionally, she felt like an empty shell of the woman she used to be.

"…so I'll leave you two to carry on."

Laura's attention snapped back to the conversation and she realized that Sam was sliding out of the booth.

"Sam!" There was panic in her voice. "Where are you going?"

"I knew you were daydreaming," Sam declared. "I've got to go, kiddo. I have to show a house very early tomorrow morning and I want to be thinking clearly when I meet the client. He's only in town for the weekend, so it's now or never for the sale. Nick, it was nice meeting you." Sam extended her hand and Nick stood, taking it in a firm grip.

"Can I walk you to your car?" he offered.

"I'm parked right at the door," she assured him. "Besides, I just spotted someone at the bar that I know and I want to stop and say hi. But do me a favor, will you? Walk Laura to hers when she leaves, no matter what she says. She's at the far end of the lot."

"Done," he said with a smile.

Laura suddenly felt like an idiot child, being talked over instead of to. "Sam, I'm quite capable of taking care of myself," she said stiffly.

"Now don't get all huffy," Sam said. "If you're with a gentleman, let him act like one. Good night, Nick."

Nick watched Sam leave and then slid into the booth again next to Laura. "I like her," he said with a smile. "Her candor is very…charming."

"I can think of another word for it," Laura muttered.

Nick chuckled. "Come on, be nice. She's obviously a good friend. She's graciously bowed out, leaving you alone with me, and she's made sure you get to your car safely. What more could you ask?"

"That she butt out?" Laura suggested. "Look, Nick, you don't have to keep me company. Actually, I was thinking about heading home. This," she said, gesturing around the crowded, noisy room, "isn't my style, anyway."

"Mine, neither. And as for keeping you company, I wouldn't have come over here if I hadn't wanted to see you."

"That's what Sam said," Laura admitted, her eyes searching out her friend, who was now carrying on an animated conversation with an attractive man at the bar.

"Well, Sam is very insightful."

"But why?" Laura turned her attention back to Nick, truly bewildered by his interest.

Nick placed his elbows on the table and steepled his fingers, staring at her pensively. Then he shook his head. "You amaze me, Laura. I told you last night. You're an extremely attractive woman. I admire your determination. You are a great conversationalist and fun to be with when you're not totally stressed out, which you seem to be tonight. Is it me?"

Laura shifted uncomfortably. "I'm not stressed," she lied, avoiding his question.

In response Nick reached over and captured her fingers. "Your hands are trembling." His thumb moved to her wrist. "Your pulse is rapid. With any other woman, Laura, I might attribute those symptoms to something else," he said bluntly. Then his voice gentled. "But you're just plain scared, aren't you?"

Laura snatched her hand away and groped for her purse, making Nick realize he had pushed too hard.

"Laura, I'm sorry. Forget I asked, okay, and don't run off. Besides, there's something I want to ask you."

Laura looked at him uncertainly. "What is it?"

"Jack and his wife, Peggy, are giving a little party next weekend. Sort of a pre-Fourth-of-July barbecue. I wondered if you'd like to go."

It took a moment for the invitation to register, and then Laura realized that Nick was actually asking her for a date. A real date, not an unexpected, spur-of-the-moment get-together.

"When is it?" she asked.

"Saturday. About four."

"I work on Saturdays, Nick."

"All day?" he asked with a frown.

"Sometimes."

"Maybe that's one of the reasons you always look so tired," he said gently, reaching over with one finger to trace the shadow under one of her eyes. "Everyone needs some fun in their life."

Laura swallowed. "I don't have time. I'm a one-person operation, Nick. Saturdays are a good time to get caught up on the books. Besides, I'm going home for a long weekend over Fourth of July, so I need to make up the time."

"We could go to the party late," he offered.

"I don't want you to miss any of it because of me," she protested.

"Laura, to be perfectly honest, I'd rather be at *some* of the party with you than *all* of it alone," he replied with a smile.

"Well…" Nick was being completely accommodating, and there was no reason to refuse. Besides, she liked Jack. They would be in a crowd, so what could happen? Sam was always telling her to make an effort to improve her social life, and this was a good opportunity.

She looked toward the bar again, just in time to see her friend heading for the door on the arm of the man she'd been talking to. Sam never seemed at a loss for male companionship. Maybe there was a lesson to be learned here, Laura thought. Her best friend had more dates than she could handle and was always telling Laura to spice up her social life. Perhaps, Laura reasoned, the Lord had put her in this uncharacteristic setting tonight so that she and Nick would cross paths. It seemed like an awfully strange coincidence to have happened purely by chance. There must be a message here. And maybe it was simply that if Sam could go out with dozens of men, she could at least go out with one. Taking a deep breath, she turned back to Nick. "Okay," she agreed.

Laura was rewarded with an ecstatic grin. "Great! I'll call you this week to firm up the plans."

"All right." She withdrew her keys from her purse. "I really have to go, Nick. It's been a long day, and frankly the smoke in here is killing my eyes."

"Yeah, I know what you mean," he concurred. He thought of suggesting a quieter lounge nearby, but decided against it. He'd already gotten more than he expected out of the evening when she'd agreed to go to Jack's party with him. He wasn't about to push his luck. "I'll walk you to your car."

"It's really not necessary. Sam's just overprotective."

"A promise is a promise," Nick said firmly.

"Well, have it your way," she capitulated.

Nick signaled the waitress again and quickly settled the bill before sliding from the booth. He reached for her hand, and, short of rudely ignoring it, Laura was left with no option but to take it. Once on her feet, she assumed he'd release it, but Nick had other ideas, tucking it into the crook of his arm. Laura's heart went into fast-forward at the protective gesture. Calm down, she told herself sharply. Nick probably treats every woman he's with the same way. You're nothing special.

As they threaded their way through the crowd, Laura wasn't even aware of the glances directed her way from the bar. But Nick was. He looked down at her, noted that her eyes were focused straight ahead and realized that she was oblivious to the admiring glances. She was a woman with absolutely no conceit, he thought. Actually, she went the other direction in terms of self-image, which wasn't good, either. Why? he wondered for the hundredth time.

As they stepped into the warm night air, Laura drew a deep breath. "I hate those kinds of places," she said vehemently.

"Then why come?"

"Sam likes them. She drags me along occasionally because she thinks it will enhance my social life," Laura joked, sorry immediately that she'd made such a revealing comment. She knew Nick was too attentive to let it pass unnoticed.

"If your social life is lacking, I can only believe it's by choice," he said.

Laura shrugged. "The business keeps me busy," she said noncommittally.

They had arrived at the corner of the parking lot, and Nick finally released her hand, making no comment. He leaned against the side of her car and folded his arms across his chest, apparently in no hurry to leave. Self-consciously, Laura fumbled for the right key and unlocked the door.

"Well...thank you for walking me to my car," she said breathily.

"No problem. I would have, even if Sam hadn't asked."

"I know." And she did. Nick's impeccable manners seemed inbred.

Nick gazed at her shadowed face and his throat tightened painfully. She always seemed so alone, so in need of loving. Without even stopping to think, tired of weighing the consequences of every action, he reached out and drew her toward him, looping his arms around her waist. Laura seemed stunned by this unexpected action and stared at him wide-eyed. Because he was leaning against the car, their eyes were on the same level, and his held hers compellingly, searchingly. At last he sighed. "Laura, what are you doing to me?" he muttered under his breath, shaking his head. He moved a hand up to cradle the back of her neck, rubbing his thumb gently over her skin as he spoke.

"Nick...I don't... You can't..." She drew in a sharp breath, tears of frustration hot behind her eyes. "Look, I'm scared, okay?" she choked, wanting to find a hole and crawl in.

Nick tightened his hold in a manner that was comforting, not threatening. "I know," he whispered hoarsely. "I just don't know why. I would never do anything to hurt you." He pulled her close, and she found herself pressed against the hard planes of his body as his hand guided her head to rest on his shoulder. He could feel her trembling, and gently he stroked her back, hoping she would relax in his arms. He felt as shaky as she did, and he forced himself to take deep, even breaths.

With her cheek pressed against the soft cotton of his shirt, her ear to his chest, Laura could hear the thudding of his heart, could feel his breath on her forehead. She knew she should pull away. Warning bells were clanging inside her head. But it felt so good to be held like this. So good. She would take this moment, take what was being offered, with no questions. A moment to enjoy being held in strong but gentle arms, that was all she asked.

Nick felt her relax slightly. Not much, but it was a start, he told himself. Whatever demons were in her past were powerful, and he'd have to be patient. If he wanted Laura, it would have to be on her own terms and in her own time.

As her trembling subsided, he eased her back, smiling at her with an achingly tender look in his eyes. "Laura, I'm going to kiss you good-night," he said softly. "I want you to know that this warning isn't part of my standard goodnight spiel," he admitted with a quirky smile, "but I don't want you to be scared. Okay?"

Laura hesitated, and then realized she was nodding. It had not been a conscious choice.

His eyes held hers for a moment longer, and then his lips gently closed over hers. Slowly, coaxingly, they began to explore, seeking a response. Her lips were stiff and uncertain at first, but when at last he felt them begin to yield, he intensified the kiss, pacing himself, allowing the embrace to progress only in small increments. Without intending to, without wanting to, she found herself responding to his touch as he fanned into life an ember of passion that had long lain dormant.

Laura didn't know how long they kissed. She just knew that the flame of passion Nick had ignited in her was more intense than any she had ever experienced. His caresses were knowing and sensitive, designed to draw the deepest possible response from her. Laura was not accustomed to such a tender touch. Joe had been her only lover, and she his. Together, through trial and error, they had learned about making love. But long before they had discovered all the things that made it so special, their marriage had started to turn sour.

Nick knew he might be pushing her too fast, and realized he had to stop, but her sweetly tender lips made the blood race through his veins. At the same time, he knew that if he kissed her any longer, tomorrow she might regret her ardent response and cut him off. It was a risk he wasn't willing to take.

With one last, lingering caress, Nick's lips broke contact with hers. Both of them were breathing raggedly, and Laura's hands were pressed flat against the front of his shirt. She stared at him, fear and wonder and uncertainty mingling in her eyes. Nick almost pulled her back into his arms, but forced himself to straighten up.

He opened her car door, and she silently slipped inside. When she rolled down the window, he leaned in and once more brushed his lips over hers.

"Until next week," he said quietly.

"Until next week," she agreed.

Chapter Six

Laura was a little surprised to find a message from Sam on her answering machine when she arrived home, considering her friend had left the bar with an attractive man. But she might as well return the call tonight, she thought with a sigh. Sam would keep bugging her until she had a full report on the evening.

"I've been sitting by the phone waiting for you to call," Sam said eagerly before even one ring had been completed. "So, did my timely departure do the trick?"

"It was a little obvious," Laura said dryly.

"I'm sure Nick appreciated it," Sam replied smugly.

"Yeah, he did," Laura admitted. "He likes you."

"Great. I like him, too. But I'm more interested in how he feels about you. What happened after I left?"

"We didn't stay much longer," Laura said. "By the way, who was your friend?" she asked, more to buy time than out of any real curiosity. She'd long ago given up trying to keep track of Sam's male admirers. There seemed to be an ever-changing cast of thousands.

"Rick? Just a guy in my office. We've gone out a

few times, had a few laughs. Nothing serious. He just walked me to my car. I have an early appointment tomorrow, remember? But why are *you* home so early?" Sam said worriedly. "Did you clam up or do something to discourage him?"

"I said I was tired and needed to get home."

"Oh, great," Sam said with disgust. "I should have hung around, after all. There would have been more action if I *had* stayed."

"No, I don't think so," Laura said slowly, playing with the phone cord.

"What does that mean?"

"Well, he asked me out next weekend."

"And you're going, I hope."

"Yes."

"All right! Now we're getting somewhere."

"He kissed me again, too."

"Well! This is definitely progress," Sam said enthusiastically.

"Sam…" Laura climbed onto a bar stool and propped her elbow on the counter, resting her chin in her hand. She frowned, unsure why she was having so much difficulty discussing this with the uninhibited Sam, who was never shocked by anything.

"Yes," Sam prompted.

"Um, Nick…he kisses…differently…than I've ever been kissed," she said awkwardly. "More…intimately, you know? And what's worse, I—I wanted him to… well, to kiss me even more. Oh, what's wrong with me?" she moaned in despair.

"Absolutely nothing," Sam said flatly. "You're a young, vibrant woman who's been living in an emotional cave for a decade. Frankly, I'm surprised those penned up hormones haven't revolted before now. Look, Laura, enjoy it. There's nothing wrong with physical affection. I understand your need to move forward slowly, and, believe it or not, I actually think it's wise. But at least move forward."

As usual, Sam's straightforward advice sounded logical enough. But move forward…how far? Laura wondered. She had never made love to a man outside of marriage. Her morals and her faith just wouldn't allow it. A few kisses didn't seem that serious. But with Nick, she feared she'd be playing with fire.

"But, Sam, I—I just don't want to get hurt again," she admitted finally.

Sam knew how much that admission had cost Laura. Since the two had become friends nearly eleven years ago, Laura had never talked about the emotional scars of her first marriage. Sam knew they were breaking new ground, thanks to Nick. He'd gotten under her skin, opened some old wounds. She realized that it was painful for Laura, but at least now the wounds would have a chance to heal.

"Laura, not every relationship is built on hurt," Sam said, treading cautiously on what she knew was shaky turf. "You've never said much about your marriage to Joe, but I could read between the lines. When I used to run into you at night school you always seemed so sad. And I saw what he did to you the night you left him," she said, her voice tightening. "You did the right thing by walking away. Randy might have been a bum, but he never beat me."

For a moment there was silence on the line, Sam wondering if Laura would deny the abuse, Laura lost in remembrance.

"Joe wasn't always like that, Sam," she said softly.

"I'm sure he wasn't," Sam said gently. "But some-times people change."

"He just couldn't take the pressure," Laura said with a sigh. "Something inside of him broke, and I didn't know how to help him fix it. He...he made me feel like his problems were my fault, and for a long time I bought into that," she said, a catch in her voice. "But I finally realized that he was sick. I knew he needed help, but it infuriated him when I suggested it. And when he started expressing his anger with violence, I was too scared to push him. Maybe I should have."

"You did the right thing," Sam said firmly. "From what I saw, you might not be around if you'd pushed."

"But what you said before, Sam, about people chang-ing...that's what I'm afraid of. How do I know Nick won't do the same thing? I survived the last time, thanks to you and my family and my faith, but I'm not sure I would again."

"Honey, I don't have the answers for you," Sam said with a sigh. "Commitment means risk, that's for sure. Relationships don't come with a money-back guarantee or a lifetime warranty. All you can do is use your judg-ment and then take your best shot."

"You know, despite my faith, I wouldn't have made it through the last time if you hadn't stuck with me," Laura said quietly.

"Of course you would," Sam said briskly. "You are one strong lady, Laura Taylor."

"Lately I haven't been feeling all that strong."

"You'll be fine. Like I said, don't rush things. Take

it slowly, if that makes you more comfortable. But give it a chance, for your own sake."

Laura lay awake a long time that night. She tried to push thoughts of Nick from her mind, but it was no use. She supposed she'd been attracted to him almost from the beginning, but her well-tuned defense mechanisms simply had not allowed her to admit it. Now that he had made his interest clear, she found that her defenses were not nearly as impenetrable as she'd assumed.

Laura thought back to her early years with Joe. She couldn't remember exactly when the disintegration of their marriage had begun. Joe's growing despondency had been the first sign, she supposed. Eventually he sought solace in liquor, which made him belligerent and abusive, both emotionally and physically. The deterioration had been a gradual thing that had slowly worsened until one day Laura realized that her life had become a living hell. In trying to appease him, to meet his unreasonable demands, she'd cut herself off from family and friends and lived in isolation, growing more desperate every day, trying to make it work, eventually realizing that she couldn't. It had taken a crisis to convince her that she couldn't go on that way anymore. She'd spent days in prayer and soul-searching, but in the end Joe's untimely death had taken the decision out of her hands. Somehow she'd pulled herself together and found the courage to start over alone, but the scars were deep.

With a strangled sob of frustration, Laura punched her pillow, letting the tears slide down her cheeks unchecked. Her stomach was curled into a tight knot, and the taste of salt was bitter on her lips. She had to let go of the past, like Sam said, and move forward—in her personal life as well as with her business. But she simply didn't know if she had the courage to take another chance on love.

By Friday, when she hadn't heard from Nick, Laura's nerves were stretched to the snapping point. He'd said he'd be in touch about Jack's party, but there'd been no call. What was he going to do, wait until nine o'clock tonight, leaving her dangling until the last minute? Or maybe he wasn't going to call at all, she thought in sudden panic.

Laura glanced at the sheet of paper in front of her. She'd been sitting at the drafting table in her office for the past hour, doodling instead of working, and she was disgusted with herself. See what caring about a man does to you? she chided herself angrily. Your emotional state becomes dependent on his whims. No way was she going to let that happen again, she told herself fiercely.

The sudden ring of the telephone at her elbow made her jump, and she snatched it up in irritation.

"Taylor Landscaping," she said shortly.

"Laura?" It was Nick's voice, hesitant and uncertain, and her heart jumped to her throat.

"Yes."

"Is everything all right?"

"Yes. Everything's fine," she said tersely.

"No, it's not. I can tell."

"Look, Nick, I said everything's fine. Let's drop it, okay?"

She heard him sigh. "I don't have the time or the energy to argue with you now, Laura. We'll talk when I see you," he said, and she realized that his voice sounded weary. "Unfortunately, that won't be until next week. That's why I'm calling."

He was canceling their date! Laura felt her heart dive to her shoes.

"Laura, are you still there?"

"Yes," she said in a small voice.

"I'm really sorry about tomorrow night. I talked to Jack, and you're still welcome to attend if you like."

"I'll probably pass," she said, her voice strained. "I have plenty of work to do."

"Laura, there isn't much in this world that would have made me break this date. But my dad had a heart attack Wednesday and I flew out to Denver on the red-eye Thursday morning. To be honest, I haven't really been thinking straight since then. I'm sorry for the last-minute notice."

Laura closed her eyes as a wave of guilt washed over her, and she gripped the phone tightly. "Nick, I'm so sorry," she said contritely. "How is he doing?"

"Okay. It turned out to be a fairly mild attack, but he had us all worried for a while."

"You sound tired," Laura ventured.

"Yeah. I am. I don't think I've had but five or six hours of sleep since Tuesday night."

"Well, don't worry about tomorrow," she said. "Obviously you need to be with your family. That takes priority."

"I hoped you'd understand. Can I call you when I get back?"

"Sure. I hope everything turns out well with your father," she said sincerely. "And get some sleep, Nick. You sound beat."

"I'll try. Talk to you soon, okay?"

"Okay."

The line went dead and Laura slowly hung up the receiver. She felt sorry for Nick and his family, but she had learned one thing. She was letting Nick become too important to her, so important that he could control her emotional state. And that was dangerous.

By the time Nick called Monday afternoon, Laura had convinced herself that, Sam's advice notwithstanding, it would be better if she didn't see him anymore except professionally. She just wasn't ready to trust a man again, it was as simple as that. Now all she had to do was tell Nick—which wasn't quite as simple.

"How's your dad doing?" she asked as soon as he said hello.

"Much better. They're pretty sure he'll make a full recovery."

"I'm really glad, Nick."

"Thanks."

"You sound more rested."

"I got in at a decent time last night and slept ten hours straight," he admitted.

"I have a feeling you needed it."

"Yeah, I did. Jack tells me you didn't make the party."

"No." She played with the phone cord, twisting and untwisting it.

"You would have enjoyed it, Laura. I'm sorry I couldn't take you."

"It's okay."

"Well, I feel like I should make it up to you. How about dinner Wednesday?"

Now was the time. She took a deep breath. "Nick, I can't. I'm going home next weekend for Fourth of July and if I want to take off an extra day I really need to put in some longer hours this week."

"But you have to eat," Nick stated practically. "Can't you spare time for a quick dinner?" he coaxed.

"Nick, I really can't."

There was silence on the other end of the line for a moment, and Laura knew Nick was frowning.

"Maybe I'll stop by one night and we can make a late run to Ted Drewes." There was a note of caution in his voice now.

"I don't think I'll have time. But thank you."

Nick stared at the wall in his office, thinking quickly. Laura was obviously giving him the brush-off. And he shouldn't be surprised, considering she'd admitted before that she was scared. It didn't take a genius to figure out what was going on here. She'd gotten cold feet, decided not to risk any sort of involvement. But he wasn't going to let her go this easily. She obviously wasn't in a receptive mood, so now was not the time to discuss it. Besides, he was sure he could be much more convincing in person. So he'd play dumb, ignore the message being sent, let her off the hook for this date, but renew the attack next week when she returned.

"I understand, Laura. I know how it is when you're trying to take a little vacation," he said sympathetically. "We'll try again next week. I'll call you soon."

"Nick, I—"

"Laura, it's okay," he cut her off. "You don't have to apologize for begging off. Duty calls. Believe me, I've been there. I'll talk to you soon. Take care, okay?"

"Yeah, I will."

Laura heard the click as the line went dead and stared at the receiver in her hand. Well, she'd certainly handled that well, she thought in disgust. Why hadn't she just come right out and said "Listen, Nick, this isn't going to work out. You're a nice guy, but I don't want any complications in my life." Period. That's all it would have taken. Instead, she'd tried the more subtle backdoor route. Unfortunately, he hadn't gotten the message. He was probably so used to women falling all over him that it had been beyond his comprehension that someone would actually not want to date him. Well, the next time he called she'd be more straightforward.

By Friday, when Nick still hadn't contacted her, Laura began to think that maybe he'd gotten the message, after all. But instead of feeling relieved, she was filled with despair. Which made no sense at all.

As Laura left her office Friday night, she was determined to put Nick out of her mind. She'd been looking forward to this rare long weekend at home for months, and she wasn't going to let anything ruin it. Once she got there, she wouldn't have time to think about him, anyway. The Anderson Fourth of July gathering was legendary, drawing family from far and wide for what had become an annual family reunion. Laura had missed several during her marriage to Joe, but none since.

She climbed into her car, depositing a portfolio on the seat beside her. Lately she'd been swamped, but she wasn't going to complain. The lean years were still too vivid in her memory. If she had to work a little more tonight at home before calling it a day, so be it. She'd have four glorious days of freedom after that.

Suddenly her stomach rumbled, and Laura grinned at the message. She'd worked through lunch, and now she was ravenous. With any luck she could have a simple meal on the table within an hour, she thought, placing her key in the ignition.

But luck was against her. When she turned the key, the engine sputtered but didn't catch. She tried again, with the same result. A third attempt was equally futile.

Laura stared at the dashboard in disbelief. Her little compact car might be old, but it had always been reliable. How could it pick tonight to act up? Without much hope, Laura climbed out of the car and lifted the hood. She had some rudimentary knowledge of mechanics, but nothing appeared to be out of order. Which meant that the car would have to be towed to the shop, she thought resignedly.

Two hours later, the mechanic emerged from the garage, wiping his hands on a greasy rag. Larry had been working on her car for several years, mostly doing routine maintenance, and Laura trusted him implicitly. He'd gone out of his way for her more than once, including tonight, staying well beyond quitting time to help her out.

"Well?" she asked hopefully.

"Sorry, Laura," he said, shaking his head regretfully. "There's nothing I can do tonight. She's got a problem, all right, but it'll take me a while to figure it out. I'd come in tomorrow, but I'm taking the family down to Silver Dollar City for the holiday. We've had the reservations for months," he said apologetically.

Laura's spirits sank. "I understand, Larry."

"I'll work on it first thing Tuesday, though," he offered.

"I guess that's the best we can do," she said, suddenly weary.

"Can I give you a lift somewhere?" Larry asked.

"Well…" Laura hesitated, loath to put him to any more trouble. But she only lived a couple of miles from the garage. "If you're sure it's not a problem…"

"Not at all. Just let me turn off the lights."

By the time Larry dropped her off at her apartment, it was nearly eight o'clock. She let herself in, too tired now to even consider making dinner. Besides, she'd lost her appetite.

Dejectedly, Laura sank into one of her overstuffed chairs and weighed her options. Sam would have been the logical one to turn to for help. But Sam had left today for a week's vacation in Chicago. Besides, asking for a ride to the office was one thing. Asking for a ride halfway across the state was another. Even if Sam was here she doubted whether she could bring herself to impose to that extent.

On a holiday weekend like this one she'd never find a rental car—at least not one she could afford. She could take a bus, but with all the stops and time spent waiting for connections it hardly seemed worth the effort. Besides, long bus rides inevitably made her feel carsick.

The apartment gradually grew dark, but Laura made no move to turn on any lights. The gloom suited her mood. She'd been looking forward to this family weekend for so long. This just wasn't fair. But then, life wasn't, as she well knew.

Laura thought ahead to the weekend stretching emptily before her. She ought to call and let her mom know she wouldn't be coming. But she knew how disappointed her mother would be, and she couldn't bring herself to do it quite yet. Maybe her fairy godmother would appear with a coach, she fantasized. There were plenty of mice in this building to turn into footmen, she thought ruefully.

Laura rested her head against the back of the chair and closed her eyes. She desperately needed some R and R. There had to be a solution to this dilemma, but at the moment she was too tired to figure it out. So she put it in the hands of the Lord. *Please help me find a way to get home,* she prayed silently. *I need to be with my family this weekend. Please.*

She must have dozed slightly, because the sudden ringing of the phone jolted her upright. Sleepily she fumbled for the light, squinting against its sudden brightness, and made her way to the phone.

"Hello."

"Laura?"

"Nick!" She was suddenly awake. "Hi."

"Hi. You didn't sound like yourself for a minute there."

"I was half-asleep," she admitted.

"At nine-thirty? That doesn't fit your normal pattern. Are you sick?"

"No. Just tired."

"It's a good thing you're taking a few days off," he said. "You need a break."

"Yeah, well, it doesn't look like I'm going to get one, after all," she said tiredly.

"What do you mean?"

"My car gave out. It's in the shop, and they won't be able to get to it until Tuesday."

"Laura, I'm sorry." The deep, mellow tones of his voice stroked her soothingly. "I know how much you've been looking forward to this. Is there any other way for you to get there?"

"Actually, I was sitting around waiting for my fairy godmother to come and conjure up a coach," she said, trying to keep her voice light.

"What?" He sounded puzzled, and she had to laugh.

"Nothing. You obviously didn't read fairy tales when you were growing up."

"Oh." She heard the glimmer of understanding dawn in his voice. "Cinderella."

"Very good. The only problem is, my fairy godmother seems to have taken off for the weekend, too." There was silence on the other end of the line, and Laura frowned. "Nick? Are you still there?"

"Yeah, I was just thinking. Listen, Laura, I may not be a fairy godmother, and my car may not be a coach, but why don't you let me give you a ride?"

There was a moment of silence while she absorbed this offer. "Are you serious?" she said at last, her voice incredulous.

"Absolutely."

"But…that's really generous of you… My family lives three hours from here," she stumbled over her words, too taken aback by the offer to be coherent. "And besides, I don't want to disrupt your plans for the holiday," she added more lucidly.

"You won't be. As a matter of fact, I was just going to go over to Jack's on the Fourth for a barbecue. I didn't have anything else scheduled. And, to be honest, I'd much rather spend the time with you."

Laura bit her lip. The temptation to accept was strong, given her desperate desire to go south and the lack of any other options. But how could she accept his offer, knowing she was planning to end their relationship? It wouldn't be honest, or fair.

"Look, Laura, I'm not inviting myself to your party. There must be a motel in town, and I'll settle for whatever time you can spare during the holiday," he said quietly.

"Nick, it's too much to ask."

"You didn't ask. I offered."

"No," she said firmly. "If you come, you come as my guest. There's always plenty of room at the house, even with all the relatives there. Mom loves company. It's no problem, and she'd never forgive me if I let you stay at the motel."

"I don't want to impose," he said firmly.

"I think you've got it backward. I'm the one who's imposing. Giving you a place to sleep is small compensation in return for the favor."

"Oh, there may be other compensations," he said lightly.

Laura stiffened. "Look, Nick. Your offer is generous. But I can't accept it if there are strings attached."

"You mean you won't even feed me?" he said disappointedly. "Man, I was hoping to at least get a good, home-cooked meal out of this."

"Oh." Laura was confused. Had she read too much into that last comment? Besides, what made her think he was that interested in her? Sure, they'd kissed a time or two. But that was probably the way he said good-night to every woman he dated. She took a deep breath. "Well, of course we'll feed you. Mom puts on quite a spread on the Fourth. In fact, it's sort of like a Norman Rockwell scene—long tables covered with checkered cloths and loaded down with every kind of all-American food you can imagine."

"Now you're talking," he said enthusiastically. "What time do we leave?"

"Well, I have a Christian Youth Outreach board meeting at eight-thirty. It should be over by eleven. I could be ready by noon," she replied. Somehow the conversation had gotten out of hand. She didn't remember ever saying she'd go with him, and now they were making departure plans.

"Do you need a ride to the meeting?"

"No, but thank you," she said, touched by the offer. "There's another board member I can call."

"Okay. Then your coach will be there at twelve o'clock sharp, Cinderella. We'll grab some lunch on the way. Now go to bed and stop worrying. We're going to have a great weekend," he said confidently.

Laura replaced the receiver slowly, wishing she felt half as confident as Nick sounded. Being in his presence for four days was more apt to be nerve-racking and unsettling than relaxing, she thought. But as long as they stayed around the family she should be safe, she told herself. Besides, instead of focusing on the pitfalls, she should be grateful for his offer. Without Nick, she'd spend the holiday weekend sitting alone in her apartment. She'd asked the Lord for help, and He had come through for her. Okay, so it was a two-edged sword. She was going home, but she also had to deal with Nick. She'd just have to make sure they were never alone, she thought resolutely. Considering the size of the group, that wouldn't be too hard to arrange. Or would it? she wondered, suddenly sure that if Nick wanted to get her alone, he would find a way. And worse, she would let him.

Chapter Seven

Laura was waiting when Nick arrived the next morning, still unsure how this had all come about, still uncertain about the wisdom of it. But Nick seemed to be on top of the world, reaching over to smooth away her frown lines with gentle fingers when he greeted her.

"What's this? Worried? Did you think your coach wouldn't materialize?" he teased.

"No, I knew you'd come. You're a pretty reliable guy."

"Thank you. Then why the frown?"

Laura crossed her arms over her chest in a self-protective hug. She'd wrestled with this problem all night. She knew she should have told him earlier in the week that she didn't want to see him socially anymore, and she should never have agreed to this arrangement. But she wanted to go home so badly, and the offer of a ride had been too tempting to refuse last night. Now she had second thoughts.

Taking a deep breath, she faced him. "Nick, I'm just not sure this is right. I feel like I'm misleading you at best and using you at worst."

"Why?"

"Because…because I…I really don't think that getting involved with each other is a good idea."

Nick felt a knot forming in his stomach. He wasn't surprised. He'd sensed earlier in the week that she was backing off. But he hadn't expected to confront it now.

"No? Why not? Don't you like me?" He grinned at her engagingly, his easy manner giving away nothing of his inner turmoil. He'd been planning to put off this discussion until after the holiday, but as long as he was going with her—and he *was* going with her, no matter what she said—they might as well get it out in the open now.

Laura found herself smiling at his teasing tone. "Of course I like you."

"Well, that's a start."

"Nick," she said reprovingly. "Will you be serious?"

"On a beautiful day like this? Mmm…that's asking a lot."

"Well, could you try for just a minute?"

"Sure. I'll give it my best effort." He settled himself on the arm of her sofa. "Shoot."

Laura moved restlessly over to the window, double-checking the lock she knew was in place. Now that she had his attention, how could she explain her reluctance? "Nick, you remember two weekends ago, in the parking lot?" she asked tentatively.

"You better believe it. It's been on my mind all week."

Laura gave him a startled look, then glanced away, nervously tucking a stray strand of hair behind her ear.

"Well, do you remember what I said about being scared?"

"Yes." Now his tone was more serious.

"I still am. Maybe more than ever. I'm just not ready for any kind of…" She stopped, fumbling for the right word, reluctant to make him think she was jumping to conclusions about his interest in her.

"Intimacy?"

She flushed. "Yes. And I have the feeling that's what you may be after."

"Guilty," he admitted readily.

She stared at him, taken aback at his unexpected honesty. The words she'd been about to say evaporated.

Nick stood and moved in front of her, placing his hands on her shoulders as his eyes locked on hers compellingly. "So now you know," he said quietly. "I like you a lot, Laura Taylor. I think something could develop here. I think you feel the same, and that's why you're scared. I've been completely honest about my feelings and my intentions, because some instinct tells me that you respect total honesty. No games. And I'm also being honest when I say that I realize you have some problems that prevent you from moving as quickly as I might want to. I also respect that. You can set the pace in this relationship."

Laura hadn't expected such a direct approach, and she was momentarily confused. Nick cared about her. He'd made that clear. Cared enough not to rush her. All he was asking her to do was give it a chance. "Nick, I—I'm not sure what to say. You may be wasting your time. I can't make any promises."

"I'm not asking you to. I'm willing to take my chances. Who knows? Maybe my charms will win you over," he said with a grin, his tone suddenly lighter. "Now, is the serious discussion over for the day?" he asked, casually draping an arm around her shoulders.

"Yes, I guess so."

"Good. Then your coach awaits."

Laura still wasn't comfortable. She respected Nick's honesty, and she'd made her position clear, so the guilt was gone. But in its place was a knot of tension so real it made breathing difficult. Because now there was no question about Nick's interest. He wanted to date her; he wanted to see where their relationship might lead. Only God knew why, considering how messed up she was emotionally, but he did. And what was worse, she was beginning to want the same thing. Nick was a hand-some, intelligent man with an engaging manner and an easy charm. But beyond that, he was also considerate and caring and gentle. Or at least he seemed to be. And there lay the problem. Laura no longer trusted her judg-ment when it came to men. She'd made one mistake, and the price had been high. More than she was willing to pay a second time. So where did that leave her with Nick?

Maybe, she thought, she should just take this one day at a time. And perhaps this weekend she should try to forget about heavy issues and just enjoy herself. After all, she'd been looking forward to this trip for weeks. Why ruin it by worrying about her relationship with Nick for the next few days? She needed to unwind, and that wasn't the way to do it.

Nick also seemed eager to relax, she thought as they headed south, through rolling wooded hills and farm-land. He kept the conversation light, chatting about inconsequential things, and even made her laugh now and then. Without even realizing it, she began to relax, her pressures and worries slowly easing as they drove through the restful, green countryside.

"So...are you getting hungry?" he said, turning to her with a smile.

"As a matter of fact, I am," she admitted.

"Well, considering that I haven't spent a lot of time down in this area, Bennie's Burgers is about the extent of my suggestions," he said, nodding to a drive-though hamburger spot off the interstate.

She laughed. "Not exactly gourmet fare, I bet. Actually, there is one place I've been wanting to try. But it's a little out of our way," she said hesitantly.

"Are we on a schedule?"

"No."

"Then let's give it a shot. Where is it?"

"St. Genevieve. It's just a few miles off the interstate."

"Ah, St. Genevieve. The old French settlement," he said. "I was there a couple of times on class assignments when I was getting my degree."

"Isn't it charming?" she said enthusiastically. "My minister's sister opened a tea room there a year ago, and it's gotten some good press in St. Louis. I've been wanting to try it, but I just never seem to find the time to drive down there. Plus, I haven't seen her in a long time, and it would be nice to say hello. We all grew up together in Jersey," she explained.

"Sounds great to me," he said agreeably.

They found the restaurant with little trouble, right in the heart of the historic district. Laura's eyes roamed appreciatively over the charming country French decor as they were led to their table, and after they were seated she turned to the hostess, a slightly plump, white-haired woman with a pleasant round face. "Is Rebecca here today?" she asked.

The woman chuckled. "Rebecca is *always* here," she said, her eyes twinkling. "Would you like me to ask her to come out?"

"If you would. Tell her it's Laura Taylor."

"Mmm, this all sounds great!" Nick said, perusing the menu appreciatively. "And very imaginative."

"Rebecca studied at the Culinary Institute of America and did internships with a couple of the best restaurants in St. Louis," Laura told him, debating her own selection before finally settling on an unusual quiche.

Just as they finished placing their order, a slender, attractive woman appeared at the kitchen door. Her delicate facial structure and high cheekbones were accented by the simple but elegant French-twist style of her russet-colored hair. But her large, eloquent hazel eyes were her most striking feature. She scanned the room, and when her glance came to rest on Laura she smiled broadly and moved quickly in their direction.

Nick rose as she approached, and Laura stood up as well.

"Laura! It's so good to see you!" Rebecca said, giving the other woman a hug.

"Thanks, Becka," Laura said, reverting to her friend's childhood nickname. "I've been meaning to come down, but what with trying to get the business established…" Her voice trailed off apologetically.

The other woman smiled ruefully. "Tell me about it."

"Becka, this is Nick Sinclair. Nick, Rebecca Matthews."

Nick smiled and held out his hand. "It's a pleasure to meet you, Rebecca."

"Thanks. It's mutual," she said, returning his firm handshake. Then she turned to Laura. "I'm so glad you stopped in. May I join you for a minute?"

"Please," Nick said, retrieving a chair from an empty table nearby.

"What brings you to St. Genevieve?" Rebecca asked as she sat down.

"We're on our way to the Anderson Fourth of July reunion," Laura replied.

"Oh, yes. I should have remembered," Rebecca said with a smile. "Those gatherings are legendary in Jersey."

"See," Laura said, glancing at Nick with a smile. Then she turned her attention back to Rebecca. "So how is it going here? I've read about this place in the papers."

"The publicity has definitely helped," she admitted. "And it's going well. Just a lot of hard work and long hours. It doesn't leave much time for anything else. But it's very gratifying to see the business grow."

"I know what you mean," Laura concurred.

"Brad tells me you're doing well, too."

"Brad's her brother—my minister," Laura informed Nick before responding to Rebecca. "Yes. I can't complain. The Lord has been good to me. Hard work really does pay."

"But too much work isn't a good thing, either," Nick interjected smoothly. "Remember that old saying about all work and no play." He turned to Rebecca. "Laura is a hard sell, but I'm trying."

Rebecca smiled at Nick. "Well, keep trying. I've

known Laura all my life, and she's always pushed herself too hard."

"Look who's talking," Laura chided teasingly.

Rebecca grinned and gave a rueful shrug. "What can I say?"

"I'm sorry to interrupt, Rebecca." The white-haired woman paused at their table, her voice apologetic. "But the repairman is here."

"Thanks, Rose. I'll be right there." She turned back to Nick and Laura. "Sorry to run. Although I suspect that three's a crowd anyway," she said, smiling as a flush rose to Laura's cheeks. She reached across and took her friend's hand. "It was so good to see you," she said warmly. "Stop by again, okay? And let me know in advance the next time. We do very romantic dinners here on Friday and Saturday nights," she said, directing her remark to Nick.

"I'll keep that in mind," he promised, rising to pull out her chair.

"It was nice meeting you," she said. "And take care, Laura. Don't work too hard."

"I'll try not to. But remember your own advice," she replied with a grin.

As Rebecca disappeared, Nick sat back down and turned to Laura with a smile. "She seems very nice."

"She's wonderful. Brad says she's making quite a go of it here. But he worries about her being alone. And about how hard she works."

"I feel that way about somebody myself," Nick said quietly.

Laura flushed and glanced down, playing with the edge of her napkin. The conversation was getting too serious—and too personal. Fortunately the timely arrival of their food kept Nick from pursuing the topic, and when the waitress left Laura deliberately turned the conversation to lighter subject matter. He followed her lead, and by the time a delicious and decadently rich chocolate torte arrived, compliments of the house, she was starting to relax again. Maybe this weekend would turn out all right after all, she thought hopefully, as they left the restaurant and resumed their drive.

Conversation flowed easily during the remainder of the trip, and as they approached her hometown, Nick turned to her with a smile. "How about a rundown on the agenda and the cast of characters?" he said.

"Okay," she agreed. "Let's start with the agenda. Today and tomorrow will be pretty low-key. We'll have dinner at Aunt Gladys's tomorrow. That's about the only real planned activity, but there will be lots of impromptu visiting going on. On the Fourth Mom has everyone over for a cookout, and then we play horseshoes or croquet and shoot off fireworks in the field after dark. Tuesday we can head back whenever we want. Now, as for the cast, there'll be my brother, John, and his family. They live in town. And my brother, Dennis, who lives in Memphis, will be up for the weekend and staying at the house. Aunt Gladys and Uncle George have five kids, most of whom are married, and a lot of them will come back for the Fourth." She paused and took a deep breath after her rapid-fire briefing. "Those are the main players, but you'll find that a lot of other relatives show up, too," she added.

"Sounds like quite a gathering. What about your dad, Laura? You didn't mention him."

Some of the brightness faded from her face and she

turned to look out the window. "He died eleven years ago," she said quietly.

"I'm sorry. You two were close, I take it."

"Yes, very. I was the only girl in the family, and Dad spoiled me, I guess. He was a real special man, you know? Sometimes even now it's hard to believe he's gone. He died right after Fourth of July—one of the few I didn't spend with the family," she said, her voice edged with sadness and regret.

"How come you weren't here? I got the impression this was a sacred ritual."

"It is now. But I missed a few years when I was married."

"Why?"

Laura shrugged, and Nick could feel her closing down. "Oh, you know how it is. Other things interfere."

Like what? he wondered. But he knew better than to pursue a line of questioning that would alienate her and erase the lighthearted mood they'd established. So he changed the subject.

"You'll need to guide me from here," he said as he turned off the highway.

By the time he turned into the driveway leading to the modest white frame house on the outskirts of town, Laura's earlier mood was restored and her eyes were shining in anticipation. The crunching gravel announced their arrival, and before he even set the brake the front screen door opened and an older, slightly stout woman in a faded apron appeared.

She turned and called something over her shoulder before hurrying down the steps and throwing her arms around Laura.

"Oh, honey, it's so good to see you," she said.

"It's good to be home, Mom," Laura answered, and Nick heard the catch in her voice. He gave them a minute to themselves before climbing out of the car.

Laura's mother appeared instantly contrite. "Oh, goodness, I completely forgot about your young man." She stepped back and smoothed her hair.

"Mom, he's not my young man," Laura corrected her, flushing. "I told you about Nick last night on the phone."

"Of course you did. I hope you'll forgive me," Laura's mother said to Nick.

"I didn't mind in the least," he assured her.

Laura's mother looked pleased. "Well, good. Now, I assume you're Nick Sinclair," she said, holding out her hand. "Welcome to Jersey. I'm Laura's mother, Evelyn Anderson."

Nick returned her firm handshake with a smile, doing a rapid assessment. The years had clearly taken their toll on Laura's mother. Her face spoke of hard work, and the once-brown hair was now mostly gray. But her eyes sparkled and her smile was cheerful and warm. While life may have presented her with difficulties, Laura's mother seemed to have met them squarely and then moved on. Much like Laura herself, Nick thought.

"It's a pleasure to meet you, Mrs. Anderson. And thank you for inviting me. It was very generous of you."

"Not at all. We're glad to have you," she said. "Now let's go in and get you both settled and then you can have some dinner. Laura, I've put Nick in John's old room, if you'll take him up. I've got a pie in the oven that's just about done."

"Okay."

"Take your time unpacking. I didn't know when everyone would be arriving so I just put on a big pot of chili. It'll keep," she told them.

Laura followed Nick around to the back of the car and reached for her bag when he raised the lid of the trunk.

"I'll take care of it," he said, moving more quickly than she and effortlessly hoisting the strap of the small overnight case to his shoulder.

"You don't have to carry my luggage," she protested.

"Neither of us packed very heavily," he said with a crooked grin, holding up his duffel bag. "I think I can manage. You just lead the way and clear the path."

"Okay," she relented, walking ahead and opening the screen door. "Up the stairs, first door on your right," she instructed.

Nick made his way to the second floor and pushed the indicated door open with his shoulder. The room was simply furnished, with a navy blue bedspread on the full-size bed, an easy chair and an oak chest and desk. Rag rugs covered the polished plank floors, and woven curtains hung at the window. As Nick set his bag on the floor, Laura spoke at his elbow.

"I hope this will be okay," she said worriedly. She'd never really noticed before how plain the house was. It had always just been home to her—warm and inviting and welcoming. But to a stranger, it might appear old and worn. Not to mention hot. She noticed the beads of perspiration already forming on Nick's forehead. "Mom doesn't have air-conditioning," she said apologetically. "All the upstairs rooms have ceiling fans, though, so it stays pretty cool at night. During the day we don't spend a lot of time up here, anyway." She paused. "I guess I should have warned you."

"It wouldn't have made me change my mind about coming," he said with a smile.

"Are you sure the heat won't bother you?" she asked skeptically. "I'm used to it—this is how I grew up, and even now, I don't use my air all that much. But most people live in air-conditioning today. Especially in Missouri in July."

"Laura." He placed his hands on her shoulders. "I told you. This is fine. It's a small price to pay for a long weekend with you. Now, where do you want this?" he asked, nodding toward her overnight case.

"I'm right next door." She bent down to retrieve the bag, but he beat her to it. "Nick, it's just down the hall," she protested.

"Good. Then I won't have far to walk."

Laura shook her head. "You sure can be stubborn, do you know that?"

"Yep."

"Okay. I give up. Besides, it's too hot to argue."

Nick followed her down the hall. He could have let her take her own bag. It wasn't that heavy, and he'd seen evidence that she was stronger than she looked. No, his reasons were more selfish than chivalrous. He was curious about the room where Laura had spent her girlhood, and this might be his only chance to see it.

"You can just put it on the chair," Laura said, entering the room before him.

Nick took his time, glancing around as he strolled

over to the white wicker chair with a floral cushion, which sat in one corner. The room was painted pale blue, with a delicate floral wallpaper border, and decorated with white wicker furniture and crisp organdy curtains. The floral spread on the twin bed matched the chair cushion, and a large print by one of the French Impressionists hung on one wall.

"Very nice," he said approvingly. "I particularly like this Matisse. Is it yours?"

"Yes."

"I'm surprised you didn't take it with you. It's a very fine print."

"Thanks. It was a high school graduation gift from Mom and Dad."

"And you left it?"

Laura turned away. "My husband wasn't a fan of impressionistic painting," she said with a shrug. "Besides, it would have left a blank spot on the wall here. I figured I could enjoy it whenever we came to visit."

"Which apparently wasn't often."

"Nick." Her eyes flew to his, and there was a note of warning in her voice. "Leave it alone."

He held up his hands. "Sorry."

She looked at him steadily for a moment, and then turned away. "I'm going to change into some shorts and freshen up. I'll meet you downstairs in about fifteen minutes for dinner, okay?"

"Sure."

Nick returned to his room and strolled restlessly over to the window, jamming his hands in his pockets, a frown marring his brow as he stared out over the distant fields. There was so much about Laura that he wanted to know. Needed to know. But she just wouldn't open up. What could possibly have happened to make her so gun-shy? He had no answers, but he did have three days ahead with Laura, in an environment where she seemed to feel safe. Maybe she would share some memories with him here. At least he could hope.

It didn't take Laura long to change. She was used to having too much to do in too little time, and she'd learned not to waste a moment. She slipped a pair of comfortable khaki shorts over her slim hips, tucking in a teal blue, short-sleeved cotton blouse and cinching the waist with a hemp belt. As she sat down on the bed to tie her canvas shoes, her eye fell on the Matisse, and she paused to look at it. The painting had always soothed her, and right now her nerves needed all the soothing they could get. Slowly she looked around the room that had been home for eighteen years, letting her gaze linger here and there. Everything was the same. The same blue walls. The same crystal dish on the dresser. The same worn spot on the rug. Everything was the same. Everything except her. So much had happened in the years since she had left this house as a bride. There had been so many hopes, heartaches and regrets....

Suddenly Laura's eyes grew misty. She wasn't prone to self-pity, so the tears took her off guard. It wasn't as if she had anything to complain about, she told herself. Yes, her life had turned out differently than she'd expected as a young bride. And some bad things had happened along the way. But the Lord had stood by her through the tough times, and her life now was very blessed. She had a successful business, a loving family, good friends and good health. The Lord always provided for her, even supplying a chauffeur for this weekend, she reminded herself.

Laura abruptly stood, brushing her tears aside. She wasn't going to give in to melancholy. Looking back did no good. She'd learned a long time ago that living in the past was a waste of time and an emotional drain. Live today, plan for tomorrow and trust in the Lord— that was her motto now.

Laura let herself out of her room, closing the door quietly behind her, and walked down the hall, her rubber-soled shoes noiseless on the hardwood floor. Nick's door was still closed, and her step faltered. Should she knock and let him know she was heading down? No, she could use a few minutes alone with the family.

Laura ran lightly down the steps and headed for the kitchen, sniffing appreciatively as she entered the bright, sunny room. John was sitting at the polished oak table unsuccessfully trying to convince eight-month-old Daniel to eat a spoon of strained peas, while Dana helped clear the remainder of three-year-old Susan's dinner off the table.

"Aunt Laura!" Susan squealed, catapulting herself toward Laura, who bent and swept her up.

"My goodness, what a big girl you are now!" Laura exclaimed, hugging the little body close to her. Susan tolerated the embrace for a few seconds, and then squirmed to be set loose.

John gave her a harried smile. "Hi, Sis. We'll clear out of here in just a minute so you can enjoy your dinner in peace."

"Don't rush on my account," Laura said, sitting down at the table and cupping her chin in her palm. Daniel chose that moment to spit out a particularly unappealing bite, and Laura laughed. "I'm enjoying this."

"You wouldn't want to take over, would you?" John asked hopefully.

"Oh, no, you're doing a masterful job. Hi, Dana. How'd you manage to get John to do the feeding chores?" she asked, turning toward her sister-in-law.

"Hi, Laura." Dana was a natural white blonde, and she wore her hair short and curled softly around her attractive, animated face. "We made a deal before we had the second one that feeding, diapering and bathing chores would be divided. And I must say, John's lived up to his side of the bargain really well."

"Did I have a choice?" he asked good-naturedly.

"No."

He shrugged and grinned. "Boy, has she gotten aggressive," he said to Laura.

"No, dear brother, the word is assertive. And good for you, Dana," Laura said with a smile.

"I should have figured you women would stick together," he lamented.

"Oh, get out the violins," Laura said, rolling her eyes.

John's grin softened to a smile. "It's good to see you, Laura."

"It's good to be home," she replied quietly, reaching over briefly to touch his shoulder. "Is Dennis here yet?"

The screen door banged. "Anybody home?" a male voice bellowed.

John looked at Laura and grinned. "Speak of the devil. We're in the kitchen," he called.

Dennis clomped down the hall and stood on the

threshold, his hands on his hips. "Who owns the sporty red number out front? Man, what a set of wheels!"

"Hello to you, too, brother," Laura said wryly.

"Oh. Sorry," he said sheepishly, engulfing her in a bear hug that left her breathless. "Good to see you, Laura. So who owns the car?"

"The guy she brought down for the weekend," John said.

"Laura brought a guy down? No kidding! Where is he?"

"Look, you've all got it backward," Laura said, exasperation starting to wear down her patience. "*He* brought *me*. My car gave out, and he very graciously offered to drive me down. He was just being nice, so don't try to read any more into it."

"Just being nice? Give me a break! No guy with a car like that drives three hours to stay in an unair-conditioned house in a town small enough to spit across just because he's nice," Dennis said.

Laura felt the color begin to rise in her face. "I knew this was a mistake," she muttered. "I just should have stayed home."

"Come on, you two. Leave your sister alone," Dana said sympathetically. "If she says this man is just a friend, then that's all he is."

"Oh, Laura! I didn't hear you come down," Mrs. Anderson said, bustling into the kitchen. "Are you and your young man ready for some chili?"

Laura looked at the grinning faces of her two brothers and dropped her head onto the table, burying her face in her crossed arms. "I give up," she said, her voice muffled.

Everyone started asking questions at once, and Laura

ignored them all—until a sudden hush told her that Nick must have appeared in the doorway. She raised her eyes and his met hers quizzically. He didn't seem uncomfortable by the attention focused on him, just curious. Laura stood, glaring a warning over her shoulder and walked over to Nick.

"Nick, this is the family. My brothers John and Dennis, and John's wife, Dana. And of course we can't forget Susan and Daniel. Daniel's the one with the green slime running down his chin and dripping onto John's shirt."

"Oh, great!" John muttered. He reached for a cloth and ineffectually wiped at the stain.

"Serves you right," Laura said sweetly, and John glared at her.

"Nice to meet you," Dennis said, sticking his hand out. "Great car."

"Thanks."

"I'd shake hands, but I think it might be better if we just said hello," John said, still struggling with the peas.

"You look like you have your hands full," Nick commented with a chuckle.

"Yeah, you might say that," John replied, juggling Daniel on one knee while the suddenly shy Susan, a finger stuck in her mouth, watched the proceedings while clinging to his leg.

"Well, let's leave these two in peace to enjoy their food," Dana said as she came to John's rescue and hoisted Daniel onto her hip. "Nick, it's nice to meet you. I'm sure we'll see a lot of you this weekend."

"We'll be back later, Mom," John said, bending over to give her a peck on the cheek.

"Good. Drive safe, now. Dennis, you're just in time for some chili," she said, turning her attention to her younger son.

"Now that's what I call perfect timing," he said with a grin, turning a chair backward to the table and straddling it.

"Nick, go ahead and find a seat," Mrs. Anderson said as she set the table with quick efficiency.

Laura was glad Dennis had shown up in time for dinner. His boisterous chatter kept Nick occupied, giving Laura a chance to think. She should have expected her family's reaction, she supposed. She'd never brought a man home since…since Joe's death. In fact, she'd never brought anyone home except Joe. It was bound to cause a stir. She'd simply have to keep Nick at arm's length and convince everyone that he was just a friend. Except he wasn't helping.

She frowned at the dilemma and looked up, only to discover Nick's eyes on her. Dennis was at the sink refilling his water glass, and Nick's lazy smile and slow wink sent a sudden, sharp flash of heat jolting through her.

"Aren't you hungry?" he asked, his innocent words at odds with the inviting look in his eyes.

"Wh-what?" she stammered.

He nodded to her almost untouched chili, and she glanced down.

"Oh. Yes, I am. I guess I've been daydreaming. You look like you're doing okay, though," she said, trying to divert his attention.

"It's great." He turned to Laura's mother. "This is wonderful chili, Mrs. Anderson. Does Laura have this recipe?"

"Oh, my yes. She's quite a good cook when she has the time."

"I know," he said. His tone implied that he knew a lot more, and he turned to smile at Laura with that easy, heart-melting look of his.

Laura swallowed her mouthful of chili with difficulty and tried to think of some response, but she could barely remember her name, let alone formulate a snappy retort, when Nick looked at her like that. In desperation, she glanced toward her mother for assistance, but the older woman was watching them with an interested gleam in her eye. No ally there, she thought in disgust.

Dennis had returned and once again monopolized the conversation, so Laura focused on her chili, her mind racing. Her family was jumping to way too many conclusions, she thought. And Nick wasn't helping. If he kept looking at her in that intimate way, it wasn't going to be easy to convince everyone that friendship was all he had on his mind. Especially when she knew better. Or worse—depending on your point of view, she thought wryly.

Chapter Eight

Laura was managing very nicely to keep Nick at bay, she thought late on Sunday, after everyone had overindulged on Aunt Gladys's fried chicken. Nearly thirty people had shown up for the gathering, including the entire Anderson clan and assorted aunts, uncles, cousins, nieces and nephews. The lively exchanges during the meal had now given way to quiet satisfaction as everyone found a comfortable spot in the shade to relax. Except for a spirited game of horseshoes undertaken by the more energetic among the group, everyone else seemed content to do nothing more strenuous than chase away an occasional fly.

From his shady spot under a tree, Nick watched Laura help her mother and aunt clear away the remains of the meal. His offer of assistance had been promptly refused, so he had sought relief from the heat under the spreading branches of this oak, which also provided him with a good vantage point from which to observe Laura. She appeared more relaxed than he'd ever seen her, he noted through half-closed eyelids, his back propped against the trunk of the tree. With her hair pulled back into a ponytail, the trimness of her figure accentuated with shorts and a T-shirt and a good night's sleep behind her, she could pass for a teenager, at least from this distance. Even up close she seemed younger, almost carefree, the lines of tension around her mouth and eyes erased. She smiled more, and Nick began to glimpse the woman she had once been, before some demon from her past had stolen the laughter from her life.

He also knew that she was doing her best to make sure the two of them weren't alone. And he was just as sure that he had to get her alone. Here, in this relaxed, safe setting, she might open up a little, give him some insight to the fears she kept bottled inside. This was his best chance to discover more about Laura Taylor, and he wasn't about to let it pass. Because until he knew the secrets she kept hidden, the source of her fears, he would be at a distinct disadvantage. The only problem was figuring out a way to spirit her away from the group.

In the end, Laura's Aunt Gladys emerged as his unexpected ally. "Land, it's a hot one," she said, fanning herself with part of a newspaper as the women came over to join him. Laura's aunt and mother opened up lawn chairs, and Laura dropped to the ground next to Nick. "Does anyone want some iced tea or lemonade? Nick?"

"No, thank you. I'm still too full from dinner to even think about putting anything else in my stomach," he said with a lazy grin. "That was one of the best meals I've had in a long time."

"Well, I'm glad you liked it," Aunt Gladys said with a pleased grin. She glanced at Laura's mother before continuing, and Nick noted the conspiratorial look that passed between them. "Laura, why don't you show Nick the spring?" she suggested casually. "It's a whole lot cooler down there."

Laura had been halfheartedly watching the game of horseshoes, listening to the conversation only on a peripheral level, but now she gave it her full attention, turning startled eyes to Nick. He saw the panic in them, opened his mouth to politely decline, but caught himself in time. Instead, he idly reached for a blade of grass and twirled it silently between his fingers.

"Oh, Aunt Gladys, it's a pretty long walk. I'm sure Nick's too full to go hiking in this weather," she said breathlessly.

"It's not that far," Aunt Gladys replied. "If I was as young as you two, I'd be heading there myself. I think Nick would enjoy it."

"It sounds very interesting," he injected smoothly. "And I'm all for finding a cooler spot, even if it does take a little effort to get there." Without waiting for a reply, he stood and extended his hand to Laura. "Come on, Laura. You can be my tour guide," he coaxed, smiling down at her.

Laura stared up at him, her mind racing. How could she refuse without appearing rude? She looked to her aunt and mother for help, but they were smiling at her innocently. It was a conspiracy, she thought, realizing she was doomed. Nick wanted to get her alone, and her mother and aunt were clearly on his side. She might as well give up.

Nick saw the look of capitulation in her eyes and let out his breath slowly. He wouldn't have been surprised if she'd refused to go with him.

Laura put her hand in his, and in one lithe motion he drew her to her feet, tucking her arm in his. She saw the look of satisfaction Aunt Gladys and her mother exchanged and vowed to get even with them later.

"We'll be back soon," she said deliberately.

"Oh, take your time," her mother said. "You won't miss anything here."

Laura gave her a dirty look before turning to Nick. "It's down the road a bit and then through the woods," she said shortly.

"If we're not back by dark, send out a search party," Nick said to the two older women. Then he paused and looked down at Laura. "On second thought, never mind."

Laura's mother laughed. "I'm sure you'll take good care of her," she said. "Have fun, you two."

Laura knew she was blushing furiously, and she turned and began walking rapidly toward the road, practically dragging Nick with her.

"Hey, whoa! What's the rush?" he asked.

"I thought you wanted to see the spring."

"I do. But it's not going anywhere, is it?"

Reluctantly Laura slowed her gait. "No," she said glumly.

"That's what I like in a tour guide. Enthusiasm," Nick said, trying to elicit a smile and dispel some of the tension.

Laura looked up at him guiltily. He'd been a good sport about all the family activities over the past two days, blending right in with his easygoing manner and natural charm, and making no attempt to monopolize her time—until now. She supposed she owed him at least this much.

"Sorry," she apologized. "I just hate being railroaded into anything."

He stopped walking, and she looked up at him in surprise.

"If you'd rather not go, it's okay," he said, knowing he had to give her an out, hoping she wouldn't take it. If she wasn't a willing partner in this outing it was doomed to failure, anyway.

Laura seemed momentarily taken aback by his offer, and he saw the conflict in her eyes. He'd promised to let her set the pace, she recalled, and Nick had been a man of his word—so far. She knew that he hoped something romantic would develop when they were alone, but if she wasn't willing, she trusted him not to push. Maybe that was a mistake, but it was one she was suddenly willing to risk. "No. Let's go. It is cooler there, and you could probably use a break from all this family togetherness."

Relief flooded through him. "I like your family a lot, Laura. But some quiet time would be nice," he admitted with a smile.

"Well, it's quiet at the spring," she assured him.

They walked along a gravel road for a while, the late-afternoon sun relentless in its heat, and Laura looked up at Nick after a few minutes with a rueful smile. "Are you regretting this outing yet?" she asked.

He took a handkerchief from his pocket and mopped his forehead. "Well…that depends on how much farther it is," he said cautiously, the shadow of a grin making the corners of his mouth quirk up.

Laura pointed to a curve in the road about a hundred yards ahead. "The path is right up there. It cuts through the woods, so at least we'll be in the shade. The spring's about a ten-minute walk from the road."

"I can handle that."

They covered the remaining ground quickly and then paused a moment after turning onto the path, enjoying the welcome relief provided by the leafy canopy of trees.

"Whew! It's a lot hotter than it seemed back at your aunt's," Nick remarked, mopping his brow again.

"Yeah. It's got to be well over ninety."

"Is this a cold spring?"

"Very."

"Good. Lead me to it."

Fifteen minutes later, they sat side by side on a log, their feet immersed in a brook that was fed by the spring bubbling up a few yards away. Laura watched Nick close his eyes and smile. "This is heaven," he pronounced.

"It is nice," Laura agreed. "When we were kids we used to spend a lot of time playing here. It was a great place to grow up—fresh air, open spaces, pastures to run in, trees to climb, apples to pick…" Her voice trailed off.

"Sounds idyllic," Nick commented.

She nodded. "It was in a lot of ways. We didn't have much in the material sense, but we had more than our share of love. You may have noticed that this weekend."

"Mmm-hmm."

"I was very fortunate to have such a wonderful family," she continued softly. "We were sort of like the Waltons, you know? When that program was on TV I used to hear people say that no one really had a family like that. Well, we did. My parents taught us by example how to live our Christian faith and gave us an incredible foundation of love to build on. Those things are a priceless legacy." She drew up her legs and wrapped her arms around them, resting her chin on her knees. "That's one of the reasons I got involved with Christian Youth Outreach. Those poor kids have no idea what it's like to grow up in a warm, caring, supportive atmosphere. Outreach can't make up for that, but it does provide programs that help instill Christian values and give kids a sense of self-worth."

Nick looked over at her, the dappled sunlight playing across her face, and noted the faint shadows under her eyes. She worked too hard, always stretching herself to the limit. Yet she still found time to give to others, living her faith in a concrete way. She never ceased to amaze him.

"You know something, Laura Taylor? You're quite a woman," he said softly.

She looked at him in surprise, a delicate flush staining her cheeks, then turned away. "A lot of people do a lot more than me," she said with a dismissive shrug. She took a deep breath and closed her eyes. "This really is a great spot, isn't it? It brings back so many good memories," Laura said, a tender smile of recollection softening her features. Then it slowly faded. "But things never stay the same, do they?"

"It must have been hard to leave here," Nick ventured, sensing a chance to find out more about her past.

She reached down and trailed her fingers through the cold water. "In some ways, yes. But I was very much in love, and when you're in love nothing else matters," she said quietly. "Besides, I had visions of recreating this lifestyle in the city. I figured there had to be some-place there with a small-town feel, and I found it pretty quickly. Webster Groves. When I was first married I used to love to drive through there and admire those wonderful, old Victorian houses. I always figured some day we'd have one." She paused and cupped her chin in her hand, resting her elbow on her knee, and the wistful smile on her face tightened Nick's throat. "It would have had a big porch on three sides, with lots of gingerbread trim and cupolas, and fireplaces, and an arbor covered with morning glories that led to a rose garden. And children playing on a tire swing..." She stopped abruptly and glanced at Nick self-consciously. "Sorry. Coming home always makes me nostalgic," she apologized, a catch in her voice.

He was tempted to reach over and take her hand. But he held back, afraid that physical contact would break the mood. "I didn't mind. I'm just sorry you never got your house."

She shrugged. "Oh, well. It wasn't in God's plan for me, I guess. At least my office is in Webster. Some-times, in the fall especially, I walk down Elm Street and let myself daydream even now," she confided.

"There's nothing wrong with dreaming, Laura."

"There is when you have no way of making those dreams come true," she replied. "If I've learned one thing in the past few years, it's to be realistic."

"No more dreams?" he asked gently.

She looked at him squarely. "No. Dreams have a way of turning sour."

"Not all dreams, Laura."

"I know. My business is a good example. But it didn't

happen by itself, Nick. It took a lot of hard work. Those kind of dreams, the ones you can control, where if you do certain things there's a predictable outcome, are fine."

"Is that why you shy away from relationships? Because people are unpredictable and don't always do what you expect?" He was afraid she'd tense up, resent his question, but the quiet of the woods, broken only by the call of an occasional bird and the splashing of the brook, seemed to have had a calming effect on her. She sighed.

"I suppose that's a fair question, Nick. You've told me how you feel, and I guess you have a right to know what your chances are with me. You were honest with me, so I'll be honest with you. I like you very much. Probably too much. But the odds aren't good."

"Because you're scared?" he asked quietly.

She hesitated, and then nodded slowly. "Yes."

"But, Laura…don't you ever get lonely?"

Laura swallowed past the lump in her throat and looked away, afraid that the tears welling up in her eyes would spill out. "I have my family."

"That's not what I mean."

She knew exactly what he meant, but chose to ignore it. "I also have my faith, Nick. Believe it or not, that helps a lot to ease any loneliness I might feel. It's a great source of strength."

Nick knew she was telling the truth. He had begun to realize just how important Laura's faith was to her. He'd seen the worn and obviously much-read Bible at her apartment, knew she attended church every Sunday. He'd been struck by the peace in her eyes during the church service he'd attended with the Anderson clan that morning—a look of serenity and fullfilment he envied. Nick hadn't attended church much since he was a teenager, and had almost made an excuse to skip the service that morning. But he had honestly enjoyed sharing the experience with Laura and even thought he might begin attending his own church more often after this weekend. But his comment had nothing to do with faith, and she knew it.

"I do believe you, Laura," he said quietly. "But even a strong faith doesn't make up for the comfort of having a human person to share your life with, a hand to hold, someone to laugh with."

Laura debated her response. She could just ignore his remark, change the subject. But he was right, and she might as well admit it. With a sigh she conceded the point. "Yeah. I know. But I've learned to handle it."

Nick watched her closely. The subtle tilt of her chin told him she was struggling for control, and he wondered what could possibly have made her so fearful, so willing to live a life devoid of human tenderness and love.

"This fear you have of relationships is really strong, isn't it?"

"I guess so."

"I assume there's a very good reason for it."

She looked at him silently for a moment and then began pulling on her shoes, concentrating on the laces as she spoke. "There is."

He reached for his own shoes more slowly, sensing that the conversation was at an end, but wanting to ask so much more. Yet he knew that she'd said as much as she planned to for the moment. Maybe more.

They tied their shoes in silence, and then Laura

stood, jamming her hands into the pockets of her shorts. "We ought to start back," she said, glancing at her watch. "We've been gone almost two hours."

Nick rose reluctantly and leaned against a tree, crossing his arms. "You don't mind if I keep trying, do you?"

She gave him a puzzled look. "What do you mean?"

"To break down that wall you've built."

She flushed and turned away. "You're wasting your time, Nick."

"I'm willing to take my chances."

"Suit yourself," she said, wishing he'd just give up and find someone without emotional roadblocks, leaving her in peace, before his persistence eventually wore down her defenses.

Laura spoke very little as they made their way back through the woods. She let Nick lead, and her eyes were drawn to the broad, powerful muscles of his shoulders, his trim waist, the corded tendons of his legs bare beneath his shorts. There was a magnetism about him that was almost tangible, and she found herself imagining what it would feel like to be enveloped in his strong arms, to feel his heartbeat mingling with hers. Lonely? he'd asked her. Oh, if he only knew! So many nights when she'd longed to be held, yearned for a tender touch, a whispered endearment. But always she went to bed alone. And lonely. Suddenly, watching Nick's strong back only inches from her, close enough to touch, a yearning surged through her so strong that she stumbled.

Nick turned instantly and reached out to steady her. "Are you okay, Laura?" he asked, studying her face with a worried frown. He noted the flush on her cheeks and the film of tears in her eyes, and his hands lingered on her shoulders.

"Yes, I'm fine," she said breathlessly, her heart hammering in her chest. "I just didn't see that rock." Her eyes lifted to his, making Nick's heart suddenly go into a staccato rhythm.

It took every ounce of his willpower not to immediately crush her to his chest, to imprison her in his arms and kiss her in ways that would leave her breathless and asking for more. He swallowed, and he realized that his hands were trembling as he struggled for control, trying to decide what to do next.

Laura stared at him, mesmerized by the play of emotions that crossed his face. With one word, one touch, she knew she could unleash the passion smoldering just beneath the surface. And she needed to be held so badly! Held by someone who cared about her, who would love her with a passion tempered by gentleness, who would soothe her with a touch that spoke of caring and commitment. Nick could give her that. Wanted to give her that. It was hers for the taking. She could see it in his eyes.

Without consciously making a decision, Laura slowly reached out a tentative hand. Nick grasped it, his eyes burning into hers, questioning, hoping, and when he pressed her palm to his lips, Laura closed her eyes and moaned softly, surrendering to the tide of emotion sweeping over her. She moved forward, inviting herself into his arms, waiting for the touch of his lips—

A sudden crashing of brush made her gasp, and, startled, she spun around as his arms protectively encircled her. A doe and fawn were hovering uncertainly only a few yards away, standing perfectly still, only their ears twitching. They remained motionless for a long moment, and then with one last, nervous look at the intruders, they bolted into the thicket.

Laura let her breath out slowly. She was shaking badly, not just because of the unexpected interruption, but because of what she'd almost done. She now knew why she'd been so reluctant to spend time alone with Nick. Just being in his presence awakened long-dormant impulses in her, impulses best left untouched. Another few minutes and she... She closed her eyes, refusing to allow her imagination any further rein. She didn't believe in casual intimacy. Never had. It went against every principle she held. But she'd never been so tempted in her life. She needed to be touched, to be held, to be loved, and the power of those compelling physical needs had stunned her. The Bible was right, she thought ruefully. The flesh really was weak. Maybe the sudden appearance of the deer had been God's way of giving her the time she needed to clear her head and make the right decision, difficult as it was.

Taking a deep breath she stepped away, and Nick's hands dropped from her shoulders. Immediately she missed his touch, missed the warmth of his hands that had penetrated her thin cotton blouse. The loss of contact was almost tangibly painful. But it was for the best, she told herself resolutely.

Turning to face him was one of the most difficult things Laura had ever done in her life. He was standing absolutely still, except for the unusually rapid rise and fall of his chest, and he looked shaken and grim. But he composed himself, running a hand through his hair and forcing his lips up into a semblance of a smile.

"Talk about bad timing," he said jokingly, his voice husky and uneven.

Laura brushed back a few tendrils of hair that had escaped from her ponytail. "We'd better get back," she said choppily.

"Laura…"

He reached out a hand, but she ignored the gesture. "Come on," she said simply. She brushed past him, walking with long determined strides toward the road.

Frustration and disappointment washed over him as he watched her retreating back. The moment was gone. But he had some consolation. The longing he'd seen in her eyes left him with hope. It wasn't much, but it was something. With a sigh he watched Laura disappear around a curve, and then forced himself to follow more slowly. At the rate she was going, she'd be back at the house before he even emerged from the woods.

He was surprised to find her waiting for him when he reached the road. "I can find my way back if you'd rather go on ahead," he said quietly.

"No. I'm sorry, Nick. That was rude of me. I'll walk with you."

She fell into step beside him, an introspective frown on her face, and though Nick tried a couple of times to lighten the mood, Laura was unresponsive and he finally gave up, lapsing into silence.

Once back, Laura's attempts to keep him at arm's length intensified. He wasn't able to say more than a few words to her in private the rest of the evening or the next morning. He realized she was running scared, frightened by what had almost happened in the woods, afraid to let that opportunity arise again. He resigned himself to the fact that the best he could hope for was to sit next to her at dinner.

By the time he filled his plate and made his way toward one of the long tables set up in the yard, however, Laura had already found a seat between her niece and her brother. As Nick surveyed the situation, juggling his plate in one hand and a lemonade in the other, John caught his eye. Nick quirked one eyebrow in Laura's direction, and John nodded imperceptibly.

"Susan, where's your fork?" John asked, leaning around Laura.

"Gone," she said, pointing under the table.

"I'll get her another one," Laura volunteered.

"Thanks, Sis."

As Laura headed for the buffet table, Nick made his move, slipping into Laura's seat. "I owe you one," he said quietly to John.

John grinned. "Laura needs a shove. She's a slow mover," he said.

"So I've noticed."

Laura was so busy talking to her aunt that she didn't realize her seat was occupied until she reached the table, whereupon she stopped short, glaring suspiciously at her brother when he turned.

"Oh, Laura. Nick was looking for a seat. We had plenty of room here." He scooted over, and Nick did likewise, leaving space for Laura to join them.

"I don't want to crowd you," she said crossly, reaching for her plate. "I'll go sit with Mom."

"We don't mind being crowded," Nick said, grasping her hand.

Laura looked around. They were beginning to attract attention, and the amused glances being sent her way made her cheeks flame. With a sigh, she squeezed in beside Nick.

"There. Now isn't this cozy?" John said brightly.

Laura gave him a withering glance. "Just whose side are you on?" she whispered between clenched teeth.

"Yours," he replied in a low voice.

She gave an unladylike snort and picked up her corn. She could feel Nick's eyes on her, but she refused to look at him. She knew she was acting like a coward, running away from a situation she was afraid of instead of facing it. Common sense told her she couldn't put off being alone with him forever. They'd be in the car together tomorrow for three hours, for goodness' sake. But at least while he was driving, his eyes and hands would be otherwise occupied, no matter what his inclinations, she thought dryly, slathering butter on her corn.

Suddenly a large bronzed hand entered her field of vision and removed the corn from her grasp. Startled, Laura turned to look at Nick, who had raised the corn to his lips.

Mesmerized, she watched as his strong white teeth took a bite of corn. Then he licked his lips and smiled with satisfaction.

"Wh-what are you doing?" she asked hoarsely, the sensuous dance of his tongue holding her spellbound.

"Nibbling your ear," he said softly, his words implying one thing, his eyes another. Her mouth suddenly went dry and she reached for her glass of lemonade and took a large swallow. He leaned closer. "This will have to do until the real thing becomes available," he added quietly.

Laura choked on the lemonade, which once more

put her in the limelight. Curious gazes were directed her way, and then she felt Nick's arm go around her shoulder solicitously. Her face was flaming, and she dabbed at her mouth with a paper napkin.

"Are you okay, Laura?"

"Yes." She coughed. "I'm fine."

"You don't sound fine."

"I said I'm fine," she repeated grimly, shrugging off his arm.

"Okay. Do you want your corn back?"

"No. You keep it."

"Thanks."

Laura ate as fast as she could, bypassed dessert and left the table to join in a game of croquet. Nick watched her go and then sent John a despairing look.

"I'm beginning to wonder if she likes me," he said.

"Oh, she likes you. You make her as nervous as a cat in its ninth life. If she didn't like you, you wouldn't have any effect on her at all."

"You think so?" Nick asked doubtfully.

"Mmm-hmm. I know my sister."

"Has she always been like this around men?"

"Laura hasn't been around men much, Nick," John said, giving the other man a frank look. "Just Joe. He was her first and only beau, as far as I know."

"So you're attributing her skittishness to inexperience?"

"Partly," John hedged.

"It's the other part I wonder about," Nick said, directing a level gaze at John.

"I don't know much else myself, Nick," John said apologetically. "Laura's always been closemouthed about her private affairs."

"Yeah. So I've discovered." Nick sighed.

"Hang in there," John encouraged him. "You're making progress."

"Yeah?"

"She let you drive her down here, didn't she?"

"She was desperate," Nick said with a shrug.

"That's not the only reason. She wouldn't share her family with someone she didn't care about."

Nick thought about John's words later that night as he prepared for bed. The weekend hadn't gone exactly as he'd planned, but he had learned a lot about Laura's roots and her family. And if John was right, there was still hope for him.

Restlessly he strolled over to the window, trying to catch a breath of air. The second-floor bedroom was especially stuffy tonight, and the ceiling fan didn't seem to be helping at all. Even though it was eleven o'clock, the oppressive heat hadn't relented. He ought to go to bed. The house was quiet, so apparently everyone else had. But he knew sleep would be elusive. Maybe if he got some fresh air, cooled off a little, sleep would come more easily, he thought.

Nick stepped into the hall, quietly closing the door behind him, and made his way down the steps, cringing as the wood creaked. But it didn't seem to disturb anyone, he decided, pausing to listen for stirrings in the house, so he continued down and headed for the back porch, holding the screen door so it wouldn't bang. It *was* cooler out here, he thought, taking a deep breath of the night air.

"Hello, Nick."

Startled, he turned to find Mrs. Anderson gently swaying in the porch swing.

"Did I scare you?" she asked in apology. "I'm sorry."

"That's okay. I thought everyone was in bed," he said, walking closer. He leaned against the porch railing, crossing his ankles and resting his palms on the rail behind him.

"Sometimes on hot nights I like to come down and swing for a while. Walter—Laura's father—and I used to do this, and I can't seem to break the habit. It's a bit lonelier now, though, so I'm glad to have some company," she said without a trace of self-pity.

"Laura speaks very warmly of her father."

"Oh, they had a great relationship, those two. Course, as you may have noticed, we're a real close family. It was hard on all of us when Laura moved to St. Louis. We figured they'd come to visit pretty often, but it didn't work out that way."

Laura's mother was being so open that Nick had the courage to do a little probing. "Why not, Mrs. Anderson? I can see Laura loves being here with all of you."

"I don't really know, Nick," she said honestly. "Laura never did talk much about her life in St. Louis or about Joe, at least not after the first couple of years." She paused a moment, then continued more slowly. "You know, Nick, you're the first man Laura's ever brought home, other than Joe. That's why you've gotten so many curious looks this weekend. I hope we didn't make you uncomfortable."

"Not at all," he said, debating for a moment whether to probe further, quickly deciding he had nothing to lose. "Joe must have been quite a guy, if Laura married him," he said, forcing a casual tone into his voice.

Laura's mother didn't respond immediately. "He was nice enough," she said slowly, as if choosing her words carefully. "But Walter and I didn't think he was right for Laura," she admitted. "He was one of those people who always seems to have their head in the clouds, building castles in the air and never putting the foundation under them. Maybe even getting angry when things don't work out, you know what I mean? Laura's just the opposite. She plans for things and persists until she succeeds." She paused for a moment. "Besides, they were so young when they got married. Too young, we thought. But there was no convincing them, so in the end we gave in. Like I said, Laura never did talk much about her life with Joe. Even when they separated, all she said was that they were having a few problems. She didn't offer any more of an explanation, and we didn't pry. Laura's always been a real private person. But she surely had a good reason. Laura isn't one to walk away from obligations or commitments, and she's a great believer in the sanctity of marriage. So for her to leave Joe—well, I can't even imagine what must have happened."

Nick stared at Laura's mother, grateful for the darkness that hid the dumbfounded look on his face. Laura had left her husband? Why hadn't she told him? And what had broken up her marriage? She'd said earlier this weekend that she'd been in love with Joe, loved him enough to make leaving her hometown and the family she cherished bearable. Knowing she was a widow, he'd more or less begun to attribute her reluctance to get involved with him to fear of once again losing a man she loved. But now that explanation didn't seem as plausible. More likely she was afraid of making another mistake, and for that he couldn't blame her. But her fear and caution went beyond the normal bounds.

Mrs. Anderson held her watch toward the dim light. "My, it's getting late! Time I went to bed." She stood and smiled at Nick. "Hope you didn't mind me bending your ear."

"Not at all," he replied, struggling for a casual tone.

"Well, I do worry about Laura. And it's nice to have someone who cares about her to share that with. Though I expect everything we talked about tonight is old news to you. You probably know much more about it than we do," she said good-naturedly.

Nick watched the screen door close behind her. *No,* he thought, *I know far less. Even less than I thought. But I'm learning.*

Chapter Nine

Laura lay in bed sleepless for a long time Tuesday night, thinking about the past four days. Nick had been unusually quiet on the ride back from Jersey, and it was clear she need not have worried about being alone with him in the car. He was probably regretting that he'd ever made the offer to take her home, she thought miserably, punching her pillow. And if she was honest about it, she couldn't blame him. From his standpoint, the weekend had probably been a disaster. Forced to take part in a family gathering where the only person he knew avoided him like the plague was not conducive to a pleasant experience, she had to admit. He had obviously come to the same conclusion, silently carrying her bag upstairs when they'd arrived at her apartment and leaving her at the door, making his escape as quickly as possible.

Well, she'd wanted to discourage him, she told herself. The success of her plan should make her happy. So then why was she so miserable? And why did the loneliness she'd long ago learned to deal with now suddenly leave her feeling so empty and restless?

Laura tossed back the covers, the hot night air feeling much more oppressive here than it had in Jersey. She briefly considered turning on the air conditioner, but the older window unit was inefficient and one night's indulgence would probably boost her electric bill twenty dollars, she thought glumly. That was more than she was willing to spend. The heat would dissipate eventually, she told herself, and sleep would come.

Sleep did come, but not until nearly three, and when the alarm went off at five-thirty Laura moaned. So much for coming back from the weekend refreshed and rested, she thought dryly as she swung her legs to the floor and yawned.

By the time she was dressed, Ken, her foreman, had arrived per arrangement to take her to the office. He had also agreed to drop her at the garage tonight so she could pick up her car.

"Morning, Ken," she said sleepily, taking a last gulp of coffee from the mug cradled in her hands.

"Hi, Laura." He tilted his head and regarded her quizzically. "You look tired."

"Yeah, well, that's what happens when you only have two and a half hours' sleep," she said wryly.

"Did you get back late?"

"No. Just couldn't sleep." She grabbed her portfolio case and headed for the door. "Let's stop by the job sites first. How did things go yesterday?"

Laura now had two crews working, and Ken filled her in as they drove, dropping her at the office by nine-thirty.

"I'll be back about four to give you a progress report, if that's okay," he said.

"Fine," she assured him. "I have plenty of paperwork

to keep me busy. It sure will seem odd to spend a whole day in the office, though," she said.

He grinned. "Yeah, the crews won't know what to think."

"Well, I'll be back on the sites tomorrow," she said with a smile. "So don't let anybody slip up."

"Don't worry. I'll keep an eye on everything."

Laura watched Ken drive away, grateful again that she'd found someone of his caliber to fill the all-important foreman role. She'd done the job herself until the volume of work became too great, but she had to admit it was a relief to let someone else share part of the burden. Ken had only been with her for about six weeks, but he was a quick study and had proven to be reliable and trustworthy. She found herself delegating more and more to him as paperwork and new design projects demanded an increasing amount of her time. The Arts Center job had been the catalyst for growth, as she had hoped it would be, and Nick was also sending other commissions her way. She was beginning to feel that maybe, just maybe, she'd turned the corner. But her cautious nature wouldn't let her go quite that far, at least not yet. Still, business was certainly booming, and for that she was grateful. Soon she might even feel secure enough to allow herself the indulgence of air-conditioning at night, she thought with a grin.

It was nearly four before Laura stopped long enough to call the garage, and as soon as Larry answered she knew there was a problem.

"I was just getting ready to call you," he said. "I'm afraid the part hasn't come in yet. I kept thinking it might still show up this afternoon, but at this point I'm beginning to doubt it."

Laura frowned and rubbed her brow. "Well, it's not your fault, Larry," she said with a sigh. "Do you think it will be here tomorrow?"

"Oh, sure. I don't know what held it up today. It'll probably come first thing in the morning. I'll call you as soon as your car's ready."

"Okay."

"I'm sorry about this," he said apologetically. "I know it's an inconvenience."

"That's okay. I'll manage until tomorrow."

Laura hung up slowly, a resigned look on her face. So much for tonight's plans. The grocery store and laundromat would just have to wait until tomorrow. She rested her chin in her hand and looked over her cluttered desk with a sigh. There was so much to do, and now she had a whole empty evening stretching ahead of her. Too many hours alone to brood about Nick, she realized. She might as well work late tonight and then catch a bus home.

Ken arrived promptly at four, and after he quickly briefed her on the day's progress, Laura told him about the car.

"No problem," he assured her. "I can pick you up again tomorrow. Besides, the guys will have another day's reprieve from the slave driver," he said with a grin.

His good humor was infectious, and Laura smiled. "Oh, yeah? Well, tell them I'll make up for it Friday."

"I'll pass that along," he said, his grin broadening. "Ready to leave?"

"Actually, I think I'll work for a while and catch a bus later."

"Are you sure?"

"Yes. Go on home to that beautiful wife and darling new baby," she said, waving him out the door.

He grinned. "You don't have to convince me. I'll see you tomorrow."

It was hunger that finally made Laura set aside her work, that and aching shoulder muscles. She was used to heavy work, but hunching over a desk and drawing table all day must use entirely different muscles, she thought, gingerly massaging her neck. She glanced at her watch and was surprised to discover that it was already eight o'clock—definitely time to call it a day.

As Laura reached for her purse her gaze fell on the telephone, and she knew that the sudden hollow feeling in the pit of her stomach was symptomatic of more than hunger. She hadn't allowed herself to think of Nick all day, but subconsciously she knew that she had been hoping he would call. Each time the phone had rung her pulse had quickened, but it was never his deep, mellow voice that greeted her. He'd probably written her off for good, she thought, pulling the door shut and turning the key in the lock. And she had no one to blame but herself.

Laura made her way dejectedly to the bus stop, telling herself it had worked out for the best, that it was what she wanted, that her life would be much less complicated without Nick in it. The only problem was that it would also be much lonelier, she admitted.

Laura had to wait longer than she expected at the bus stop, and by the time she finally boarded and was on her way dusk had descended. She hadn't taken the bus in a long time, and apparently they ran much less frequently in the evening than she remembered.

That conclusion was borne out at the next stop, where

she waited about twice as long as she expected for her connection. By the time she finally disembarked two blocks from her apartment, it was dark and she felt so bone tired that her walk home seemed to stretch out endlessly ahead of her. The lack of sleep was finally catching up with her, and all she wanted to do at the moment was stand under a warm shower, eat something and go to bed. She watched the bus disappear in a cloud of noxious fumes and, wrinkling her nose in distaste, turned wearily toward home.

Once off the main street, Laura was surprised to discover just how dark the neighborhood was at night. She didn't make a practice of wandering around once the sun set and had never noticed that the streets were so poorly lit. Since the side streets were not heavily traveled, the darkness wasn't even broken by car headlights. Nick had asked her once about the safety of the neighborhood and she had dismissed his concern, but now she looked at it with a fresh eye. It wasn't the best part of town, she'd always known that, but she'd never had any problems. So why was she suddenly nervous?

With an impatient shake of her head, she dismissed her sudden, unaccountable jitters. It was just the power of suggestion, intensified by her weariness, she told herself.

Laura had almost convinced herself that she was being silly when she felt a strange prickling at the back of her neck. It was an odd, unsettling sensation that sent a cold chill coursing through her body. Her step faltered, and she turned to look behind her. Nothing. Just shadows. Nevertheless, she picked up her pace, hugging her shoulder bag more tightly to her side.

Laura gave a sigh of relief when she at last turned the

corner to her street and her apartment came into view. Now that home was in sight, her jitters eased. After all, there was only one more patch of darkness before she came to the entrance of her building.

Laura had very little warning before it happened. There was the sudden sound of running feet close behind her, and then she felt her purse being jerked away from her shoulder. Instinctively she tightened her grip. Dear God, she was being mugged! she thought incredulously.

The attacker was momentarily taken aback by Laura's resistance, and they both froze briefly, stunned. Laura noted that he had a hat pulled low over his eyes, but in the darkness she couldn't tell much else about him except that he was tall and broad shouldered. The freeze-frame lasted only a second, and as he moved back toward her fear coursed through her body. She responded with a well-placed knee, and his grunt told her that she'd hit pay dirt. Without pausing, she snatched the purse strap out of his hands and began to run, hoping her aggressive response would discourage him.

She heard a muttered oath of anger, but instead of abandoning the attack, the man pursued her. She didn't get more than a few steps before a hand closed on her arm. She stumbled, and then was jerked roughly around. She didn't even have time to scream before a powerful fist slammed into her face.

Laura's head snapped backward from the impact of the blow, and she staggered, then fell, the breath knocked completely out of her lungs. Her nose began to bleed profusely, and one eye was watering so badly she couldn't see. She gasped in pain as she once again felt the assailant relentlessly tugging on her purse.

"Let go," he muttered, "or you'll get more of the same."

Laura heard his words, but her fingers didn't relinquish their viselike grip on the purse.

"Okay, you asked for it," he muttered.

Laura looked up, just in time to realize his intention, but too late to do anything to protect herself. A second later the hard toe of his boot viciously connected with the tender skin over her ribs, and she gasped as a searing pain shot through her side. With a moan, she curled into a tight ball in a posture of self-protection and fought the waves of blackness that swept over her.

Hazily she realized that the assailant had once again gripped her purse, grabbing a handful of her blouse at the same time. The buttons gave way in response to his vicious yank, and Laura heard the fabric rip. She moaned softly, each breath now an agony of effort, and once more blackness descended.

Nick pulled to a stop in front of Laura's apartment, hoping for an impromptu trip to Ted Drewes. As he turned off the engine his eyes scanned the deserted neighborhood. It was obviously not a place where couples and families took evening strolls, he thought wryly.

Or was it? he wondered idly a moment later, his eyes caught by a movement in the shadows down the street. He grew instantly alert, however, when he realized that a struggle was taking place. One of the two figures was prone on the sidewalk while the other, clearly male, tried to grab something—a purse, he noted.

Nick sucked in a sharp breath and then reacted instinctively, his heart hammering as adrenaline pumped through his body. He flung open the door and sprinted toward the mugger, shouting furiously.

"Hey! You! Leave her alone!"

The mugger whirled around, saw Nick and, after one last, futile tug on the woman's purse, abandoned the attack and took off running in the opposite direction.

In a split second Nick decided it was more important to go to the woman's aid than chase the mugger. He turned to her, and it took only a second for sudden suspicion to turn into terrible certainty. Panicked, he dropped to his knees beside her, the mugger forgotten. Her blouse had been nearly torn off and blood covered her face. One eye had already swollen shut and she seemed barely conscious, her breathing labored. The color drained from his face and he felt his stomach turn over.

"Laura?" Dazed, he reached out a tentative hand, feeling as if he were in a terrible nightmare. But her soft moan made it clear that the attack had been all too real.

"Laura, can you hear me?" he asked urgently, gripping her shoulders. Her only response was to curl into a tight ball, holding her side. Nick withdrew his handkerchief and held it against her nose, glancing around desperately for help. He couldn't leave her here and he was afraid to pick her up. He had no idea how severely she was injured.

Nick could barely remember the last time he prayed, but he suddenly found himself sending an urgent plea for assistance. *Dear Lord,* he pleaded silently, closing his eyes. *Please help us. Please!*

Suddenly, as if by miracle, Nick heard a siren, and his eyes flew open. A police car, its lights flashing, was turning the corner. His shoulders sagged in relief as he mouthed a silent thank-you, and he stood and waved. The car rolled to a stop and an officer got out.

"What happened?" the policeman asked, kneeling beside Laura.

"She was mugged."

"I'll call an ambulance," he said, rising.

Laura's eyes fluttered open, and though she had trouble focusing, her hearing was fine. An ambulance meant a hospital, and the last time she'd been to a hospital was the night she'd left Joe. She had no wish to return to a place of such unpleasant memories.

"No," she said hoarsely.

Nick took her hand. "Laura, sweetheart, you have to go to the hospital. You could be seriously injured," he said gently.

Laura's eyes turned to his. "Nick?" Her voice quavered, and he felt as if someone had kicked *him* in the gut.

"Yeah, honey, it's me."

"No hospital," she repeated stubbornly.

The police officer hesitated, and Nick looked up at him. "Call an ambulance," he said curtly. Then he turned his attention back to Laura. "Laura, I'll stay with you the whole time, okay? I won't leave you."

Laura looked up at him, and even in the dim light she could make out the lines of worry etched in his face. She tried to reach up and smooth them away, but the attempt brought a searing pain intense enough to make her realize that Nick was right.

"Okay," she said raspily.

"That's my girl," he said, squeezing her hand, making an effort to smile reassuringly.

Laura tried to smile in return, wanting to reassure him that she was okay, but the effort was beyond her. Instead, she closed her eyes, taking comfort in the warm clasp of his hand.

Nick saw her eyes close, wondered if she'd lost consciousness again and began to panic.

"So where's the ambulance?" he snapped when the officer rejoined them.

"It will be here any minute," the officer reassured him. He glanced down at Laura. "She looks pretty banged up," he said.

"Yeah."

"I take it you know her?"

"I was on my way to see her. She lives in an apartment over there," he replied, pointing out Laura's building. "I had just parked when I saw them. I don't know what would have happened if I hadn't..." His voice broke, and the officer reached out a hand to grip his shoulder.

"It was lucky for her," he agreed.

The faint echo of a siren was the most beautiful sound Nick had ever heard, and though he knew it must have taken only minutes to arrive, he felt as if he'd lived a lifetime. Laura's eyes flickered open as the two paramedics bent over her and Nick relinquished her hand.

"Nick?" Her voice was frightened.

"I'm right here, honey," he said.

The paramedics performed a quick examination and then went to retrieve the stretcher. Nick squatted beside Laura again. "I'll ride with you in the ambulance."

She nodded gratefully, her eyes clinging to his with

a vulnerability that made his heart contract. He was filled with a sudden rage at the injustice of this, and at that moment he felt capable of murder.

As the paramedics bent to lift her to the stretcher, Laura moaned, and Nick saw the tears running down her cheeks.

"Can't you guys be a little more gentle?" he barked, wishing it was him on that stretcher instead of her.

The paramedics glanced at the policeman, who just inclined his head toward the ambulance. Then he turned his attention back to Nick. "I'll follow you to the hospital. I'll need a statement, since you were a witness, and hopefully the victim will be able to talk to me later."

"Her name is Laura. Laura Taylor," Nick said, his voice tight. Then he strode toward the ambulance and climbed in beside her, noting how icy her hand felt when he took it in his.

"Her hands are cold," he said shortly as the ambulance pulled away from the curb.

"Shock," one of the paramedics replied.

Nick lapsed into silence, and Laura didn't open her eyes again until she was being wheeled into the emergency room. He stayed beside her, determined to honor his promise despite the nurse who was bearing down on him.

"Sir, you can wait over there," she said.

Nick glared at her. "No way. I said I'd stay with her, and I intend to do just that. I'll keep out of your way."

The woman took one look at the stubborn set of his jaw and nodded. "I'll let the doctor know."

"You do that," he said, his eyes never leaving Laura. As they rolled to a stop, he bent over her and stroked her forehead. "Laura," he said gently, taking her hand.

Her eyes flickered open. "We're at the hospital. I've got to stand back so the doctor can take a look at you, but I'll only be a few steps away, close enough to talk to, if you want." Her eyes were frightened, but she nodded and he released her hand.

Nick moved to the side of the room while the nurse removed the tattered remnants of her blouse and eased the jeans down her hips. Nick swallowed and looked away, respecting her modesty, knowing she would be embarrassed by being so exposed before him. With an effort, he kept his eyes averted as the doctor did a cursory exam and spoke with the nurse in low tones. Not until she was wheeled to X ray did he leave her side, reassuring her that he'd be waiting.

Wearily he made his way toward the waiting room, where he found the policeman. After one look at Nick's face the officer disappeared into a side room, reappearing a moment later with a cup of coffee.

"You look like you could use this. Actually, you look like you could use something a lot stronger, but the closest thing they have in this place is rubbing alcohol."

Nick accepted it gratefully, noting in surprise that his hands were shaking. He took a long, scalding swallow, then he let his eyelids drop, forcing himself to take several deep breaths. It helped, but he still felt unsteady. When he opened his eyes, he met the policeman's sympathetic gaze.

"If I sounded a bit short-tempered before, I'm sorry," Nick said hoarsely. "I know you all were doing everything you could. And you sure showed up at the right time."

"A neighbor called and reported a disturbance," he

explained. "And there's no need to apologize. I understand the strain you were under. Is she okay?"

Nick sighed and sank down into a plastic chair, the kind he always found so uncomfortable. Only tonight he didn't notice. "I don't know. She's in X ray."

"Can you tell me what happened?"

"Only what I saw. I think I must have come along toward the end," Nick explained.

The officer took notes as Nick spoke, looking up when he paused. "Could you give me a description of the assailant?"

Ruefully, Nick shook his head. "It was too dark. The guy took off before I got close enough to see anything, and he had a hat pulled low over his eyes. All I know for sure is that he was big—football-player type."

The policeman nodded. "Maybe Ms. Taylor will be able to add something to this," he said.

"I'm not sure she'll be up to talking to you tonight," Nick cautioned.

"If she's not, we'll do it another time," he said easily.

Nick's attention was suddenly distracted as he saw Laura being wheeled back into the examining room, and he was on his feet instantly. She had been left alone for the moment, and he moved close, alarmed by her pallor. Her face looked as white as the sheet drawn up barely high enough to cover her breasts. His eyes flickered across the expanse of skin, noting the long, angry bruise that marred the creamy flesh at her shoulder, apparently inflicted by the strap of her bag. He also noted something else—a three-inch-long scar of older vintage near the top of her right breast. He frowned, wondering about its origin. But before he could speculate, Laura called his name softly and his eyes flew to hers. Her hand reached for his through the bars of the gurney, and he gripped it tightly, reassuringly. His other hand smoothed the hair back from her face. The blood had been cleaned away, but her nose was puffy and one eye was purple and swollen nearly shut. His throat tightened painfully and he found it difficult to swallow.

"I guess I don't look so hot, huh?" she said, trying to smile.

"You look beautiful to me," he said hoarsely. Her eyes filled with tears, and he leaned closer, his breath warm on her cheek. "It's okay, sweetheart. It's okay to cry."

"I ne-never cry," she said, her words choppy as she fought for control.

"Well, maybe you should make an exception this once," he said softly.

The door swung open and, after one more worried look at Laura, Nick straightened up. The doctor glanced at him before his gaze came to rest on Laura. "Would you like him to stay while we discuss your condition?"

"Yes."

"All right." The doctor moved beside her. "You're a very lucky woman, Ms. Taylor. No broken bones, no internal injuries as far as we can determine. You've got quite a shiner, though, so I'd suggest an ice pack when you get home. The nose will be tender for a few days, but it will heal without any help. The ribs are another story. None are broken, but they're badly bruised. You'll need to take it easy for at least a week or so to give them a chance to start healing."

"A week?" she asked in alarm.

"At least," he confirmed.

"But, Doctor, I—"

"I'll see that she takes care of herself, Doctor," Nick interrupted, ignoring her protest.

Laura turned her head on the pillow and stared at him, but she remained silent.

The doctor looked from one to the other and gave a satisfied nod. "Good." Then he turned his attention to Laura. "There's a police officer here who would like to talk to you if you feel up to it."

Laura's hand reached for Nick's again. "I suppose I might as well get it over with."

"I'll send him in," the doctor said. "Then the nurse will help you dress and we'll give you something to relieve the pain so you can rest." He moved to the door and motioned to the officer.

Laura's details of the attack were even more vague than Nick's, and she looked at the policeman apologetically. "It happened so fast, and it was so dark… All I know is that he was big. And strong."

"Age? Race?" he prompted.

She shook her head slowly. "I'm sorry."

"Do you usually walk at that time of night?"

She shook her head. "No. I had taken the bus home, and—"

"Wait a minute," Nick interrupted. "What happened to your car? I thought you were picking it up tonight."

"It wasn't ready."

"Then why didn't you call me for a ride?" he demanded angrily.

"Mr. Sinclair." There was a warning note in the officer's voice.

Nick sighed and raked a hand through his hair. "Sorry."

"Go on, Ms. Taylor."

Laura finished her story and then looked at him resignedly. "I suppose there's not much chance of catching him, is there?"

"Honestly? None," he admitted frankly, closing his notebook. "He didn't get your purse, did he?"

"No. I had a pretty good grip on it."

"Let me leave you with one piece of advice, Ms. Taylor," the policeman said in a matter-of-fact tone. "I hope this never happens to you again. But if it should, forget your purse. Let it go. Your life is worth a lot more. That man could have had a gun or a knife. And I can guarantee you that if he had, you wouldn't be here right now. You'd be in the morgue," he said bluntly. Laura stared at him, tears welling up in her eyes. When he spoke again his voice was gentler. "I'll wait outside and give you folks a ride home whenever you're ready."

Nick could feel Laura trembling, and he stroked her head. "He's right, you know."

"But that guy was trying to take my purse," she said stubbornly.

"So let him have it! Good grief, Laura, was it worth this?"

"It's mine," she said, squeezing her eyelids shut. "I won't let anyone take what's mine. I won't be a victim again," she said fiercely, the tears spilling onto her cheeks. She opened her eyes and looked up at Nick. "Take me home, please," she pleaded.

He hesitated for a fraction of a second, still trying to figure out her last remark, and then reached down and smoothed the hair back from her face. "I'll get the nurse."

He waited outside while the woman helped Laura dress, and the doctor came over to speak to him. "I've given her a pretty strong sedative. She's had a bad shock, and the pain from her injuries will get worse before it gets better. This will knock her out for about twelve hours. By then her eye and nose should feel a little better. But those ribs are going to be sore, so she'll probably need this by tomorrow," he said, handing Nick a prescription. He paused for a moment before continuing. "She really shouldn't be left alone tonight."

"She won't be."

The doctor nodded. "That's what I thought."

The nurse appeared at the door, supporting Laura, who was walking hunched over, one hand pressed to her side. Her blouse, damaged beyond repair, had been replaced by an oversize surgical shirt that made her appear small and defenseless. Her face was gray with pain, and Nick moved to her side. "Maybe you should stay tonight," he said worriedly.

"No! I want to go home, Nick." Her eyes pleaded with him and, though it was against his better judgment, he relented.

"Okay. But not to your place. I'm not leaving you alone tonight. I want you close where I can keep an eye on you. You'll stay with me."

Laura looked up at him and opened her mouth to protest, but after one glance at his stony face she shut it. It was obvious that arguing would get her nowhere, and she wasn't up to it, anyway. She'd be perfectly all right alone, of course. But she had to admit that his concern had done more to relieve her pain than any drug the doctor could have offered.

Chapter Ten

By the time they got back to Laura's apartment, the sedative she'd been given was making her feel strangely light-headed, She was grateful for Nick's steady arms as he eased her into the front seat of his sports car, then squatted down beside her.

"Laura, is there anything you absolutely have to have from your apartment tonight?" he asked slowly, enunciating each word.

She frowned, trying to concentrate, but her mind felt fuzzy. "No, I don't think so."

"Okay. Then we'll head over to my place. It won't take long," he said, giving her hand an encouraging squeeze before gently closing the door.

Laura dozed as they drove, rousing only when he stopped at a drugstore.

"I'll only be a minute, and I'll lock the doors," he said, turning to her. "Will you be all right?"

"Yes."

He studied her carefully, a frown on his face. "I know you're hurting, sweetheart. But hang in there. We're almost home."

Oddly enough, she wasn't hurting. In fact, every bone in her body had gone limp and she felt as if she were floating. It was a pleasant sensation, and she let herself drift off again, hardly conscious of Nick's return and completely unaware of the worried frown he cast her way.

But reality came back with a vengeance when they arrived at Nick's condo and she tried to get out of the car. Even though he was helping her, a sharp, piercing pain shot through her rib cage, rudely assaulting her senses and leaving her gasping for breath.

Nick leaned in when she hesitated, took one look at her face and, without a word, put one arm under her knees and another around her shoulders, lifting her effortlessly out of the car. Even that hurt, though he'd been as gentle as possible, and tears stung her eyes. She bit her lip to keep from crying out, burying her face in his chest and clutching the soft cotton of his shirt as he cradled her in his arms.

Nick looked down at her bowed head, felt the tremor that ran through her body and wished he had some magical way of transporting her upstairs. But this was the best he could do. And the fact that she hadn't protested being carried told him more eloquently than words just how badly she was hurting.

Taking care to jostle her as little as possible, he pushed the door shut with his foot and strode to his condo, his step faltering only when he reached the door. He paused uncertainly and then leaned close to her ear, his breath comfortingly warm against her cheek as he spoke. "Laura, honey, I've got to put you down while I open the door. Can you stand on your own for a minute?"

Laura wasn't sure she could sit, let alone stand, but there was obviously no choice, so she nodded.

Carefully Nick lowered her legs to the ground, keeping one arm around her shoulders as he reached for the key. "Okay?" he asked gently.

She gave a barely perceptible nod, trying desperately to keep her knees from buckling.

From the way she clung to him, Nick knew that she was on shaky ground. The moment he had the door open he once again lifted her gently into his arms, and she nestled against him in a trusting way that made his throat constrict with the realization that, for the first time in this relationship, he felt truly needed. And surprisingly, for a man who'd studiously avoided the demands of a serious relationship, he found that it felt good. Amazingly good.

Laura shifted slightly in his arms, which effectively forced him to refocus his thoughts. Without bothering to turn on the lights downstairs, he quickly made his way through the dark living room and up the stairs to his bedroom, flicking on the light with his elbow as he entered. Laura felt herself being lowered to the bed, and when his arms released her she opened her eyes, took a deep breath and smiled at him shakily.

"I'm impressed," she said.

Nick was relieved that she was able to smile at all after what she'd been through, and he squatted down beside her. "What do you mean?"

"You must lift weights or something to be able to lug me all the way from the parking lot to the condo and then up those stairs."

"Well, I didn't want to tell you, but Superman was my cousin. Muscles run in our family," he teased gently.

"When you feel better, I'll show you my cape." He was rewarded by another smile. "I'm going to fix an ice pack for that eye," Nick said, straightening up. "Just lay there and rest until I get back."

"Gladly."

By the time he returned, Laura was dozing, and he paused in the doorway for a moment, his throat tightening as he studied her bruised face, his simmering rage once again threatening to erupt. If only he'd gotten to her a few moments sooner. She, who had always been so independent and strong, now seemed so fragile and vulnerable. He was surprised by the protective instinct she'd brought out in him, finding it a heady, but not unwelcome, feeling.

He moved beside her then, and her eyes fluttered open as he reached down and stroked her cheek. "Laura, I've got the ice pack. But first you need to change into something more comfortable. Jeans are great—but not for sleeping."

"I don't have anything," she said, her words slightly slurred.

"Well, I have a pajama top that might work." He moved to his dresser and rummaged in a drawer, looking for the rarely-used piece of clothing. The pajamas had been a gift from his mother, and he'd never worn them. In quick decision, he removed the bottoms as well as the top from the drawer before returning to her side.

"Laura, can you manage this?" he asked.

"I think so," she replied, looking at the pajama top he was holding.

"Okay. I'll wait outside. Let me know when you're ready."

Nick closed the door and leaned a shoulder against the wall, folding his arms against his chest. He took a deep, harsh breath and then expelled it slowly as a sudden, numbing weariness swept over him, the traumatic events of the past few hours finally extracting their toll. The sound of running water in the bathroom told him that at least Laura was able to move around a little, although what it cost her he couldn't imagine. Then he heard the water go off, and Nick waited expectantly for her to call to him. After several minutes, he frowned and knocked on the door. "Laura? Can I come in?"

There was a brief pause before she responded. "Yes."

He opened the door and found her still dressed, standing, one hand gripping the bedpost.

"Laura, honey, what's wrong?"

She looked at him, tears of pain and frustration in her eyes. "I can't get undressed," she said, her voice quavering. "It hurts too much."

"Then let me help you," he said without hesitation, quickly moving beside her. Noting the uncertainty in her eyes, he placed his hands on her shoulders and forced himself to smile. "Now, don't tell me you're worried about my intentions. I promise you I've never seduced a woman with a black eye."

Laura's lower lip trembled. She hated being so helpless, so dependent. But like it or not, she needed assistance tonight. Nick was available and willing, and if she had to rely on a man, there was no one else she would have chosen. "I guess I don't have a choice," she said with a sigh.

"Not tonight, I'm afraid. Now what exactly is the problem?"

"It hurts when I try to pull this thing over my head," she said, gesturing to the surgical top.

"Does it hurt when you lift your arms?"

"A little. But I can manage it."

"Okay, then just sit here," he said, easing her down on the side of the bed, "and lift your arms while I do the pulling. I'll stand behind you," he said easily. "It's okay if I look at your back, isn't it?" he asked with a grin.

She smiled shakily. "Yeah. I guess so."

He moved around to the other side of the bed, and she felt the mattress shift under his weight as he came up behind her. "Okay, sweetheart, let's give it a try."

Obediently she raised her arms, and Nick gently lifted the surgical top over her head. As it skimmed her sides he glanced down, his eyes arrested momentarily by the huge blackish-purple bruise stretching across her rib cage. He paused, a muscle tightening in his jaw, his stomach churning with anger and sympathy. She must be hurting—badly—yet she hadn't complained once.

"Nick?" Laura's voice was muffled, but he could hear the puzzled tone.

"We're doing great," he assured her, smoothly completing the maneuver. Then he turned to lay the garment aside, giving her a moment to slip her arms into the pajama top. By the time he came around to the other side of the bed, she was huddled miserably, her face once again pale and drawn. He dropped to one knee and took her hands between his, caressing the backs gently with his thumbs.

"I'm so sorry, Laura," he said, his voice laced with anguish. "I wish there was something I could do to help."

"You've done more than enough already. I'm sorry to have caused you all this trouble."

"It's no trouble. Believe me."

Laura looked into his eyes and believed. Unquestionably. Not knowing how to respond, unable in her present state to deal with complicated emotions, her gaze skittered away.

Sensing her discomfort, Nick rose and placed his hands on his hips. "What about the jeans?"

"I can get them down to my knees. I have trouble after that."

"Okay." He nodded, turning around. "Get them that far and I'll take care of the rest." He heard her stand, heard the zipper, heard the friction of the coarse denim fabric against her skin.

"All right, Nick."

When he turned back she was lying on the bed, the pajama top pulled down as far as possible but still revealing a long expanse of thigh and leg. He took a deep breath, forcing himself to focus on her pain. Any other thoughts were totally inappropriate at the moment, he told himself sternly. With an effort he drew his eyes away from the hem of the pajama top, and noted that the jeans were bunched around her knees. Silently he reached over and quickly eased them down her legs.

"Shoes," she said.

"What?" he asked distractedly.

"Shoes," she repeated, pointing to the athletic shoes and socks she still wore. "I don't think the jeans will go over them. And besides, I don't usually wear shoes to bed."

Nick flashed her a grin and bent to remove them, quickly stripping off her socks, as well. "Well, what's this?" he asked in surprise, cradling her foot in his hand.

"What's what?" she asked, puzzled. When he tapped one of her rosily polished toenails, she blushed. "Oh. You've discovered my one concession to vanity," she admitted sheepishly. "I've always envied women with beautiful nails, but unfortunately in my line of work that's not very practical. This is the next best thing. It's good for my ego, if nothing else."

Nick smiled at this unexpected facet of her character. He would never have believed it if he hadn't seen it for himself. With her sensible nature, Laura just didn't seem the type who would indulge in something like polished toenails. But apparently even she had a frivolous side. Which was fine as far as he was concerned. He had begun to think she never did anything for herself. Painted toenails weren't much, admittedly, but they were a start.

"You think it's silly, don't you?" she said, her cheeks still flushed.

"On the contrary. I think it's charming."

She smiled shyly and closed her eyes as everything began to grow hazy again. "I think I'll rest for a bit," she mumbled sleepily.

"Good idea. I'll hold this ice bag on your eye for a while, okay?" She nodded, wincing when he first placed it against her skin, but then gradually drifting into welcome oblivion.

Nick stayed with her for another half hour, and when he was satisfied that her deep, even breathing indicated sleep, he pulled the sheet up and tenderly brushed his lips across her forehead before turning the light off.

Once in the hall, he wearily rubbed the back of his

neck. Laura was docile tonight because she was hurting. But he knew when she woke up tomorrow she'd be hyper about her business, so diversionary tactics were needed. He frowned, trying to remember the name of her new foreman. Ken something. Nichols…Nolan… Nelson, that was it. With any luck, he'd be in the phone book.

Ten minutes later, after a satisfactory conversation with Ken, he headed back upstairs to the loft sitting area that overlooked the living room and opened up the sofa bed, glad now that he'd had the foresight to buy it. Although he'd never imagined that he'd be the first to use it, he thought ruefully.

By the time he took a quick shower downstairs and made up the bed, it was nearly two in the morning. But though he was bone tired, he still felt too keyed up emotionally to sleep. Rather than even try, he prowled around restlessly, verifying that he had breakfast food in the kitchen, going through his mail, looking over a few plans in the downstairs bedroom that he'd turned into an office, checking on Laura every few minutes. When at last his body revolted, he climbed into the sofa bed, yawned hugely and turned out the light.

Sleep came more quickly than he expected, a deep sleep that dulled his senses. So it took a long time for him to wake up, brought back to consciousness by something he couldn't immediately identify. Groggily he glanced at the illuminated dial of his watch and groaned. Three-thirty. His eyes flickered closed and he was beginning to drift back to sleep when Laura's soft sobs suddenly penetrated his sleep-fogged brain. Instantly alert, he swung his feet to the floor and moved quickly down the hall, pausing briefly on the threshold of her room, which was illuminated only by a dim night-light. In the shadows, he heard Laura thrashing fretfully around on the bed, mumbling incoherently, sobbing quietly. She must be having a nightmare, he thought, moving quietly beside her, and he wasn't surprised, not after what she'd been through. She'd probably be plagued with them for months, only the next time he wouldn't be there to comfort her, he thought, a muscle clenching in his jaw. He bent to gently touch her shoulder when suddenly Laura flung out an arm.

"No, Joe, don't! Please don't hurt me!" she cried.

Nick yanked his hand back at her impassioned plea, and his heart actually stopped, then lunged on, hammering painfully against his chest. She wasn't having a nightmare about tonight's attacker. She was having a nightmare about her husband! What had that bastard done to her? he wondered in sudden fury.

Laura's thrashing grew more intense, and Nick became alarmed, fearing that she would injure herself even further. He crouched beside the bed, reaching over to gently stroke her hair. "It's okay, sweetheart. It's okay," he murmured soothingly, aware that her whole body was trembling.

Her eyes flickered open, and she stared at his shadowy figure dazedly. "Nick?" Her voice was barely a whisper.

"It's me, honey," he said huskily. "Everything's okay. You just had a bad dream, that's all. Try to relax and go back to sleep."

"Could…could you stay with me for a little while?" she asked in a tremulous, little-girl voice that tore at his heart.

"Sure." He took her hand, and she grasped it with a steel grip that surprised him. "I'll be right here."

He continued to stroke her hair, murmuring soothing words, and slowly she relaxed. Her breathing grew more even and gradually her grip on his hand loosened as she slipped back into sleep.

When she seemed to be resting easily, Nick carefully extricated his hand and gingerly stood up, much to the relief of his protesting calf muscles. He frowned as he stared down at Laura, her face now at peace as she slumbered. He ought to go back to bed, he supposed. But he just couldn't leave her. Not yet, anyway. He wanted to be at her side if she awoke again in the grip of another nightmare.

Wearily he sank down in an overstuffed chair near the bed. It had been a very long day. And it looked like it was going to be a very long night.

Nick let his head drop onto the cushioned back and stared at the dark ceiling, torn by conflicting emotions that he didn't understand. He cared about Laura. Deeply. But what was he getting himself into? She was obviously troubled, clearly scarred emotionally, and he was no psychologist. He ought to get out of this relationship while he still could.

Only it was already too late, he acknowledged with a resigned sigh. He couldn't walk away, not now. Not after he'd seen the vulnerable look in her eyes tonight. And maybe not ever. But they couldn't go on as they had. He'd heard too much tonight, learned more from those few words spoken in sleep than he'd learned from all of their waking conversations. The time had come to demand some answers, to examine the reasons why she was so afraid of commitment. It wouldn't be easy for her. But psychologist or not, he knew with absolute certainty that until they confronted the demons from her past, they had no future together.

Laura awoke slowly, disoriented and sluggish. It was a struggle just to open her eyes. She raised her arm and stared at her watch, squinting as she tried to make out the time, but for some reason she had trouble focusing.

One thing did come suddenly—and clearly—into focus, however: her attire. She was wearing a man's pajama top! And just where exactly was she anyway? she wondered in sudden panic, her gaze sweeping over the unfamiliar surroundings. It jolted abruptly to a stop on Nick's sleeping figure, slumped uncomfortably in a chair near the bed, his leg slung over one of the arms.

Suddenly memories of the night before came rushing back—the horror, certainly, but even more prominently the care and tenderness of the wonderful man just a touch away. In sleep, his face had an endearing, boyish quality that she'd never seen before. His hair might be tousled, and he might look rumpled and unshaven, but as far as she was concerned he was the handsomest, most appealing man she'd ever seen.

Of course, the bare chest might have something to do with that perception, she admitted, her eyes drawn to the T pattern of dark, curly hair that rose and fell in time with his even breathing. Her own breathing was suddenly none too steady, and she had a sudden, compelling urge to reach over and lay her hand close to his heart, feel the rise and fall of his broad chest beneath her fingers.

At just that moment, as if sensing her gaze, Nick

awoke—abruptly, immediately and fully. His gaze locked on hers, his stomach instinctively contracting at the purple, swollen eye and puffy nose, harshly spotlighted in the brightness of day. He rose stiffly from his uncomfortable position and then moved toward the bed in two long strides, squatting down beside her.

"Good morning, sweetheart," he said, his voice still husky from sleep. He reached over and stroked her hair, his eyes never leaving hers. "How do you feel?"

She frowned and gingerly touched her face, then her side, wincing at even the slightest pressure. "I'm a little sore," she said breathlessly, her voice unsteady.

"I have a feeling that's the understatement of the year," he replied with a frown, his lips compressing into a thin line.

"I'll be fine," she assured him. "But…did you sleep in that chair all night?" she asked, her eyes wide.

"What was left of it," he said with a wry grin.

"You must be exhausted! I'm so sorry to cause all this trouble," she apologized, her eyes filling with tears.

Nick reached over as one spilled out to trickle down her cheek, wiping it away with a gentle finger, his throat constricting painfully. "Laura, you were no trouble. Trust me," he said, his own voice uneven. She still looked unconvinced, and his instinct was to kiss away her doubts. But given her physical—and emotional—fragility at the moment, that was probably not wise. Mustering all of his self restraint, he tenderly touched her cheek and then stood up. "I'll run downstairs and get you a pill, okay?"

She nodded silently, still feeling off balance and uncharacteristically weepy.

His concerned eyes searched hers, and then he turned and rummaged in the closet for a shirt and slacks. "Just stay put till I get back," he said over his shoulder, sliding the door shut and making a quick exit.

When he reached the loft, he rapidly pulled on the cotton slacks and thrust his arms into the hastily retrieved shirt, distractedly rolling the sleeves to the elbows. Based on her pallor and lines of strain in her face, Laura needed a painkiller quickly. He took the steps two at a time, and returned in record time with the pill and a glass of water.

Laura was up, gripping her side and leaning against the bedpost for support, when he entered the room. "I thought I told you to stay put," he said with a frown.

"Nick, do you know what time it is?" she asked, panic edging her voice.

He glanced at his watch. "Nine o'clock."

"I should have been at work an hour ago... Ken won't know what happened... He was supposed to pick me up at seven-thirty... My car's ready today," she said disjointedly.

"Relax, honey," he said, depositing the pill and water on the dresser and easing her back down to the bed. "I called Ken last night. Everything's under control. He'll fill in until you feel well enough to go back."

"But I have so much to do. I can't take another day off. I can at least go to the office. That won't be too taxing, and—"

"Forget it, Laura," he said flatly, cutting her off.

She stared at him. "Excuse me?"

He sighed, regretting the dictatorial approach. Maybe logic would work better. He sat down next to her and gently took her hand. "Look, Laura, you're in no shape to get out of bed, let alone go to the office. Do you honestly feel up to doing anything today?"

She stared at him, savoring the warm clasp of his hand on one level, thinking about his question on another. The truth was, she didn't. But that had never stopped her before. She hadn't been able to let it. It hadn't mattered how she'd felt; the job had to be done. But then again, she'd never felt quite this bad. Her ribs ached, she could barely see out of her left eye and her nose was almost too tender to touch. Besides, every muscle in her body felt as if it had been pulled taut. But there was work to be done. "No, I don't," she admitted. "But I can't afford to lose a day," she said resolutely.

"For the sake of your health, you can't afford not to," he told her bluntly.

She looked at him in exasperation. "Nick, you just don't understand. I'm it. Taylor Landscaping is a one-person show at the management level. You have someone to fall back on. I don't. I can't take a day off."

Laura took a deep breath and stood, gripping the headboard to steady herself. Tears pricked her eyes and she forced them back, but she couldn't do anything about the trembling in her hands. And Nick wasn't blind.

He remained on the bed for a moment, looking up at her back, ramrod straight, and the defiant tilt of her head. She was probably going to hate him after this, he thought ruefully, but there was no way he was letting her set one foot outside this condo today. He wouldn't be surprised if her stubborn determination carried her through a day at the office. Laura wasn't a quitter, that was for sure. But by tonight she'd be a basket case. He steeled himself for her anger and stood, moving to face her, placing his hands on her shoulders.

"Laura, I'm sorry. No way. I've already called Ken, who sounds very competent, and he's handling everything. You're not leaving here until tomorrow."

"Tomorrow?" she stammered.

"Tomorrow," he declared.

"Nick, you can't do this!"

"I can and I am. I'm bigger than you are. And you're in no shape to resist. I'll sit on you if I have to, but I hope it won't come to that."

Nick saw the anger and defiance flash in her eyes and prepared to do battle. But then he watched in amazement as the flame of anger slowly flickered and went out. Her shoulders suddenly sagged and she carefully sat back on the bed, dropping her head to hide the tears that shimmered in her eyes. He squatted in front of her and took her hands in his, taken aback by her unexpected acquiescence. He'd expected a struggle; instead, she'd caved in. Had he pushed too hard, been too heavy-handed? He knew her emotions were tattered. "Laura, I'm sorry for being so obstinate about this," he said gently. "But I'm doing it for you."

"I know," she said softly, struggling to keep the tears from spilling out of her eyes, but the tenderness in his voice just made it more difficult. It had been so long since she'd felt this cared for, this protected, this cherished. Her heart overflowed with gratitude…and something else she refused to acknowledge. Instead, she met his eyes and tried to smile, but didn't quite succeed. "I'm very grateful. It's been a long time since…" Her voice trailed off and she looked down at the strong, competent hands that held hers so comfortingly.

Nick didn't move. He just stared at her bowed head, struggling to regain his own composure. It wasn't easy, not when his emotions were pulling at him like a riptide, threatening to sweep him off balance, a protective instinct emerging on the one hand, a purely sensual one on the other. The latter instinct urged him to take her in his arms, to kiss away her tears, to love her as she deserved to be loved. She seemed so desperately in need of loving.

"Laura," he said at last, the unevenness of his voice making him stop and clear his throat before continuing. Her head remained bowed. "Laura," he repeated, squeezing her hands, this time forcing her to meet his eyes, which held hers with a compelling intensity. "You are very special to me. Special, and precious. When I think about what could have happened last night…" He closed his eyes for a moment and took a steadying breath, struggling for composure before fixing his intense gaze on her once again. "You're not in great shape," he said, reaching up to her eye with a whisper touch, "but you'll be okay. You'll be okay," he repeated more forcefully, as much to convince himself as to reassure her, touching her as he spoke—her arm, her cheek, her hair. "And I don't want you to ever be alone and frightened again."

She stared at him, swallowing with difficulty. "Is that why you slept in the chair last night?"

"Yeah. You had a nightmare," he said quietly. "I wanted to be close in case it happened again."

She studied his eyes—dark, intense and filled with integrity. He seemed too good to be real, and she reached over and tentatively touched the angled planes of his face. A muscle twitched in his jaw, and she watched as the smoldering sparks of passion in his eyes burst into flame. Alarmed, she tried to draw her hand away, not wanting to create false expectations. But he held her fast, his fingers tightening on her wrist.

"Laura?" his voice was gentle, his eyes probing. "What is it?"

"I—I'd really like it if you would just hold me," she said, so quietly he had to lean close to hear. "But that's not fair to you. I can see that...I mean, you want more and right now...I can't promise that."

He placed his fingers against her lips, and her eyes searched his. "Sweetheart, if being held is what you need now, that's what I'll give. Okay?"

Her head nodded jerkily, and he eased her back on the bed, then stretched out beside her, carefully gathering her soft, bruised body into his arms. It was some minutes before he felt her tension ease, and then he brushed his cheek against her hair. "Better?" he asked.

"Yes. But, Nick...I know this isn't enough for you."

"It's enough," he assured her. But then he added a qualification. "For now."

Chapter Eleven

The persistent ringing of the phone slowly penetrated Laura's consciousness. Tenderly cradled in Nick's arms, feeling utterly safe and content, she had drifted off to sleep. When the ringing of the bedside phone continued, she opened her eyes and glanced up questioningly. "Nick?"

"Mmm-hmm."

"The phone's ringing."

"I know."

"Aren't you going to answer it?"

"I don't think so."

"But it might be something important."

"It's probably just the office."

The ringing stopped, and Laura's eyes grew wide. "The office! What are you doing home? Shouldn't you have been at work hours ago?"

"Normally, yes," he replied mildly.

"So?"

"The past eighteen hours haven't exactly been normal," he reminded her wryly.

"No, I suppose not," she conceded. "But I'll be okay here. You don't have to baby-sit."

"Work can wait," he insisted.

Suddenly the phone rang again, and Nick glanced at it in irritation. But Laura also saw the concern in his eyes, and she nudged him with her shoulder. "Go ahead. This will drive you crazy."

He sighed. "Yeah, I guess so." He reached over to pick up the receiver. "Jack? I told you this morning, we'll have to postpone it. I'm not leaving Laura today." Silence, while he absently continued to stroke her shoulder. "Yeah, yeah, I know, but you don't need me for the presentation." Silence again. "Look, just cover for me. Tell him…I don't know, tell him anything."

Laura frowned. Nick obviously had a commitment, apparently an important one. The thought that he was willing to forgo it on her behalf filled her with a warm glow, but at the same time, she'd struggled long enough herself to know that it was never wise to upset a client.

"Nick," she whispered.

He glanced down. "Jack, hang on a second." Depressing the mute button, he reached down to stroke her cheek, his brusque, businesslike tone of moments before suddenly gentled. "What is it, honey?"

"Go to your meeting. It sounds important."

"You're more important," he insisted.

She smiled her thanks, but shook her head. "I'll feel guilty if you don't go. There's no sense in both of us falling behind, and I'll be fine." She could see the flicker of indecision in his eyes, and with a determined smile she gently eased herself away from the warmth of his body and swung her feet to the floor, trying not to wince at the sudden pain in her side. Carefully she stood, and by the time she turned back to him her features were placid. "Come on, you'll be late," she urged lightly.

Nick hesitated a fraction of a second longer and then released the mute button, glancing at his watch. "Okay, Jack, I'll be there. But not until one-thirty. That will give us time to look over the presentation and make sure we're in sync before Andrews arrives... Yeah, I know."

Nick replaced the receiver and stood, facing Laura across the bed. "I hate to leave you," he said with simple honesty.

"I'll be fine," she assured him again. "And you'll be back."

"You can count on that. And as soon as possible," he said huskily. Laura felt the warmth creep up her cheeks at his tone and glanced down, tugging self-consciously at the brief hem of the pajama top she wore. Nick cleared his throat. "Do you need anything from your apartment? I could stop by on the way back."

"Other than my toothbrush, I think I'm okay for another day. Except...do you have an old shirt or something with buttons I could borrow? I'd rather not put that thing on again," she said, gesturing distastefully toward the discarded surgical top.

"I'm sure I can find something. And I may even have a spare toothbrush." He returned triumphantly a few moments later with the latter item, still cellophane enclosed, and quickly riffled through his closet. "Will this work?" he asked, withdrawing a striped cotton shirt.

"Perfect. I'll just roll up the sleeves and it will be fine."

"Can you get dressed on your own?"

"I think so. But I'd like to take a shower first."

Nick nodded. "I'll put some fresh towels out for you and come back in a few minutes."

It took Laura a lot longer to shower than she expected. First, a glance in the mirror over the sink made her stop in midstride, alarmed at the extent of the damage. She looked terrible. Her nose wasn't too bad—just slightly puffy—but the purple-and-red eye, still half-swollen shut, made up for it. She wished she had some makeup, but she doubted whether anything would be able to disguise the discolored area. She'd barely come to grips with the appearance of her battered face when she'd been shocked by the huge, ugly blue-black swath of skin splayed over her ribs. It had made her momentarily queasy, and she'd forced herself to take a few deep breaths, telling herself that she was okay, that the bruise would eventually fade. But no wonder she hurt so much!

Carefully she stepped into the shower, adjusting the water temperature before turning on the spray. The sudden force of water against her ribs, however, made her gasp in pain, and she quickly angled away from the spray, shielding her side. Nick had been right about her going to work today, she admitted. She was in no shape to sit at a desk, let alone visit the job sites. Just the exertion of taking a shower had drained her. But the warm spray felt good, and she let it massage her body with its soothing caress.

At last, Laura reluctantly turned off the water and toweled herself dry, carefully avoiding the injured areas.

She dressed slowly, easing the jeans over her legs, grimacing as she bent to pull them up. The voluminous shirt was easier, and as she slipped her arms into the sleeves she caught the unique scent that she had come to associate with Nick—warm, vibrant, slightly spicy... and very masculine. For a moment she buried her face in its folds, wistfully inhaling the essence. Then with a sigh she slipped it over her head.

Laura pulled a comb from her purse and carefully worked the tangles out of her wet, tousled hair. By the time she finished it was almost dry, hanging loose and long, with a few stray tendrils curling around her face.

"Laura, are you okay?" Nick's soft knock and worried voice came through the door.

"I'm fine. I'll be right out," she called. After neatly folding the wet towels and placing them on the edge of the tub, she picked up her purse and opened the door.

Nick's perceptive eyes swept over her. "How are you feeling?"

"Better. The shower helped."

He grinned and folded his arms, tilting his head as he looked at her. "You know, that shirt looks a whole lot better on you than it ever did on me," he said.

"It's a little big," she said, a smile hovering around the corners of her mouth.

"Big is in. It's a very attractive look."

Laura shrugged. "I don't feel very attractive," she admitted.

If any other woman had said that to him, Nick would have assumed she was angling for a compliment. With Laura, the remark had been artless and without pretense. He moved toward her and placed his hands on her shoulders. "Sweetheart, you are the most irresistible woman I've ever known," he said huskily. And then he lightened his tone. "Even with that shiner."

Laura looked up at him in surprise, suddenly realizing that he'd been using terms of endearment ever since last night. They seemed to come so naturally to him, and had sounded so natural to her, that it had taken all this time for the fact to register. Before she could evaluate its significance, however, he was leading her out the door.

"I'm afraid I'm not much of a cook, but you can't afford to skip any more meals and I didn't want you to have to fix anything yourself," he said over his shoulder. "I hope this is at least palatable."

He stepped aside when they reached the loft, where a tray rested on the coffee table in front of the now-made-up sofa sleeper. Laura's eyes grew wide. It wasn't so much the contents—scrambled eggs, toast, an orange that had been carefully peeled and separated into chunks, a steaming cup of coffee—but the thoughtfulness of the gesture that stirred her heart. Her throat constricted with emotion, and when she turned to Nick the warmth in her unguarded eyes made him catch his breath. "Nick, I... After all you've already done, this makes me feel so..." She gestured helplessly.

He grinned, inordinately pleased by her response, and took her hand, steering her toward the sofa. "Don't say anything else until you've tasted it," he warned teasingly. He settled her comfortably and then glanced at his watch. "Do you mind if I get dressed while you eat?"

"No, of course not."

By the time she'd finished the last bite of what she

would always remember as one of the best meals of her life, Nick reappeared, dressed in a lightweight charcoal gray suit, crisp white shirt and paisley tie. He smiled when he saw the empty plate. "Well, I guess it wasn't too bad. Or else you were starved." When she started to speak, he held up his hand. "No, don't tell me which. I prefer to keep my illusions."

Laura smiled. "Thank you," she said simply.

His expression grew suddenly serious and he sat down beside her, grasping her hand as he studied her eyes. "Laura, are you sure you'll be all right? I can still stay if you want me to."

"I'll be fine," she assured him again. "I took the pill you left on the tray, and I already feel very relaxed and sleepy. I'm just going to nap this afternoon, and it makes no sense for you to sit around and miss an important appointment while I sleep."

Nick bowed to the logic of her argument. "Okay. But I'll be back early—no later than five. Do you like Chinese food?"

"Love it."

"I'll pick some up on the way home." He stood, taking the tray with him.

"Oh, Nick, let me take care of that," she protested.

"No way. You're not to lift a finger today. Promise me that, or I'm not leaving."

She shook her head. "You really do have a one-track mind."

"Promise?" he persisted.

"Promise," she agreed.

Laura's day went almost exactly as predicted. She took a few minutes to explore Nick's condo, admiring his spare but tasteful and obviously expensive furnishings. The cathedral-ceilinged living room, overlooked by the loft, featured a two-story wall of glass that offered a restful view of the wooded common ground. She peeked into his office, impressed by its neatness, and through the window she glimpsed what looked like a clubhouse and swimming pool. Compared to this, her apartment really was the pits, she thought. No wonder he had remarked on the neighborhood a few weeks ago. And rightly so, she thought wryly, wincing at the twinge in her side as she turned.

After a quick call to Sam, who was shocked by the mugging but clearly pleased by Nick's attentiveness and concern, Laura took another pill and lay down. Within minutes she was asleep.

The sound of Nick's voice calling from downstairs awakened her later in the afternoon, and by the time she had oriented herself and was struggling to sit up, he appeared in the doorway, his jacket already discarded, his face a mask of concern. He moved beside her immediately, his intense, dark eyes critically examining her. For a moment he hesitated, and then he reached over and touched his lips to her forehead. "I'd like to give you a better hello, but that's about the only spot I know of that isn't bruised," he said huskily, brushing her hair back from her face as he spoke.

Laura smiled hesitantly. "My lips are okay," she said softly.

Nick's momentary surprise was quickly followed by a pleased chuckle, and the deep, throaty sound of it sent a hot wave of desire crashing over her. "Are you saying you'd like to be kissed?" he asked with a smile.

She swallowed. "Only if it's what you want."

"Oh, I want," he said huskily, and the ardent light in

his eyes left little doubt about his wants. "I just don't want to hurt you."

Laura's mouth went dry. Already her lips were throbbing in anticipation of his touch. "We'll be careful," she whispered.

Nick gave up the fight. He'd told himself she was in no shape, physically or emotionally, for intimacy right now. He'd told himself that he would keep his hands off until she was stronger. He'd told himself that she wasn't herself, that the trauma of the previous night could make her needy in ways she would later regret. But he was only human, after all. And the tender, welcoming look in her eyes was too much for him. With a soft groan he lowered his lips to hers, gently nipping at their pliant fullness, until her mouth stirred sweetly beneath his. He felt her shudder as he tasted the warm sweetness of her mouth, and her response nearly undid him. Gently he lowered her to the bed and stretched out beside her, cradling her head in his hands, his fingers lost in the thick fullness of her hair. How he'd waited for this moment, to have her close to him. His lips left hers, moving down to her neck, and she arched her throat for his touch, breathing heavily. Her arms clung to him, urging him closer. Nick let one hand travel downward until it rested lightly at her waist. Laura was so lost in the magic of his touch that it took her a moment to realize that his hand was gently but firmly tugging her shirt free.

Laura knew where this was leading, knew she was breaking every rule she'd ever made about allowing any man to get close to her again, knew that it went against everything she believed about casual intimacy. And yet she seemed powerless to stop what was happening.

When Nick had appeared in the doorway tonight she'd had no plan to initiate this embrace. But he'd looked so wonderful standing there, so dear and so handsome and so very special. And she was very grateful for all he'd done for her. Yet she was honest enough to admit that gratitude wasn't the only explanation for her behavior. Last night had been like déjà vu, a bad dream come again to life, awakening old memories and old pain. Today she felt vulnerable, needy, scared—aching physically and emotionally. Nick, with his gentle touch and caring concern, could make her fears and pain disappear, at least for a little while. Her Christian faith put strict limits on intimacy outside of marriage, and she knew she was pushing those limits. Tomorrow she'd probably be sorry. But for now, she needed to be held, to be cared for and protected, to bask in the warmth of his caresses.

Laura felt her shirt being pulled free, felt his hand hesitate briefly at her waist before sliding slowly up her back. The warmth of his fingers against her bare skin made her sigh. "Oh, Nick," she breathed, her own fingers kneading his hard, muscled shoulders. He urged her closer, his lips once more capturing hers with an urgency that stole her breath away.

It was her sudden, sharp intake of breath that stilled his hands and made him draw back. Her face had gone white and tears glimmered in her eyes. "Nick...I'm sorry," she said breathlessly. "My side... I forgot..."

Her voice trailed off at the stricken look on Nick's face. "Oh, sweetheart," he whispered, cradling her face in his hands, stroking her cheeks with his thumbs. "I'm so sorry! Did I hurt you?"

"It's okay. It just...surprised me. It doesn't hurt now."

She wanted to smooth out the deep creases that had appeared on his brow, ease the sudden tension in his jaw, erase the self-recrimination in his eyes.

"I told myself not to touch you. I knew better," he said angrily.

"Nick, it's my fault. I—I more or less asked you to."

"Yeah, well, you're not thinking straight. You're probably half out of your mind in pain and you're doped up on those high-powered pills. Laura, let me take a look, okay? I promise not to hurt you. I just want to make sure I didn't do any more damage."

Laura knew he needed to reassure himself, so she nodded silently. With utmost care he pulled up her shirt-tail, sucking in his breath at the bruise that extended from her breastbone to the bottom of her rib cage. "Dear God, it looks worse than yesterday," he declared in dismay.

"Bruises usually do," she said lightly, easing the shirt back down. "But it will fade, Nick."

"No thanks to me."

"Nick, I'm okay. And hungry. Where's that Chinese food you promised me?" she asked, trying to divert his attention.

For the rest of the evening he treated her like spun glass, helping her up and down the steps, getting a cushion for the back of her chair while they ate, wrapping an afghan around her before they settled in to watch an old movie on video that he'd brought home.

When he tucked her in for the night, gently pressing a chaste kiss on her forehead, Laura smiled. "You'd make a good mother," she joked gently.

"Laura, believe me, my feelings for you are anything

but motherly," he said with an intensity that left no doubt about exactly what his feelings were. "My restraint is the result of sheer terror. I never want to hurt you, sweetheart, and if touching you hurts at the moment, I won't touch. The important thing right now is for you to heal."

Later, as Laura began to drift to sleep, she thought about Nick's parting words. She would heal—physically. It would just take time. It was the emotional healing that still troubled her. Today they'd been closer physically than ever before. Not because he'd pushed, as she'd feared all along, but because she'd pressed him. He'd responded readily, and she couldn't blame him; he'd long ago made his intentions clear. But they'd been heading for a level of intimacy that she believed should be reserved for a committed relationship. And even if he had suggested that, Laura knew she wasn't yet ready—just needy. And that wasn't enough. For either of them.

Nick didn't sleep well. His body was still vibrating with unrelieved tension, and his conscience was battering him for letting his emotions and physical needs cloud his sensitivity and judgment. It was the early hours of the morning before he finally fell into a restless sleep, and even then he only slept lightly, half expecting to again hear Laura's anguished cries, as he had the night before. But all was quiet.

It seemed he had just drifted off when he felt someone prodding his shoulder. "Come on, sleepyhead, wake up," an amused voice said.

Nick opened one eye and stared up at Laura, fully

dressed, standing with her hands on her hips next to his bed. "What time is it?" he asked groggily.

"Seven-thirty."

He groaned and buried his head in his pillow.

"Nick Sinclair, even if you have time to loaf, I don't. I need to get to the office."

Nick sighed. It had been hard enough to hold Laura down for one day. He'd pretty much figured two days were out of the question. "Did anyone ever tell you that you're a hard taskmaster?" he growled.

She prodded him again. "Come on, Nick. Here, try this. Maybe it will help." She waved a fragrant-smelling cup of coffee under his nose.

He sniffed appreciatively and grasped the mug in both hands, taking a long swallow before he even opened his eyes. And this time he took a good look at her. Her nose seemed back to normal, her eye was slightly less swollen—though no less purple—and he could only speculate about her ribs. But her face had more color than yesterday, and she seemed to be in good spirits.

"How do you feel?" he asked, watching her over the rim of his cup as he took another swallow.

She shrugged. "Compared to what? Better than yesterday, worse than last weekend. It's all in your point of view. But I'll live."

She was her spunky self again, which meant that she really must be feeling better. Nick was glad, of course, but he felt a sudden, odd sense of loss. For the past thirty-six hours she'd needed him—really needed him—and though the circumstances had been less than ideal, the feeling had been good. Now, suddenly, he felt less needed, less important in her life. He took another sip of the coffee and, trying to throw off his melancholy mood, he glanced at his watch. "Okay, give me fifteen minutes and we can roll."

At her request, Nick dropped her off at the garage to pick up her car, coming around to open the door for her when they arrived. "Do you think you're up to driving?" he asked worriedly.

"Of course," she said with more confidence than she felt.

He sighed and raked his fingers through his hair. "Laura, will you promise me something? If you get tired, go home and rest. Don't force yourself to put in a full day."

"I'll be fine, Nick. Okay, okay." She held up her hands when he opened his mouth to protest. "I'll try not to push myself."

"Promise?"

"Promise."

"Okay. Now, what would you like for dinner tonight?"

"Tonight?" she asked, startled.

"Mmm-hmm. Does pizza sound okay?"

"Well, sure. But, Nick, you don't have to feel obligated. I can manage."

"Yeah, I know. I just hoped you might like to have dinner with me. Besides, you may feel perky now, but I have a feeling that you're going to fade by this afternoon, and I doubt whether you'll be in the mood to cook." More likely she'd just fall into bed without eating, he thought, and skipping meals was not something she could afford to do.

"Well…thank you. That would be great."

"I'll see you about six," he said, walking around to

the driver's side of his car and opening the door. "And, Laura...?"

"Yes?"

"Will you take it easy today?"

"I'll try," she hedged.

Nick rolled his eyes and shook his head. "You're stubborn, do you know that?"

She grinned. "Yeah. But it takes one to know one." Then she grew more serious. "Nick...I want to thank you for...well, for everything. You've been really great. I don't know how I would have managed without you. Knowing you were there—just having you with me— made all the difference."

He looked at her for a long moment before speaking. "Hold that thought," he said at last. Then he slipped into the low-slung car and was gone.

Chapter Twelve

Nick called Laura several times during the day. Though she kept her voice determinedly cheerful, he could hear the underlying weariness that intensified with each call. She stuck it out most of the day, despite his urging to go home and take a nap, and by the time he arrived at her apartment with the pizza he wasn't sure what shape she'd be in.

Not good, he thought the moment she opened the door. Her face was as pale as it had been at the hospital two nights before, making the dark, ugly colors of her bruised eye stand out in stark relief.

Nick opened his mouth to tell her she had pushed too hard, took another look at her weary face and changed his mind. She'd clearly already had all she could take today. What she needed now was support, not criticism.

"Rough day," he said quietly. It was a statement, not a question.

"Is it that obvious?" she asked ruefully, shutting the door behind him.

"Mmm-hmm," he replied, aware that she was moving stiffly and slowly—and trying to hide it.

"You look tired," she said, studying his face.

He hadn't really thought it, but she was right. The strain and worry had taken their toll on him, too. "Yeah. I am."

"Why don't you sit down and I'll get you something to drink. I'm sorry about the heat. I turned on all the fans, but I know you're used to air-conditioning. At least you changed into something cooler before you came. Would you like some iced tea, or—"

"Laura." His quiet voice stilled her.

"Yes?"

"Would you please sit down before you fall down? You look half-dead. I did not come over here tonight to be waited on." He took her arm and guided her to the couch, and she went unprotestingly, the stream of adrenaline that had kept her on her feet all day suddenly running dry. All at once she was overcome with a numbing lethargy, and she sank down gratefully onto the soft, chintz-covered cushions of her couch.

"Would you like a cold drink?"

She gazed up at him, her eyes slightly dazed with fatigue. "Yes, I think I would. There's some soda in the fridge."

She heard the clatter of ice and then he was back beside her, a glass in each hand. "I put the pizza in the oven to warm for a few minutes."

She nodded, silently sipping the sweet liquid, fighting a losing battle to keep her eyelids open. When her head began to nod, Nick reached over and gently took the glass from her fingers, then he pulled her against him, carefully avoiding contact with her bruised ribs.

She nestled into the crook of his arm, her cheek resting against the hard contours of his chest, and sighed.

"I'm not much company, am I?" she said apologetically.

"Don't worry about it. I didn't expect you to play hostess."

"I'm just so tired."

"I know." What Laura needed tonight was food and sleep, in that order and preferably as quickly as possible, he concluded. What he needed was beside the point, he thought longingly as her firm, supple body molded to his caused stirrings of emotion best held in check. This was not the time. "How about some pizza?" he asked, his chin resting on her hair.

Laura wasn't hungry. Just tired. But she knew she needed to eat, and Nick had gone to the trouble of bringing food, so she nodded.

She perked up a little as she munched on the spicy, rich pizza, enough to remember that she wanted to invite Nick to dinner the next night. He protested at first, suggesting instead that they go out so she wouldn't have to cook, but she insisted.

"I really want to, Nick. It's Saturday, so I can rest all day. And I like to cook. It's not exactly strenuous, and I find it relaxing. Besides, I want to thank you for everything you've done these past couple of days."

"You don't need to do that, Laura."

"I want to. Unless…that is…well, I understand if you have other plans," she said, her voice suddenly sounding uncertain.

He reached across the table and took her hand, forcing her to meet his eyes. "I don't have any other plans," he said firmly. "I'll be here." He gave her fingers a gentle squeeze and then released them, standing to clear away the remnants of their meal. When she started to help, he placed a hand firmly on her shoulder. "Just sit," he commanded.

"Can I at least move to the living room?" she asked with a tired smile.

"Sure. I'll be right in."

By the time he rejoined her, she was sitting in a corner of the couch, her legs tucked under her, her head resting against the back, her eyes closed. He thought she might have dozed off again, but when he quietly sat down next to her, her eyelids flickered open.

"Dinner was great. You're going to spoil me," she said with a smile.

"You could do with some spoiling."

"Well, I'm not used to it, that's for sure."

Nick reached over and took her hand, gently stroking the back with his thumb. "Laura?"

"Mmm-hmm?"

"Will you be okay here tonight by yourself?"

"Of course," she lied. In reality, she was as nervous as the deer they'd spotted in the woods, but she wasn't about to admit that to Nick. He'd insist on spending the night on her couch and he looked wiped out. After the past couple of days, he deserved a decent night's sleep in his own bed.

"I could stay," he offered.

"No. You need to get some rest. I'll be fine."

"But what if you have another nightmare?"

"I won't. I was fine last night, wasn't I?"

"Yeah, but subconsciously you knew I was close by."

She couldn't argue with that. The simple fact was

she *would* sleep better with Nick here. She was still spooked from the attack, and she knew that when quiet descended on the apartment after he left, every sound would seem magnified—and menacing. But she couldn't live the rest of her life afraid. "Nick, please... I've got to stay by myself eventually. It would just be postponing the inevitable," she said resolutely. "The memory of the attack will fade in time."

"That's true. But at the moment I'm more concerned about other memories."

She frowned. "What do you mean?"

"I mean the nightmare you had the other night wasn't about the attack," he said quietly.

"How do you know?"

"Because I heard what you said. Laura...it was about Joe."

A stricken look crossed her face, and she bit her lip. "Oh," she said in a small voice, turning away.

He reached over and stroked her arm, and then his hand strayed to the top of her right breast, his fingers resting lightly on the spot where he'd seen the scar two nights before. "Did he do this to you?" he asked, a sudden edge to his voice.

He felt her stiffen even before she pulled away. "What?"

"The scar. I saw it at the hospital."

She drew a deep, shaky breath. "Nick, what happened between Joe and me is in the past. Let's leave it there."

"I'd like to, because I know it's painful for you. But I can't. Because whatever happened between the two of you is coming between us, whether you want to face that or not. We've got to talk about it, Laura."

She wrapped her arms around her body and shook her head. "No."

With a muttered oath he stood abruptly and walked away from her, the rigid lines of his back speaking more eloquently than words of the strain of the past two days and his longer-term frustration. He was clearly a man on the edge, pushed to the limit of his patience, struggling to maintain control. Laura had never seen him this upset, and it frightened her. Not in terms of physical danger, the way such anger once might have frightened her, but in the knowledge that Nick could very well walk away—and with very good reason. He deserved to know more than she was willing—or able—to tell. She just didn't have the courage to dredge up her painful past for anyone—not even Nick.

It seemed as if an eternity passed before he at last turned and looked at her. When he spoke, she could hear the anger—and the underlying hurt—in his voice. "How long is it going to take for you to realize that you can trust me, Laura? Can't you see how much I care about you? Why won't you share your past with me?"

Laura huddled miserably on the couch, the sting of tears hot behind her eyes. "Nick, please. What happened with Joe is over."

"No, it isn't! If he wasn't already dead I could kill him with my bare hands for what he's done to you! For what he's still doing to you," he said savagely.

She stared up at him, her face devoid of color. "It wasn't like that," she whispered.

"No? Then explain to me why you're so terrified of commitment, so afraid to trust. Explain that," he said, pointing to the scar.

Laura blinked back tears. She felt hollow inside, and

a deep emptiness echoed within the walls of her heart. "If you need answers, Nick, I can't give them to you," she said wearily. "I told you at the beginning it was a long shot with me." Her voice broke and she swallowed, struggling for control. "Maybe you better just give it up."

Nick looked at her for a long moment, and then he took a deep breath. "Maybe I better," he said tiredly, his anger suddenly spent. "Because I sure can't continue like this. When I saw what that mugger did to you, I felt like somebody had kicked me in the gut. It's tearing me up inside right now, wanting to share this with you, wanting to share everything with you, and watching you retreat behind your wall, knowing that the door is locked and I don't have a clue where to find the key."

"I—I'm sorry, Nick."

He sighed heavily. "Yeah. Me, too." He jammed his hands into his pockets and walked over to the window, staring out into the darkness. The ticking of her clock echoed loudly in the oppressive stillness that had descended on the room. "What do you say we call it a night?" he said at last. "You need to get some rest."

"I am tired."

He nodded. "Lock the door behind me, okay?" She rose shakily and followed him to the door. He turned and looked at her for a long moment, one hand resting on the frame. "You've got to get out of this place, Laura. It's not safe."

She nodded. "I know. I was planning to move anyway when my lease is up."

"How long is left?"

"Seven months."

"Seven months! That's too long. You need to move now."

"I can't break the lease, Nick."

He sighed, recognizing the stubborn tilt of her chin. He hesitated, as if he wanted to say more, but in the end he didn't. "Good night, Laura."

"Good night," she whispered.

Then he turned and was gone.

Nick ran his finger down the phone listing. Ralph Reynolds. Robert Reynolds. Rudolph Reynolds. Samantha Reynolds. That was it. He quickly punched in the numbers, praying she'd be home. He'd had all night to think about his evening with Laura, and he knew he should never have started that discussion with her. The timing was lousy. If he hadn't been so tired, so stressed out, he would have realized that. She had been in no shape for a confrontation, for a true confessions session, and he had been wrong to press her. But he had to have some answers, and Sam was his only hope.

Nick recognized the voice that greeted him and slowly let out his breath, relief washing over him. "Sam? This is Nick Sinclair."

"Nick?" The surprise in her voice quickly changed to alarm. "Is Laura okay?"

"Yes, she's fine," he assured her. "Or as fine as can be expected after what happened. Would you by any chance have time to meet me for lunch?"

There was a fractional hesitation, a question hovering palpably in the air, and Nick was grateful when Sam left it unasked. "Sure. I have to show houses at ten and two, so how about around eleven-thirty?"

"Fine. Just name the place."

Nick arrived early at the designated restaurant and was waiting in a quiet, secluded booth when Sam appeared in the doorway, her striking red hair announcing her arrival even before he caught a glimpse of her face. When she turned to scan the room he motioned to her, rising as she joined him.

"Nick, it's good to see you."

"Thanks for coming."

"It sounded important," she said as she slid into the booth.

"It is." A waiter appeared, and Nick glanced at Sam questioningly.

"Iced tea, please," she said.

"The same for me," Nick told the waiter, then turned his attention back to Sam. "I'm sure you're wondering why I asked you to meet me," he began.

"You might say that," she replied mildly.

He sighed. "The trouble is, I'm not sure myself. It's just that I don't know where else to turn." He paused as the waiter deposited their drinks and they gave their orders. Then he took a long swallow of his iced tea.

"You really do have a problem, don't you?" Sam said.

"Yeah. Laura."

"I figured as much."

He twirled the ice in his glass and stared broodingly into it. "Sam, I care about Laura. But she's running scared. It's like she puts up a No Trespassing sign on certain areas of her life."

Sam nodded. "I know. She's a very private person."

"I realize that. I also realize she's been burned.

Badly. From what I can gather, her husband was not only a first-class jerk, but abusive."

"Did she tell you that?"

"No. I just put two and two together. Her mother casually mentioned the separation when we were there for the Fourth. Then I saw the scar above Laura's right breast at the hospital. And the night of the mugging, she had a nightmare. Not about the attack. About Joe. She was pleading for him not to hurt her." A muscle in his jaw twitched convulsively, and his lips compressed into a thin, white line.

"I knew it was bad, but it must have been even worse than I thought," Sam said in a subdued voice. "He really did a number on her, didn't he?"

"It sure looks that way." There was a moment of silence, and then Nick leaned forward intently. "Look, Sam. I don't want you to betray any confidences. But is there anything—anything at all—you can tell me about what happened to Laura in that relationship? I want to help, but my hands are tied. I don't know enough."

Sam toyed with her glass. "Don't you think this should come from Laura?"

He sighed and raked his fingers through his hair. "Yes. And I've tried to get her to open up. I pushed pretty hard last night, in fact. Probably too hard. All I succeeded in doing was upsetting her. I came to you because you're her best friend, and I thought…" He shook his head. "I don't know what I thought. I'm desperate. Because the truth is, I'm falling in love with her."

Sam quirked an eyebrow. "Have you told her that?"

"Are you kidding? She's frightened enough as it is, and love can be a very scary word."

Sam eyed him speculatively. "I see what you mean."

Their food arrived, and Sam stared down at her plate for a long moment, her brow furrowed. Nick waited, praying she'd trust him enough to tell him something. Anything. Finally she looked up. "Okay, Nick," she said in sudden decision, and he slowly expelled the breath he'd been holding. "It took me a long time to win Laura's trust, and I'm not about to jeopardize our friendship. But she does have blinders on when it comes to men, and I like you. I think the two of you could have something really special if she'd only give it a chance. So I'll tell you how we met, and I'll tell you what I know about the night she left Joe, because I was involved. But that's it. And to be honest, I don't know much more, anyway. Laura has never talked much about her marriage, and even with my big mouth, I sometimes know when to keep it shut."

She speared a forkful of tuna salad and chewed thoughtfully. "Laura and I met when we were both in night school. In the ladies' room, of all places. Not exactly an auspicious beginning," she said dryly. "Anyway, I remember thinking that she looked like she could use a friend. We ran into each other a few more times, and something just clicked. I can't explain it, because we're obviously Mutt and Jeff. She's a lady through and through, discreet, polite, considerate. All that good stuff. I'm more the irreverent loudmouth, the class clown, the kid who was always getting in trouble. But despite our differences, we became friends.

"It hasn't been easy for Laura, that much I know," she said pensively. "Not that she's ever complained. That's not her style. You've seen her apartment? Well, that's a palace compared to where she and Joe lived. It was a dump," she said bluntly. "But it was all they could afford, and she refused to ask her family for help. To be honest, I doubt whether she's ever told them the real reason she left Joe. Anyway, she's had to fight every step of the way to get where she is, and she did it with sheer guts and determination."

"Tell me about when she left Joe," Nick prompted, when Sam paused.

She laid her fork down carefully. "That was a bad night," she said with a frown. "Laura called me from a pay phone at the corner of her street, hysterical and almost incoherent. When I got there, she was still in the phone booth, shaking like a leaf, not so much hysterical anymore as in shock. She was wearing a jacket, even though it was warm that night, which I thought was odd. After I got her into the car, I asked her what happened, and she said that Joe had gotten drunk again and that he'd hurt her. Then she opened the jacket and I saw the blood all over her blouse."

Nick clenched his napkin into a tight ball, closed his eyes and swallowed convulsively.

"Nick?" Sam paused, and with a worried frown reached over and touched his hand. "Are you okay?"

He opened his eyes and expelled a long breath, then reached for his drink. "Yeah. Go on."

She hesitated briefly, then continued. "Well, at first she wouldn't let me look, but I insisted. And I can be pretty pushy. It's a good thing I *was* pushy that night, because when I saw that cut I took off for the emergency room like a bat out of…well, you get the picture. The hospital took one look at her physical and emotional state, came to the obvious conclusion and called the cops. Laura wouldn't press charges, no matter how hard we tried to convince her to, but she did decide to leave Joe. That night. She insisted on going home to collect her things, so I drove her back to their apartment and waited at the door. Joe was sleeping it off by then, so there was no problem. I guess she left him a note. I never asked. Then I took her back to my place."

There was a momentary pause as Nick stared into his glass, then he looked up at Sam. "Did Joe try to get her to come back?"

"I think so. I know he called a lot. Fortunately I answered one of the first calls and told him to keep his distance or I'd bring in the cops. I guess I was pretty convincing, because as far as I know he never actually came over."

"And Laura never went back?"

"No. But it was really hard on her, Nick. I'm sure you've discovered by now how strong her faith is. She really believes in the sanctity of marriage and she took those 'for better or worse' vows seriously. In case you haven't figured it out, she lives by the book—the good book, that is. She doesn't just talk about her Christian principles—she practices them. Anyway, I know she felt guilty about leaving Joe, despite what he did to her. She never once mentioned the word divorce and always acted as if their separation was only a temporary thing. I know she tried to get Joe into counseling for his problem. But he wouldn't go. She did tell me that she talked to her minister, who advised her to put her personal safety first, and I put my two cents in. But I think she might actually have gone back to him one day, if Joe hadn't been killed."

"What happened to him?"

"He was in a car accident two weeks after Laura left him."

There was silence for a long moment, and then Nick spoke quietly, the anger in his voice barely held in check. "How many times did he hurt her before the night she called you?"

"I have no idea."

He rested his elbows on the table and interlocked his fingers, his untouched lunch forgotten. "I guess I suspected all this. But I was hoping I was wrong. No wonder she's so petrified of intimacy!"

Sam nodded. "I've been talking to her like a Dutch uncle, but I'm afraid I haven't made much of a dent. Maybe you'll finally break through."

"I don't know, Sam. That's a pretty impenetrable fortress she's built around her heart."

"Hang in there, Nick," she said, touching his hand. Then she glanced at her watch. "Good grief! I've got to run," she said, gathering up her purse and jacket. "I'll tell you something, Nick," she said as she slid to the edge of the booth. "She's a fool if she lets someone like you get away. You don't happen to have any brothers, do you?"

He quirked his lips up into the semblance of a smile. "Afraid not."

Sam lifted one shoulder in resignation. "It figures."

She stood, and he rose and took her hand in a warm clasp. "Thank you."

She shrugged. "I didn't tell you much more than

you'd already figured out. I know this isn't easy on you, but Laura's worth waiting for."

But for how long? he asked himself in despair as he watched Sam disappear in the crowd. And with what results?

Chapter Thirteen

Laura had no idea if Nick intended to keep their dinner date, but she went ahead with preparations anyway, guilt pricking at her conscience as she worked, telling her that she wasn't treating Nick fairly. She took and took, but gave nothing back. Not even trust. And he deserved that at least.

Distractedly she rolled the chicken cordon bleu in bread crumbs, placed them in a pan and put them in the oven. Why was she so afraid to share her past? Was it pride? Embarrassment that she'd let herself be treated so badly? Concern that her bottled up anger and resentment would be destructive once released? Fear that the information would be used against her? Or the guilt she had never been able to fully put to rest?

Probably all of the above, she thought with a sigh as she laid a linen cloth on the table and set out crisply starched napkins and sparkling wineglasses, placing two long tapers in candlesticks.

Laura didn't know why she was so afraid. All she knew was that the fear was real. Why was Nick even bothering with her? she wondered in dismay as she riffled through her closet. There were probably thousands of women out there who would spill their guts to him and welcome him into their arms—and their hearts.

Laura's hand paused on her one good summer dress as she recalled the strength and comfort she had found in his embrace. And she'd found something more as well, she acknowledged. A tide of yearning, so strong it left her flushed and breathless, swept over her. No one had ever made her feel like this, not even...not even Joe, she forced herself to admit. With Nick it was different. Was it because she'd been so long without male companionship? Or was it more than that?

She slipped the teal green silk shirtwaist over her head, cinching the belt and leaving the bottom button open to reveal an enticing glimpse of leg. Then she turned her attention to her face, noting resignedly that the black eye hadn't faded one iota. No cosmetic magic was going to camouflage this shiner. She had to content herself with mascara on her good eye, lipstick and blush. Finally she brushed out her hair, leaving it loose and full. Usually it was too hot in the apartment to wear it down, but tonight she'd splurged and turned on the air-conditioning.

Should she tell Nick about her marriage? she wondered again as she distractedly fiddled with the buttons on her dress. Or maybe the more pressing question was whether she wanted to continue this relationship. Because if she did, this was the moment of truth. Nick had made that clear last night.

Restlessly she moved around her bedroom, tugging at the uneven hem of the comforter, straightening a picture, adjusting the blinds. The room was neat as a pin already, though, leaving her little to do. Her eyes did one more inspection, coming to rest on the nightstand where she'd left her Bible. Slowly she walked over and picked it up, paging through to the familiar twenty-third psalm as she sank down on the side of the bed. *The Lord is my shepherd, there is nothing I shall want,* she read silently, slowly working her way through the verse. As always, the lyrical beauty as well as the content refreshed her soul and brought her a sense of peace. Now if only she could decide whether to share her past with Nick!

Laura returned to the living room and inspected the small, carefully set dinette table, caught a glimpse of her meticulous appearance in the hall mirror as she passed, and smelled the aroma of the special, time-consuming dish she rarely prepared. And she realized with surprise that she'd already made her decision. She'd orchestrated the setting and ambience to show Nick she cared; now all she had to do was follow through with words. She closed her eyes. *Dear Lord, please stay beside me tonight,* she prayed silently. *Let me feel your presence and your strength. I don't know if Nick will even come, but if he does I owe him the truth. Give me the courage to share it with him.*

The sudden buzz of the doorbell startled her, and her eyes flew open, her heart soaring. He was here! He'd come, after all! With shaking fingers she slid back the locks and pulled open the door.

At first all she could see was a huge bouquet of long-stemmed red roses and baby's breath. Then Nick's face appeared around the greenery, an uncertain smile hovering at the corners of his mouth. "Hi."

"Hi."

"I wasn't sure I'd be welcome."

"I wasn't sure you'd come."

"Laura, I'm sorry about last night. I was completely out of line. You were in no shape for a heavy discussion."

"Well, I feel better tonight," she said, stepping aside for him to enter. Then she reached over and touched one of the velvet-soft petals of a rose. "These are beautiful," she breathed softly.

"Not very original, though. I don't suppose flowers are anything special for someone in your business."

"These are," she said simply. "Thank you, Nick."

"It was my pleasure." As she took the vase from his hands, he sniffed appreciatively. "Hey, something smells great!"

"Dinner. It's ready, if you're hungry."

"I'm starved. I haven't eaten much today."

She placed the roses on the coffee table, and when she turned back she found Nick studying her. His eyes caught and held hers, and there was a warm light in their depths that made a bolt of heat shoot through her. "That's a lovely dress. And you look wonderful in it," he said quietly.

Laura felt a flush of pleasure creep onto her cheeks at the compliment. "Even with a black eye?" she teased.

"Mmm-hmm."

"I think you need to have your vision checked."

"My taste buds are working," he said hopefully.

She laughed and shook her head. "Go ahead and sit down. I'll have dinner on the table in a minute."

She turned away, but he caught her hand and she looked back in surprise.

"How are you feeling?" he asked, scrutinizing her face.

She smiled. "I'll live." She tried to turn away again, but he didn't release her hand.

"Let me help."

She shook her head firmly. "Not tonight."

His eyes traced her face once more, and finally, with obvious reluctance, he let her go. He strolled over to the table, noting the linen, the crystal and the candles, and he glanced questioningly at Laura, who was hovering in the doorway. "You went to a lot of trouble."

"Not nearly as much as you went to for me," she said quietly.

Although Laura kept the conversation light as they ate the gourmet fare she'd prepared, he sensed an undercurrent of tension. By the time they settled on the couch after dessert, he knew something was up. She seemed distracted and preoccupied, and when he reached over and gently touched her arm, she jumped.

"Oh!" Her hand went to her throat and her startled eyes flew to his. "Sorry," she said with a shaky laugh.

"Laura, what's wrong?"

She stood and restlessly moved around the room, touching the flowers, straightening a picture on the side table, adjusting a lampshade. Finally she sank down into a chair across the coffee table from Nick. He remained silent, guarded, a slight frown on his face and an unsettled feeling in the pit of his stomach.

"Nick…about what you said last night," she began hesitantly.

"I said a lot of things last night. Most of which I regret."

She shook her head. "No. You were right. You've

been incredibly patient as it is. Why you're interested in someone with as many hang-ups as me..." She shook her head uncomprehendingly. "But the fact is you seem to be. You've never shown me anything but kindness and understanding, and you've shared your past with me. So I—I want to do the same with you."

Nick drew in his breath, not sure whether to believe his ears. It seemed too much to hope for, and he watched her silently.

When he didn't respond, she twisted her hands in her lap and looked down. "That is, if you still want to hear it," she said hesitantly. "It's a rather sordid tale." She tried to smile to lighten the mood, but didn't quite pull it off.

"I'd like to hear it. But I need to tell you something first." He took a deep breath, knowing that honesty was the only course. "I had lunch with Sam today."

Laura's head flew up in surprise. "Sam?"

He nodded and leaned forward earnestly, his forearms resting on his thighs, his hands clasped in front of him. "I didn't know where else to turn. I care about you, Laura, but you wouldn't let me get close. I thought maybe if I understood what happened to make you so afraid, I'd know how to address it."

"What did Sam tell you?"

"Not much. She made it clear that she wasn't about to betray any confidences, and I didn't expect her to. She just told me how you two met, and about her role the night you left Joe."

"She told you I left Joe?" Nick could see the hurt in her eyes, the look of betrayal.

"No," he corrected her quickly. "Actually, your mother told me."

"My mother?" she asked incredulously.

"In a roundabout way. The last night we were there I went out for some air and found her on the porch. In the course of conversation, she mentioned your separation. She assumed I knew."

"Oh."

"That's the extent of my knowledge, Laura. No one violated your confidence."

She nodded, still assimilating what he'd just told her. "You know a lot. More than I expected. Which may make this easier." She drew a shaky breath and stared off into a blank corner, carefully keeping her face expressionless and her tone factual. "Joe and I were what romantics call childhood sweethearts," she began. "I never went out with anyone else. We were always a pair, from the time we were children. When I was eighteen and he was twenty, we decided to get married. My parents never did think we were right for each other, but when they realized we were determined, they supported our decision."

She leaned her head back against the chair and transferred her gaze to the ceiling. "Joe had an associate's degree in data processing, which made him well educated for Jersey, and he had great dreams. So we moved to St. Louis, with not much more than hope to sustain us. As it turned out, the competition here was a lot more fierce than Joe expected, and he just couldn't compete with four-year degrees and MBAs. He finally got a low-paying job, as a data entry clerk, and I worked in a department store to help make ends meet.

"As time went on, Joe began to lose heart. It was clear that his only hope of advancing was to get more education, but he had no interest in going back to school. I finally realized that if we were ever going to have a better life, it was up to me. So I went instead. I'd worked every summer in a greenhouse at home, so I got a job at a nursery and began to take classes in landscape design. I discovered I had a knack for it, and decided to go on for my degree."

Her voice grew quieter. "I don't exactly remember when it started to get really bad. It happened so gradually. I think Joe resented my ambition, for one thing. And I know he was frustrated. Anyway, he started to drink—heavily—and a side of him emerged that I'd never seen before. He'd get belligerent when he was drunk, and push me around physically. And he would belittle my efforts to get an education. Then he started making fun of the way I looked, especially my weight, which was dropping steadily. He...he even laughed at my faith. He began to lose jobs, one after another, and finally he just quit working. Our life grew more and more isolated, and I felt so cut off and alone. If I hadn't had school, and Sam, and my church, I doubt I would have made it. Those were the only normal things in my life—those, and my family," she said with a catch in her voice. She paused and took a deep breath.

"I told myself that he was sick, that what was happening wasn't my fault," she continued. "But the guilt was there, anyway. I tried to convince him to get help, but whenever I brought it up he got angry. The last time I suggested it was the night I left. Believe it or not, it was our fourth anniversary."

Nick didn't know when the tears had started. He just knew that suddenly they were there, twin rivers of grief running silently down her cheeks. The unnatural lack of sound unnerved him, and he sat there helplessly, silently cursing the man who had done this to Laura. He longed to reach for her, to hold her, to tell her that he'd never let anyone hurt her again. But he held back, knowing there was more, knowing that she needed to finish what she'd started. "What did he do to you that night, Laura?" he asked gently.

Her head swung around, and her startled eyes met his. It was almost as if she'd forgotten he was there. She swallowed with difficulty, and her eyes flitted away again. When she spoke, her words were choppy. "It was late. I was asleep. A crash from the living room woke me up, and I ran in to see what had happened. There was a broken whiskey bottle on the floor, and I went over to help Joe clean it up. But he…he slapped me, and he started saying…terrible things." Her voice quavered, and she paused, struggling for control. "I got scared and I backed away, pleading with him to get help, but he was yelling… I started to turn away, so I didn't even see it coming until it was too late."

"See what, Laura?" Nick prodded gently.

"The bottle. He threw the broken bottle at me. I had on a nightgown…my shoulders were bare… It hit me here." Her voice caught and she gestured toward her right breast.

Laura was close to losing it, she knew. Only superhuman control and the Lord's help had let her get this far without breaking down. That was why she'd physically removed herself from Nick. One touch from him, and she knew her fragile control would shatter.

Nick watched the struggle taking place on Laura's face. There was no way he could make this any easier for her. All he could do was let her finish and then be there to hold her, to stroke her, to love her.

"I guess I finally admitted then that things were probably over between us," she said unevenly. "So I left. Sam took me in, bless her heart. Joe kept calling, begging me to come back. Sam told me I'd be a fool to give him another chance. So did my minister, in a more diplomatic way. But I still felt an obligation to try everything I could to straighten out our marriage. I was raised to believe that it was a sacred trust and something to be preserved at all costs. Except maybe physical danger," she admitted. "I finally realized that the next time Joe got drunk I might not get off with only a three-inch scar. My safety was literally at stake. Besides, the love I'd once felt for Joe had just about died. All that was left was fear. So I finally made the decision that I wasn't going back unless he got some real help and we went into counseling together. I told him he had to truly change before I'd come back. He was so angry and upset the night I called to tell him..." Her voice trailed off for a moment, and he saw her swallow convulsively. "A few days later, he was killed in a drunk-driving accident." She paused and blinked rapidly. "You want to hear something funny?" she said, choking out a mirthless laugh. "He wasn't the one who was drunk. All those nights I'd lain awake, terrified that he'd run down some innocent person..." She fell silent, her mind clearly far away, but after a few seconds she resumed her story.

"After I pulled myself together, I got an apartment, applied for a grant, went to school full-time and worked a forty-hour week. Eighteen-hour days were the norm. Money was tight, and I lived on peanut-butter sandwiches and macaroni-and-cheese for years. But I made it. I finished school and I got a job with a landscaper.

I had Joe's insurance money, which I'd saved, and that gave me the seed money to open my own place after I'd accumulated a little experience. That was six years ago, and I've poured every cent back into the business since then. Now, thanks to the Arts Center job, I think we've finally turned the corner." She paused and expelled a long breath, then turned to face Nick. "So there you have my life story," she said, trying for a light tone and failing miserably, fighting to hold in the sobs that begged for release.

Nick moved for the first time since she'd started speaking. He stood and walked swiftly over to her, reaching down to draw her to her feet. Then he wrapped his arms around her and buried his face in her soft hair, holding her as tightly as he dared. Her whole body was trembling, and she was breathing erratically. Without releasing her, he reversed their positions and sat down, pulling her into his lap and cradling her in his arms.

"It's okay to cry, Laura," he said softly, stroking her hair.

She had struggled valiantly for control, but she finally surrendered, giving in to the deep, gut-wrenching sobs she'd held inside for so long. Her ribs ached, but once released, the tide of tears could not be stopped. She cried for so many things—for the lost illusions of youth; for the guilt she still carried over Joe's deterioration and death; for the lonely years with no hand to hold and no one with whom to share her life; and for her empty heart, and the fear that prevented her from giving love another chance.

Nick just held her, because there was nothing else he could do. His heart ached for the woman in his arms, and he was filled with a deep, seething anger at the injustice of the world.

When at last her sobs subsided, she spoke against his shirt. "How could I have been so wrong about someone I'd known all my life?" she asked in a small, sad voice.

"Not everyone reacts well to adversity and disappointment, Laura. You had no way of knowing what would happen when Joe was put to the test."

"All these years I've felt guilty," she admitted. "I keep wondering if there wasn't something I could have done or said that would have made a difference. Maybe he'd still be alive if I'd stayed."

"And maybe you'd be dead," Nick said bluntly. Then his tone softened. "What happened wasn't your fault, Laura. You stuck it out a lot longer than most people would have. Probably too long."

She shifted in his arms and looked up at him. "Nick?"

"Mmm-hmm."

"After everything I've told you, do you still...I mean, I'd understand if you wanted to cut your losses and get as far away from me as you can."

"Do you want me out of your life?"

"No," she said softly. "But I'm still scared."

Nick let his breath out slowly. Fear he could handle. Withdrawal was something else. But they'd just bridged that hurdle. "I know, sweetheart," he said gently, running a finger down her tearstained cheek. "But we'll work on it together, okay?"

Laura searched his eyes—tender, caring, filled with warmth and concern—and nodded, her throat constricting. "Okay," she whispered. "But I still need to move slowly."

"Slow is fine," he said. "Just as long as we're moving."

Gradually, Laura began to forget what her life had been like before Nick. He became such an integral part of her existence that just as she once could not imagine life *with* him, now she could not imagine it *without* him. He became her wake-up call, making her smile as she sleepily reached for the phone each morning. His was her last call of the day, the deep timbre of his voice lingering in her mind long after the connection had been severed. And in between, he was there—pulling her away for impromptu picnics, dropping by at night to take her to Ted Drewes, clipping funny articles he thought she'd enjoy. She grew to love his dependability, his gentleness, his enthusiasm, his ability to make her laugh, and slowly the lines of tension in her face eased and the shadows under her eyes disappeared. She gained a little weight, and the angular contours of her face softened and took on a new beauty. As her bruises healed, so, too, did her heart.

Nick watched the transformation with gratitude and pleasure. As her skittishness eased, he began to weave small, undemanding physical intimacies into their relationship. A welcoming kiss whenever they met; an arm casually draped around her shoulders at the movie theater; his hand holding hers when they walked. If she grew accustomed to the small intimacies, he reasoned, the bigger ones would come naturally in their own time. And he could wait. He'd promised to let her set the pace, and he intended to honor that vow. But he planned to set the direction.

Though it was slow going, Nick was not unhappy with the progress of their relationship. Laura was more relaxed than he'd ever seen her, laughing more readily, touching more naturally and easily. Her touches—initially tentative, as if she was afraid that they would be rejected—gradually grew bolder under his welcoming encouragement. She was learning to love all over again, cautiously, but with a restrained eagerness that delighted him and did more for his libido than any of the amorous ploys of the more sophisticated women of his acquaintance. As her confidence grew and she became more secure in their relationship, gradually she began to initiate physical contact on her own.

Nick had known from the beginning that physical closeness frightened her. She hadn't spoken about her intimate relationship with Joe, and Nick hadn't asked, but he imagined that making love had probably become a nightmare for Laura as the relationship deteriorated and the love had disappeared. And, given her background and her strong faith and Christian values, he also knew that she didn't take physical intimacy lightly. She was the kind of woman who equated making love with commitment, and she'd been avoiding that like the plague for years. He couldn't expect her to change overnight.

But slowly he guided her toward change, finding ways to touch her that were not threatening but that brought a flash of desire to her eyes. In time she grew to not only allow these touches, but to welcome them. He'd learned to keep his desires on a tight leash, though, and at her slightest hesitation he pulled back. He had come to realize that Laura's values were deeply entrenched and that she simply didn't believe in intimacy outside of marriage. He admired her for her beliefs and intended to respect them. But keeping his desires under control was hard, and getting harder every day.

Laura locked the office and glanced at her watch. She was due to meet Nick at one-thirty, and it was already one-twenty. Fortunately, the client's house was only a short distance from her office, she noted, consulting the address Nick had provided.

Laura rolled down the window as she drove, breathing deeply of the crisp October air. She loved fall, especially here in Webster, when the old, established maples put on their most colorful frocks. Her route took her through the heart of the small community, and she glanced admiringly at the wonderful turn-of-the-century houses.

When Laura reached her destination, she sat for a long moment in the car without moving, letting her eyes roam lovingly over the old frame Victorian. It was set far back from the street, on about an acre of ground, and was everything a Victorian should be. Painted a pale peach, it was embellished with white gingerbread accents, making it appear to be trimmed with lace. A wraparound porch hugged the house invitingly, and tall, stately maples stood on the front lawn. She saw Nick waiting for her on the front porch and waved as she climbed out of the car.

He watched her approach, his body stirring as it always did in her presence. She was dressed as she had been the day they'd met—jeans, work boots, a worn blue work shirt and sunglasses—and her hair was pulled back into a ponytail. But her greeting was certainly different. She ran lightly up the steps and reached on tiptoe, raising her face expectantly. Nick smiled and leaned down, grasping her shoulders and pulling her toward him hungrily for a lingering kiss.

"Mmm," she said dreamily, closing her eyes.

He chuckled, and the deep, seductive sound of it made her feel warm despite the slight chill in the air. "Well, what do you think?" he asked, gesturing toward the house.

"It's wonderful!" she said.

"I thought you'd like it."

"I take it the new owner wants to make some changes?" she said, nodding toward the For Sale sign on the lawn.

"A few. I've already been over the inside, so we can skip that and just go around back. Unless, of course, you'd like to take a look?" He grinned and dangled the key enticingly in front of her.

"Are you kidding!" she exclaimed, her eyes shining. "I've been dying to get inside one of these houses ever since I moved to St. Louis."

Nick fitted the key in the lock and then stepped aside. "After you."

Laura stepped over the threshold—and into the house of her dreams. It was everything she had always imagined—tall ceilings, gleaming hardwood floors, private nooks and crannies and alcoves, fireplaces, a wonderful L-shaped stairway in the foyer that hugged the wall, a gorgeous art glass window and plenty of light and space. She examined it all rapturously, reverently running her hand over the fine wood moldings and marble mantels. When she'd explored every inch, she turned to Nick. "I don't know what the new owners have in mind, but I wouldn't change a thing. It's perfect."

"If all my clients were that satisfied with the status quo, I'd be out of business," he said with a grin.

"You aren't going to do anything to change the character, are you?" she asked worriedly.

"Nope. Just some minor updating. Ready to take a look at the grounds?"

"I suppose so," she said reluctantly, casting one more lingering, longing look at the foyer before stepping outside. "Can't you just imagine this house at Christmastime, Nick?" she said softly. "Snow on the ground, golden light shining from the windows, smoke curling above the chimneys, a wreath on the door... It's a perfect old-fashioned Christmas house. So warm and welcoming." She sighed. "What a wonderful place to call home."

"You make it sound very appealing," Nick said, locking the door and taking her arm as they strolled around the back.

"I don't have to try very hard. It's a very romantic house."

Laura pulled up short when they reached the backyard. It was heavily shrubbed on the edges, affording complete privacy, and several big trees were spaced over the lawn. Little had been done in the way of landscaping, but Laura could visualize the potential.

"Are your clients open to suggestions?" she asked.

"Yes."

"Well, my first thought is a gazebo—white lattice, of course. And a formal rose garden is a must. Somewhere there should be a trellis, overflowing with morning glories, that leads to a private area with a bench and a birdbath. And there's plenty of room for an English woodland country garden, sort of wild, yet controlled, you know? That's what gives them their charm. But we have to leave lots of open space for a croquet court. This is a perfect yard for that." She paused, and Nick heard her soft sigh. "It could be so lovely here. I hope the client will let me do this right."

There was a wistful note in her voice, and Nick squeezed her hand, then tugged her gently toward the back of the house. "Let's sit for a minute, Laura."

She followed, still scanning the grounds, visualizing the perfect backdrop for this house. It was the kind of home she'd always hoped to have, and even if that was never to be, perhaps she could create her dream for someone else to enjoy.

Nick pulled her down beside him on a small stone bench set under a tree near the house, and stroked the back of her hand with his thumb. "Laura?"

"Hmm?" With an effort she pulled her eyes away from the yard and forced her attention back to Nick.

"Laura, I…" He stopped, as if he didn't know what to say next, and drew in a deep breath. He seemed at a loss for words, which was completely unlike him, and Laura stared at him curiously. "About the client for this house…"

"Yes?" she prompted, when his voice trailed off.

"Well…it's me."

Her eyes widened in shock. "What?"

"I've put an option on this house."

"You? But, Nick—it's a wonderful house, don't get me wrong—it's just so big for just one person."

"I know. I was hoping that you might share it with me."

Chapter Fourteen

Laura stared at him, her eyes wide with shock. "Nick…are you…are you asking me to marry you?" she stammered.

"I guess I'm not doing a very good job at it, am I?" He tried to grin, and then drew a deep breath, letting it out slowly. "Laura, the simple truth is I'm not getting any younger. The years have gone by a lot faster than I expected. I want a home, and a family, and a house with a white picket fence and a tree swing—the whole nine yards. And I want it before I'm too old to enjoy it." He stroked the back of her hand absently with his thumb, his eyes locked on hers. "I've been involved with my share of women over the years," he said honestly, struggling to find the right words because it was vitally important that she understand exactly how he felt. "But I've never really been 'involved,' not in the true sense of the word. In fact, I went to great lengths to *avoid* involvement, because I didn't want the complications and responsibilities that go with it. And then you came along, and suddenly everything was different. I *wanted* to share your life—and your responsibilities."

He paused and searched her eyes. "I guess that's what happens when you fall in love," he said quietly.

Laura tried to swallow past the lump in her throat. For the past few months she'd gone blithely along, relishing her developing relationship with Nick, refusing to think about the inevitable day of reckoning. Now it had come, and she wasn't ready. All the old fears, which had gradually subsided under Nick's gentle nurturing, resurfaced with alarming intensity. He was talking love and commitment and vows, and it scared her to death. There was no question that she loved Nick. But she'd loved Joe, too, and that had been a mistake, one that was still exacting a price.

Nick's eyes were locked on hers, trying to gauge her reaction to his proposal, watching the play of emotions cross her face. He'd known it was a risk to ask her to marry him, but it had been a calculated one. He knew Laura well enough to know that she was completely without guile or pretense. The affection she so willingly returned could be taken at face value as a true measure of her feelings. He'd hoped those feelings would be strong enough to overcome her fears, but now, searching her troubled eyes, he wasn't so sure.

"Nick, I—I don't know what to say."

"'Yes' would be nice." When she didn't respond, he took a deep breath. "Things have gone well between us, haven't they?" he asked gently.

"Yes. But why can't we just leave them as they are?" she pleaded.

"For how long?" His voice was sober, direct.

"I—I don't know," she replied helplessly. "It's such a big step. And I made a mistake once before."

"That was a long time ago, Laura. You were only

eighteen years old—just a kid. And you had no way of knowing what would happen to Joe."

"But…but I'm so afraid it could happen again," she whispered.

Nick didn't say a word. He tried to understand, tried to remind himself that Laura's traumatic past was clouding her judgment, but he was still deeply hurt by her lack of trust. He'd done everything he could to prove that he was different than Joe, that he was trustworthy and dependable and even-tempered, that he cared about her and loved her unconditionally. And he had failed. Instead of the joy he had hoped to see in her eyes, there was only doubt and uncertainty. He glanced away, feeling as if his heart was being held in a vise, the life slowly being squeezed out of it. He gazed at the house he'd allowed himself to dream of sharing with the woman beside him, and felt something inside him begin to die. Finally he looked back at her.

"I don't know what else to do, Laura," he said wearily. "I'd hoped the fear had dimmed by now. But I'm beginning to think it never will."

Her eyes filled with tears, and she blinked them back. She wanted to tell him she loved him, but the words wouldn't come. Just saying them seemed too much of a risk. But she didn't want to lose him. Without Nick, her life would be empty, emptier even than before. She touched his arm and looked up at him desperately. "Nick…maybe we could just… Lots of people live together nowadays," she said.

He gazed at her in surprise, completely taken aback. Yes, lots of people did live together. But Laura wasn't cut out to be one of them. It went against everything she'd been brought up to believe about love and commitment, flew in the face of her deeply held Christian principles. Her willingness to even consider compromising her values spoke more eloquently than words of the depths of her feelings for him. But it would impose a very heavy burden of guilt on her and, in the end, she would come to not only regret such a choice, but resent him for forcing her to make it. It just wouldn't work.

Nevertheless, Nick was tempted. He was losing her—she was slipping away even as he watched—and now she'd thrown out a lifeline. Maybe this was better than nothing, he thought, trying to convince himself. But how long would the arrangement last, even if she did go through with it, which he doubted? Would she ever feel secure enough to marry him? And if not, then what? What if she walked away, somewhere down the road?

As hard as it would be to let her go now, it would be even harder once they'd lived together intimately.

Slowly he shook his head. "I'm sorry, Laura," he said, his voice filled with regret. "I love you. I want to build a life with you—for always. It's got to be all or nothing."

Laura began to feel physically ill. Her world was crumbling around her, and she felt powerless to stop it. The man she loved was about to walk away, taking all of the sunlight and warmth and tenderness out of her life. The tears that had welled up in her eyes slowly overflowed and trickled down her cheeks.

"Nick, I can't marry you," she said brokenly. "I'm not ready for that step and…and I don't know if I ever will be."

He took her hands, his gut twisting painfully at the shattered look in her eyes. She seemed so vulnerable and defenseless that he almost relented, just to ease her pain. Almost. But in the end, he shook his head.

"Laura, I love you," he repeated, his voice hoarse with emotion. "Part of me always will. I wish we could have made this work." Gently he released her hands and slowly stood.

Laura's heart was pounding in her chest, her eyes desperate. "Nick, I…" She tried again to say "I love you," but the words stuck in her throat. "I'll miss you," she said instead.

"I'll miss you, too." He bent down and placed his lips gently and lingeringly on hers, in a kiss as light as the wayward leaves that drifted down around them.

"Will I see you again?" she whispered.

"In the spring, I guess, when the landscaping starts for the Arts Center." He desperately hoped that by then the pain of this parting would have dulled. "Goodbye, Laura. And good luck. I hope someday you find someone who can bring you the happiness you deserve."

As the sun darted behind a cloud, she watched his back, ramrod straight and broad shouldered, disappear around the corner of the house. The air grew chilly, and so did her heart.

With Nick gone, there was an empty place in Laura's life that couldn't be filled. She tried working even longer hours, but that once reliable distraction barely eased the pain. She went back to doing more outdoor labor, but the physical tiredness couldn't mask her emotional fatigue and despair, nor did it help her sleep any better. Night after night she lay awake, thinking about what might have been, wondering if Nick missed her as much as she missed him, aching for the closeness she had grown to cherish. She had never felt more alone in her life.

Even her best friend seemed to desert her. Sam had always been the one she'd turned to for support during the difficult years after Joe died and through all the tough times when she'd been trying to establish her business. But Sam offered little sympathy. Laura knew her friend thought she was a fool for letting Nick walk away. She'd pretty much said so to her face, in her blunt, outspoken way.

Her family was too far away to be able to provide much consolation, even if she'd told them about her relationship with Nick, which she hadn't. All her mother knew was that they had been seeing each other, never that it had grown serious. As much as she loved her family, it had never been her custom to share the intimate details of her life.

Even in her darkest days she'd always found solace in talking over her problems with the Lord, but even He seemed distant. She just couldn't find the words to pray, beyond a desperate plea for help and guidance. But God worked in His own time, and no direction had yet been provided.

So Laura was left alone with her pain. She tried to tell herself that she'd done the right thing, that entering into a relationship when she wasn't ready would be wrong for everyone involved. At the same time, she couldn't blame Nick for walking out. She'd made it clear that marriage wasn't an option at the moment, maybe never would be. He wanted to share his life with someone on a permanent basis, to raise a family, to create a home, and she couldn't offer him that. Because Joe had left her with a legacy of fear that was debilitating and isolating, had shaken her confidence in her own judgment so badly that even now, ten years later, she was afraid to trust her heart. Nick had tried his best to convince her to risk loving again, and he'd failed. And if Nick—with his integrity and gentleness and love— couldn't succeed, she doubted whether anyone could.

Laura carried that depressing thought with her into December, through two long, lonely months without the sound of his voice each morning and night, without his impromptu visits, without the laughter he'd brought into her life. Her solitary existence, once carefully nurtured, now seemed oppressive.

Laura didn't even bother to put up a tree, a custom she'd never abandoned, even at the worst of times. But her heart wasn't in it this year. The Christmas decorations looked garish, the carols sounded flat and the weather was dismal. Her only concession to the holidays was the small crèche she always displayed on the mantel. As she placed the figure of baby Jesus in the manger she reminded herself that the Lord had never promised an easy road in this world. She accepted that. She always had. But did it *always* have to be so hard? she cried in silent despair. Weren't there ever happy endings?

And then, with a jolt, she realized that the key to a potentially happy ending *had* been offered to her. She had refused—because she was afraid. And the simple fact was that despite the emptiness of the past two months, she still carried the same oppressive burden of fear.

Her loneliness only intensified as the holidays grew closer. Laura's mother had decided to visit her brother's family in California, and though Laura had been invited to spend Christmas with John and Dana and the kids, trying to look cheery for several days in front of her family seemed too much of an effort. Sam had gone to Chicago. Laura told everyone she was too busy to take time off anyway, but in reality business was slow. People typically didn't think about landscaping at Christmastime. They were too busy planning holiday gatherings and buying gifts for family and friends.

On Christmas Eve Laura closed the office at three o'clock, realizing as she slowly walked to her car that she had nowhere to go until the evening service at seven. Her cozy apartment, once a welcoming haven, now seemed empty and hollow. She tried strolling around a mall, but the laughing crowds, so at odds with her depressed mood, only made her feel worse.

In the end, even though the service wasn't scheduled to start for an hour and half, she just went to church. Maybe here, in the Lord's house, she could find some peace and solace.

Laura sat forlornly in the dim silence feeling more alone and lost than she had in a very long while. *Oh, Lord, show me what to do!* she pleaded. *I love Nick. And yet I let him walk away because I'm afraid. I need to move on with my life, find the courage to trust again. Please help me.* She closed her eyes and opened her heart, and slowly, as she poured out her fears and confusion to the Lord in an almost incoherent stream of consciousness, she began to feel a calmness steal over her.

The church was filling with people when she at last opened her eyes, and by the time the candles were lit and the service started, she had attained some measure of peace, though no insights. But she had faith that the

Lord would offer those in His own time. If she was patient, He would show her the way.

As Brad Matthews stepped to the microphone, she forced herself to put her problems aside and focus on the words of her childhood friend. He was a wonderful minister, and he had offered her a sympathetic ear and sound advice during her darkest days. He was also an accomplished speaker, and she always found value in his thoughtfully prepared sermons.

Tonight was no exception. In fact, it almost seemed as if the end of his talk had been prepared especially for her, she thought in growing amazement as she listened to his words.

"And so tomorrow all of us will exchange gifts with the ones we love," he said in his rich, well-modulated voice. "They'll be brightly wrapped, in colorful paper and shiny bows. But let's not forget that those gifts are only meant to represent the true gift of this season—the gift of love. My friends, that is why we are here tonight. Because God so loved the world that he sent his only Son to save us. That gift of love is what makes this day so special. No one who knows the Lord is ever truly alone or unloved, because His love is never ending and He is always with us.

"God gave us the gift of perfect love when he sent us His Son. And that love is manifested here on earth in many ways, most beautifully in the love we have for each other. Love one another as I have loved you. That was His instruction.

"Well, all of us know that, as humans, we can never achieve the perfection of God's love. But it should stand as a shining example of what love is at its very best. It is unselfish. It is trusting. It is enduring. It is forgiving. It is limitless. And it is unconditional.

"On this Christmas Eve, let us all reflect on God's love and the gifts of human love with which we are blessed in this earthly life. And let us remember that God never promised us that love was easy. It isn't even easy to love the Lord. Christianity is a celebration, but it's also a cross. And it certainly isn't always easy to love each other. But love of the Lord, and the reflection of that love in our relationships with the people in our lives, is what sets us apart as Christians.

"So during this Christmas season, give yourself a special gift. It won't be as flashy as a new CD player or a computer, but I promise you it will be longer lasting. Because CD players and computers break. And love can, too. But the difference is that love can not only be mended, but strengthened. Sometimes all it takes is two simple words, spoken from the heart: I'm sorry. The power those two words contain is amazing.

"At this season of God's love, which manifested itself in the humble birth of a baby two thousand years, show the Lord that you've heard His voice. Mend a broken relationship. And I guarantee that the joy of Christmas will stay in your heart long after the gifts under your tree are just a memory.

"Now let us pray…"

As the service continued, Laura reflected on Brad's beautiful words, which deeply touched her heart. He was right. Love was a gift, both the divine and human forms. And both kinds of love required trust and a leap of faith to reach their full potential. Maybe that was what made love so unique and special.

A gentle snow was falling when she emerged from

the church after the service, the soft flakes forming a delicate, transparent film of white on the ground. As she climbed into her car, an image of the cozy Victorian house Nick had so lovingly chosen for them suddenly flashed unbidden across her mind.

It was probably filled with laughter and music and love as the new owners enjoyed their first Christmas there, she thought wistfully. Without consciously making a decision, Laura put the car in gear and drove slowly toward the house that had come to represent Nick's love and the life he had offered her. Dusk descended, and the snow continued to fall, lightly dusting her windshield as she drove.

When she reached the street, Laura approached the house slowly, surprised to find the windows dark and the For Sale sign still on the lawn. Sam was always complaining that the real estate market was soft, but Laura found it surprising that a gem like this would still be unsold.

The street was lined with cars, so she had to drive a few houses away before she found a spot to park. Then, digging her hands into the pockets of her wool coat, she trudged up the sidewalk, stopping in front of the house. Her eyes filled with longing as they lovingly traced the contours of the structure. It was just as beautiful as she'd remembered it, but so empty and alone. Just like me, she thought, allowing herself a moment of self-pity. Both of us could have been filled with the magic of Nick's love, but instead we're cold and dark.

She walked up the pathway to the front door and slowly climbed the steps, running a hand over the banister, touching the brass knocker on the door. Then she sat down on the top step, folded her arms on her knees and rested her forehead on the scratchy wool of her sleeves. An aching sense of regret flooded through her as she faced the fact that something beautiful had been within her grasp and she'd allowed it to slip away. Brad had said that love required trust, and a leap of faith. And there were certainly no guarantees. She knew that. Life—and love—didn't come with warranties. But which was worse—to shun risk and spend her life alone and miserable, or to take a chance on love with the most wonderful man she'd ever met? Put that way, and in the context of the past two lonely months, the answer suddenly seemed obvious.

Brad had said that love could be mended, she reflected. But she had hurt Nick deeply. The look in his eyes when she'd admitted her fear was burnt into her memory forever. Because that fear also implied lack of trust. No wonder he'd walked away that day. Love without trust was just an empty shell, and he deserved better than that. If only she could retract her words!

But that was impossible, and it made no sense to yearn for impossible things, she thought bleakly. She just wished she could find a way to make him understand how deeply she loved him, to ask his forgiveness. All she really wanted, or could hope for, was a second chance.

Though her eyes were clouded with tears, Laura realized with a start that the toes of two boots had appeared in her field of vision. Probably a cop, about to cite her for trespassing, she thought dejectedly, quickly brushing a hand across her eyes before looking up.

"I'm sorry, I didn't mean…" The words died in her throat. Nick stood at the base of the steps, his hands in the pockets of a sheepskin-lined jacket, snow clinging to his dark hair, his eyes shadowed and unfathomable, with a fan spread of fine lines at the corners that hadn't been there two months before.

"Hello, Laura."

"Nick?" She took a great gulp of cold air.

"Fancy meeting you here," he said lightly, though his tone sounded forced.

"I—I thought it would look pretty in the snow," she stammered, still not trusting her eyes.

He nodded. "Yeah. Me, too." He glanced at the shuttered windows and placed one foot on the bottom step. "I remember the day we were here, how you said it would be beautiful at Christmastime, so I thought I'd take a look. I see it's still for sale."

A door opened nearby and the sound of carols and laughter drifted through the silent air.

"Yes, I noticed."

"I'm surprised you didn't go home for Christmas."

She shrugged. "I wasn't in the mood."

They fell silent, and Laura looked down, shuffling the toe of her shoe in the snow that was rapidly accumulating at the edge of the porch, trying to make some sense out of her chaotic thoughts. If Nick didn't still care about her, he wouldn't be here tonight, would he? Maybe, just maybe, it wasn't too late to salvage their relationship. She looked up and found that he was watching her. This was the second chance she'd wished for. *Please, God, don't let me blow it!* she prayed. *Help me find the words to make Nick understand how much I care and how sorry I am for hurting him.*

"Nick…I've missed you," she began tentatively.

"I've missed you, too," he said quietly.

"I've had a lot of time to think these past couple

of months, and I was wondering… Is there… Do you still…" Her voice trailed off. She was making a mess of this!

"Do I still what, Laura?" Nick asked, his voice cautious.

She took a deep breath. There was no easy way to say it. "Do you still…do you still want me?" she asked artlessly.

He hesitated. "I've always wanted you," he replied, his voice guarded.

"No…I mean, do you still want to marry me?"

Instead of replying, Nick grabbed her hands and pulled her to her feet. She gasped in surprise as he hauled her up onto the porch and over to a dim light by the door that offered only marginal illumination. Then he turned her to face him, his jaw tense, his hands gripping her shoulders almost painfully, his eyes burning into hers.

"Laura, what are you saying?" he asked tightly.

He wasn't going to make this easy for her, she thought. He wanted her to spell it out, and after her previous ambiguity, she couldn't blame him. She drew a deep breath and looked directly into his eyes, willing him to see the love, the sincerity, the apology, in her own. "Nick, I'm sorry for what I've put you through. I'm especially sorry for being afraid to commit to you, for not trusting you, when I've never met a more trustworthy person. But when I left Joe, I vowed never to get involved with anyone again. And I did pretty well, till you came along."

When she paused, he prodded. "Go on."

"These past two months have been miserable," she said, her voice breaking. "Maybe even harder emotionally than when I left Joe. Because when you left you took the sunshine with you. Oh, Nick," she cried, clinging to him. "I want the same things you want—the rose garden and the picket fence and the family. I realize I'm no bargain, that I still have a lot of problems to work through. But I'd like to work on them with you beside me. I'd still like a lifetime warranty, but I'll settle for an 'I'll do my best to make you happy.' And I'll do the same for you."

He studied her face, wanting to believe, but afraid that this was all an illusion, much as he'd thought *she* was an illusion when he'd first seen her slumped on the steps. Then, too, he realized, she hadn't yet said the three words that really counted.

Laura watched his face, saw a flicker of disappointment in his eyes and her stomach knotted into a tight ball. She panicked. He was going to tell her to forget it, that it was too late.

"I...have the feeling...that the offer is...no longer available," she said choppily. "I...know I hurt you, and I guess I can't blame you if...if you can't forgive me."

"It's not that, Laura." He released her and turned to walk over to the porch railing, leaning on it heavily with both hands, facing away from her. "I *was* hurt. Deeply. But I never really blamed you. If anyone ever had a reason to be wary, it was you. It was egotistical of me to think I could overcome years of debilitating fear in just a few months. In the end, I was just sad. For both of us. But there was nothing to forgive. You were a victim of your circumstances."

"Then what's wrong?" she pleaded.

"I still want to marry you, Laura, but..."

"But what?" she asked desperately.

"You say you're lonely, and God knows, I can relate to that," he said with a sigh. "But that's not reason enough to get married."

"But it's not just that. I want to be with you, Nick. For always."

"Why?"

"Why?" she parroted blankly. Then suddenly her taut nerves shattered. "Well, why do you think?" she snapped. "Nick, I love you! What more do you want?"

He was beside her in one quick step, pulling her roughly against him, burying his face in her hair as he let out a long, shuddering sigh. "That will be plenty," he said huskily.

"Then do you mind telling me what this was all about?" she asked, still mildly annoyed, her voice muffled by his jacket.

He took her by the shoulders and backed up far enough to look down into her eyes. "Laura Taylor, do you realize that this is the first time you've ever said, 'I love you'?"

She frowned. "Yes, I guess it is. But I assumed you knew."

"How could I know?"

"Well, by the way I acted. I tried to show you how I felt."

"Showing isn't the same as telling."

She smiled, a sudden, euphoric joy making her heart soar. She sent a silent, fervent prayer of thanks to the Lord for granting her a happy ending after all.

"Are you saying you'd rather have words than actions?" she teased, tilting her head to one side and reaching up to run a finger down his cheek.

She heard his sharply indrawn breath and grinned.

"Well, action is good, too," he conceeded.

"I thought you'd agree." She slipped her hands inside his jacket and gazed up into his face, the ardent light in her eyes playing havoc with his metabolism.

"You can count on it," he said huskily, pulling her roughly against him, his mouth urgent and demanding on hers. Laura responded eagerly, tasting, teasing, touching.

"Excuse me…are you folks lost?"

Startled, they drew apart, their breath creating frosty clouds in the cold night air. An older man stood looking up at them from the sidewalk.

Nick put his arm around Laura and drew her close. "No. Not anymore," he said, smiling down at her. "We just came home." Then he turned back toward the street. "We're going to buy this house," he called, and the jubilant ring in his voice warmed Laura's heart.

The man chuckled softly. "Now that's what I call a Christmas present!"

Epilogue

❦

Nick brought the car to a stop and turned to Laura with an intimate smile that made her tingle all over. "Welcome home, Mrs. Sinclair," he said huskily.

Her throat constricted at the tenderness in his eyes, and she swallowed with difficulty. "I love you, Nick," she said softly, her voice catching as her own eyes suddenly grew misty.

"Believe me, the feeling is mutual," he replied, reaching over with a feather-light touch to leisurely trace a finger down her cheek, then across her lips. He drew an unsteady breath and smiled. "Shall we go in?"

She nodded mutely, not trusting her voice, and tried unsuccessfully to slow her rapid pulse as he came around and opened her door. He took her hand, drawing her to her feet in one smooth motion, then let his arm slip around her waist, pulling her close. She leaned against him with a contented sigh as they stood for a moment in the dark stillness to look at the old Victorian house, its ornate gingerbread trim and huge wraparound porch silhouetted by the golden light spilling from the windows.

"It's beautiful, isn't it?" she said, her eyes glowing.

"Beautiful is a good word," he agreed.

She turned to find his eyes on *her,* not the house, and she blushed.

"You're even more beautiful when you do that," he said with a tender smile, touching her nose with the tip of his finger before taking her hand. As they climbed the steps to the porch he turned to her. "Are you sure you wouldn't have preferred the Ritz tonight?"

"This *is* my Ritz," she said softly, letting her free hand lovingly glide over the banister as they ascended.

"I agree," he replied with a tender smile. For both of them, the house had come to symbolize their love and the promise of a rich, full life together.

When they reached the door, he fitted the key in the lock, and before she realized his intention he swept her into his arms and lowered his lips to hers, drawing a sweet response from deep within her. Only when the kiss lengthened, then deepened, did Laura reluctantly pull away.

"Nick! The neighbors might see us!" she protested halfheartedly.

He grinned. "They're all in bed. Speaking of which…" He stepped across the threshold, pushed the door shut with his foot, and started up the curved staircase.

Laura didn't say a word as a wave of excitement and delicious anticipation swept over her. She just nestled against his chest, enjoying the feel of his strong arms as she listened to the rapid but steady beat of his heart against her ear.

When they reached the bedroom, he carefully set her on her feet and removed the light mohair wrap from around her shoulders. Soft, classical music was playing and the room was bathed in a gentle, subdued light.

"I want to show you something," Nick said, taking her hand and leading her to the antique oval mirror on a stand that stood in one corner of the room. He positioned her in front and then stood behind her, his hands on her shoulders. "What do you see?"

She gazed at their reflections, a tender smile on her face. She saw Nick, tall and incredibly handsome in his tux, the elegant formal attire enhancing his striking good looks and broad shoulders. And she saw herself, dressed in her wedding finery. Her peach-colored tea-length lace gown softly hugged her slender figure, and the sweetheart neckline and short, slightly gathered sleeves added an old-fashioned charm that perfectly complemented her femininity. Her hair hung loose and full, the way Nick liked it, and the soft waves were pulled back on one side with a small cluster of flowers and lacy ribbon, giving her a sweetly youthful appearance. But mostly what she saw was the two of them, together, for life.

"Well?" Nick prompted.

"I see a miracle," she replied softly, her eyes glowing with happiness.

"I'm inclined to agree with you on that," Nick concurred with a smile. Then his voice softened and his tone grew serious. "Do you know what I see? The most beautiful bride that ever lived and the most wonderful, desirable woman I've ever met."

"Oh, Nick," she said, her eyes misting. "I never thought I could be so happy!"

"Well, get used to it, Mrs. Sinclair. Because happiness is exactly what I have planned for you for the next sixty or seventy years," he said, turning her to face him, taking both her hands in his as he bent to trail his lips across her forehead. "Now don't go away. I'll be right back," he said huskily, his breath warm against her face.

She closed her eyes, letting his touch work its magic. "I'll be here," she whispered.

When Nick left, Laura turned slowly and let her gaze roam over the lovingly decorated room they'd created together—their first priority when they bought the house. The English country style suited the house, as did the canopy bed that was draped in a floral print of rose and forest green. The thick carpet was also rose-colored, and two comfortable chairs in complementary striped fabric stood close to the fireplace. Yes, this was far preferable to the Ritz, Laura thought with deep contentment. Tonight marked a new chapter in their relationship, and she wanted it to start here, in their own home.

Nick had clearly gone out of his way to make this night special, she thought with a soft smile, her eyes filled with tenderness at his thoughtfulness. Two champagne glasses rested on a low table, and the subdued lighting and soft music created the perfect ambience for their first night together.

Nick quietly reentered, pausing a moment to let his eyes lovingly trace the contours of Laura's profile, bathed in the warm glow of the golden light. It was hard for him to even remember a time when she hadn't been the center of his world. She brought a joy and completeness to his life far beyond anything he could ever have imagined. Today, as they'd recited their vows, he'd felt as if he'd truly come home. Gazing at her now, he was overwhelmed with joy and gratitude for the gift of her love.

Quietly he came up behind her and nuzzled her neck. "Did you miss me?"

"Mmm. As a matter of fact, I did," she said, leaning back against him.

"I brought some champagne."

"I saw the glasses."

"Will you have some?"

"Mmm-hmm."

He popped the cork, poured the bubbly liquid into the two waiting glasses and bent to strike a match to the logs. They quickly flamed into life, sending shadows dancing on the walls. It was chilly for the first day of spring, and Laura moved closer to the welcome warmth.

"Cold?" Nick asked as he handed her a glass.

"A little," she admitted.

He gave her a lazy smile. "I think we can take care of that," he said, his eyes twinkling.

Laura flushed and looked down, a smile playing at the corners of her own mouth. "I was counting on it," she said softly.

"But first...I'd like to make a toast." Nick raised his glass, and Laura looked up at him, the love shining from her deep green eyes. "To new beginnings—and a love that never ends," he said softly.

Laura raised her glass, and the bell-like tinkle as they clinked resonated in the room.

They both took a sip, and then Nick reached over and gently removed the glass from her trembling fingers. He set the two glasses side by side on the mantel, turned, held out his hand. And as she moved into his arms, Laura had one last coherent thought. The good book was right. To everything there was a season. And this, at last, was her time to love.

* * * * *

Dear Reader,

Ever since I could put pen to paper, I've enjoyed writing. It's a very special gift for which I am deeply grateful.

Love is a gift, too. A precious and beautiful gift that requires courage and faith and trust—and yes, even risk—to reach its full potential.

It is a great joy for me to write about people like Nick and Laura, who find love and romance without compromising their moral values. And I am delighted to be part of Steeple Hill's Love Inspired line, which recognizes that readers want books that reaffirm the existence of character and honor and principles in today's world, despite media messages to the contrary.

I truly believe that good, old-fashioned romance lives even in this modern age. Virtues and values never go out of style. And heroes like Nick are out there, waiting to be found. I should know. I married one!

Happy endings…that's what romance is all about. May you find your own happy ending—and a lifetime of love!

Irene Hannon

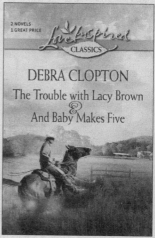

REQUEST YOUR FREE BOOKS!

2 FREE INSPIRATIONAL NOVELS
PLUS 2
FREE
MYSTERY GIFTS

When Texas Ranger Benjamin Fritz arrives at his captain's house after receiving an urgent message, he finds him murdered and the man's daughter in shock.

Read on for a sneak peek at DAUGHTER OF TEXAS by Terri Reed, the first book in the exciting new **TEXAS RANGER JUSTICE** *series, available January 2011 from Love Inspired Suspense.*

Corinna's dark hair had loosened from her normally severe bun. And her dark eyes were glassy as she stared off into space. Taking her shoulders in his hands, Ben pulled her to her feet. She didn't resist. He figured shock was setting in.

When she turned to face him, his heart contracted painfully in his chest. "You're hurt!"

She didn't seem to hear him.

Blood seeped from a scrape on her right upper biceps. He inspected the wound. Looked as if a bullet had grazed her. Whoever had killed her father had tried to kill her. With aching ferocity, rage roared through Ben. The heat of the bullet cauterized the flesh. It would probably heal quickly enough.

But Ben had a feeling that her heart wouldn't heal anytime soon. She'd adored her father. That had been apparent from the moment Ben set foot in the Pike world. She'd barely tolerated Ben from the get-go, with her icy stares and brusque manner, making it clear she thought him not good enough to be in her world. But when it came to her father...

Greg had known that if anything happened to him, she'd need help coping with the loss.

Ben, I need you to promise me if anything ever happens to me, you'll watch out for Corinna. She'll need an anchor.

I fear she's too fragile to suffer another death.

Of course Ben had promised. Though he'd refused to even allow the thought to form that any harm would befall his mentor and friend. He'd wanted to believe Greg was indestructible. But he wasn't. None of them were.

The Rangers were human and very mortal, performing a risky job that put their lives on the line every day.

Never before had Ben been so acutely aware of that fact.

Now his captain was gone. It was up to him not only to bring Greg's murderer to justice, but to protect and help Corinna Pike.

For more of this story, look for DAUGHTER OF TEXAS by Terri Reed, available in January 2011 from Love Inspired Suspense.

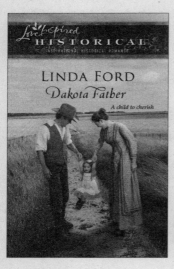